'*Arslan* starts with a strong science fiction premise – and then raises it to the level of the greatest tragedies . . . by the end of the book, exhausted and fulfilled, you will realize you have read something that stands head and shoulders above the other fiction of its time'   Orson Scott Card

'This is wonderful and terrifying SF . . . certainly *Arslan* is the best political novel I've read in more than a decade'
                                                                                Samuel R. Delany

'Engh's performance is as perversely flawless as Arslan's'
                                                                                New York Times

'A compelling story'   *Publishers Weekly*

'*Arslan* makes for compulsive and disturbing reading, largely because of its intriguing central character, who combines cruelty with heroism and fierce pride . . . a genuine cult favourite'   *Booklist*

Arslan

M. J. ENGH

Copyright © M. J. Engh 2010

The right of M. J. Engh to be identified as the author
of this work has been asserted by her in accordance with
the Copyright, Designs and Patents Act 1988.

This edition published in Great Britain in 2010 by
Gollancz
An imprint of the Orion Publishing Group
Orion House, 5 Upper St Martin's Lane,
London WC2H 9EA
An Hachette UK Company

1 3 5 7 9 10 8 6 4 2

A CIP catalogue record for this book
is available from the British Library

ISBN 978 0 575 09501 4

Typeset at The Spartan Press Ltd,
Lymington, Hants

Printed in Great Britain by
Clays Ltd, St Ives plc

The Orion Publishing Group's policy is to use papers that
are natural, renewable and recyclable products and made
from wood grown in sustainable forests. The logging and
manufacturing processes are expected to conform to the
environmental regulations of the country of origin.

www.orionbooks.co.uk

For Fritz Leiber:
friend, heartener

INTRODUCTION

M. J. Engh's *Arslan* (previously released in the UK under the rather timid *ars*-avoiding alternate title *A Wind from Bukhara*) contains two of the most shocking scenes in post-war science fiction. The first is in the opening chapter. The novel's titular Turkic military dictator-of-the-world arrives in the mid-America small town of Kraftsville, Illinois, and makes his base in the local school. Having barracked and feasted his troops, he rounds the evening off by raping one school girl and one school boy in front of this appreciative audience of soldiery.

A Communistic Asiatic tyrant forcibly occupies middle America, crushing democracy, shooting opposition, raping women and children and outlawing trade and technology. It's an iteration of a particular US paranoid invasion fantasy: from Floyd Gibbons's *The Red Napoleon* (1929) to *Red Dawn* (1984), US popular culture has luridly imagined the one military catastrophe – occupation by a foreign army – that the USA has never, in actuality, suffered. Engh's contribution to this raises the transgression to deliberately hyperbolic levels.

The second shocking scene is less obvious, perhaps, but in its way more shocking. It comes near the end, when an older, physically weakened Arslan returns to Kraftsville. He builds a fortified house in the middle of town, and when a gang of marauders threatens to rape systematically the town's women. Arslan organises the defence, and rebuts the assault. The shocking part is: we realise, by this point in the novel, that *we are rooting for him*. Engh, without ever directing or manipulating the reader, has managed to shift the balance of empathy around: a figure who starts the novel positively Mephistophelean ends it with his charisma elided from diabolical to heroic. It's an extraordinary piece of novelistic sleight-of-hand; but it's much more than that. What makes this novel so very special is the depth of its understanding of the way 'force' does more than enable the domination of one human being over others; that way it shows how it also informs the electric glamour that is the currency by which all adoration is bought.

About a third of the book is given over to the narrative voice of Hunt, one of Arslan's initial victims; and through him we learn that 'adoration' is not too strong a term. The journey he, and we as readers, travel is pithily summed-up by the other narrator, Franklin Bond: 'Arslan's old theme: first the rape, then the seduction'. It gives Engh a point of purchase against which to lever her critique of the political 'cult of personality' that has foisted so many dictators on the world, from the Roman Caesars onward (Engh, when she is not writing SF, is a historian of the Roman Empire). But more than this, it becomes a means of dramatising the sort of *love* that is the novel's true theme. Love, this novel is saying, is rarely a rational process of negotiation and free exchange. It is more often likely to be a phosphorescent blaze of overmastery that the individual must, by a process of resistance rather than surrender, somehow work to integrate into his or her everyday life.

Engh runs a fearsome risk here; for no sane writer wants to give readers the impression that the sexual abuse of children leads into loving adult relationships between abuser and victim. And I don't think any sane reader would take that moral away from this novel. But by framing the story the way she does, Engh is suggesting that large-scale political and small-scale personal emotional dynamics are not separate things.

In fact *Arslan* is neither an apologia for tyranny nor a one-dimensional critique of it. Actually (and I don't say this to deprecate the book so much as identify its real focus), Engh's apprehension of the logic of fascism is pretty narrowly conceived. In the world, Fascism is always a *societal* event; a mass phenomenon. *Arslan* reduces all the large scale aspects of its story to background embroidery, often only nebulously rendered. Precisely how, we ask ourselves, does this warlord from a country smaller by population than Baltimore or Manchester become tyrant of the entire globe? There's some handwaving about a 'laser missile defence' system, and a brief, melodramatic vignette of him holding a pistol to the head of the Soviet premier; but not even the most naïve political theorist would believe global *realpolitik* works that way.

The point of all this, though, is not to negate the novel's plausibility; it is to move it, forceably, to a different arena. Actual Fascist or Communist dictators, having invaded a town, do not select a local schoolteacher, hand him a gun and offer him the chance to commit tyrannicide. Actual dictators, when faced with the assassination of a family member, would not singlehandledly wrestle the perpetrators to death in a town square display – nor would they limit their retribution to only four individuals. Actual dictators are always much more bureaucratic than gladiatorial. Engh knows this; it's just that she's not interested in the affective logic of bureaucracy. She is interested in writing a story about the extent to which love parses pain and bliss into versions of one another. She is interested in the *practical* person-to-person business of running a small town, or a school, or a family; and especially interested in the way these things contain within them the same intensities of justice and injustice, freedom and unfreedom, as Genghis Khan's governance of all Asia. Engh's genius as a novelist is the particular, not the general. Her account of the practical *details* of life, love and struggle in this novel is impressively involving and powerful, particularly given her deliberately repellent opening gambit.

Even without the sexual abuse of children, it would be a bold enough and perhaps even reckless textual strategy to take as one's hero a pitiless tyrant whose aim – we discover as the book proceeds – is nothing less than complete autogenocide, the elimination of all humanity. In fact it is a dangerous truth of art that we find it easy to 'enjoy' almost any villain; to transform bloody deeds, cruelty, atrocity into drama, and thereby make the perpetrators protagonists. And in the political arena, what calls forth our admiration is not, I think, any respect for political pragmatism – the sense that a person cannot run a country, or a town, if they are too squeamishly tender-hearted. *Arslan*, as novel, goes far beyond that. I think the novel's boldness is predicated upon an understanding that what makes the ruthless dictator weirdly admirable is a certain sort of *authenticity*. Being above the law is something dictators have in common with poets. They have the strength to break and remake notions of right and wrong in the service of winning free space for their own actions, the expression of their will. Of the three main characters in Engh's novel, two compel our respect by virtue of their pragmatic, flexible yet inviolable refusal to compromise their principles: Arslan himself and Franklin Bond (the third, Hunt Morgan, is a more complex case).

One deep consonance in the novel is its decision to represent the logic of charismatic dictator via a focus on childhood, children and childishness. There is, for instance, something of the precocious, energetic child about Arslan, I think. Ian McEwan in his novel *Saturday* (2005) muses on the nature of dictators via the example of Saddam Hussein (still, when that novel came out, alive):

> It's only children, in fact, only infants who feel a wish and its fulfillment as one; perhaps this is what gives tyrants their childish air. They reach back for what they can't have. When they meet frustration their man-slaying tantrum is never far away. Saddam, for example, doesn't simply look like a heavy-jowled brute. He gives the impression of an overgrown, disappointed boy with a pudgy hangdog look, and dark eyes a little baffled by all that he still can't ordain. Absolute power and its pleasures are just beyond reach and keep receding. He knows that another fawning general dispatched to the torture rooms, another bullet to the head of a relative won't deliver the satisfaction it once did.

What I especially like about this quotation is the way it suggests that children are always being dragged unwillingly along in the wake of 'growing up' so that the instantaneous joy of desire/ gratification is always receding further and further away from them – a loss they feel acutely, if incoherently. Hitler's mad tantrums; Stalin's ludicrous ego; these are meagre substitutions for the original *jouissance*.

But rather than slot her novel into the easy groove of satirical caricature, Engh takes the more challenging and, ultimately, more rewarding approach of drawing Arslan as a fully rounded character. Arslan is a novel absolutely interpenetrated all the way through with a deep interrogation of 'childishness' and 'adulthood'; with what is gained and lost in growing up, with questions of parental authority good and bad. We might say, and truly, that Arslan is a profoundly 'grown-up' novel; but that is not to say that it is a novel purged of childish intensities. Quite the reverse.

This is one reason why Engh structures the story around a plot to do away with children altogether: the simultaneous forced maturing and extermination of the human race. And this is why Hunt has such a pivotal role in the book: raped as a child, abandoned by his biological father, torn between the 'good' paternal figure of Bond and the 'bad' paternal figure of his abuser and mentor Arslan, it is Hunt who gets the last word. In the retrograde American pastoral imposed on the world by Arslan, Hunt goes hunting for a deer, in doing so mediating adulthood and childhood. 'Though for years past I had delighted to play with bows (making of civilization's wreck an excuse to return to my childhood's toys), for this hunt I chose a graver weapon . . . Arslan's gun.' It might misfire, he thinks, but accepting that risk was only being fair to the deer. And then he says: *'fair:* a sweeter, truer word than *just.'* Justice is what politicians talk about; but children, with no sense of connection to that 'adult' concept, nevertheless intensely comprehend the power of 'fairness.' Justice is general; fairness is personal. The shocking scene with which this extraordinary novel opens is bitterly unfair for the children caught up in it; but the strength of this fiction is in the way it bridges the space between this initial shock and the rather different shock that grows on us at the end – that, like a brilliant child, ingenuous, impulsive and unflagging, Arslan himself has worked his way into our affections.

Adam Roberts

PART ONE
FRANKLIN L. BOND

1

When his name first cropped up in the news reports, it was just one more foreign name to worry about, like so many others. And like so many others, it graduated in due time to the level of potential crisis. But before it had gone any further than that, suddenly all the rules had been changed when we weren't looking, and if you said 'he' without an obvious antecedent you were talking about Arslan.

On TV and in the news weeklies he'd looked no different from a lot of them: young, jaunty, halfway Oriental like the second-row extras in *Turandot*, and every one of them a major general at the very least. 'Turkistan – is *that* independent now?' Luella had asked me, one of the first times he showed up.

'I think it always has been.' I meant to look it up in the big atlas at school; but I was busy planning for quarterly exams, and that intention went the way of a lot of other things I meant to do. I never did get around to it till after the Emergency Broadcast Network began its terse announcements that martial law had been proclaimed throughout the United States and that all US armed forces were under the command of General Arslan. Among other things that hectic day, I looked at the map of Central Asia. *Turkistan. Cap: Bukhara. Pop: 1,369,000.* Even South Vietnam would have been able to handle a place that size. Still, with China on one border and Russia on another, and an oil field begging for development, it was small wonder Arslan had made a splash at the UN.

'Stay off the highways,' the EBS kept saying. Whether that was a friendly voice or a hostile one was anybody's guess. 'Only military transport is permitted on state, interstate, and national

3

highways.' *Military transport* – that included, apparently, the great commercial trucks that rolled past the square and on through town. We stood and watched them in the early dusk, and I wondered if it was good luck or bad that Kraftsville happened to lie on a main highway.

'I've got to get home,' Paul Sears protested. 'I can't help it if I *live* on the hardroad.'

'If I were you, Paul, I'd go around by the back road.' That was Arnold Morgan, knowing all the answers. 'Once the President invokes his emergency powers, we're required to follow his instructions. That's Federal law.'

Paul snorted. 'It didn't sound like the President to me.'

'I'd feel better if I knew who that General Arslan was,' somebody else put in. Which was about par for Kraftsville. Plenty of people in town had never heard of Premier Arslan, or didn't remember it if they had.

'He's the one that's been talking to Red China,' I said. The last news I remembered hearing about him, Arslan and the Chinese premier had been in Moscow by invitation, presumably discussing their border dispute. The Russians had been offering for months to mediate it. Turkistan had been cagey, China had emphatically refused; but at last they had agreed to a Moscow summit meeting, agenda unspecified. Now, a few days after the meeting started, Arslan was Deputy Commander in Chief of the United States armed forces. And the trucks were rolling. It didn't make a whole lot of sense.

Everybody was on the telephone. Long distance calls were getting through to some places, but none farther away than Louisiana, where Rachel Munsey talked to some of her relations and found out there was fighting going on down there. Maybe riot or maybe war – Rachel had managed not to find out that little detail; but there were people with uniforms and people without, and black and white in both categories. We couldn't make connections with the East Coast or the West Coast, and even Chicago was cut off cold. There were open lines to St Louis, our nearest city, for just two days. Then they went dead, sometime in the night.

And the next morning we got word from Monckton that a real,

4

genuine army was driving west on Illinois 460, which meant straight towards us. But Kraftsville, Illinois, wasn't likely to be anybody's military objective, and the highway didn't pass the school; I saw no reason to declare a holiday.

It was just after lunch when Luella came hurrying across Pearl Street to my office. 'I thought I'd run over and tell you instead of tying up the phone. Helen Sears just called, and she says they're passing her place right now; they ought to be in town in a few minutes.'

'You shouldn't be alone,' I said. 'Why don't you go over to Rachel Munsey's?'

'No, I'd rather be in my own house. And somebody might call.'

'All right. Call me or come over if you hear anything that sounds important. Otherwise just stay put. I want to know where you are.'

From Nita Runciman's eighth-grade room, which was the southwest corner of the top floor, you could see a little bit of the highway four blocks away. I told Nita to post one or two of her students there as lookouts and let me know as soon as they saw anything. In less than ten minutes she was on the intercom. 'They're coming through,' she said. 'Mr Bond—' Her voice crackled. 'Some of them are turning down Pearl Street. Trucks and jeeps.'

They didn't pass the school; they stopped beside it. I watched them from the south window of my office while I talked on the intercom. They pulled up in a line right in front of me, their engines still running, stretching nearly the full block. The last jeep of the string drove past the others and turned into the parking lot. There was a driver, and a man with a submachine gun, and one passenger. I didn't know what I had been expecting, but when I saw him, my heart went down a notch. He was too young, too young and too happy.

I had no doubt of who he was, much as I could have used a little doubt right then. The news pictures that had seemed so anonymous suddenly flashed into vivid focus. He gave orders exuberantly, waving his hands. Soldiers swarmed out from Pearl Street in both directions, into the schoolground and into the yard of my house. I searched the upstairs windows for a sight of Luella.

But I didn't have much time to look. Soldiers were at the south door, a few steps from my office, some of them with rifles reversed – ready to smash the glass if the double doors were locked, or maybe just for fun. I got there first, and they waited grinning while I opened up. We might be wanting those doors intact.

They pushed in. Whatever they were, they weren't Americans. I got in front of a sergeant (I didn't bother to count his stripes, but he looked like a sergeant) and braced my legs. 'Wait a minute!' I said. He looked at me without much interest and gave an order, and three men backed me into my office. I guessed this was what was called token resistance; anyway, it seemed like the best idea available at the moment. Now it was my teachers' turn. They had instructions to sit as tight as possible, cooperate without objection, volunteer nothing, and keep the children still. There wasn't much else we could do on such short notice.

Boots thudded along the hall, up the stairs, down into the basement. Doors opened, doors slammed. A long barrage of thumps told me they were opening the desks. Then most of them came trooping back and out of the door. It had only taken a few minutes.

The sergeant held the south door open, saluting smartly, and General Arslan strode in, with quite a retinue behind him. He was stocky, but he moved with lightness and bounce, like a good welterweight boxer. He turned into the office as if he knew his way around. The soldiers let go of my arms and fell back, and I was face to face with him.

'You are in charge of this school?' His English was very clear, his voice a quick baritone.

'That's right,' I said. 'I'm the principal.'

'What is your name?'

'Franklin Bond.'

He had been smiling all the time. Now he tilted his head in a little hint of a bow, never taking his eyes off mine. There was nothing else impressive about him that you could put your finger on, but he did have the most piercing eyes I'd ever seen. 'Good,' he said. 'You will show me your school.'

'Gladly. But I'd like to know what you're here for.'

He strode out, and a bayonet prodded the small of my back, in

6

case I hadn't gotten the message. My legs were a good deal longer than his; I caught up in two steps, and we went down the hall side by side. He glanced up at me with amusement. 'I shall bivouac in your town.' Well, that sounded temporary. 'I shall hold a dinner here tonight. You will be my guest.'

I showed him the new west wing first, with the kitchen and cafeteria and the wide folding doors opening into our gym that doubled as auditorium. He took it all in with those eyes of his, as if the fate of the world hung on everything he looked at. Then the library and the audio-visual room and the music room. Then I had to lead him back into the main block of the school.

'And what is this?'

'That's the fire door.' Where he came from, it might be a revolutionary concept. 'In case a fire ever broke out in one part of the building, we could pull this steel door down and keep it out of the other part.'

He nodded and ran his left hand up the tracks. 'It is good,' he said. A connoisseur's appreciation.

It wasn't much different from a start-of-school guided tour for the PTA. A little pack of soldiers – half a dozen, maybe – seemed to be tied to General Arslan's heels. I showed him the shop, the furnace room, the washrooms, the teachers' lounges, the broom closets. We looked into every classroom. He asked the name of every teacher. The children sat subdued and uneasy at their desks; I was proud to see that the teachers were keeping them quietly busy.

The only classroom we actually went into was Nita Runciman's eighth grade. Arslan paused a moment at the open door, resting his hand lightly on the frame, and then stepped in with a broad smile. He stood with arms akimbo, surveying the class. For the first time I noticed he wore a pistol on his left hip. The children watched him blankly.

Suddenly he stepped forward, down one aisle and back another, swiftly tapping three children on the shoulder as he passed. He was saying something, chuckling, to his men as he came back toward the door. Immediately the three were pulled from their seats and hustled after him. It was two girls and a boy – Paula Sears, LouAnn Williams, and Hunt Morgan. He had picked, very possibly, my three best eighth-graders.

7

'Wait a minute,' I said. He had to stop or walk into me. He stopped. 'Where are you taking these children? And what for?'

He put on an expression of mocking innocence. Yes, he was too young. He shrugged. 'Is it important that you should know this? However, I tell you. They will serve at my dinner tonight.' He stepped forward, and the faithful bayonet prodded me out of his way.

Back in my office, one hip perched on the edge of my desk, he lit cigarette after cigarette, smoking each one down in intense short drags till the live coal touched his fingers, flipping the smoldering butts onto my floor. He had a window opened, which let in a cold draft without clearing the air much. Meanwhile he was busy. The three eighth-graders had been led out and driven away in a truck. Soldiers kept coming and going, reporting to Arslan and receiving orders. Every one of them looked like a kid getting ready for a birthday party. I'd never seen so many jubilant faces on grown men at one time before. Whether it was a good sign or bad remained to be seen.

He wasn't just planning a bivouac and a dinner. It was to be a feast. It was to be, all too obviously, a victory celebration. The cooks were put to work, not just in the kitchen but in the home ec room, with Maud Dollfus in charge there. Five of Maud's best students were drafted to help, and so were the music teacher (Hunt Morgan's mother Jean) and our new little librarian. The freezers were emptied. There was a regular procession of soldiers carrying cases of liquor. My phone kept ringing, and Arslan kept answering it himself, sounding brusque and casual in his ungodly language. I wasn't much acquainted with the ways of generals, but it seemed to me he was an almighty informal commander.

I'd settled down in my desk chair at first, to keep him out of it; but the intrusion was getting to my stomach, and pretty soon I had to stand up and move around. I was just pacing back from the big window when he suddenly swung toward me with a friendly smile and announced, 'Now it is your turn.' He waved his hand hospitably toward my phone. 'You have three hours, twenty minutes; at five P.M. the telephone service stops. You will inform the parents of your students that their children are held as hostages for the good behavior of all citizens. You will inform

8

them that they will surrender all vehicles and all weapons and ammunition to my soldiers on demand. You will inform them that each time one of my soldiers is attacked or resisted, two children will be executed – if possible, children belonging to the family of the guilty citizen. You will inform them that they may bring one blanket for each child, to be delivered to the southwest corner of the school grounds by five-thirty P.M. You will inform them that for each citizen seen outside his or her home after six P.M., one child will be executed – if possible, again, a child belonging to the family of the guilty citizen.' He straightened up suddenly from the desk and stepped close to me, thrusting his face up toward mine. He was alive with eager pleasure. 'Have you understood?' he demanded exultantly. 'Do you believe that I can do what I say – and that I will do it?'

Maybe and maybe not. I pushed past him, bumping his shoulder hard, and picked up the phone. He was still grinning as he led his retinue out.

There were about two hundred families represented in the school, and not all of them had telephones. I called first the ones who were most likely to be of help and gave each of them a list of others to contact, ticking off names in the school register. It wasn't just a matter of spreading the news. Everybody had to be convinced. Everybody. The middle of southern Illinois might not be a very likely spot for military atrocities, but I was damned if I'd call his bluff. I wasn't going to have children slaughtered – not my own students, not in my own school. And he looked like a man who could have a taste for blood.

The second call I made (I wanted to let Arslan's men get out of the office first) was to Luella. 'They've been here,' she said grimly. 'They took the couch and the green armchair, for some reason. And they turned the whole house wrong side out. They just ransacked everything. It'll take me *days* to get it cleaned up.'

'But they didn't hurt you?'

'No, no. I just stayed out of their way.'

I gave her a list of names to work on and told her to be careful – good advice in a cyclone, but there wasn't much else to say.

I was still on the phone at five, checking with people who'd helped make calls. The line went dead almost on the second by the master clock. That was it. I rubbed my face and said a little prayer.

They had left me alone all this time, and when I stepped out into the hall nobody bothered me. I walked down to the cafeteria and through it into the gym. My living-room couch was standing in the center of the stage at the opposite end, with my coffee table in front of it. Some of the cafeteria tables had been moved into the gym, and between them the floor was crowded with chairs – all of the school's folding chairs, teachers' desk chairs, and a medley of chairs that must have been confiscated from people's homes. No doubt my armchair was in there someplace. I strolled back into the main block of the school.

Relays of children were being led into the A-V room and the shop room, and a couple of Arslan's officers were interviewing them there. The officers were polite, but it wasn't likely they'd get much information, considering that the scared kids couldn't understand one word in four of their accented English. A lot of blankets had already been delivered, and more were coming all the time. Grinning soldiers were distributing them, as friendly as you please. Little Betty Hanson was very shaky, but the rest of the teachers made me proud. I sent Nita Runciman down to help Betty with her third grade, and took Nita's class across the hall to join the other eighth-grade class under Jack Partridge.

This time there was a colonel in my office. He was in the process of going through my desk, taking a few notes and helping himself to a few of my papers, which he filed neatly in a large folder. He glanced up when I came in and introduced himself in an atrocious accent. It went with his dark, sharp features and wolfish eyes; he would have made a pretty good villain in an old movie. I couldn't make out the name very well, but part of it sounded like Nizam. I stood and watched him till he got through with my desk and applied himself to the file cabinet. Then I sat down and watched him some more. He breezed through the files very rapidly, not seeming to find anything worth taking, thanked me, and stalked out.

After the five-thirty deadline no more blankets were accepted, though a few more people showed up with them. Maud Dollfus organized teams of seventh- and eighth-grade boys to carry supper trays to the classrooms. (She was about to use the girls from her home ec classes, till I told her I wasn't going to have girls running around with the halls full of soldiers.) It was a slow way to feed three hundred children, but keeping them out of the way was worth a little inefficiency.

Six o'clock came and went, and I felt my stomach tighten as the hand of the clock moved past that curfew mark. What I wanted most of all right then was to sit down somewhere and pray, but I wasn't about to do it with all those grinning Turkistanis (assuming that was what they were) bustling around. Besides, the supper business was keeping me busy. We finished a little before seven-thirty. I was eating my own meal at last when a certain stir among the soldiers told me Arslan was coming back. He carried a sphere of motion and excitement around him. I knew the phenomenon very well. We didn't see it so often in grade school, but it happened every few years in high school, whenever the basketball team had a star player who inspired the rest of the kids with pride instead of envy. There was exactly that feeling obvious in the looks of the Turkistanis; wherever Arslan went was where the action was.

He certainly moved with the style of an athlete riding a wave of popularity. He came in swinging along as if he heard cheers on every side. 'Now.' He faced me, about a foot too close, considering the liquor on his breath. 'You should see that your children are disposed for the night. Very soon they will be locked in their classrooms.'

'Quite a few of them are going to need to go to the bathroom in the night.'

'There will be a man on duty here.' He tapped the intercom on my desk. 'The door will be opened for any adequate cause.' He grinned arrogantly. 'You see, I am not unreasonable. You will return to this office with those members of your staff who are not required in the classrooms or in preparing food.' The corner of his mouth drew itself into a deep dimple of amusement, and he paused for just a second before he added, 'Including Miss Hanson,' and it was only then that I began to understand what we were really in for.

'Miss Hanson is required in her classroom.'

'This is not true,' he told me reprovingly. 'Mrs Runciman is competent to replace her there. You yourself have arranged this.'

'By what authority are you acting, General?' It was a question I'd forgotten to ask before. He carried his credentials in his eyes.

He pursed his lips. 'By authority of the President of the United States of America.'

I made sure that things were squared away in all of the rooms, and the intercom working. I said a few words to each class, and a few more to each teacher privately. Last of all, I brought Betty Hanson out. There was a lone soldier in my office now. We stood in the empty corridor. She hadn't been crying for a while, from the looks of her, but she was shaking. I squeezed her arm, and she took a deep breath and tried to calm herself. 'How old are you, Betty?'

'Twenty-three.'

'That makes you our youngest faculty member. But remember, Betty, there are about three hundred people in this building who are younger than you. A lot is going to be demanded of you, but a lot is being demanded of them, too. They're my responsibility, and they're your responsibility, and every teacher's here. You understand that, don't you?' She nodded. She'd stopped trembling, and a little color was coming back into her fragile face. 'Nobody's asking us to do anything heroic, Betty. I'm just asking you to remember you're a teacher. I expect you to behave accordingly. Will you promise me that?'

She took another shuddering breath. 'Yes, Mr Bond.'

'Good girl. I know you will.' I put an arm around her and shepherded her into the office, which comforted her and saved me from having to look at her directly. She was too young and too scared – too pretty, aside from the temporary effects of the tears. Arslan's hands had looked very hard.

It was mainly to provide cover and comfort for Betty that I pried loose Maud Dollfus and Jean Morgan from the cooking. Perry Carpenter had been helping the janitor bank down the old furnace. As shop teacher and coach Perry hadn't had much to do all day, and he was pretty nervous. The six of us waited in the office, and at first nobody spoke.

'Franklin,' Jean said sharply, when she saw me watching her, 'if you're wondering whether to tell me that they took Hunt, I already know about it. But that's all I know, so if there's anything else, for Pete's sake tell me.' Her chin was up and her voice firm. I didn't need to worry about Jean Morgan.

'You know as much as I do, then, Jean. Hunt's a level-headed boy.'

'That's what I'm telling myself,' she said doggedly.

The soldier lounging at the door came to eager attention. 'Here it is,' I said. But Arslan didn't bother to enter the office; he just returned the soldier's salute and gestured us towards the cafeteria. Two of his followers dropped off to herd us down the hall after him.

The tables bristled with liquor bottles. The folding doors stood wide open, and we threaded our way through into the gym. It was filling up fast with soldiers. The moment Arslan appeared, they raised a shout of joy. There was no doubting the spontaneity of that cheer. He waved his arms and shouted back at them. He loved it; and to all appearances they loved him.

They were streaming in from the back door, filling the gym and starting now to flow on into the cafeteria, so that Arslan, in his progress toward the stage, breasted the full stream of them. They opened a path for him, closing in again in little eddies around us, and as he passed they laughed, shouted, shook their fists triumphantly. It was an impressive thing to walk through.

They were fresh and spruce. They didn't look as though they'd been in any battles very recently, but it was a dead certainty they'd been in battles. Not a man of them but looked older and grimmer than their general, though there was nothing grim about their mood at the moment. In one word, they looked tough – not the desperate boy-toughness I'd seen in so many American veterans, but the unpretentious toughness of professionals.

Near the back door we were halted by the pressure of the stream. Arslan stood flushed and laughing – shaking hands, slapping backs, waving over shoulders at faces beyond. In half a minute we were cut off from him by the swarm, and gradually . forced backwards. I steered us up against the wall, and we stuck there stubbornly.

No matter how well you knew your teachers, you could never

predict for sure how they would act in a completely new situation. But you could make a pretty darned good guess – especially if one of them had been your next-door neighbor for four years. Perry Carpenter worried me. Perry with his breezy ways and red hair and long-handled basketball reach had been the most convenient hero for the boys of his teams and classes, but not a man I'd ask for anything out of the ordinary. Now, scared rotten, he was ready to sell the school or the whole country, whichever was in demand, to whoever held the gun. I couldn't blame him, any more or less than I blamed myself for having a bad stomach. It was just another aggravating factor that had to be taken into account.

At last the stream stopped flowing. The tiers of seats were packed; the tables were crowded. Whoever had decided how many troops were to be squeezed into the gym and cafeteria tonight had figured it pretty close. But they were all in; I could see that only a couple of sentries were left outside when the door finally closed. Arslan waved his arms, and the soldiers jostled down into their seats. Now only he, and we, and the little pack that must be his bodyguard, were left standing. He turned to us, and the look that lit up his face made me stiffen. It was a devil's look, a look of white-hot pleasure.

'You are my guests,' he said. Without turning his eyes away from us he gave an order, and suddenly his guards were at us, pinioning our arms, wheeling us face-forward against the wall, and in what seemed seconds we were helpless as papooses, our arms roped tight (they had had those ropes mighty handy) and our mouths choked with cloth gags. All except Betty Hanson.

They turned us again to face Arslan. He let his eyes drift relishingly over us all and settle on Betty. She was leaning against the wall beside me, trembling so hard that I felt it through the plaster. Slowly and thoughtfully he stretched out his left hand and closed it on her right breast. Slowly and thoughtfully he caressed it. 'You,' he said tenderly, 'will wait.' He nodded to one of the bodyguard, and instantly she was grabbed by the arm and hustled out the back door. The troops shouted applause and groaned disappointment. He threw them an acknowledging grin. Then he took two easy steps to stand in front of Perry Carpenter at my other side. The gleam of his eyes was intensely mocking. 'You are not worth keeping alive,' he said. And he turned to another one of his men and gave a brusque order. The soldier looked regretful.

It wasn't necessary to know the language. A quavering whisper of sound came from Perry, and he pitched limply against my shoulder. 'You should not worry,' Arslan said consolingly. 'I have ordered him to play no games with you. He will kill quickly.'

So he was willing to murder a man to make a point. The soldier who'd received the order pulled Perry off of me and prodded him to the door. Arslan looked us over coolly, wheeled, and mounted the steps to the stage. He waved down their cheers and settled himself on my couch, stretching out full length and sinking his head and shoulders luxuriously onto a pyramid of cushions in the corner. And the feast began.

Maud's scared boys served it – not bringing the food all the way, but forming a bucket-brigade line from the kitchen to just inside the gym door and passing the trays along it. From there the soldiers took them, and they flew, wavering wildly, through a forest of reaching arms, hand to hand up to the highest rows. There weren't enough trays to go around, of course, and well before all the tiers were served, plates began to appear – confiscated plates, no doubt. All things considered, it was a pretty efficient operation.

And whether it was from being under their general's eye or some other reason, for a mob of celebrating soldiers they were pretty gentlemanly. That dawned on me against my will when I saw the emptied trays being passed back. And so far as I'd been able to see all day, not a man had made an improper move – not a serious one – toward any of the girls or the women teachers. They looked wild, they sounded wild, but they were better disciplined than any troop of Boy Scouts I'd ever seen.

As fast as the top tiers finished their noisy meals and politely handed in their trays, they started to sing. There must have been a couple of hundred voices joined in by the time I realized that singing was what it was. It puzzled me, the mindless, tuneless, inhuman noise that came out of them, till I realized this must be what passed for music in Turkistan. Then it grated on me, hard. As noise, it was acceptable. As music, it was desecration.

How long we stood there, deserted and ignored, I wasn't sure.

Jean beside me held herself stiff as a poker and alert as a sentry, her face awkwardly strained around the gag. For myself, I was aching just to move – longing just to stretch, just to change position, just to shake off the ropes. I shook my head, shifted my feet, flexed my shoulder muscles. I felt like yelling and stamping and throwing a few things. The worst of it was the gag. It was a lot more than uncomfortable; it was insulting.

Meanwhile the show went on. Maybe we were an exhibit ourselves, but we were something else, too. General Arslan was on stage, all right, and playing to a double audience. It wasn't enough that his own men should respond to him like an orchestra; some representatives of Kraftsville had to hear the performance and watch him conduct. Now he was in his glory. He proposed the toasts, he led the songs. The whole gym echoed and reeked with drunken happiness. Still there was a waiting air, an overture feeling, as if there was some expected climax yet to come. And it came.

Arslan, propped on one elbow, swung his glass arm's-length high; at once they were all attending eagerly. He bellowed a few sentences at them, and each one drew its response of cheers and laughter. Then he drained off his drink, shouted a brisk order backstage, and sank again into his cushions.

A long, welling, multitudinous sound rose out of the relative silence that followed his last word; a growing, blossoming, self-renewing disharmony of whistles, laughter, cries, applause. Paula Sears was being led out from the left wing of the stage. Each of her elbows was gripped by a studiously poker-faced soldier. She was naked. She was thirteen years old.

They kneed the coffee table away, to give the spectators an unobstructed line of sight. They forced her down on her knees in front of the couch, and as Arslan's hand went under her arm and clasped her back they released her and sprang aside, each to one end of the couch, and stood there at attention.

The khaki wave-trough of the gym grew suddenly rough and ragged, as men fought for a better view, climbed on chairs and tables, waved their arms enthusiastically. She was struggling, but it was hardly what you could call a contest. Already he had got her stretched out against himself, rolling upon her hard. The noise took on coherence and rhythm, and in a surging chant they cheered him on. When he was through, he heaved himself against the back of the couch, and with one knee and one elbow he nudged her off onto the floor. She lay tumbled there till the two soldiers hauled her up and walked her stumblingly off the stage and down the steps at our end. They passed within a yard of us on their way to the back door. I saw her face, and I saw the blood that drabbled her legs.

That would have been enough; surely, that would have been enough. But no – any man could have raped one little girl. He took time to enjoy another drink. Then he turned his head and gave his sharp order once more. And this time, to their delirious whoops, it was Hunt Morgan who was led naked onstage.

He was walking docilely enough when I first caught sight of him; but from the second he realized the scene that had been set for him, he was fighting. And the troops were crazy with delight. The whole gym shook with their shouting and stamping. Arslan had trouble keeping Hunt under. The boy fought with flailing arms and legs; the soldiers screamed and bellowed with a new ferocity; and I felt my flesh sag with a cold sadness. Then through a lull in the din I heard Hunt's cry – a muffled, wordless squawl of anguish and shame and rage. It was a signal that set off their cheers again.

Jean Morgan was leaned against the wall, not slumped, but tense and quivering, her face drained. They led Hunt off and past us, and he walked upright, not half-collapsed like Paula, not struggling now, either, but with eyes fixed on the floor, his dark hair falling raggedly around his closed face, and his naked shoulders looked thin and pitiful.

When he was gone, and the troops had settled down a little, Arslan stood up. He made a little speech, and they cheered him, and the liquor detail hauled more bottles out from under the stage and started passing them out. A wiry little corporal, serious as a judge, suddenly bounded up on the stage and knelt to tie the lace of Arslan's shoe, and the soldiers guffawed with happy humor. Arslan made as if to pat the man's head, and then bowed gravely to him instead, doubling the joke. Finally he stooped to finish off his last drink, flipped the glass high over his shoulder in a comedian's gesture, and walked down the steps.

He stopped directly in front of us. Whether the bronze of his skin was suntan or native color, it gave him a discordant look of wholesomeness. He was brimming with glee, glowing, disheveled, with heavy, drunken breath; and I swam in pure fury.

He cocked his head at Jean, his eyes crinkling with laughter. 'You should be proud of your son, madam. He fights well – well.' He faced me square and laid the flat of his left hand lightly on my chest. Involuntarily I twisted. 'You, sir, you give me much pleasure. You are good – good.' And the hand gave one real, very gentle pat. He beamed intensely on us, and passed us by.

In a little while they took us to the teachers' lounges, unbound and ungagged us, and locked us in. For a long time yet the noises of the feast went on. I lay on the cot, trying to pray away the pain in my stomach and chest, concentrating everything I had on that simple task – to burn away, dissolve, drain out somehow some part of the killing hate that swelled in me. It was too much. It was too much.

2

'I have seen your mayor and your aldermen. I have seen your county supervisor and your commissioners. They are not adequate even for normal times. Their government is now dissolved. If they attempt to revive it, they will be executed. You, sir, will work with my officers. I have assigned an interpreter to you. Your task is to convert your district to self-sufficiency.'

It was morning. I was sitting at my desk, and he was sitting on it, or as near as made no difference – perched sideways on the far edge, his right hand planted flat on my papers and his weight leaned on it squarely. 'What do you mean, "my district"?' The difficulty I had talking to Arslan was physical. My lips and tongue and vocal cords simply resisted. It was obscene and unnatural to use human speech to him.

'Approximately your county. The boundaries will be demonstrated to you. Any citizen attempting to cross those boundaries is liable to execution. Within the few simple rules that I have given, sir, your people are entirely free.'

They were simple enough. Anyone out after sunset (which he considerately defined for me as the moment the sun disappeared below the horizon) was liable to be shot on sight. Anyone resisting or disobeying a soldier was liable to be shot summarily. Anyone found in possession of firearms or ammunition was liable to be executed – no qualification on that one. Now the boundary rule. And the cruellest of all, the teaser, the killer, the one that knotted up my stomach in the worst spasm I'd felt in years: the billet rule. Every household – whether it was old Billy Moss living alone in his little ramshackle house, or Junior Boyle and his bride in their trailer behind his mother's place, or the Felix Karchers with eight kids, two grandmothers, and a hired girl – every household was to have one soldier billeted in it. If any one of these soldiers died of any cause or was attacked in any way, anywhere, at any time, by anybody, all the members of 'his' household were to be executed. Summarily, no doubt. I didn't like the distinction between *shot* and *executed*, either. *Shot* was at least definite; it eliminated a lot of possibilities. As for my household, the billet rule didn't quite apply to us. We had something a little extra. We had Arslan.

Upstairs we had four rooms and a bathroom. They had all been intended as bedrooms, but we'd never needed that many, and since the little boy died a dozen years ago, we'd needed only one. Luella used one of the smaller, back rooms for her sewing, and I had fixed up the other one as a den and home office, where I could play Verdi records as loud as I pleased, and work out the plans for next semester and next year that there was never enough time for in my office at school. The east front room we kept as a guestroom, and we slept in the other ourselves. I assumed that Arslan had taken over the guestroom.

I hadn't been home yet; didn't know, as things stood now, if I would ever get home. It looked as though the bivouac was settling into an occupation. The Turkistanis were busy after their debauch. A considerable arsenal was being collected in the school music room, as they brought in confiscated shotguns and rifles. The billet rule sounded like a permanent substitute for hostages; Arslan wouldn't have any excuse for holding the children much longer. And while I didn't expect that fact to influence him the way it would a human being, I did expect it to bring a turning point of some kind. Whether I was willing to 'work with his officers' was doubtful, to say the least, but it might depend a lot on the direction of the turn.

We had served a breakfast of leftovers, as soon as possible after they had unlocked us. Only Jean Morgan stayed in seclusion in the women's lounge. I'd known Jean through many years and more than one trouble, and it had taken this to daunt her. We put all the classes to doing calisthenics, and then a singing session, and got started on schoolwork at almost the normal time.

It was barely ten when Arslan appeared, with his twinkling eyes and his few simple rules and the news that he had quartered himself in my house. And gradually I got my vocal apparatus under control. *Entirely free*, he had said. 'What about your soldiers? Aren't there any restrictions on *them*?'

He smiled swiftly. 'There are restrictions. It is not desirable that your people should know exactly what restrictions. This would encourage disputes and misjudgments. I myself will judge my men.'

I looked at him. 'How old are you?' I asked him. My voice was still a little thick.

He gave my look back steadily, and soberly for the moment. Then he straightened up. 'Twenty-five years,' he said softly. 'Come.'

He motioned me ahead of him, into the cross-hall and out through the south door into the parking lot. It was the first time I'd been outside since yesterday morning. We had had a late fall, with off-again on-again weather that had put the forsythias in bloom at Thanksgiving, and now in the first week of December it was like October again, mild and sunny and breezy. The air was delicious.

There were soldiers all over the lot, buzzing in every direction like bees at the door of a hive. A good deal of their traffic was straight across Pearl Street to my house. That sharp-eyed colonel was expounding something, without gestures, to a little cluster of noncoms, making them look first west, then south, then east. Arslan spoke, and they all saluted him and stared at me, the noncoms grinning, Colonel Nizam with a mortal frown.

We crossed the street, but when I started up my front walk, Arslan laughed. 'This way.' Some kind of armored truck was parked in my driveway – my car had disappeared – and a Land Rover behind it on the lawn. He slid into the driver's seat of the Land Rover and motioned me toward the seat beside him.

I got in. He threw it into gear and plowed straight across the lawn and one of Luella's flower beds before he turned down the Morrisville road. Even so, he drove well. He handled the car like a man who made his living driving. There wasn't a bump or a pothole on the road that he didn't foresee and compensate for. He was looking very smug.

'Would it be easy to kill me?' he asked pleasantly.

21

I imagined not. In any case, I wasn't about to try it, with the school full of children and Luella alone with his soldiers. And it didn't make any obvious sense for him to drive out into the country with me, alone and unguarded; there had to be a catch. 'That's not why I'm watching you,' I said. 'I was thinking you may make some pretty big headlines, but this is the first time I've seen you do anything for yourself. It takes a corporal just to tie your shoes.'

He stopped the Land Rover right there in the middle of the road, turned off the engine, leaned his left elbow on the wheel, and slewed around on the seat to face me full. His eyes fairly danced, exactly like some fourth-grader bound to stir up mischief at any cost. And by God, it made me ache to look at him – ache to get my hands on his neck or my foot in his face. We were already out of sight of town, just before the road turned west, with Sam Tuller's fields on our right and the woods of the old Karcher place on the left. There wasn't a sign of life anywhere.

'I have brought you here for two reasons, sir. One, that you should tell me about these farms. Two, that you should see that I do things for myself.'

The little breeze stirred the heavy, dead-black hair above his foreign face. He was breathing fast and easily. His eager eyes were no more than two feet from mine. And I felt my blood surge up like a river rising. 'Are you daring me to attack you?'

'Yes, sir,' he said softly.

I took a deep breath. 'You're a good seventeen years younger. You're armed, and you're a professional soldier. I'll be damned if I'm going to throw away whatever chance I've got just to satisfy your sadistic whims. If you want to kill me, you'll have to do it on your own initiative.'

He didn't move a muscle; only the whole expression of his face changed. The smile was still there, but the eyes were serious. 'Good.' He stared at me as if he was reading the fine print on the inside of my skull. 'Your language has a beautiful saying, "Strike while the iron is hot." Now, sir, you are hot. You would like to kill me, yes. But you are afraid that if you tried, you would fail; and this is true. Also you are afraid that if you succeeded, my soldiers would take a great vengeance; and this is also true. But there will be times when it will be easy to kill me, for you or for others. I tell you now what will happen if I ever die within the borders of this district – even of what you call . . . natural causes.' His smile tightened. 'Every effort will be made to exterminate the entire population of the district, beginning with Kraftsville, which will be surrounded and burned to the ground.'

I swallowed a swell of rage. 'What you mean is, those are the orders you've given.'

'This has been sworn to me by Colonel Nizam,' he said portentously – there should have been a dark bass chord of accompaniment – but all at once he grinned. 'Yes; yes, sir – orders and oaths are no more immortal than men. So I tell you this, sir: my soldiers are like a pack of hungry wolves; they need no whip to drive them to the kill.' He fished a cigarette out of his shirt pocket and lit it without taking his eyes off mine. 'It is important for your people that you should understand this. Do you understand?'

I nodded. I understood it.

'Do you believe it?'

I nodded again. I believed it very well. Whatever was going on in the rest of the world didn't matter much – *this* was what was happening in Kraftsville. 'Do we have anything to gain by *not* killing you?'

He smiled sweetly – sweetly is the word. 'That, of course, you cannot know with certainty. But it is a chance, and you cannot afford to lose any chance.'

I cleared my throat. 'Second question. What if somebody decides to kill you anyway? How are you going to stop them?'

He shrugged. 'That is your problem, sir.'

'I'd say it's yours.'

He pursed his lips – considering, probably, how to make it sound plausible. 'I desire to live, yes. But the desire ceases with the life. And the process of dying does not deter me. I am a soldier. Sir, I am Arslan. You should not expect me to think like a citizen of Kraftsville.'

No, not a citizen of Kraftsville. Looking into his eyes was like looking into the bottomless pit. 'If you don't mind dying,' I said, 'why go to all this trouble?'

He smiled again. 'I have said that I desire to live. It gives me pleasure; also there are plans to be fulfilled before I die. Therefore I take certain precautions. But when I am dead, I shall not remember these things. Only the living can suffer.'

'That's a matter of opinion.'

'I urge you to believe that it is my opinion.' He cocked his head. 'I have a question for you also, sir. Why are you not afraid of me?'

'Because I can't afford to be.' I'd no sooner said it than I felt my insides jerked by a cold convulsion. He must have seen it in my face, because he exploded suddenly into a laugh, gay and contemptuous. That made me hot again. 'I've got a bad stomach,' I said steadily. 'If I got upset, it would interfere with my work.'

'And exactly what is your work, sir?'

'I'm responsible for my school. If you don't know what that means, I can't tell you.'

He studied me. 'I can make you afraid.'

'Maybe so, General. But why bother to try? I can't do you any good if I'm disabled.'

He nodded agreeably. He finished his cigarette in silence, crushed out the butt between his thumb and fingers – he could be very careful, I noticed, when it suited him – and flipped it onto the road. 'Now, sir, we shall show each other something. I shall show that I mean what I say; and you will show whether you have understood.' For the first time since he stopped the car his eyes left my face, as he unholstered his pistol. He took it loosely by the barrel and held it out to me.

I had to lick my lips before I could speak, and I could barely hear my own voice through the blood singing in my ears. What made him think he could play games with me? 'You wouldn't offer it to me, except you're sure I won't take it.'

'Ah, no,' he said quickly. 'There is always risk. In every battle there is risk of death – even when victory is sure.' He smiled. 'It is loaded, sir; with live ammunition.'

I thought that when I reached for the gun, or at least when I touched it, he would simply jerk it back. But he didn't. For just an instant we both had hold of it, and I felt the solidity of that casual-looking grasp. And then it was all mine. It was years since I'd held a handgun, a lot of years. It felt very effective.

He wasn't smiling any more, but his whole air was too comfortable. I could well imagine the gun wasn't loaded, or was loaded with blanks. It was the sort of joke that might tickle his fancy. And if I fired a trial shot at something else, the report – if there was one – would bring his men down on me as fast as if I'd really killed him. No doubt the woods and fields were full of them already. But he was right about one thing – I couldn't afford to pass up any chance.

'Start the car.'

'No,' he said. 'You are not my master; I am yours.'

I had hit him – as hard as I could, lefthanded and backhanded in that cramped space – literally before I knew what I was doing. He took it full in the face without flinching, and it knocked him back against the frame. But as I struck, his hand came up and touched my left wrist – not a grab or a blow, just a touch like a cat's playful pat.

He straightened up and leaned on the wheel again. Still, that had gotten to him. It took a minute for his eyes to clear – ten seconds, anyway – and when they did, he looked really hard for the first time, like a man fighting. 'It is not your fault,' he went on smoothly. 'You have the strength, and the courage, and the brain, and now the gun. You lack only the army.' I could see he was swallowing blood. 'If my troops were not occupying your town, I should act differently. Perhaps I should even start the car. But now, sir, if you kill me' – he smiled thinly, swallowed again, and shrugged – 'it is the end for me, but it is the beginning of very bad things for you and for Kraftsville, and for many other places.'

'Your little Turkistani wolf pack looks pretty small in the middle of the United States of America, General.'

His mouth pursed with amusement or a good imitation of it. 'Do not forget, sir, that I command the armed forces of the United States of America.'

'You can't tell me they'd fight for you.'

Another shrug. 'Was it necessary for the armed forces of Vichy France to fight for Hitler? Do not deceive yourself with false hopes, sir. There is no United States government to help you.

There is no Soviet government. There is no government in Canada, in England, in France, in Germany, in Egypt, in Israel, in Turkey, in India, in China, in Japan, in Australia. I am the government. I am the leash that holds my wolf packs. If you kill me now, sir' – he smiled a real smile – 'hell breaks loose.'

'As far as I can see, it already has.'

He shook his head gently at me. 'Then you have not seen war.'

'What happens if I don't kill you now?'

He turned and spat over his shoulder, and wiped his mouth on the back of his hand. 'You will not be punished. You have asked how I can prevent others from killing me. There is no certain method. But you, sir, can help. Do you understand?'

'You mean spread the word that you're worse dead than alive?'

'Exactly.'

'Before I did that, I'd have to believe it. And I'm not about to believe anything till I know a whole lot more about the situation. Just what the hell have you done, General? What the hell are you planning to do?'

He said nothing. He looked at me, cool and level. The gun felt warm and heavy in my hand. 'Do you think I am some politician,' he said at last, 'to feed upon power and praise?'

'I think you're a devil. I think you're a barbarian Hitler. Your idea of fun is raping children in front of their mothers.'

'Fun, yes,' he agreed comfortably. 'If you cannot endure this, sir, shoot – and let my soldiers have their turn. But I have not conquered the world for . . . fun.'

Up the back of my neck I felt my scalp prickling. 'There's a lot of world not covered in that list you reeled off.'

An empty smile flitted across his face. He looked very thoughtfully at the pistol in my hand. 'Well, I am a soldier. I do not pretend that I would have let the chance go by, once I saw it. But also I saw another chance.' He met my eyes suddenly. 'More difficult, sir. But if I work quickly, it is conceivable that I can do it.'

I had to wet my lips again. 'Do what?'

'Make the world a good place in which to live.'

I heard myself make a snorting noise. Somehow I had expected better from him.

He smiled innocently. 'Or I could say, "destroy civilization," if you prefer that I should be . . . diabolical. But what is that civilization, sir? Is it so worthy of preservation? Tell me, what was wrong with the world, sir?'

'I'll tell you exactly what *is* wrong with it. Too little Christianity.'

His eyebrows went up. 'Christianity has had its chance. Now I have mine. No, sir; the two great curses of mankind are very simple: hunger and crowding. Crowd human beings together, and all miseries multiply. And there is no greater misery – believe me, sir – than hunger. Therefore there are two great needs: more food, more land. And this has always been true, even when food and land were absolutely plentiful. It is a problem of distribution.'

I stared at him, amazed as much as disgusted. It was incredible that a two-bit warlord from nowhere, infected with some out-moded Middle Eastern strain of agrarian socialism, could be kinging it over my town – let alone my whole country. I had it in my hand, if the gun was loaded, to end it right now. And if he was as crazy as he must be, it might really be loaded, and we might really be alone. I didn't think it would take two weeks for this country to shake off Arslan's wolf packs. If the gun was loaded.

And I would have the gun and the Land Rover, and maybe a little time. My hand was slippery with sweat. Good God, I had thought of the noise – why hadn't I thought of silencing it? But with what?

'So you're going to redistribute the wealth,' I said. 'It's been tried.' I scooted back as far away from him on the seat as I could get.

'No, sir. I am going to redistribute the people.' I flipped the chamber open, flipped it shut. It was loaded. Arslan watched, but he didn't move. 'And I am cutting lines of communication,' he said. 'I intend that every community should be self-sufficient. It should produce everything it consumes, and contain no more people than it can support in comfort.' He was speaking dully, absently. His eyes were on the gun.

I had started to take off my suit coat. And just now, when I needed every speck of coolness I could manage, sweat ran into my eyes and I kept seeing faces in the corner of my mind's eye: the children's faces, Hunt and his mother, Betty white with fear, and

27

Colonel Nizam's face, and faces of soldiers; and over and behind what Arslan was saying now, I heard him saying to Perry, 'No games,' and the noise Perry made.

'I thought there were too many people to go around.' I had my left arm out of the sleeve. I reached across my chest and pulled the coat loose from behind me, pulled it down from my right shoulder, leaving my right arm in its sleeve, and began to wrap the loose folds around the gun.

'Of course. It is too late to solve the problem by distribution alone. But it is better to die quickly than by starvation or malnutrition. And those who remain alive will have enough. Also, there is more land than you may think, sir. Very much is now wasted.' He watched the gun. It was the first time I had seen that face dead serious, without a trace of mockery or humor. *No games*, I heard his voice saying, and I saw the soldier's rueful look, and Paula's face.

'Destruction of civilization sounds like a good name for it, all right. What about industry?'

'Only local industry. No trade. Total self-sufficiency based on the land.' He glanced from the gun to my face and smiled faintly. 'Yes, these are clichés. You yourself live by clichés, sir. But mine are enforceable.'

'Not for long.'

'No. But for long enough to change the pattern of society, the pattern of human life. If I succeed, I think it will be several hundred years before the world becomes again as bad as it was last summer.'

'In other words, you want to set the world *back* several hundred years. What about medicines? What about training doctors and dentists?'

'They can be trained like other craftsmen, by apprenticeship. There will be less disease, because conditions will be more healthful; less contagion, because less travel. Medicines enough can be produced locally.'

'What are you doing *here*? Why Kraftsville?'

'There was a cause for celebration. It was convenient to halt here. And then—'

It was the first time I'd seen him hesitate over anything. 'And then?'

His grin came back, just for a second. 'Kraftsville pleases me.'

I had the gun as well muffled as I was likely to get it. 'You said there's no United States government. What happened to it?'

'It abdicated to me.'

'That's unbelievable,' I said. 'And I don't believe it. Any of it.'

No, he wasn't really very much interested in agrarian socialism at the moment. Blood showed rusty at the corner of his mouth. 'Believe this, then, that I will not die easily. I have put my death into your hands, sir; but at the end I must fight it. The range is very short, yes, the caliber is large; but I am very quick, and I am strong. And do not hope to disable me and hold me as hostage. This pistol is not a precision instrument. You will not stop me with less than a fatal wound.' He paused, his eyes preoccupied with the gun, and went on again. 'If you kill me, sir, I think your best chance will be to fire the town yourself, immediately.' I stared at him. 'Do not imagine that you can surprise the school. But with a few good men and a sufficient diversion, you might save very many of the children.' Slowly he fingered another cigarette out of his pocket, but he didn't put it in his mouth. 'Your wife,' he said, 'sleeps in your own bedroom. The boy Hunt is in the southwest room. There is a guard on the stairs, and one on each side of the house outside.'

'Where are those two girls?'

'At the high school.'

'Where's Betty Hanson?'

'In the northwest room.'

'Why are you telling me this?'

He shrugged. He put the cigarette in his mouth. He looked at me. And I felt an anger that burned and ached to my fingertips. *He* had started this. He had come here, occupied my town, taken over my school. And now he was passing the buck to me, to decide, on the shabbiest sort of data, which of two intolerable directions the world should take. Well, I didn't want it. I wasn't God. The most I could do was choose for myself, for Luella and the children.

'All right,' I said finally. 'You can light your cigarette.'

29

He lit it in a hurry, and dragged deep. Apparently he was part human, at least.

'What happens,' I asked, 'if I just get out of the car and go away?'

He shook his head. 'I will stop you.'

I shifted the gun to my left hand while I got the coat off of myself and it. I opened the breech and took out the cartridges. I half turned, and flung them broadcast into Sam Tuller's oat field, and the gun after them.

Arslan didn't seem to have moved an eyelash. He offered his cigarette pack, and I shook my head. I felt sick and cold. His whole face was shiny with triumph.

'You threatened me with a weapon, sir,' he said quietly. 'I threatened you with a more powerful one. I still hold that weapon. I could use it now to make you search this field on hands and knees until you found every cartridge. But I do not.' He straightened in his seat and switched on the ignition, and that little flick of the fingers was a swagger in itself. 'I wish to know about the farms we pass: who lives in each house, how much land, what crops, what livestock. You should not lie to me about anything today, sir. It is important for your people.'

We covered practically the whole of Kraft County, and a little of three neighboring counties. We went down roads I hadn't been on in years, and some I'd never been on. In fact we covered, by actual driving or by sight, every passable backroad in the whole area. He wasn't interested in the main roads; or maybe he thought he knew them already. And all the way he kept me busy with his questions. 'Who lives there? How old? How many sheep? Is that wheat? Is that soybeans?' (He was always right.) 'What is their water supply? Is there a basement in that church? Does this stream flood?' And every now and then, 'What bird was that?'

I usually hadn't seen the bird. I was busy thinking a few miles ahead, searching for something that I *could* profitably lie to him about. The thing was to save any weapons we could, and a reserve of people willing and able to use them. He didn't ask me about guns, but he asked me a lot about people and about farm equipment. And it was on those points that I did slip in a few outright lies and several exaggerations.

When we pulled up at the south door of the school and got out and he faced me across the car and said pleasantly, 'You will find ways, sir, to spread the word,' I couldn't speak – couldn't have spoken if my life depended on it, which for all I knew it did. It was the most I could do to hold myself upright against the pain in my stomach. I just looked at him. He smiled and turned away toward the street – toward my house – and a soldier behind me opened the school door.

But it wasn't for me; it was for Colonel Nizam coming out. He passed me with a carnivorous look and saluted his general. Everybody in the parking lot was looking very attentively at Arslan's face. His mouth and cheek were swollen, with a little discoloration around the lips; and even while my stomach was rolling into itself, it made me proud to see the mark of my fist on him. Nizam asked him something, sharp and low, and Arslan answered briefly, with a smile and a sidelong glance at me. But the look that Nizam turned my way was pure murder. I gave him one straight stare for answer, and went in. So now Colonel Nizam had it in for me, and General Arslan thought it was very amusing.

Well, there were two things I could hold on to. For one, there were a high-caliber pistol and eight cartridges somewhere in Sam Tuller's oat field. For another, this earth-shaking Arslan had a suicidal streak a mile wide. And both those facts might be useful; but they might also be very dangerous.

3

I dreamed about it. It seemed to me I dreamed about nothing else for weeks. I had the pistol in my hand (sometimes it was so real I could feel it) and I was facing him – in spitting distance, as my father used to say. Sometimes I did spit in his face. We were in the Land Rover, or my office, or different rooms of my house. We talked, talked, talked. Once in a while we would be fighting hand to hand; but every time it switched back to the thick gun butt against my palm and the little distance between us. Sometimes I pulled the trigger, with various results. The gun would refuse to fire; or the bullet would have no effect; or, on the other hand, it would blow him into bloody pieces that kept on struggling stubbornly. Most often I woke up before I did anything. But sometimes I threw the gun away, or hid it under something, and sometimes I even handed it to him. Now and then I turned it on myself and pulled the trigger; and nothing happened.

That same evening, before the first of my dreams, the school-bus drivers were brought in, glum and scared, and the children were loaded up and driven home. Three soldiers rode with every busload. I didn't begin to breathe easier till the first bus got back and the driver told me they really had taken the kids home – even delivered every child to his own door. That made it a long evening.

The teachers went with the last loads. When the buses were all back and the drivers were escorted away (the confiscation of motor vehicles had started, and they weren't allowed to drive home), the young officer who seemed to be in charge gave me a pleasant smile and waved me toward the south door.

The street lights weren't on, though it was past nine o'clock.

None of the soldiers wandering in the darkness paid much attention to me. As an experiment, I turned west past my house – almost anything was worth a try – but I wasn't surprised when a rifle turned me back.

A sentry on my front porch eyed me insolently as I opened the door, though he didn't make a move. There was a hot, hard fireball burning in the pit of my stomach. But the first thing I saw was Luella sitting stiffly in the green armchair. She jumped up and touched my arm. 'You haven't had any supper, have you? I'll get you something right this minute.'

The couch was back, too, and the coffee table, both of them strewn with papers. The rug was littered with cigarette butts. Two soldiers lounged on the windowseat, and two more leaned against the built-in bookcase, their elbows on the shelves among Luella's bric-a-brac, all smoking, all looking very much off duty. They broke off their chatting to eye me for a minute.

I followed Luella into the kitchen. Another soldier was sitting at the table, also smoking, also much at his ease, dropping ashes on his dirty plate. 'Just give me a glass of milk,' I said. She looked pained, but she managed to pour it without a word. 'Where's Arslan?'

'The General? He's upstairs,' she said gloomily. 'And the Morgan boy,' she added. 'And Betty Hanson.'

'I know.' I took a drink of my milk and looked at the soldier. 'All right; you can bring me a plate in the dining room. And you sit down and tell me everything that's happened and everything you've heard.'

There wasn't much I didn't already know or at least expect. Betty had been brought over straight from the banquet and locked into the sewing room, and that was when the guards were posted around the house and on the stairs. Luella had been in the bedroom when Hunt was brought in; she had just got a quick sight of him in the hall, but that was enough to stop her from asking any questions. She hadn't seen Arslan come in at all, but she had heard him, sounding like a whole new invasion. 'And then this morning,' she said, 'Betty started screaming.'

And that morning at ten-fifteen he had been in my office,

saying, 'Your people are entirely free,' with a face like a cat just wiping the feathers off of its mouth.

Neither Hunt nor Betty had been out of the rooms since they went in, except for one guarded trip each to the bathroom. That was after the one meal Luella had been allowed to fix for them, carried up on trays a while after noon by Arslan's men. She hadn't seen them; hadn't heard any sounds out of the rooms since the screaming stopped, a little while before Arslan left that morning. He had come back around suppertime, eaten a big meal, and disappeared into the guestroom. Since then everything had been very quiet.

She hadn't been out of the house the whole time since the Turkistanis arrived, hadn't seen anybody else or heard anything else. And she was almost at the end of her rope. By the time she had finished her story she was shaking all over, just the faint animal quivering of weariness and strained nerves. 'I'm sorry, Franklin,' she said. 'I've had all I can take for one day. I'll be all right tomorrow.'

And she would, I knew that. I could rely on Luella. But unfortunately the world wasn't made of Luellas.

If you couldn't use your anger constructively, it poisoned you; I'd found that out a long time ago. Raging and raving against Arslan would just get in the way of working against him. And I was beginning to see that I could work against him. Not that I hadn't done a beautiful job of asking all the wrong questions; but I'd learned a few things, in spite of myself, and I was going to make the most of them.

By next morning, Arslan's version of normality was already in force. *Entirely free.* I made myself eat a good breakfast, ignoring all spectators, and walked out of my front door as if I still owned it; and the first civilian I met was Wallace Ford, coming to look for me. His pale face colored up with relief.

'There you are. They wouldn't let me get into school, and I was afraid—'

I steered him out of the crowded parking lot, and we strolled quietly toward the square. It was silly not to have any place to go, but that was the truth of it. 'All right, let's hear *your* story,' I said.

He looked hopefully back toward the house. 'Any chance you could invite me to sit down? I walked in to town this morning, and I didn't get any sleep much last night.'

Wallace Ford was principal of Kraft County Consolidated High School. Their new school building was located a mile out of town, which had raised considerable opposition from the people who thought the only place to build a new building was where the old one was torn down.

'I could invite you to sit down, and I could offer you some breakfast, too. But any talking we do had better be outside.'

He shrugged hopelessly. 'Forget it, then. That's all right, I've had breakfast; I stopped at home a minute. I just thought—' He ran a shaking hand through his hair. 'What are they going to do with the kids, Franklin?'

'Nothing – not with *my* kids. They'll be safe at home unless some grown-up does something stupid.'

He gave me a wild look, the very picture of a man longing to go crazy and get away from it all. '*My* kids are still locked up at school.'

'Then why in heaven's name aren't you with them?'

'They sent the faculty home this morning.'

And he had let himself be sent. 'All right, Wally, tell me about it.'

'Oh, my God, Franklin.' But that was something of an exaggeration. What he had to tell wasn't much. I'd known from the first day that the high school had been shut up the same as we were; some of the parents I phoned had already heard from Wally about their older children. 'But the kids are still there,' he mourned. 'Franklin, you've had a night's sleep, at least. I just can't think any more. What in God's name am I supposed to *do*?'

'That's your problem, Wally. I've got all the responsibility I need right now.' It was a shame to disappoint Wally when he wanted to impress me, but I just didn't feel inclined to hold his hand for him. I had both hands full. 'What you really ought to do is go back home and get some sleep yourself. Come on, I'll walk you over.'

By dawn the next morning the high school was empty. During

the day and night every single student had been trucked away toward the west.

He hadn't abducted my students, but in the next two weeks he did a pretty thorough job of taking over my school. He informed me that my office was now his office – meaning, in a nutshell, that it wasn't my office any more; he never did any work there, to my knowledge. He was all over the rest of the school, though, directing operations I didn't like the look of. Electronic equipment, canned goods, and God only knew what else, was being brought in by the truckload and installed on every floor. Floodlights were mounted all around the schoolground. There were more and more rooms I wasn't allowed to enter. The whole building rattled with carpentry. Walls were torn down, partitions set up. All of the children's desks were knocked apart and the pieces neatly stacked on racks in the basement. 'Firewood,' Arslan explained with lifted eyebrows, as if it was the most obvious thing in the world. He was stockpiling a real conglomeration of things, from pumpkins to transistors. It looked as though he couldn't make up his mind whether to expect a Vicksburg siege or a computerized space battle.

Meanwhile, Colonel Nizam had quietly moved into Frieda Althrop's house. Frieda's place was one of the biggest in town, built by her grandfather back when people knew how to build big houses, and modernized a time or two since then. It also commanded the intersection of Pearl Street and Illinois 460, looking north from its high-shouldered yard to the square, east to the school, and south along the hardroad out of town as far as the curve. Here my wolfish colonel had established his own headquarters – whatever it might be headquarters for. He disappeared into the house like a broody termite into a timber, and that was that.

The Althrops were out-of-county people to start with, and Frieda had never married, so she didn't have many relations in town. She moved in with her neighbors, the Schillingers, till she could get a place of her own. Frieda had lived alone for a long time, and she didn't want to change. 'She's not thinking about the billet rule, though,' Luella remarked to me.

We gave her a day to get settled at the Schillingers', and then paid her a call. And while Luella led Mrs Schillinger into another room to talk about some sort of women's business, I had a little conversation with Frieda. Frieda had done all her own cleaning in that big house, except once or twice a year when she'd get a woman in to help with some of the heavy jobs; and I just felt it would be a good idea for somebody else in town to have a clear picture of the structure and layout of all three stories.

Two nights later, Frieda Althrop died in her sleep. That was the first death, except for Perry, that we owed directly to Arslan. Frieda was getting on in years, and, as people said, it was too much for her to be uprooted that way. But we'd all been uprooted, and we couldn't all afford the luxury of dying.

The sixth day – the day after Frieda died – a new army marched into town. People stood around dumbfounded, watching as if it was some kind of a parade. We had one of the best views in town. Like Arslan's first army, they came in from the east and turned down Pearl Street; but these marched straight on past the school, headed out of town towards the fairground. I made Luella stay inside, but I stood out on the front steps to watch them. I wasn't about to crawl into a hole.

It was a very different bunch from the others, and that went beyond the different uniform they wore. They were younger and fairer than the swarthy veterans of the first wave, and not half as well disciplined. They stared and craned their necks and grinned, like a gang of kids on an outing.

There were long gaps now and then between blocks of marching men, which meant people could cross over every so often to compare notes with the opposite side, and there were more grown-ups than children trotting along parallel with the parade. Fred Gonderling was one who came down my side of Pearl Street, working his way briskly along from one watcher to the next. I waved him up onto my porch steps. 'What's the news from the square?' I asked him, which was a favor I was in the habit of doing him. He'd moved into his new office on the square that very spring.

'Morning, Franklin. I suspect that they'll be out of your school before long.'

'Why?'

'A detachment of these fellows is taking over the Court House. I should imagine that that will be their new headquarters.'

'I hope so.' As a matter of fact, I hoped not. If we had to have them at all, I was just as glad to have their pulse right under my fingers.

'Incidentally,' he added after a minute, 'I assume you know who these are.'

One time a news item in the Kraft County *Register-Blade* had referred to Fred Gonderling as a 'rising young attorney,' and he had been almighty pleased. Personally, I wasn't exactly sure how far he would rise, or would have risen. He was a spruce little fellow, intelligent and well-spoken; but it had always seemed to me that he was more interested in making a good show than in doing a good job. He was just at the point in his career of deciding whether he'd rather grow up to be a big frog in Kraftsville's puddle or go seek his fortune someplace else. I'd had my try at that when I was his age and found out I could make a lot more money in the city, and aim for a lot bigger position, but I'd also found out I didn't want it – not at the price of being cut off from the people I understood and the things I believed in. And till Arslan turned up, I never doubted I'd made the right bet.

'Invaders,' I said sourly.

'They're Russians.'

'*Russians!*'

'You bet they are. I remember that uniform from TV. And I've *heard* Russian. I took it in college.'

'Can you tell what they say?'

He shook his head shamefacedly. 'They talk too fast for me. To tell the truth, I don't remember it that well. But it's Russian, all right.'

They camped on the fairground. They took over the existing structures, and next day they went right to work building more, with lumber from the local lumber yards. Fred Gonderling's prediction was dead wrong. The Russian detachment stayed in the Court House just long enough to seal it up pretty thoroughly – every window barred, and every door locked. Colonel Nizam and his boys had already nosed through the county records and carried off heaven knew what to his den in Frieda Althrop's house. Every citizen in the county must have been recorded in some form or another in the Court House. And it did occur to me that one way to find out what Nizam considered interesting enough to take would be to have a look at what he'd left.

The high school stood empty, but not for long. On the heels of the Russians, a regular little truck convoy delivered the new occupants to the door. They were girls – not women, girls; girls in their teens. As well as you could judge from a distance, they were American, and scared stiff. 'But what—' Luella began, when I told her about it, and stopped.

'I'm afraid that tells us what happens to about half the high-school student body when Arslan moves in.'

Maybe it was his version of a sense of decency that prompted him to stock his brothel with out-of-county girls. More likely it was his idea of how to avoid trouble. And if you started from the premise that there had to be a brothel and that it had to be staffed with conscripted American high-school girls, that was about as unprovocative a way as you could find to do it.

There was a Russian captain in charge at the high school and another one in charge of the new stable they were building on the little stretch of dirt road that connected the Morrisville road with the highway. There were plenty of horses in the county. Nobody with a field to plow lacked a tractor, but Kraft County didn't let go of anything in a hurry; there were still work horses to pull an occasional mudboat or work in the woods or brush where anything on wheels or tracks would look silly. There were mules – in fact, there were still a few people proud of their wagon mules; and there were enough saddle horses to stock a couple of dude ranches. Arslan was rounding them all up.

He might have international affairs on his mind, but his hands would have made him a pretty good farmer. He not only knew how to pick a good horse, he knew how to handle one. Every decent saddle horse in the district was brought around for his personal inspection. The really good stock went to the Russian camp. The others were returned to their owners. He saved out a few – ultimately four – for himself and had the storage shed behind my house cleared out, built a little longer, and fitted up to stable them. He didn't give the same individual attention to the work horses and mules, which meant that people with enough sense were able to save some of their good stock. Even so, the Turkistanis and Russians didn't seem to be any more fools than other people, and they ended up with a pretty good stable.

'I won't say this is the *only* way to look at it,' Fred Gonderling said, hedging his bets as if he had something to lose, 'but it's one way: we only have Arslan's word for *anything* outside the district.' At any rate, it was a pretty good seal. There was a half-mile-wide sanitary cordon all around the perimeter. The people who lived there had been moved out – 'chased out' would be more accurate – and a mixed guard of Russians and Turkistanis had moved in. Any citizen sighted within that border area was liable to be shot on sight. And since the half-mile limit wasn't very clearly defined by any landmarks for most of its length, people generally chose to be on the safe side and gave it a wide berth.

On the other hand, saying we had to take Arslan's word for everything was a little bit like saying we'd had to take the Weather Bureau's word for the weather. Maybe we didn't get explicit information from outside the district, but we got evidence, even if it was mostly negative – just as no cordon of armed foreigners could keep the clouds from sailing across the border. And any time you were tempted to think that it was somehow a fake, that the normal United States existed right over there on the other side of the boundary, you came smack up against the fact of what *didn't* come across.

We still had radios, and nobody was broadcasting any jamming signals. After dark in the old days – meaning two weeks ago – you could pick up stations as far away as Canada and Mexico, Philadelphia and Salt Lake City. Now there was nothing, not even the EBS – nothing except on shortwave, where we listened in on Arslan's business, and might have learned God only knew what, if any of us had understood Russian or Turkistani. I made a special effort to locate the Cuban propaganda station we used to hear sometimes. There wasn't a sign of it. TV screens showed nothing at all, except some variegated static.

Then there were the maps. Arslan was forever on the move, shuttling up and downstairs, in and out of the house, to school, to

Nizam's, to the stable, out of the district, and back to my house every time. And the maps followed him. There always seemed to be a messenger trotting up with another bunch of them. Arslan labored over those maps morning and night, brooding, scribbling, comparing, like a boy who'd just discovered the new world of geography. And since he did a good deal of it on my coffee table, it didn't take the CIA to figure out that Kraftsville was being turned into a nerve center for some intercontinental operation. Which was all very interesting, of course; but for right now the question of what Arslan and his army were doing in America and the rest of the world had to take a back seat – pretty far back – to the question of what they were going to do in Kraftsville.

Arslan was as good, or as bad, as his word. The interpreter he provided was a pleasant-faced, serious-faced young lieutenant with a mustache, whose name I never did exactly catch – something that started with a sharp 'Z' sound. He escorted me silently to Frieda's – Nizam's – wearing a peculiar strained look all the way. I didn't know enough yet to recognize it as the expression of a frustrated longing to practice English small talk.

The big front room was being transformed into Colonel Nizam's office, though a burrow would have been more appropriate. He looked hunched and blinking, at his desk in the middle of that spacious parlor. The big windows let in too much light, even in December, and opened too many walls. He was doing what he could to make himself a homey atmosphere, though. Filing cabinets stood among Frieda's overstuffed divans and shelves of bric-a-brac. There were three subsidiary desks, all busy. Two soldiers in a corner were putting a just-uncrated tape recorder through its paces. A crew of half a dozen or so seemed to be operating on the house wiring, yelling at each other up and down the big staircase that climbed from the back of the room. A piece of the wall was knocked open there, and thick black electrical cords trailed around the floor and up the stairs like endless leeches, barely alive enough to wriggle and suck.

We stood in front of Nizam's desk, observed but not acknowledged, till he deigned to look up. My polite little lieutenant saluted – not very snappily, I thought – and presented me.

Colonel Nizam's eyes scraped over my face like claws. If I'd known where we were going, I'd have had one of my stomach pills before we started, or maybe two. Then he lowered his eyes to his deskful of papers and uttered a quantity of Turkistani in an unencouraging voice. The lieutenant translated, with about as much feeling for the original as a sixth-grader reading Shakespeare: 'Mr Bond, will you please supply all the information about the conditions of District Three-Two-Eight-One?'

'What?' I said blankly. The words registered, but they didn't mean anything. He repeated them. 'I don't know what District 3281 is. I certainly can't supply all the information about it.' Not that I'd undertaken to supply anybody with anything.

Lieutenant Z looked apologetic and surprised and a little uncertain – running over his English lessons in his mind to see if he'd forgotten anything vital. He made a little circular gesture with his hand, forefinger pointing down. 'District 3281 is *this* district,' he said.

So there it was, and Colonel Nizam was to be the officer I worked with.

4

The colonel and I didn't make a very good team. That first day I got off on the wrong foot by declining to pour forth 'all the information about the conditions' at the flick of a switch. But I was as tactful as I could figure out how to be in those circumstances. I very politely indicated that I couldn't answer him on such short notice and very politely asked him just exactly what he wanted to know and just exactly what he wanted to know it for.

I got the impression that Colonel Nizam had a constitutional impediment to answering questions. But after a certain amount of dickering he unbent enough to give me, via Lieutenant Z, a very lucid account of what was wanted. Arslan was serious about his economic theory, at least as far as Kraft County went – or District 3281, which wasn't quite the same thing. There was no telling – not right now – how good a seal that guarded border was from the military point of view, but there was no doubt about it economically. My role in the Turkistani scheme of things was to work out a plan that would keep the local economy from collapsing altogether. If I could get it done before anybody starved, fine; if not, well, it would have been an interesting experiment. Nizam was ready, Lieutenant Z assured me, to cooperate in every way; but the plan was my responsibility.

It was clear enough. I thanked him – for the clarity – and I got to work.

That evening, in the kitchen, Arslan passed me with a knowing smile. 'You are busy, sir?'

I was scribbling figures while I ate. 'It's a long winter yet, General.' Already the food was sticking in my throat. A long, hungry winter.

He paused beside the table, resting the blunt fingertips of one hand on my papers. He had his shirtsleeves rolled up, and his bare forearms were burly but smooth, like a store-window dummy or a polished statue. 'You will not find Colonel Nizam unreasonable. Probably some form of relief can be arranged.' With the other hand he was holding the wrist of a very pretty, very bored-looking girl, the way he might have held a dog's leash.

'Can you do something with this another time?' I asked Luella, pointing to what was left on my plate.

'Oh, yes,' she said abstractedly. 'It will keep.'

I pulled my papers out from under his hand and got up, starting for the door and upstairs. With a broad grin he shouldered in ahead of me, dragging the girl against me and past. I went on steadily up the stairs behind them.

So, like it or not, I was in the economic planning business. It didn't suit my politics or my experience, but it looked like a job somebody had to do. There wasn't time enough to let supply adjust itself to demand – or supply enough, maybe. I got the basic figures from the County welfare people, and went at them with old-fashioned arithmetic.

I had to take Arslan at his word. We were cut off from the rest of the world, and we had to survive with what we were and what we had – survive maybe two weeks, maybe two years. It might not be true at all, but there wasn't anything to gain from betting it wasn't.

Back in the eighteen-hundreds, southern Illinois had done pretty good business in castor beans, sunflower seeds, sorghum, cotton, and tobacco. Times had changed, and the crop land had nearly all gone into newer cash crops – corn and soybeans, mostly, then oats and wheat. Well, we could grow the old crops again. There were still private patches to seed from. There were sheep in the county, beef cattle, clean milk cows, good hogs, good poultry, some beehives. Deer and small game hunting was pretty good, fishing just passable but with a few good spots. Plenty of vegetables, plenty of fruit and nuts. Wood to burn, and stoves that could burn it. It would be primitive, all right, but Kraft County wasn't going to suffer as much of a shock as a lot of places might.

And there were worse things than old-fashioned smoked ham and hot cornbread with sweet cream butter and sorghum molasses on it.

Nizam's English turned out to be nearly as adequate as Lieutenant Z's, when he chose to exercise it, except that his accent was a lot nastier. The lieutenant was dispensed with after our first few meetings. I was sorry to see him go. For one thing, it nearly broke his heart, to judge from his woeful look; and for another, it meant I had to deal with Nizam directly, without a shock-absorber.

I took care of the real work of planning in my own bedroom. When I needed information from the Turkistani side, I went to Nizam. At first that meant a wait of anywhere from one hour to six on Frieda Althrop's front porch, in full view of Pearl Street and the hardroad – and if Nizam didn't have enough business on hand to keep me waiting that long, he would find some. As soon as that became clear, I quit waiting. If he wasn't ready to see me when I got there, or within a few minutes, I went away and came back exactly two hours later. The longest streak of such visits we ever worked up to was a day and a half, with time out for a night's sleep. After that, I never had to come back more than once, and those few occasions I was perfectly willing to put down to genuine business.

I never tried to analyze Nizam's motives, any more than I'd analyze a snake's; but I learned to tell which way he was likely to wriggle. And by a combination of growling and playing possum, I managed to get some fine cooperation out of him. But it was a hassle and a haggle, day after day, and no Sundays off. It gave me a feeling like listening to a record played at the wrong speed.

The relief operation alone took an almighty lot of dickering. Colonel Nizam's ideas of what constituted adequate sustenance were based on Turkistani standards, maybe, or else on a desire to starve us gradually. It was possible to reason with him, but not pleasant. Every little thing had to be argued out, with figures and documents.

The food Nizam delivered – and he did deliver it, and delivered on schedule, or pretty nearly so – was U.S. government surplus, the same as had been doled out to us as part of the old school lunch program. The question that came to mind was, how many districts could be nursed through the winter this way? Presumably there *was* food – Arslan's mere existence didn't alter the world's food supply – but, to put it in his own terms, it was a problem of distribution. He'd cut the normal distribution channels very effectively in Kraft County, and it took my best efforts and Colonel Nizam's organization to replace them. Nobody could tell me that that was being duplicated in a minimum of three thousand two hundred and eighty other districts.

Unfortunately, Arslan's troops didn't limit themselves to confiscating movable goods. They had taken over for their own use an area that included most of our best corn land, the two biggest beef herds in the county, and the only commercial dairy herd. The farmers inside the confiscated area weren't evacuated, they were simply reduced to their houses and yards.

That made things harder. The Government surplus wouldn't last forever; and I not only had to get us through this winter, I had to figure on getting us through the next one. There was more to it than raising the crops and the livestock, too. We did have a feed mill; and according to Morris Schott, the manager, it might just as well turn out cornmeal and crude wheat flour. But that looked unlikelier after the twenty-first of December.

By now I was well used to Nizam's standard procedure. He accepted a sheaf of papers from me, shuffled it to the bottom of a stack and cleared his throat a little in preparation for English. He very seldom looked at me, except to deliver one of his venomous stares, and he didn't look at me now. 'You will extinguish the power plant before midnight twenty-four December,' he said.

'You mean close it down?'

He watched the top paper of his stack, as if it had made a suspicious move. 'Yes,' he decided.

'Colonel, if it has to be closed at all, which I fail to see, is there any strong reason for that particular date? Two or three days later could save you some opposition.'

He nodded – at least I thought it was a nod – and shuffled the suspicious paper to the bottom of the stack. 'Midnight twenty-four December,' he repeated. 'You are dismissed.'

That night, I put the question to Arslan. 'We can do without electric lights and electric stoves,' I said. 'But that power plant

46

pumps our water, and it's the only practical hope I see for grinding our grain.'

He looked at me without expression. 'I have assigned your task,' he said. 'Do you forget?'

I could feel myself getting hotter. 'Self-sufficiency was the word you used. What's wrong with producing our own electricity?'

'Nothing, if you can also produce your own fuel and your own spare parts. Remember that henceforth your district imports nothing. Nothing.'

That wasn't even true; but if I reminded him that we were already starting to import food, he might just decide to cut off the supply. 'I see your point,' I said. 'But the plant's there, General. Wouldn't it be more efficient to let us down a little bit easy?'

He laughed. 'With all deliberate speed, as your country integrated its schools? No, sir, I have no time for this.'

'Then why not put us back to stone axes right now and get it over with?'

'Again, I have no time for this. I am directing you to follow the path of greatest operational simplicity.'

'All right, then. But why Christmas Eve? I assume that's not coincidental.'

'My soldiers are Moslems, sir.'

'Your soldiers. What about you?'

'Yes, sir, I am a Moslem – as you are a Christian.'

'Most of your troops are Russians. *They're* not Moslems, are they?'

He grinned sardonically. 'Even worse, they are Communist. On the other hand, they have vestiges of Christian tradition. Those who desire to celebrate this Christmas will be permitted to do so. But they will do it without benefit of electricity. Why should your citizens enjoy privileges that my troops lack?'

'General,' I said, 'tyrants have been trying to stamp out Christianity for a couple of thousand years, and it hasn't worked yet.'

'Ah, no, sir!' he cried exuberantly. 'I do not plan to stamp out any religion. On the contrary, sir! Perhaps I shall crucify one of your citizens, to help the others understand what is involved in Christianity.'

47

'Do *you* understand?' I asked as coolly as I could.

He looked good-humoredly up at me from under his eyelids. 'Ah, perhaps not, sir. No, in candor, I do not understand Christianity. Can you explain it to me?'

'I don't know. But I'd like very much to try.'

'Good. But not at present.'

'Of course not. You have no time for this.' That made him grin, and I took the opportunity to go on. 'If you don't have time for me to tell you anything, how about you telling me something?' He lifted his eyebrows inquiringly. 'You say the Government abdicated to you.'

'Various governments.'

'The only reason I even consider believing that, is that it's too unbelievable to be a lie. What pressure could the Premier of Turkistan bring to bear on the President of the United States?'

He put on one of his sweet and gay looks. 'Why do you assume that there was pressure? Perhaps it was entirely voluntary.' I didn't say anything. He discarded that look and added smoothly, 'Or perhaps the Premier of Turkistan was more powerful than you knew. Or had more powerful allies.'

'China? Or Russia? China *and* Russia, wasn't it? That was a summit meeting in Moscow, not an arbitration.'

He shrugged, shutting off the conversation right there. 'You have your instructions, sir. I think that you understand them now.'

'China, Russia, and Turkistan. Who's running the show, General?'

The look that flared from his eyes was like an axe-stroke. 'I run it,' he said quietly.

Black Christmas. That was what we called it. There were gifts given, and maybe a few people had the heart to sing a few carols in their own homes, in spite of the billeted soldiers. God knows there were prayers said.

But electricity wasn't really basic. What was basic was fuel.

On any ordinary-scale map, we were located in the coal belt of southern Illinois, but in fact there wasn't a single coal mine in the district. I gave some thought to the possibility of starting one ourselves, and gave it up; no matter how you figured it, the thing just wasn't feasible. Coal was one of the oldest industries in the state. This whole area had been surveyed and explored and evaluated time after time, and Nizam had reluctantly pulled the local records out of the sealed Court House for me. There was certainly coal in Kraft County, but it was too low-grade and too hard to get at; and while we would have gladly settled for a lot less than commercial quality, we didn't have the equipment or the know-how to mine anything that didn't just about jump out of the ground at us.

That left wood, wind, and muscle. A windmill and a good rationing system might be all we needed for our water supply. But the wind wasn't reliable enough for anything that needed steady power. I set all the local talent I could scrape up onto putting together a wood-burning steam engine for Morris Schott's feed mill. I was proud to see that Kraftsville people *could* work together, even if it took a catastrophe or the end of the world to get them started. It wasn't all smooth, either.

I ran into Leland Kitchener on foot one day, which was unusual. He was a shabby little old fellow to look at (probably not as old as he looked, for that matter), but there was more to Leland than showed on the outside.

'Morning, Mr Bond. How's your house guest?'

'Making himself very comfortable, Leland. What's new?'

He walked with his hands in his pockets and his head and shoulders hunched forward, so when he looked you in the eye he had to peer through his eyebrows. He grinned up at me. 'Well, to hear people talk, I guess about the newest is you buying Perry Carpenter's house.'

'What do they say about it?'

'Well, there's some says it don't look just right.'

'Then there's some that don't know what they're talking about, Leland. I'm buying that house as a kindness to Christine. She can't live there alone, a young widow and a baby – not with this billet rule. And she won't want to be responsible for a house. This way she's able to move back in with her folks and forget it. I'm taking the responsibility off her hands.'

'That's what I tell them, Mr Bond. Nobody wouldn't think any different if it wasn't for him being your coach at school, and the house being right next door to yours. They're saying – *some* people are saying – you bought it for these Turks.'

'I tell you what, Leland. We're all in this together, and we can't afford not to trust each other. You tell them so. I didn't buy the house for anybody else, and nobody's going to be able to say I did. By next week there won't *be* any house.'

His smile went sly and sweet. 'You need any help, Mr Bond, I'm your man.'

It was true the Turkistanis looked interested in Perry's house. It would be convenient to barrack the bodyguard, at least, next door to General Arslan. But it would be more convenient from my point of view to have an empty lot there. The house belonged to me now, and legally I could tear it down any time I wanted to, but it was just as well not to confront Arslan head-on – not with anything less than a *fait accompli*.

That meant getting busy before the Turkistanis moved in and made it impossible. Even now, it was tricky. We had to get the fire well started before they noticed it; and there was some remote chance of it blowing across the side yards and catching on my house. But we were lucky enough to have a dry, windless night. The Turkistanis got there with the city firetruck in time to save the shell of the house, nothing else.

That brought me on the carpet before Arslan himself. I didn't deny I'd had the place burned.

'Why do you destroy your own property, sir?'

'Why take over the world and then start tearing it down?'

He laughed outright, but his face hardened again in a hurry. 'Who are your subordinates? Who have helped you?'

'You wanted me to spread the word, General. I can't do that unless people know they can trust me.'

He eyed me steadily for a while – and those eyes could be pretty damned steady. Then the hardness relaxed, and he nodded thoughtfully. 'Yes,' he said. 'Let them trust.'

There were other kinds of planning besides economic, and other kinds of survival. Above all, there was one thing I was anxious to keep from getting started. It didn't need a preacher to tell me that the best of us at the best of times were no more than poor ornery sinners. And Arslan had put a terrible weapon within our reach – a weapon to use not against him but against ourselves: the billet rule.

I didn't think there had ever been a murder in Kraft County in my lifetime, or, in the normal course of things, ever would be. But who was to say there might not have been, if there had been a really sure and safe and well-established method handy? Now we were living in a time of violence and stress and permanent emergency, and we had that kind of a method. To get rid of your enemy and his whole household, you only had to throw a rock at his billeted soldier. There were risks, of course, but they didn't amount to much, compared with the certainty of the return. There was the little matter of incidentally murdering maybe three or four innocent children; but these were desperate times, and anyway, you wouldn't have to pull the trigger on them yourself.

I worked as hard at it as I'd ever worked at anything. What with this, and laying the groundwork for the economic plan, and a few other things, I had become a first-class rumor mill. I started a lot of talk under the pretense of just passing it on, and I learned to convey a lot of information and opinion by asking questions. Some people I could talk to straight, which was more comfortable, but most of it was sideways and round-about.

We had to keep up the faith that there was a viable United States and a viable Christian Church somewhere over the boundary of District 3281; that the old rules were still essentially valid, however much we might have to twist them to fit new cases, and that the old penalties would descend all the harder after the time out.

We needed that assurance. Arslan's brothel was more than a convenience for his soldiers; it was a deliberate focus of corruption for the county. In other words, it was free and public. There would even have been a useful side to that, except that the American girls were reserved for the troops. A truckload of foreign girls (it was one of them that Arslan had led up the stairs, and not the last one) had been installed in the north wing of the high school, and that wing was open to all comers. It emerged –

emerged pretty fast for a supposedly Christian town – that these girls were Russians. And, not to make it worse than it was, most of the north wing's business was Russian soldiers. You might put it down to homesickness.

There were bound to be a few failures; you couldn't expect any better. I came home one day and found Luella waiting for me in the bedroom.

'I just couldn't face it down there,' she said. *Down there* was downstairs, among Arslan's men.

'What's the matter?'

Her face was anguished. 'You know Mattie Benson, don't you?' she said tremulously. 'Howard Benson? Mattie was a Schuster. I can't remember their boy's name. He graduated from high school about three years ago and went to Chicago or somewhere.'

'That would be Paul Benson. I don't remember ever knowing his folks especially. What about them, anyway?'

She looked away from me desolately. 'Well, you know the billet rule . . .'

The soldier had been jumped down by the railroad embankment and beaten – how badly, and by how many, nobody seemed to know. He was said to be one of a bunch who had raped a young farm wife near Blue Creek a couple of weeks before. Whether that was true or not didn't matter. Whether the soldier deserved his beating, whether Kraftsville was satisfied or shocked – all that was immaterial. The billet rule had been broken.

'I'll try to see Arslan.'

He saw me readily enough, but only to put me under temporary arrest (he actually called it that) till the executions had been carried out. That was interesting, too. Because just what was it he was afraid I might do in the interval?

We got used to people being killed. Arslan's rules were one hundred percent enforced – which was, after all, a lot better than unpredictable terrorism. He had a peculiarly unattractive way of disposing of the bodies. They would be dragged behind a jeep or truck, like Hector's corpse in the *Iliad* – dragged all the way out to the city dump, which was three miles on a dirt road, and deposited there. Some of us saw to it that everybody got buried eventually. It wasn't pleasant to collect the remains of your kinfolk from out there, and some people didn't have kin. There were two funeral parlors in town, but of course their hearses had been confiscated. Two months later, they were still discussing deals for suitable conveyances, and meanwhile anybody that wanted to be buried had better have his own transportation.

But Leland Kitchener had been shrewd enough to trade himself into a wagon and a team of lethargic but durable mules within two weeks of Arslan's arrival. They were too old, slow, and dilapidated to tempt confiscation, but they served Leland's turn all right. They were just about exactly the unmechanized equivalent of the old stave-sided truck he'd limped about his business with, before Arslan. The business was junk and trash generally, but he would haul anything that could take a rough ride. It was Leland who always made the trip to the city dump.

We could have used a lot more like Leland. It was funny how many people didn't really believe in Arslan – seemed to take him for some sort of optical illusion that would probably disappear when the weather changed. Meanwhile they went on doing what they'd always done, like a bunch of stubborn robots trying to march forward with their noses pressed against a wall. Then there were those who fell all over themselves to lick Arslan's boots before he kicked them. I preferred Leland's attitude.

5

You couldn't accuse Arslan of laziness, anyhow. He would be up and working long before daylight, and he didn't really stop till after supper – sometimes long after. He *worked*, too, he didn't just diddle with papers and assign jobs to other people. He worked, though God only knew what he was working at, and though he was restive as a hot-blooded colt, interrupting his day at odd times for a bath, a shave, a meal. He had the appetite of a field hand in harvest-time, and he washed every meal down with milk. The liquor didn't come out till the day's work was done.

He'd taken over everything except our bedroom and as much of the kitchen as Luella absolutely required for cooking. Anywhere else in my own house I might be refused admittance – at the very best, I had to share space and facilities with a bunch of enemy aliens – and those three upstairs rooms were completely off limits to me, where he presumably slept and certainly practiced his obscenities. What this came to in terms of practical living was one continual aggravating hassle. The bathroom had to serve a minimum of eleven people, counting Arslan's bodyguard, and with the daily and nightly comers and goers there seemed to be no maximum.

It cost me an effort to open my bedroom door in the morning; and coming back to the house from outside, I could feel my neck prickle as soon as I got near the front walk. I had had that house built when I could ill afford it, when Luella and I were first married, the year after I came back to Kraftsville for good; and nobody but my family and myself had ever lived in it, and nobody had ever set foot in it without my invitation till now. And now I might as well have invited a circus in.

None of his soldiers lived in the house, strictly speaking. But there was an orderly forever popping up (the same corporal who had jumped onto the stage to tie his shoe), and there was a bodyguard of six men attending him every moment of the day and night. I counted seventeen individual guards, once I learned to tell them apart. They relieved each other according to some complicated system of rotation, so there always seemed to be a different combination of them on duty. 'If it was my bodyguard,' I told Luella, 'I'd have them set up in teams. You can train a team to work together.'

'It does seem inefficient this way,' she agreed. But maybe it wasn't. They kept on their toes; they didn't all get bored at once. Besides, it meant sharing the goodies all round. Because that bodyguard was with him enough to make voyeurism one of the main fringe benefits of their job.

Betty Hanson was still cloistered, if the word can be applied, in the northwest room. A cot had been brought in for her, and – after I insisted on it to Arslan – Luella's sewing machine had been brought out. Luella cooked her meals, but one of the bodyguards always carried them up. As far as we were concerned, she might as well have been invisible. Even her trips to the bathroom were guarded sneak operations.

I could have wished, if only for Luella's sake, that she was inaudible, too. She seemed to go into an explosion of some sort every few days – screams of what might have been fear or pain, sounding unpleasantly genuine sometimes; or long, heartbroken wails of sorrow; but most often just an outburst of assorted hysterics. There wasn't anything to be done about it, short of suicide, so I got into the habit of ignoring these commotions right away. There was enough on my mind that I *could* do something about. But it was hard on Luella, no question of that.

Maybe it didn't mean anything, but I noticed that Hunt Morgan rated a real bed, even if it was just a little rollaway. I didn't ask for my record player out of that room; I thought it might be of some help to him. But I never heard it play except when Arslan was in there. There were no disturbances from Hunt. I'd have felt better if there had been.

*

Arslan must have been born in a crowd – or maybe picked up in the middle of a desert. Whatever the reasons, he couldn't seem to get too much of human company. He was literally never alone, as far as I could tell, or not more than five minutes at a time now and then.

Not just human company, either, and not just the horses. Sam Tuller told me the fairground camp was full of dogs and puppies; and in a very short time my house was, too. 'Every time he goes out in that Land Rover,' Luella complained to me, 'he brings back another animal.' The first pup was a beagle. The next was a bluetick hound. Then came a German shepherd bitch with a litter of puppies that didn't look much like German shepherds. In between he had picked up half a dozen kittens and Paula Sears's pet monkey. All of them except the monkey had the run of the house, and all of us were under orders to let them in or out whenever they wanted – which wasn't the kind of order I was going to pay any attention to.

Luella had to feed them most of the time and clean up after them all of the time, but it was Arslan who trained them, and did it very well, too – if you didn't count the monkey. 'To be fair,' I told Luella, 'I don't think you *can* housebreak a monkey.'

She sniffed. 'Not without trying, I'm sure of that. But if he just won't, he could at least keep it in a cage. Paula had a perfectly nice, big cage for it.'

He kept it in the coal bin. A couple of his men shoveled what little coal there was left into a corner of the furnace room, and mopped out the bin. From then on, it was Luella's job to go in every day and clean up; and of course that was on top of all the damage it managed to do around the house when Arslan had it out. I objected, not only because it was a dirty, mean job, and it was his monkey, or rather Paula Sears', but because Luella was getting physically worn out.

'You are wrong, sir; it *is* woman's work. My men have other occupations.'

'Then let one of those girls help her – or Betty. It wouldn't hurt Betty to do a little work around here.'

He shook his head. 'They do woman's work also,' he said cheerfully, 'but of another type.'

*

I hadn't ridden a horse in ten years, hadn't owned a hunting dog in six, and I had missed them. In a way, it did me good to have them around the place again. And Arslan was undeniably good with all of the animals. He would pet a cat about the same way he petted his girls – expertly and with interest, but a little off-handedly. I'd never had anything against cats, but it still looked peculiar to me, a grown man fondling one like a little girl with her doll. What was beautiful was to see him with the dogs. He reminded me of a good teacher – the kind whose technique is so good it looks like all rapport and no technique. The dogs *wanted* to please him, wanted to understand what he was telling them to do, and do it; and he could make them understand. He knew something about training, no doubt of that.

Which didn't mean I liked having my house transformed into something between a barracks and a menagerie. Just the smell disgusted me every time I came in the door: the smell of the monkey, of too many cats and too many dogs, of too many soldiers and too many muddy boots, of too much cooking and too much laundry, of liquor, of tobacco. And it was never really quiet. There were always people moving around, if not inside the house, then in the yard. All day there was tramping in and out, up and down the stairs, doors slamming, foreign voices. And there was always some uproar or other likely to erupt at any hour of the day or night. It would be a dog fight, or Betty Hanson in hysterics, or some indecipherable Turkistani crisis that had soldiers gallumphing down the walk, radios crackling, Arslan machine-gunning out orders. I was used to spending my workdays amid noise and confusion – yes, and some smells, too; but I was used to peace and quiet and cleanliness in my own house.

Along about lettuce-planting time, which was February 11 by Kraft County tradition, I had the year's outline pretty well set. The details remained to be filled in. 'I can't do all this from an office chair,' I told the Colonel. 'I've got to get out and talk to people, and look at what we've got.'

He contemplated his cigarette, while he constructed his clauses. 'You will give me two lists. Of people to whom you wish to talk. Of things at which you wish to look. Before noon tomorrow.'

I gave him his lists first thing in the morning. A little past ten he sent for me. Lieutenant Z and two soldiers were waiting in his office. 'You will follow this route,' said Nizam, holding up a paper for me to take. He didn't bother to look at me; after all, he'd glanced up when I came in. 'You will return between noon and curfew, eighteen February. Dismissed.'

Nizam, or his staff, had laid out a very sensible route. It not only took in all the people and places on my lists with just about the minimum of wasted miles and minutes, but it also made allowance for the type and condition of different roads. In fact, unless we were just peculiarly lucky, it made allowance for the visibility from different spots. I'd learned to respect the Turkistani organization, if nothing else. They were thorough, and they digested information fast. I came back with two notebooks full of data, and raring to get on with the job. Lieutenant Z watched me sidelong but wide-eyed. It was the first time he'd seen me with my hands on really solid material I knew I could work with.

We checked in with Nizam first, and from there I started home on foot. But Leland Kitchener's wagon came moseying out of the last alley before my house. Leland had a very handy way of just happening to run into you when he wanted to tell you something. We said hello, and I asked him how things had been while I was gone.

'Pretty quiet. The Commies got their stable about finished. Nothing new out of your houseguest, that I know of – except he's sent Miss Hanson somewhere out of county, and he's got a girl for Hunt Morgan.'

'A *what?*'

'A girl – you know what I mean; one of them little Russian girls. A girl for Hunt. Now ain't that something?'

Arslan wasn't in the living room, or the dining room, or the kitchen. The guard at the guestroom door put his rifle to my chest. I wasn't there to beg anybody's permission. I opened my mouth and yelled, 'Arslan!'

Instantly his voice came back, what sounded like a single word in his ungodly language, and the guard moved aside. I opened the door and slammed it behind me.

He was sitting on the edge of the bed. There were dented pillows behind him, just starting to swell back into shape, and maps and papers on the bed and the floor. The rest of his bodyguard were distributed around the room, like statuary in an old-fashioned garden. He had a glass of beer in his hand (he had taken up beer lately) and he was smiling. 'Welcome home, sir.'

I walked up to him. I wanted to be at close range, and maybe I wanted to see him looking up. 'Leave Hunt Morgan alone,' I said.

He did look up, and looked down at his glass, and drank; and when he looked up again it was his smart-aleck look, a look that begged for a spanking. He gestured toward the chair. 'Will you sit, sir?' he said silkily. 'We can talk.'

I hit the glass sideways with the heel of my hand. He didn't drop it; beer and shattered glass sprayed like an explosion. And at the same time his left hand came up and closed on my wrist, and he wrenched me down onto the bed beside him. For a little bit I couldn't see much, let alone speak. I hadn't known till then that a simple twist of the wrist could be so effective. 'Now, sir,' I heard him saying, 'you should tell me what you mean.'

'You know damn well what I mean.'

'Unfortunately no.' I could see him all right by now. He looked interested. The guards had surged forward a step, their faces dangerous and confused. 'What do you wish me to do?'

'I want you to stop systematically corrupting that boy.'

'I am wooing Hunt,' he said smugly. 'First the rape, then the seduction.'

I shook my head. 'What are you getting out of it – another kick?'

'Do you imagine that I require "another kick," sir?'

'Some people never lose their appetite for cheap thrills.'

He put on a little studied frown – giving courteous consideration to a silly idea. 'Is every pleasure a cheap thrill? Thrills of any price do not attract me; but it is true that I enjoy pleasure. For what else do we live?'

'I thought you didn't conquer the world for fun.'

'Your memory is good, sir. Most men forget. Yes, this is also true. There are patterns to be completed without regard to pleasure.' He tilted the broken stub of glass in his right hand and let the last of the beer dribble onto my rug. 'And yet you know, sir, that every pleasure has its own character, its own . . . shape. For example, under certain circumstances, rape gives a very beautiful pleasure, a unique pleasure.'

I felt my throat swell. 'What about that girl? What kind of pleasure do you get from turning a boy over to a whore?'

He looked at me sidelong and humorously for a moment. The glass dropped quietly, and he wiped his wet hand on the bed-clothes. 'Consider. When a woman is raped, then she is perhaps by so much more a woman – do you understand? But when a boy is raped, he is by so much less a man. And at Hunt's age, a boy questions already whether he can attain manhood. I wish Hunt to know that he is a man.'

'He's not a man. He's a child. You're not doing him any favor. You put him into hell, and now you're trying to make him like it.'

He smiled broadly at me. 'Yes, sir. Yes, sir. This is true. And if he must live in hell, do you not also wish him to be happy there?'

'No, I don't.'

He raised his eyebrows. 'Why not, sir?'

'Because in hell only the devils are happy.'

He threw back his head and laughed. 'Good! And you believe that I am a devil. Good! Then you can well believe that I desire to make Hunt happy.'

'Leave him alone. You've played with him long enough.'

'Yes, I have played. I am not playing now.'

'Then let him go.'

'Not yet.'

Sometimes his eyes were as deep as hell itself. But I wasn't about to let him stare me down. 'Why not?'

'Because, sir,' he answered slowly, 'I have taken something from Hunt. I desire to give him something.'

'And what do you think you have to give him?'

'Strength. Strength. And if I cannot give him enough, then I shall do him the favor of killing him.'

'Why do you care?'

Very slowly his mouth pursed into a half smile, and the creases of amusement showed around his eyes again. 'Why do you care what happens to your wife, or to the children of your school?'

I looked at him in disgust. 'I don't think you could understand why.'

'Yes, sir, I understand.' He held up two fingers, and touched one of them. 'You are connected with them. If they are hurt, you feel the pain.' He touched the second finger. 'Also you are responsible for them. If they are hurt, you have failed in your duty.' He nodded assertively. 'It is the same with Hunt and me. I am connected. I am responsible.'

He kept the boy with him most of the time, physically beside him; and the rest of the time he kept him locked in that back upstairs room, either alone or with the girl. Hunt never left the house. Getting ready to go out, Arslan himself would turn the key in Hunt's door and pocket it. But when he came in, he was as likely as not to toss the key, without a word, to one of his bodyguard, and the grinning soldier would tramp up the stairs and tramp down again with Hunt docilely at his heels. Or when Arslan was busy and had no time for Hunt, he would send him upstairs with a curt word, handing the key to the nearest guard. And he talked about giving the boy strength!

The girl couldn't have been more than sixteen. Even so, she was enough older than Hunt to matter; and in some ways, of course, she was ages older. She was slight and dark, pretty in a gypsy way, and her whole occupation, outside of whatever she did in bed, seemed to be singing songs and beautifying herself. She was a cheery little creature, I had to say that for her, but at absolute maximum she was worthless. Most of her time was spent in Hunt's room or monopolizing the bathroom – though she didn't dare start that till Arslan was definitely out of the house. In between, she would wander airily around the house, getting into everybody's way and poking into everybody's things, chattering saucily in what she seemed to think was English. She was absolutely the first child I'd ever met (and in every way except her profession she *was* a child) on whom I couldn't seem to make any impression – and there were times when I was red in the face from shouting at her. She was a little too old, and the situation a little too touchy, for me to turn her over my knee. Even so, I was mightily tempted.

She made herself very scarce whenever Arslan appeared. I saw him look at her sometimes, but I never heard him speak to her. For that matter, I didn't hear him say much to Hunt. 'Read to me.' That was his usual greeting. He would pluck a book from the shelves, or his pocket, or most often from one of the piles that littered the floor and the furniture (Luella wasn't allowed to touch them), and flip it carelessly at Hunt. If the boy caught it clumsily or missed it altogether, the bodyguard would grin in derision. And Hunt, God help him, was still vulnerable enough to flush.

He would read – read until he was hoarse, until sometimes his voice cracked and broke, and Arslan would stop him impatiently, as he might have switched off a staticky radio. He read while Arslan ate, while Arslan was being shaved, while Arslan skimmed through reports and pored over maps. He read to him in the bathroom, in Arslan's bedroom and his own – or at least they carried a good many books in and out. He read, read; and it was touching to see him lose himself in his reading. Since that first night, he had hardly spoken voluntarily. Every move he made, every look of his dark eyes, showed how badly he was being hurt. But when he read aloud, you could literally see and hear him sink into the words, shutting out everything else. He had always read well by school standards, two or three grade levels ahead of himself all the way; but now he was beginning to read really well, not just 'putting in the expression,' but living the words.

So I was concerned about *what* he read. It was certainly a strange mixture. They always had about half a dozen different books in process, scattered around the house. Arslan seemed to pick up whichever one was handiest. Most of them came out of my bookcases, and to tell the truth I was surprised to be reminded of what all I had on hand. They read Shakespeare, and Shaw, and Oscar Wilde, and an old manual of beekeeping, and *Stories of the Great Operas*, and the introductions to Luella's cookbooks, and *Paradise Lost*, and (so help me God) Fowler's *Dictionary of English Usage* from cover to cover, and books on vegetable gardening and evolution and hunting rifles, and *Moby Dick*, and Nietzsche, and the Bible. Those were all from my shelves, and so were the old histories: Prescott's *Conquest of Mexico*, and *Cook's Voyages*, and a few volumes left from a nineteen-hundred set of histories of the principal nations of the world. The books that Arslan produced from somewhere were mostly histories, too, but modern ones, and technical works on electronics, medicine, biology.

And it was this hodgepodge that Hunt read day by day, sitting a little hunched with the book on his knees, never looking up except for occasional furtive glances at Arslan, and all the life of his young body and soul concentrated in his voice.

> Is this the Region, this the Soil, the Clime,
> Said then the lost Arch-Angel, this the seat
> That we must change for Heav'n, this mournful gloom
> For that celestial light? Be it so, since he
> Who now is Sovran can dispose and bid
> What shall be right.

And as Hunt read, Arslan listened. Sometimes his eyes would take on a tranced expression, his eyelids would droop, and he would look, for the time being, genuinely Oriental.

> For we cannot call it reasoning to make pain a presumption of death, while, in fact, it is rather a sign of life. For though it be a question whether that which suffers can continue to live for ever, yet it is certain that everything which suffers pain does live, and that pain can exist only in a living subject.

Meanwhile, if it was one of his irregular mealtimes, he would be chewing slowly, seeming to consider and savor every mouthful. He liked to eat like a Roman emperor, reclining on the living-room couch, with his meal on the coffee table. Chairs certainly weren't invented for Arslan. If he wasn't standing up, or riding something, he was sure to be stretched out somewhere.

> His movement was prompt and his hand heavy; the staff of Ivan IV. seems to have passed into his grasp. We have seen him strike with his cane the greatest lords, Prince Menchikof

among the number. He bent to his will men, things, nature, and time; he realized his end by despotic blows.

Or he would be leaning back in my armchair beside the kitchen sink, in the blissful trance of a hot shave, the little orderly operating with all the grim delicacy of a brain surgeon. And Arslan would look like a petted cat.

Locks so grey did never grow but from out some ashes! But do I look very old, so very, very old, Starbuck? I feel deadly faint, bowed, and humped, as though I was Adam, staggering beneath the piled centuries since Paradise.

It was strange fare for a Turkistani general. He never commented, never asked questions; and, almost always, he was doing something else while he listened. But he listened. Sometimes a passage would make him smile. More often, he would turn his snake's eyes abruptly on Hunt, with an expressionless spotlight intensity that it almost hurt to watch. Hunt seemed to feel it, always; a flush would start upward from his neck, and his voice would burn all the more earnestly. But those were never the times when he stole his glances at Arslan.

His mother had been after me all along to arrange some way for her to talk to Hunt. She had lost weight, and she'd never had a lot to spare. Her freckled face was pinched and grim, but she went about business as briskly as ever. On my way to Nizam's – or more often on my way back, because I'd be in better humor – she would waylay me. 'Any chance, Franklin?'

'Nothing new, Jean, but you know there's always a chance.'

What was less common was for me to hear anything from her husband. Arnold Morgan was generally considered the best attorney in town, or anyway the sharpest, and in my opinion he'd raised a fine son; but I didn't think any the better of him for the way he was acting now.

I caught up with him one day just coming out of his office. Business was still being conducted, Arslan or no Arslan. A lot of legal requirements were in abeyance, for lack of a government, and we weren't allowed to hold court, but there was still plenty to keep the lawyers busy. 'Hello, Arnold.' I slowed down to fall into step beside him, and he looked a little annoyed.

'Good afternoon, Franklin. How's it going?'

'Not too bad.' I waited; sooner or later he would have to ask about his son.

'Of course, Jean keeps us pretty well posted about Hunt,' he said reluctantly, 'and I know he's in good hands at your house. The best thing we can do for him now is not make waves.'

'He's in General Arslan's hands,' I said.

He threw a furious look at me and checked himself. 'Fortunately, Hunt has been brought up to think for himself. He's a very mature boy.' He settled his hat more firmly on his head, and added, 'All this must be pretty hard on your ulcer.'

'It's not an ulcer. It's a spastic pylorus.'

'I beg your pardon.'

What that came to was that Arnold Morgan was in no hurry to get his son back. A bright, polite, good-looking child was an asset, no matter how much it took to support him, but now Hunt was tainted. It wasn't a question of morals. It would have been the same if he had lost his looks, or his grade average. But Jean was dying for him.

It wasn't often Hunt was alone with Luella and me, or either of us. But sometimes Arslan would trot upstairs for a few minutes, or swing out of the house for half an hour, leaving Hunt unoccupied. He would sit in his little pool of self-consciousness, waiting for whatever somebody might choose to do to him next. I always took the opportunity to speak to him and try to get some reaction, if it was nothing but a faint nod in response to some remark on the weather.

'Isn't there a poem with something about Bukhara in it? Something about "lonely Bukhara"?' Arslan had just gone out with one of his officers, and the word *Bukhara* hung in the air.

Hunt nodded. He got up silently, took an old high school literature book from the shelf, and leafed straight to the page he wanted. He held the book out toward me without a word.

'Will you read it to me, please, Hunt?' I didn't want him to feel that reading was just part of the regimen Arslan inflicted on him.

He sat down, docile as always. 'Matthew Arnold,' he said

quietly, smoothing the page. ' "Sohrab and Rustem." ' He began
to read. I didn't pay much attention to the words at first—

My terrible father's terrible horse—

But Hunt was reading it as if he'd been born to read it.

O Ruksh, thou art more fortunate than I;
For thou hast gone where I shall never go,
And snuff'd the breezes of my father's home.
And thou hast trod the sand of Seistan—

It didn't sound exactly like what I remembered.

—But I
Have never known my grandsire's furrow'd face—

His voice shook with feeling. It was a question whether he would
make it through.

But lodged among my father's foes, and seen
Afrasiab's cities only, Samarcand,
Bokhara, and lone Khiva in the waste,
And the black Toorkmun tents; and only drunk
The desert rivers, Moorgab and Tejend,
Kohik, and where the Kalmuks feed their sheep,
The northern Sir; and this great Oxus stream,
The yellow Oxus, by whose brink I die.

He stopped. 'That's all,' he said, without lifting his eyes. 'It's
not much.' But he was struggling to bring out something else, so I
waited. 'He,' he began, swallowed hard, and then got it out
steadily enough, 'he told me they really do ferment the milk of
mares. I was surprised.'

It didn't matter much what he had said; he had said something.
His hands jammed the book shut convulsively, and he shot me a
naked, stricken look – confessing everything, that he was a child,
that he was alive, that Arslan was his grown-up. His eyes fell

again; his shoulders shook, but before I could cross the room to him he stiffened again, and the look he flung at me this time stopped me dead – it was so plainly a look of fear.

I held out my hand for the book, and I saw his shoulders relax. 'Thank you, Hunt,' I said.

6

'That Morgan boy's a pitiful case, isn't he?' Fred Gonderling made it sound sympathetic, which was better than most people managed to do.

'He's in a tough spot, if that's what you mean. But he keeps his wits about him. I think he'll come out of it all right.' It made me a little mad to hear Hunt Morgan dismissed as pitiful, like a failing patient in a nursing home. There was no telling what kind of a future lay ahead of that boy, except that it wouldn't be an easy one; but I thought he had more of a future than most of the people who were shaking their heads over him. There was something in Hunt that could hold out for a long time against everything Arslan was doing to him – given a little luck, long enough to come through on the other side.

By midsummer, he had been granted some of the trappings of freedom. He was never locked up now. He was allowed to come and go pretty much at will, except when Arslan had a use for him. He was even allowed to take a horse out of the Russians' stable and ride anywhere in the district, apparently. But the district was sown with soldiers, and I thought one of the permanent duties of every one of them was keeping an eye out for Hunt Morgan. Every time Jean had tried lying in wait along his usual routes – and she had tried it often enough, if not more – some Russian or Turkistani had sent her about her business. After a while I persuaded her to quit trying and wait till I could arrange something. Partly I wanted to keep her out of official trouble, and partly I wanted to keep her from finding out in the bluntest way that Hunt didn't want to see her.

'She's on your side, Hunt,' I told him. 'Forget about everybody else.'

Usually his answer was silence; but once he brought himself to say, 'I *know* her opinions.'

'Forget about opinions. And when you do see her, never mind what she says to you. When it comes to family, those things don't really matter – not if you can remember they're just words.'

'Sticks and stones,' he said.

In a way, Arnold Morgan had been right when he called Hunt mature, but not in a very important way. Compared to most of his classmates, with their raw country boyishness, he'd always seemed both younger and older. But that had been superficial, just the self-confident sophistication of any well-bred child. Now he was definitely, irreversibly older. It had been close, but Hunt had proved me right. He had had just barely the necessary toughness to get him through. He didn't blush any more.

Hunt would survive, no doubt of that. What I worried about now was what kind of a person he would survive as. He listened when he was talked to – listened seriously but distantly. There was a kind of impediment in his communication. He volunteered practically nothing, and when he answered a question it was most often with a shrug, a sidelong look, or a cool stare.

Toward Arslan, he had the manner of a well-trained servant – sometimes he was disconcertingly like the little orderly. Arslan was the sun around which Hunt had to revolve, and it was only on the side illuminated by Arslan that he showed much sign of life. On that unique subject he was able and willing to talk, or at least answer questions articulately. And then again he would clam up, and I couldn't get any more out of him except a shrug and 'He doesn't tell me everything.'

Either he told him an almighty lot, or Hunt had a very fertile imagination and didn't mind farming it. 'He says he has American troops in Russia and China, and Chinese troops in Europe, and European troops in the Middle East, and Arab and Israeli troops in Africa. All commanded by his officers.'

'Hunt, I don't see how he could *have* that many officers.'

'That's what he told me.'

'Why does he stay in Kraftsville? Has he told you that?'

One of the things I'd noticed about Hunt lately was that he held his head upright even when he bowed it. His shoulders might hunch and droop, his eyes and chin might sink, but his spine stayed straight and tall. Now he lowered those big eyes and shrugged his little shrug, and his mouth stirred briefly.

'Of course,' I said, 'we don't have to believe everything he says.'

'Free will,' he observed constrainedly.

'And common sense. If he'd really conquered the world, would he set up his capital in Kraftsville, Illinois?'

He took on a struggling look – trying to enunciate an answer that would suit me – but after a minute he gave it up and relaxed in silence.

'And what's he doing with those troops, if he commands them all?'

'Dividing the world into small, self-sufficient communities,' he parroted patiently.

'How ready does he have to be, General?'

Arslan looked up blankly from his coffee-tableful of papers. He had sent Hunt upstairs a few minutes before, and he had called for a bottle, but it still stood unopened. Lately he had started to break his unstated rule of no hard liquor while there was still work to do. 'How ready?'

'How strong. Strength was the idea, wasn't it?'

He fingered the top of his bottle. 'He is ready now,' he said finally. 'Let him go to his people.'

I wasted no time setting up a meeting between Hunt and Jean – and when it came right down to it, Hunt raised no objection. They talked in what had been the music room at school and was now an office supply storeroom. (The Turkistanis used a considerable amount of memo paper.) Hunt was back in twenty minutes, and I felt better as soon as I saw his face. There was a freshness and childhood there that had been missing for too long. And a vulnerability. He didn't say anything; he just started to pack a little toilet kit. Hunt didn't have very many belongings. Still, he managed to put off his departure till after supper, dawdling through his preparations and taking individual leave of every animal on the place. Arslan wasn't there.

And when Arslan came in at last, not half an hour after he finally left, he didn't mention Hunt.

A little after dark (it would have been about eight – there was no Daylight Saving Time this year) we heard a single rifle shot, not far away. On the couch Arslan swung himself upright, his face gone hard, and spoke an order. Two soldiers jumped to put out the lights, and another one rushed past me and out of the door. I heard low voices, running feet, one cautious shout; then in scarcely a minute the man was back with a word to Arslan, the door was shut, the lamps being lit again.

'What's the matter?' I demanded. But Arslan was giving more orders, brisk and easy. One man disappeared through the kitchen door, another up the stairs. Luella came in from the kitchen, white-faced. There was a pause. We were all on our feet, except Arslan.

He knew too damned well what was coming, and I knew it, too. Anger was building up in me like compressed air, so tight I could hardly hear the slow steps on the porch. A guard held the door open for Hunt and closed it after him.

He looked straight towards me. 'Would you mind if I came back, Mr Bond?' His voice was clear, level, and bitter.

'As far as I'm concerned you *are* back, Hunt, and always welcome.'

Luella came to him anxiously. 'What happened, Hunt?'

'Forget it.' He was leaning against the door, his little bag in his hands. His eyes flared at me as he burst out, 'He's willing to take me back – *on conditions*! How about that? If you've got any conditions, I'd appreciate hearing them now.'

'No conditions, Hunt,' I said. 'Never.'

Luella gasped wordlessly, and I followed her look. Hunt's left pant leg was streaked with wet from thigh to ankle; the blood dribbled silently off his shoe onto the rug. 'Yeah,' he said. She was trying to help him away from the door, but he leaned against it stubbornly. 'I can walk very well, thanks.' His eyes were alight with fury. I touched Luella's arm, and she stepped back.

It was Arslan's turn now. He stood up at last, and Hunt limped across the room and allowed himself to be let down onto the couch. Arslan was on his knees beside him in an instant, ripping open the pant leg with his knife.

Luella surprised me. 'You get your hands off him!' she snapped. 'You're the one that had him shot!'

'My own fault,' Hunt said calmly. 'I know the curfew rule. I'm surprised, though,' he added to Arslan. 'I thought you had better marksmen. Or don't they shoot to kill?'

Arslan glanced up appreciatively. 'Not to kill, no. To immobilize. It is often desirable to question those who break rules.'

'I wasn't even immobilized,' Hunt said tightly.

'Yes. The sentry will be reprimanded.' The guards were reappearing with water, bandages, medicines. There was a well-rehearsed air about the whole thing. 'For your information, Hunt,' Arslan was saying, 'I have given standing orders not to fire on you unless you should actually attack me. Otherwise you would have been shot as soon as you left your parents' house. But the man who fired was unable to recognize you in the darkness. I consider him justified.'

'How about a doctor?' I said.

'Unnecessary. It is a very simple wound.'

Maybe it hadn't quite been rehearsed. Conceivably – just conceivably – the shot had been accidental. But, to whatever extent he had manipulated for it, I didn't doubt that this was exactly the scene Arslan had planned. But Hunt had come to my house for shelter, and I'd given it, without conditions. That was what mattered.

I went to see Arnold Morgan first thing the next morning. He looked half relieved to see me and half belligerent. 'Did Hunt get back to your place all right?' he demanded.

'Well, he got there, and by good luck he's only got a bullet hole in his leg. Didn't you people ever hear of the curfew?'

He went as white as if he'd been bleached. 'We tried to keep him, Franklin. I did everything I could. How is he?'

'He's all right. What I'd like to know is, if he started off intending to stay with you, and you did everything you could to keep him, what made him come back?'

He firmed up at that, and flushed angrily. 'When Hunt comes home, it's going to be the real thing, Franklin. Nobody's going to use *my* house as a . . . a . . .'

'In other words, you sent your son out to be shot at because he couldn't promise he wouldn't be assaulted.'

'No, sir – and you ought to know me better than to say that to me. I didn't send him anywhere. The only thing I asked for was that he wouldn't *volunteer* himself to that greasy devil. For God's sake, Franklin, what do you expect me to do – encourage him?'

'I did expect a little Christian charity and a little understanding for your own child. But it looks like that was too much to ask for.' We weren't quite shouting yet, but we were getting close.

'You're not in a very good position to—'

'—So how about a little common sense instead? The only things you've accomplished are convincing Hunt he *can't* get back to a normal life – not that anything's normal these days – and pushing him right into Arslan's corner. His own father drives him out, and who takes him in? Arslan! Arslan! Just putting it bluntly, Arnold, anytime Arslan wants his body he can have it, and neither you nor I nor Hunt can stop him; and it doesn't matter whose house he's living in, either. What you've done is help Arslan get hold of his soul.'

'That's a hell of a thing to say to me.' His voice shook. 'That's exactly what I'm trying to stop. He wouldn't even agree—' He broke off, waving his open hand spasmodically, as if he was looking for something to hit with it. 'As far as I'm concerned, it's not too late even now. My door's open whenever he's ready to come home.'

'On your terms.'

'Now, listen, Franklin. If you've got anything practical to tell me, go ahead and say it. But if you're just here to pass insults, let's call a halt right now. Jean's upstairs trying to get some rest, and I've got better things to do.'

'Yes, I've got one thing very practical—'

But he was so worked up now that he couldn't let me go on till he got in his counterattack. 'And I'll tell you something, Franklin, there's a lot of people who don't think much of the way you've toadied up to that stinking Turk. Collaborator's a dirty word, but that's exactly—'

'I didn't come to discuss myself.'

'No, you came to pull that holier-than-thou act because I've insisted on a little basic morality and loyalty – and coming from you it doesn't look very good. Ever since they came shooting their way in here—'

'Nobody shot their way in.'

'—you've been preaching. "Cooperate! Cooperate!" Well, I say that's just the coward's way to pronounce "collaborate." '

'If you think so, why haven't you done something about it?'

'If we'd had a chance, we would have! You were so damn quick to inform on anybody who had a gun.'

'Do you have any idea what this town would look like now if we'd tried to fight?'

'We'd be able to hold our heads up, anyway.'

'After you'd scraped them out of the mud, maybe. I'm not hanging mine. Now, just shut up and listen to me for five seconds. For God's sake – for Jean's sake, Arnold – get word to Hunt that you want him back, no strings attached. Don't do it through me if you don't want to. You're welcome to think whatever you want to about me, but it's more important what you do about your son.'

I left that little scene with a feeling of satisfaction, all in all. Collaborator. Well, in a sense I certainly was. I'd gone all out to get people to do what Arslan and his henchmen demanded, and I'd been working hand-in-glove with Nizam on the economic plan. What Arnold Morgan didn't know about – what nobody knew much about, I hoped, except a few people like Sam Tuller's family and Leland Kitchener the junk man – was a little non-existent organization that we called the Kraft County Resistance.

Arslan's pistol and its eight cartridges were hidden in nine separate spots. They might as well be separate, for now. There was no possible way for that gun to do us any good tangibly, except the way I'd failed to use it in the Land Rover; but the fact that it existed was a solid rock to build a faith on. Sam Tuller and two of his boys had crawled in that oat field night after night, till they found every last cartridge. It had to be careful crawling, too.

Aside from the matter of getting out of the house and back in again without disturbing their billeted soldier, it was likelier than not that Arslan would have the field watched. But we got them all, and got them safely squirreled away, without rousing the least suspicion. Or so we had to tell ourselves.

I had thought long and hard before I told Sam about the gun in his field. But he was a reliable man, the kind who could shoulder a risk like that, and I felt justified in giving it to him. If there was going to be any real Resistance at all, quite a few people would have to take quite a few risks. And, by God, there was going to be a Resistance.

That was why I had planted some rumors within a week of Arslan's banquet. People needed something to hang onto, if it was only a name or an idea, and they needed it right from the start. It didn't hurt that there was nothing to back it up at first – you couldn't arrest a name without a body. The real organization developed very slowly. It had to be solid. It had to be built man by man.

Naturally, there was a lot of resistance, with a small 'r', to Arslan, and not everybody had the patience to wait for a solid organization. There were other names besides ours going the rumor rounds, names with 'Freedom' and 'America' in them. It was partly by talking to people who seemed to be getting themselves involved with those things that I had gotten my reputation, in certain circles, as a collaborator. Some of those people were the gun-owners I had informed on, as Arnold chose to call it. But I'd managed to discourage others before it was too late – good people who didn't need to throw away their lives for nothing.

The would-be patriots hadn't found much to do but talk – except, of course, that some of them were responsible for the death of Howard and Mattie Benson back at the beginning of spring. There hadn't been any noticeable investigation of that incident. Arslan – or Nizam – apparently felt the deterrent effect of promptly enforcing the billet rule was enough, and apparently he'd been right. But one night at the end of August somebody tried to set fire simultaneously to the stable, Nizam's head-quarters, and my house. Nizam's men were not only waiting for them with open arms; before the night was over, they had also arrested not just the entire membership of the particular organization that had undertaken the arsons, but every other resistance movement in the district. Except, of course, the Kraft County Resistance.

7

It was mid-October when I came upstairs one evening to find my door open and Hunt sitting listlessly on the windowsill.

'Take a chair, Hunt.' He stood up hastily – remembering his manners – and I closed the door and waved him towards my armchair.

'Thanks.' He sat down awkwardly and gave me a smile as an afterthought. One thing Arslan had done for him was destroy his gracefulness. He had been one of those easy-moving boys that take to bikes and horses and skis as if they'd been born in motion. Now he acted like somebody who'd been bedridden and hadn't quite got his muscles under control yet. It made me wonder sometimes how much sheer physical abuse he had to put up with.

I turned my desk chair around to face him, sat down, and stretched out my legs. Hunt had never visited me in my room before, and it obviously meant something to him, but he wasn't going to open up without some priming. So I began to talk, about what I'd done that day, about the weather prospects, about the dogs and the cats and the monkey.

'I hate the damned monkey,' he said suddenly. He hated something, all right. His voice shook and his cheeks flamed. I nodded. He dropped his eyes. 'I'm going to kill him.'

'Well, you know, a monkey can't really help itself.'

He sank back in the chair, turning his face half away – wondering, I realized, whether it was worth the trouble to disabuse me. 'I didn't mean the monkey,' he said. 'I meant *him*.'

Well, there it was. I heaved a sigh. No, under the circumstances, I didn't think he was going to kill anybody. Hunt had been building up steam for nearly a year now, and with a little bit more, maybe he *would* have killed Arslan, or tried; but now he had let it out in words. And, after all, he was only fourteen. He was breathing deeply now, and his face was exhausted and calm.

'Why tell me about it?' I asked gently.

'I thought you might want to make preparations.'

'Thank you.' He looked at me at last, rolling his head against the chair back, and smiled wanly. I took a deep breath and leaned forwards. 'Hunt. Just what preparations do you think I could make that would save Kraftsville from absolute destruction? I'm not God.'

'Neither is Arslan,' he offered mildly.

And on that cue the door opened, quietly but not stealthily, and Arslan stood leaning against the doorframe. He had a bottle under his arm and a roll of papers in one hand. He looked as if he might have been there a while.

We were as still as mice. Gently Arslan lifted his hand and tossed the papers, and they splayed out across the bed and onto the floor at Hunt's feet. He took the bottle by the neck, hefting it thoughtfully for a minute as if he was considering it as a weapon. Then he tossed it after the papers. It bounced softly on the bed. 'I am tired, sir,' he said matter-of-factly.

I looked hard at his face and the set of his body. Was it possible for Arslan to be tired? His eyes were bloodshot and a little puffy, and there were lines around them, but the rest of his face was smooth and fresh-looking, neither drawn nor drooping, a very youthful face. There wasn't a trace of slump in his leaning. He was relaxed like a coiled copperhead or a dozing cat – comfortable, but ready to kill on a split second's notice. Still, he would probably look like that if he was about to drop from exhaustion. It was no wonder Arslan ate so much; he must have used up a lot of energy just standing around.

He lit a cigarette, took one drag, looked at it, and pinched it out, dropping it back into his shirt pocket. 'Africa and South America may be the most difficult problems in the end,' he said conversationally, 'but Asia is of course the most massive problem.' He turned his steady, humorous gaze on me. Yes, I thought he looked tired. 'It is probable that I shall fail in Asia.'

Probable. It would be silly to forget that everything he said had a purpose. But all the same, that one word *probable* lit a little blaze of hope. If he failed anywhere, he failed everywhere; unless every wall stood, his house of cards would come tumbling down.

He came on into the room, shouldering the door shut behind him, leaned back against it, and surveyed us. 'I give myself six years. Six years. Then, if I have not succeeded, I will apply my second plan.'

I nodded involuntarily. I'd seen too much of Arslan to be sure his grand scheme would fail, but on the other hand, I couldn't really imagine it succeeding; and when it failed, Arslan wasn't the man to go home to Bukhara and raise sheep. There figured to be a second plan, and I had a kind of an idea what it would be.

'Plan Two is also difficult,' he went on, 'but it is more practicable, and also more permanent.' He straightened himself, and smiled coolly at me as he crossed over to the bed. 'You have refused to drink with me in your kitchen and in your living room, sir. Will you drink with me in your bedroom?'

'I don't drink,' I told him for the twentieth time. 'Anywhere.'

He stepped over my feet, swept the scattered papers to one side, and settled himself on the bed, with my pillow tucked behind his shoulders and his shoes on Luella's clean bedspread. 'Strong drink is raging,' he said, carefully opening his vodka. 'You have promised to explain Christianity to me, sir. I am ready to listen.' He tilted the bottle with loving care and took a long, slow swallow.

'I don't think so.'

He lowered the bottle long enough to shrug, and drank again, drew a deep breath, and prodded his papers with the butt of the bottle. 'These are the messengers that tell me my failure is probable,' he said. 'Hunt, pick up those.' Hunt stooped and gathered up the papers from the floor; he looked blankly across Arslan as he laid them on the bed, and met my eyes. 'The current demographic analyses. Always they insist upon this message. I cannot make them change their story.' He smiled to himself. You could literally see the liquor hitting him. Something like a shudder went down the length of him, as if he were settling more comfortably into his skin; the lines around his eyes smoothed out, and his face flushed.

I watched him pretty sourly. I didn't like his dirty boots, and I didn't like his jibes at religion. 'Does that mean you're giving up?' He made a little grunt of amusement. 'At any rate,' I said, 'it means there's a little bit of hope for the world.'

'Hope,' he said thoughtfully. He drank deep again, and then suddenly he collected himself like a cat going into a crouch. He turned to me, leaning hard on his elbow, his face and voice indignant and venomous. 'You are not a child, sir. You have seen something of life and death. Tell me, are they what you have pretended them to be? You call yourselves a Christian people; and that, sir, is a lie, and you are wise enough to know that it is a lie. You would have called Kraftsville a safe and pleasant place to live, before I came, would you not? But answer this for yourself, sir. How many households do you know personally in Kraftsville? Two hundred, perhaps – three hundred? How many of these are free of serious evil – *serious* evil, sir? Aggression, exploitation, cruelty – lust to possess, lust to destroy – hatred, envy, deceit – have not these been always commonplace in Kraftsville? I did not import pain, sir; it is a local product.' His mouth tightened emphatically. He went on staring at me with remote eyes while he bit at his underlip. 'And yet it is true,' he announced sternly. 'It is true that Kraftsville was a safe and pleasant place, in comparison with other places. Your hungriest paupers have been better fed than the chiefs of towns. Your people have slept in security. They were free, they were healthy, as human health and freedom go. They had never suffered war. But you know that in most of the world, sir, there has been war and war again, and again, and again war, so that every generation learns again. Strange. It is very strange.' He shook his head like a man in real puzzlement.

'What is?'

'More than one hundred years without war. A strange way of life.'

'What do you mean, without war? My God, we've—'

'You have *made* war, you have not suffered it! Your nation, sir, has been perhaps the happiest to exist in the world. And yet consider its history. The natives despoiled, displaced, cheated, brutalized, slaughtered. The most massive and the most cynical system of slavery since the fall of Rome. A civil war spectacular in its dimensions. A century of labor troubles, of capitalist exploitation and union exploitation. And in the very ascendancy of your power, disintegration! The upheaval, the upswelling, of savagery, of violence. Not revolution, sir, for revolution requires coherence. Not eighteenth-century France, but fifth-century Rome. The exposure, the revelation, of that all-pervading rottenness that is the fruit of your hypocrisy.' He pursed his mouth like a disapproving old woman. 'Grotesque, sir, this combination of a primitive puritanism and a frantic decadence; very like the Romans whom you so much resemble. Name me a happy nation, sir!'

'Switzerland,' I hazarded.

'Ah, Switzerland! The parody of Protestantism! All lusts sublimated into the pure lust of cleanliness and profit. The prudent, virtuous nation fattening upon the viciousness and greed and folly of all the world. Would you exchange your own life, sir, your life now or a year ago, for the life of those pious, prosperous people?' He shook his head dogmatically. 'I tell you, sir, not even the Japanese have been more rigidly inhibited.'

I wasn't entirely surprised at this tirade. After all, as he'd said himself, you didn't conquer the world for fun – nor for theory, either. There had to be some kind of emotional force powering Plan One. Why it came out now, this particular evening, was understandable enough, if he was really tired, if his plan was really in trouble, if he'd just heard Hunt plotting to murder him.

He leaned a little towards me again, blazing at me like an evangelist on fire with his message. 'Sir, you have been shocked by things I have done in Kraftsville, by things my soldiers have done. But I tell you we have been restrained, my soldiers and I. I tell you – and, sir, you know this already, you have known it for years – all these things, and worse, much worse things than these, have been done every day, in every country, all over the world, for thousands of years. You knew this, sir; your history, your newspapers, your eyes, your brain, your body and blood have told you. Were you shocked then? Was your Christian faith shaken? Did you vow vengeance for those wrongs?'

He leaned back abruptly against the pillows and drank again. It was my turn. 'All right, General, let me tell *you* something. You don't shake my faith, either. Sure, I know about the hell that goes on in this world. That's the whole point of Christianity – to keep from sinking into it all the way. It takes all the strength a man has, to deal with evil – that's nothing new. But that's what we're alive for. And let me tell you something else, General; we can win. You're trying to tar the whole world with one brush; you're saying it's all bad, and that's a lie. Kraftsville certainly wasn't perfect before you came, but it was paradise compared to what you've made of it, and it was a better and happier place than a lot of other places.'

'Yes, sir, yes!' He was smiling his triumphant, now-you-understand-how-right-I-was smile. 'Have you read *Candide*, sir? Three hundred pages of catastrophe and misery and injustice, of which the moral is, "We must cultivate our garden." Was not this the virtue of Kraftsville, that it cultivated its own garden? Sir, I am trying to reduce the world to Kraftsvilles.'

' "Reduce it"! You're reducing it, all right, reducing it to a wasteland. You think you get gardens out of ashes?'

'No!' he cried gladly. 'Out of death and excrement. Out of garbage and corpses. You cut the weeds before you sow the crop, do you not? Consider the world as it was before I came, sir. Throughout Asia hunger, disease, fear, tyranny of landlords or of rulers, and war or the threat of it. In Africa, chaos and corruption. In South America, unconquerable poverty breeding still new revolutions. And everywhere, dread of nuclear war and busy preparation for it. Was this a happy world, sir? A safe and pleasant place to live?'

His voice rang and throbbed, a parade-ground voice – except, I realized, he wasn't actually speaking very loud. His eyes burned. He looked as if he'd hit anybody who dared to answer one of his rhetorical questions. On the other side of the bed, Hunt was watching him with a kind of motionless frenzy – frozen on the verge of some explosion.

'And this was not an accident of the times. What came before, sir? Colonialism; and I assure you – I assure you, sir – that the evils of colonialism have not been exaggerated. Before the Second World War, the First. Before that, more than half a century of revolutions, and the Industrial Revolution that powered them all. Before that, the wars of Islam and the wars of Christianity. How far back do you wish to go, sir? Do you remember the Chinese general who took Canton in fifteen-hundred and gave that perfect order to his troops: "Kill, kill, kill, kill, kill"? Can you smell the stink of the galleys, sir – the most elegantly efficient means of transportation for twenty centuries? An invention of the Romans, sir, those famous practicians. Do you remember the battle of Lepanto, which saved the West for Christianity and proved the virtue of heavy firepower? Was there a really significant difference between the stench of the Turkish Moslem galleys and the stench of the Spanish Christian galleys? On the one hand the smell of Christian slaves and Moslem convicts, on the other that of pagan slaves and Christian convicts. There were still galleys in the nineteenth century, sir; and the latest belonged to France, that most humane flower of Western civilization. Which do you prefer, sir? That holy St Vladimir of the Russian church who used cavalry to drive his subjects to the river to be baptized or drowned; or that holy Emir of my country who kept a snake pit into which uncooperative ambassadors could be lowered; or those prudent American pioneers who massacred a village of Christian Indians as a preventive measure; or those loyal Vietnamese patriots who tied their Communist neighbors together in live bundles and dropped them into rivers – a technique they may have learned from a study of French history? An English soldier of Cromwell's army was surprised to see the little children of a woman dead of starvation eating the flesh of their mother's corpse, and yet there is a natural logic in this. Passing over gas ovens and human vivisection, penal colonies and sharecropping, you have heard of the battered-child syndrome?' He gave me a blank ghost of his angelic smile. 'A worldwide, an age-old phenomenon, though perhaps especially a modern American one. Are these things tolerable? Clearly yes; they have always been tolerated. But there are more important things. Consider, sir. It is natural to man to build a civilization, and it is natural to civilization to destroy itself and to wreck the world.'

'You think so?' I broke in roughly.

He glared at me a moment, and then half-relaxed – remembering, no doubt, that he was talking to humans. 'I think so, yes. If war were not natural to man, there would be no wars. And what is natural is inevitable. Do you know the fable of Venus and the cat? No?' He laughed. 'Read it.' He waved his hand impatiently, disposing of the human race with a gesture. 'Man is a mistake of evolution. He is too potent. Any species will foul or exhaust its habitat in time, unless it is checked by counterforces.' He wiped his hard palm across the mouth of his bottle and drank in violent gulps. Something seemed to have given way in Hunt. He sat docile and still now, his eyes following automatically every movement Arslan made. 'Counterforces,' Arslan said, 'internal or external. When the food supply is inadequate, the does drop fewer fawns. But man, man is too strong. He fouls and exhausts too rapidly, and nothing checks him for long. There is only one end for such a species: extinction; quick extinction. It only remains to be seen if the end comes by holocaust or by poisoning and starvation.' He chuckled. 'A bang or a whimper.'

I started to speak, but again he crowded in ahead of me. 'Is this important? Not in itself, except to those who die. But man has taken all the world as his habitat. *Therefore* this is important. Not man alone, but the whole world is dying. Your scientists have spoken of the web of life. Yes. It is a web, in four dimensions. And man hangs in the web above the void. But man has strained and twisted and torn the web. Man has pruned the web to make for himself a cozy hammock, and now' – he snorted a contemptuous laugh, or maybe it wasn't a laugh – 'now he dangles, now he feels the runs and ravels in the fabric, and the void is so cold, so cold!' He drew a harsh breath through his open mouth, and nodded dogmatically. 'Yes, sir. The natural is the inevitable.'

'Then what's the use of what you're doing?' I got in.

He nodded again. 'Good. A good point. If man is set back to his beginnings, will he not build another civilization? If he can, yes; but he must have the raw materials, and his environment must not be too strong for him. Now, sir, do you understand?'

'No, I don't. You say what's natural is inevitable, and I say that at least what we've done before we can do again. Man has *proved* he can handle any environment in the world – and out of this world, too. If you're talking about depletion of natural resources, a civilization just getting started doesn't need the resources that we've depleted.'

'On the contrary, sir! It is exactly the resources it needs that are gone forever. Where now is the ore that can be mined and smelted without modern equipment – the equipment that I am destroying? Where is the coal that lay exposed on hillsides, the oil that oozed from the ground? There is wood, yes, I grant that, there is water, yes, there is air, and these will survive – if I succeed. If I succeed.' He stopped for another drink, a hasty one this time. 'But consider the environment, sir, the environment as a whole. Drought, flood, fire, vermin, disease, all the enemies that man boasts of controlling – he has armed them, trained them, fed them, laid himself down in their path. Man has unbalanced the world, unbalanced so literally, sir, that he creates earthquakes. Earth breaks beneath his tread and he falls, he drowns in his leaking oil. He burns the oxygen of the land, he smothers the oceans with his grease. These abuses must cease, sir – I tell you, these abuses must cease at once! You have complained' – his face twisted in a genuine sneer of contempt – 'because your little pollution machines have been turned off – your clumsy little coal-burning power plant—' Something internal interrupted him; his eyes went blank and private, and he chuckled and muttered. He was drunk.

'So we cut down the trees instead,' I said.

He grunted and shrugged. 'Reversible. Correctable. You understand? What you do to the trees is very little. Man is man; yes. But it is possible to eliminate the practices that cause irreversible damage. It is possible to reduce the population within tolerable limits. District by district.'

'I thought you'd already stopped everything, abuses included.'

'I have halted these abuses, sir. It is the first step – only the first step. No doubt the world can heal itself, but already it has been permanently scarred – disfigured – maimed. This is my hope, sir: that, once destroyed, civilization will not rise again, or at worst will rise only very slowly.'

I heard Hunt draw a long, weary-sounding breath. Arslan was tending to his bottle again, and I said bitterly, 'If civilization's going to destroy itself anyway, why do you have to step in and do it?'

He waved his hand impatiently. 'Is this so hard to understand?

I do it for two great reasons. The first, but the less important, is this, to save mankind from much suffering.'

'Save it!' I was on my feet and he was looking up at me. 'You call this saving mankind from suffering?'

'Yes, sir,' he said coolly. 'But in any case, my second reason is sufficient.'

'And what is that?'

'To save the world from mankind.'

I swung away from him and paced around the room, stopping at the foot of the bed to face him. 'Plan Two,' I said. 'What's Plan Two?'

A new kind of smile spread across his face, thin and cold. 'If civilization cannot be thoroughly eradicated, it remains necessary to exterminate the human species.'

'That's what I thought. Damn you, that's what I thought.' My own voice sounded small and thin in the silence before it and after it.

'This plan contains its own problems,' he was saying. 'The Nazis eliminated with difficulty only a few million persons. And passing over all operational problems, the final problem remains: Who will exterminate the exterminators?' He dropped his head back on the pillow and smiled at me. 'There are, however, other approaches. For example, a program of disease dissemination could be managed to end with the spread of contagion to my armies.'

I stared down at him. His smile deepened and faded, and his eyes flicked away, finished with me, to rest on the ceiling. I raised my hand, and let it drop again. I would no more have hit him than I would have hit a corpse.

'But there are unavoidable risks,' he went on after a moment. 'Your liberals have prattled of the dangers of biological weapons, the danger of inadvertently destroying mankind. But in fact it is very difficult. No disease can be trusted to produce perfect mortality. There is always, always, the possibility of undiscovered pockets of survivors. Are you familiar with the screwworm fly, sir?' He turned his bland face back to me.

'Screwworms,' I said, when that non sequitur had gotten through to me. 'I'm familiar with screwworms.'

'Then perhaps you know that they were exterminated in Florida by releasing sterilized males into the wild population for two consecutive years.'

I shook my head, partly to clear it, partly because that didn't sound logical.

'Yes, sir.' He was warming to his subject again. 'Naturally, the species was particularly vulnerable to such treatment. With the human species, one entire sex would have to be sterilized. There are certain advantages of sterilization over killing, as no doubt you can see. There are two possible disadvantages; death is irreversible, sir, and it is recognizable.' And again he gave me a small, horrible smile.

I turned slowly back to my chair and sat down. We were walking through a mine field; but there were ways out of it, if we could just feel our way into them. *Who exterminates the exterminators?*

It dawned on me presently that for a minute, or a few minutes, or maybe more, we had all three been silent, sunk and oblivious in our separate contemplations of the same horror. Well, contemplation didn't win wars. I took a deep breath and cleared my throat.

'General,' I said, 'I don't know the details of how you came to power in your own country. We didn't get too much news of it, and frankly I've forgotten most of what little we did hear. But I have an idea you started out as a patriot.'

'My country,' he mocked throatily. 'My country.' He pressed himself back into the pillows, stretching his legs and lifting the bottle at arm's length, then relaxed again. 'This I have never understood,' he said mildly, 'how people forget. By what mechanism do your minds shut out parts of themselves? I, I do not forget.'

Hunt laughed haggardly. Arslan looked at him, and slowly an intense, warm smile lit up his face. 'I do not forget,' he said again. 'You speak of my country, sir. Do you think Turkistan is a country? Ah, no. Turkistan is an invention, sir, of the British.'

It was interesting to hear bitterness in Arslan's voice. It helped bring him down to size. Now he was drawing maps in the air with his hand. 'Turkistan is a dying fish. In the time of Herodotus – not so very long ago – *here*' (he stabbed the air with his bottle) 'was a great sea. What is it now? A salt pond – a puddle – fifty, sixty feet deep. And here the Caspian; a great sea still, but also dying. Once rivers flowed into these seas from the mountains here on the south. The mountains still stand. The rains fall, the snows melt, the rivers start out bravely into Turkistan. But only two are strong enough to live. And the others, that flow into nothing, that are blotted up by the desert and the sun, they are not rivers, sir. Can you call them rivers?' He drank, and added to his imaginary map. 'Here, the Amu Darya, the famous Oxus. Northeast, the Syr Darya, the little brother of the Amu.' Hunt's eyes, across the bed from me, glinted like wellwater. 'These are the only streams that feed our salt puddle, which is called the Aral Sea. But the Aral Sea is a Russian lake. Do you begin to understand?' Another stroke at the air. 'Between the Syr and the Amu live a people with Mongol eyes and little leather caps.'

'Not your people,' I said. Not if you could judge from his tone of voice.

'Not my people, but my mother's people.' What kind of a mother could Arslan have had, I wondered. 'They call themselves Uzbek, the people of Uzbek Khan, who led them across the Syr Darya a few hundred years ago – not so very long. But between the Syr and the Amu they found Bukhara – Bukhara the old city. Bukhara the Noble; the Dome of Islam; the city of the pure faith. Bukhara, my city; not my mother's city. And beyond the Amu they could not go, because of the Turkmens.' He drank again. His voice had turned heavy with the liquor. He managed his words and his sentences all right, but you could hear him managing them. 'Turkmens – Turkistan – Turkey – you understand? If my people had traveled a little farther west, as their cousins did, I would have been born a Turk. The Uzbeks, too, call themselves Turkish; but in the old language Turkmen means "pure Turk."' A drunken frown darkened his face. 'Although some have claimed "Turk-like"; but that is a lie. In any case, you see, sir, there are differences . . .' He faded out for a moment, and then collected himself again. 'All over the map of Central Asia, sir, you will find Turkistans – towns, provinces, regions. Sinkiang is not Chinese, and its right name is not Sinkiang; it is East Turkistan. Afghanistan south to its center is not Afghan; it is another Turkistan. My country,' he said again, and chuckled. 'This is not a country, it is a . . . diaspora. And this Turkistan that the British made and sold to the Emir of Bukhara – is not even Turkistani, except for my Turkmens. My father's Turkmens. You understand, sir, that the British were very anxious to stop the expansion of Russia in Central Asia. Russia itself was not a country, it was an empire, and an empire has no natural boundaries. Therefore the British manufactured their buffer states and sold them to the greediest local rulers: Iraq, Afghanistan – and the northern borderland, the most expendable buffer, Turkistan. So the Emir of Bukhara ruled over Turkmens and Uzbeks and Tajiks, and the British had their buffer state, their treaty of friendship, and their oil concession.

'Did I begin as a patriot? Ah, no, sir; I began as a child of a general of the Air Force, the air force that the British had given. My father was the patriot, who bombed the Emir's palace and began the civil war – the Generals' War. When it was over, there were no generals except my father.

'But before it was over, he had allowed my mother to take her children to Samarkand – Samarkand the city of delights, the city of Uzbek Khan and Timur the Lame. She believed that we would be safer among Uzbeks. Nevertheless, it was an Uzbek general who imprisoned us, and took time from his revolt against my father to rape personally my mother – my first experience of rape, sir, although not, as you know, my last. But it was a time of countercoups and counterrevolts. We were freed, and we fled into the desert of the Black Sands – my first and last experience of flight. We reached Bukhara, the city of wisdom, exactly in time for the countercoup of the loyalists – loyalists, you understand, to the dead Emir. So we were imprisoned again. This time my father came with his fighter-bombers. He sent a warning to the loyalists that if his family were not released within six hours he would strike. The loyalists replied that if he struck, his family would be killed. We were not released. He struck. And while the bombs fell, we were stoned in the courtyard of the old prison.' He smiled thinly. 'Until my father ordered the courtyard strafed.'

He lifted his eyes questioningly to the ceiling, took a long breath, and went on. 'So in due time the attack was successfully completed, and I was removed from the rubble, and survived, as you regret to see. Do you care to consider this, sir – how merely another stone, or another bullet, or another hour would have spared the world the affliction of Arslan? But the past is what we have.'

Suddenly he sat up, crossing his legs under him, making the bed shake. 'Yes, Hunt, yes, this is a disillusionment. Yes, it is sad, is it not, to find one's angels or one's devils driven also? The superman himself is human-all-too-human.' He groped in his pocket for a cigarette, looking humorously from one to the other of us. 'You have considered me a monster, and indeed you have reason. But – alas for the sublimity of your feelings! – the monster is also a man. I must confess this in humility.'

Certainly Hunt was hanging on his words, pale and tense. Arslan's bottle was empty. He rolled it off the edge of the bed, and got his cigarette lit with a little difficulty. 'Did I begin as a patriot, sir? In ten years my father was as powerful, and as rich, as any emir of Bukhara had been, and ready to send his only surviving son to Oxford like any satellite princeling. But I did not choose to be sent to Oxford. I studied one year at Moscow, two at Peking. You will understand, sir, that the Chinese saw me as a tool which they might shape for their own hands. When I returned to Bukhara, I took charge of the army – the simple utility, sir, of being a dictator's son. However, I disagreed with my father on several points of policy, and I was not disposed to obey his orders on those points. For these reasons he arranged to have me assassinated. It was a good plan, you understand. Whether the assassination succeeded or failed, he could put the blame on certain rebellious elements in the army, whom he very rightly suspected of plotting against him, and thus arm himself with an excuse to crush them.' He paused and smiled. 'Nizam,' he said fondly, 'was one of these. And Nizam's private intelligence system, even then, was better than my father's. It was Nizam who raised the revolt, but he raised it in my name, broadcasting a full confession by one of the assassins.

'I was not prepared to execute my father. I owed him something, did I not? I planned only to hold him in protective custody. But the choice was not given me. We took Bukhara, but not my father. He had preferred to shoot himself.'

'I think that was the first news we heard of you,' I said.

'And yet you could believe that I began as a patriot?'

'I'm curious, General. What makes you so eager to deny that you might have been one?'

'But I do not deny it! Ah, no, sir. If love and hate are brother and sister, why not pride and shame also? You understand, then, that I have had four years in which to rule my country. My country. Yes. My artificial buffer state. And for four years I worked hard to do what I am now undoing: to unite, to centralize, to modernize. It is possible that I would have made Turkistan a country that could have patriots.' Abruptly he swung his feet to the floor and stood up, swayed and recovered, and laughed softly. 'Bring them, Hunt,' he ordered, gesturing loosely towards the papers on the bed, and walked out.

Hunt stooped slowly to the papers, his face withdrawn and haggard. I got up and put my hand on his arm. 'Give him a minute,' I said. 'He may go to sleep.'

He nodded. He sat himself stiffly on the edge of the bed and began brushing away at the dirt Arslan's boots had left. 'Mr Bond.'

'Hunt,' I said, 'I'm not your principal any more. I wish you'd call me Franklin.'

He nodded again, and moved his mouth in his little inward humorless smile. 'It would be very useful,' he said at last, 'to be brave.'

'I believe you're as brave a person as I've ever known.' We looked at each other. 'Hunt, I'll talk to you again later. I'm not just sure yet what has to be done. Will you try not to rock the boat for a little while?'

'Okay,' he said wearily. He straightened the papers and stood up. 'Thanks for something.'

8

One week later, Arslan was standing across the table from me as I finished my breakfast, his knuckles on his hips, his garrison cap on his head. He beamed with youth, health, and vitality. 'I am saying goodbye, sir,' he announced. 'I leave Nizam in command. Krafts-ville has given me much pleasure.'

I was on my feet by that time. 'You're leaving? For good?'

He laughed happily. 'For good, for evil, who knows? It is very possible that I shall return. In a year, two years, twenty years perhaps. If not, sir' – his dark eyes flashed and fixed me hard – 'I am very happy to have known you.'

Hunt was standing in the kitchen doorway. Arslan swung halfway around, to follow my look. 'Yes, sir, Hunt goes with me.' The whole idea tasted good to him. He stood there for a minute watching the boy and rocking a little on his feet. 'Go, Hunt,' he ordered cheerfully.

'Wait a minute,' I said. Hunt hesitated just inside the living room. I clasped his right hand in both of mine. His face flushed; his eyes were bright with fear and excitement. 'Do you want to go?'

His head twitched. 'Yes,' he said huskily, and followed that with a quick, painful grin. 'Under the circumstances.' His eyes fell. 'I'm sorry . . .' he began indefinitely.

'Can I do anything for you here? Can I tell your folks anything?'

He made a little sardonic grimace. 'Could they tell me any-thing? Tell them goodbye, I guess.' Now he looked up, faintly returning my handclasp.

'Come back if you can, Hunt,' I said. 'But whatever happens, don't give up.'

He gave me a sudden wild look. Luella had followed from the kitchen, wiping her hands. 'Hunt—'

'Goodbye, sir,' he said. 'Also thank you. Both.' He walked out briskly, eyes straight ahead.

Arslan stood where I had left him, smoking a cigarette, his eyes dancing. 'I suggest that you cooperate with Nizam, sir. You should not expect as much indulgence from him as from me.'

'I have a pretty good idea what to expect. How many of these troops are you taking with you?'

He grinned delightedly. 'Have I appointed you my adjutant? What you need to know, you will learn without my help.' He touched his cap in salute, or what passed for a salute with him – almost correct, almost genuine, like a good amateur actor who wants his audience to know he doesn't have to make his living at it. 'Good luck,' he said.

'It could be worse, Mr Bond,' Leland Kitchener said. 'There's no taxes, anyway.'

There were no taxes, and no forced labor – except for the girls in the brothel. But there was the sunset curfew. There was the no-meetings rule. There was the soldier billeted in every home. Arslan hadn't moved a one of them, but he had taken all the surplus Turkistanis – the ones from the camp. A few days later, about half the Russians followed, or anyway headed east. And District 3281 belonged to Colonel Nizam.

NOTICE. The following items are declared contraband: Wire, all types. Electrical equipment, all types. Engines, all types. Petroleum products, combustible.

By February, Nizam's notices didn't bother to include the instructions any more. Everybody knew the blacklisted items had to be delivered immediately to the school, the camp, or Nizam's head-quarters. *Immediately* (we had learned the definition the hard way) meant *today*. The notice would be up at daybreak; if you didn't see it, or understand it, or have the means to comply with it, that was your hard luck. The next day, and unpredictably after that, there would be spot checks and sometimes sweeping searches. Possession of contraband was punishable (not always punished, though) by death. So we kept a sharp and early eye on the notice boards, and passed the word fast.

That had come to be the most obvious function of the Kraft County Resistance: to watch the boards, to pass the word, to help people shed their 'contraband.' The KCR was an established fact of Kraft County life now, but it was an invisible fact. Everybody knew it existed – which meant we had to assume Nizam knew it – but nobody called it by name. It was always 'they' or 'people' or 'somebody.' Keeping the membership secret was easier than I'd expected, for the very good reason that nobody wanted to know. 'Somebody told me' was all the authorization needed, and instructions were passed along from neighbor to neighbor just as efficiently as gossip used to be. That first spring of Arslan's absence, we had it down so pat that we could inform every household in the district inside of two hours. Then there would be a quietly frantic time. Definitions were matters of life and death. Was paraffin a combustible petroleum product? What about plastics? Did you have to cart your whole useless refrigerator to town, or was it good enough if you brought the motor? Did you have to take down your wire fences? What about phone wires and electric lines, that weren't exactly in anybody's possession?

We took down the fences. We climbed poles and took down the wires. We carted refrigerators. We ran regular wagon trains through the district all afternoon, picking up stuff. We tried to put ourselves in Nizam's place and imagine what he had in mind (though that didn't work entirely – one thing he had in mind was that at least part of whatever we decided would be wrong), and in cases of doubt we figured better safe than sorry. We also cached a few thousand feet of electrical wire, two generators, and about two bushels of assorted radio equipment.

Arslan had been satisfied to let us wither on the vine; Nizam went at us with an axe. You could say that Arslan had hit us like an avalanche, but after the dust had settled he really hadn't tried to shake us any further. You might even say he'd been fair, according to his lights. At least he'd stuck by his own rules. But Nizam's whole idea was to shake us and keep us shaken.

He had a little bit of a problem. Wherever Arslan was now, it was pretty evident he was still keeping a tight rein on his colonel. The look in Nizam's eye told me very plainly what would happen to me if the choice were up to him. It wasn't one of my biggest worries. Nizam was nothing if not scrupulous, and he had to play by Arslan's rules, too. It was Nizam who assigned a loud-mouthed corporal to my house, making me as vulnerable to the billet rule as the Bensons had been; it was Arslan who must have decreed free medical service for all citizens, including inoculations against all the foreign diseases his troops might have brought in. It was Nizam who instituted a system of bribing informers with extra rations; it was Arslan who had seen to it that nobody would have to starve in District 3281.

Even working within limitations, Nizam showed himself an expert at pure, plain harassment. He was keeping the district in a state that varied from nervous tension through misery and frustration to panic. Not to speak of the families of the people who were shot.

That *Petroleum products, combustible* was a typical example. At one unexpected stroke it deprived us of all our lights. No kerosene for lamps, no paraffin for candles. The town went black – except for Nizam's termite nest. Meanwhile every housewife was muttering unladylike things under her breath about the paraffin seals she'd had to pry off her jelly jars. It was a confiscation with no material excuse for it. If he wanted our kerosene, why wait till it was practically used up? If he wanted to deprive us of it, why not just wait a little longer, till we ran out? But about two weeks later, Nizam informed me that kerosene would be issued on a strict ration to selected households.

'We don't need it,' I told him. Selected households meant collaboration and broken morale. Rationing meant black-marketing and dependence. I already had a little project started for the manufacture of tallow candles, and we were experimenting with sunflower-seed oil.

The households were selected and the kerosene ration authorized. Nobody came to the camp to pick it up. All the lucky families had received a message from the KCR the same day they got their notification. Everybody had lived without kerosene for better than two weeks now. Some of them really wanted it, but not badly enough to cast what amounted to a vote for Nizam and against America. Not when it was put to them clearly in those terms. And the first tallow candles were being distributed free. After that, it would be a commercial enterprise.

So we had our successes. We held the line. But it wasn't only people we had to contend with. That year the bugs began in earnest.

Naturally Nizam had confiscated all the pesticide and herbicide and fertilizer he could find in the district for the troops' use. And their fields looked to be in relatively good shape. I thought it was only relative. Because that summer was like nothing I'd ever seen before, unless it was Arslan's advent. It was heartbreaking to see the potato bugs demolish a field in a day. People began to panic. We had worked hard the year before, but we had worked with confidence. Men had been masters of Kraft County for a long time, and just taking away their tractors didn't change that. But this year we were fighting for our lives. It wasn't possible there could be a famine in Kraft County, we kept telling ourselves. But we weren't exactly Kraft County any more. And then another blow hit us.

The corn was blighted. The stalks had tended to be leggy and a little pale from the start, like a slight case of mineral deficiency – nothing to worry anybody much. But the ears just didn't fill. What kernels did form were small and misshapen. Sweet corn wasn't very much affected. But all the field corn was hard hit; and our precious hybrids, that the County Farm Advisor had literally made by hand on his seed plots the year before, were a total loss.

And it was right then, while I was figuring how many livestock we could winter on practically no corn, that Roley Munsey brought me the news of *Evergreen*.

Roley was the youngest Munsey boy. He would have been in high school if he hadn't dropped out in his freshman year. As a matter of fact, he had just barely managed to graduate from eighth grade, a year behind his age. But he was a good boy – a good-natured kid, clever with his hands, and one who tried his best. And, very importantly for us, he had been a radio ham. Not Citizens' Band stuff, but a real, licensed amateur. There had been some others in the district, before Arslan, but it was remarkable how many of them had been high school students.

What radio equipment we had saved from Nizam's confiscations didn't look too impressive, but it was plenty for Roley to work with. He had a shortwave receiver that picked up signals, sporadically, from all around the world. Unfortunately, not one of them in the past year had ever sounded like anything but the internal communications of Arslan's organization. It was that fact, more than any other, that made me believe in the reality of Arslan's Plan One.

'Mr Bond, I hate to bother you when you're busy, but I never heard nothing like this before.'

'Just sorry I couldn't get here faster. Tell me about it.'

'Well, it was an American voice, no damn Turk. The only words I could make out was, "Both sunk. Sorry about that, Arslan. *Evergreen* signing off." But he laughed, see? He said "Sorry about that, Arslan," and he laughed. So I figure he *got* to be American.'

'Where did it come from?'

'East. I don't know where from, only east of here. It come in clear enough.'

'Nothing else?'

'No, sir, nothing, not a thing. He just said "sunk." "Both sunk."'

'Roley, you mean to tell me there are still American ships at sea? After nearly two years?'

'I don't *know*, Mr Bond, I sure don't know. But I know he said "sunk."'

'Well, if we heard it, Nizam must have heard it, Roley. You can bet Arslan's organization knows a lot more about it than we do.'

Roley nodded, which he always did, but he rubbed the back of his head doubtfully. 'Well, yeah, sure, Mr Bond, but *maybe* not. Maybe not. Like if they wasn't expecting it, they likely wouldn't be listening on that band. If they wasn't right there on the right frequency at the right second, they wouldn't of heard it. That signal never lasted but half a minute.'

'Roley, you figure out exactly what you'd need to hook into Nizam's power. We just might want to transmit a long-distance signal. I'll talk to you later. You boys be sure there's one of you listening every second. Now get on it and stay on it.'

Evergreen. It sounded more like a code word than the name of a ship. I felt ten years younger. My mind was happily jumping to conclusions. *Evergreen.* It would be appropriate for, say, a nuclear-powered ship, or a group of them. What else *could* be still functioning? Hunt had told me, and it sounded plausible, that Arslan was destroying fuel production facilities. He would have taken over the navies as he had the armies, of course; but it would be a lot easier for a recalcitrant ship to hold out against him than a recalcitrant regiment. He could have starved out any conventional-powered ship by this time, for lack of fuel. But even if you commanded the combined fleets of the world, it wouldn't necessarily be easy to track down one or two or a dozen nuclear-powered vessels, especially if some of them were submarines. And he couldn't actually have the combined fleets of the world in operation; he must have felt the fuel squeeze himself, long since, plus all the maintenance problems that would intensify as he phased out industries or smashed them cold.

Evergreen. It would be appropriate, of course, for any unit of resistance that had survived the cold wave of Arslan's first great sweep. Suppose a mosquito fleet of private boats had maintained itself in the creeks and coves of some ragged coast or island chain – motorboats that could operate for years on a few well-rationed barrels of oil, reconverted steamers burning wood, sailboats. It wouldn't be much of a combat navy; but suppose there were a hundred such little fleets. It was the old, old story; no force, *no* force could destroy a popular movement, if it was popular enough. Not without destroying the population.

Evergreen . . . The fields looked naked, stripped, like burned-over ground. A potato plant or a beanstalk with all the leaves eaten off was awkward and obscene, not like the honest stubble of any harvested field. I knew it had gotten to me the day I found myself clenched up with fear, not for the county but for my personal stomach. The medicines that Doc Allard had kept me in shape with were all used up, and I had to depend on diet and willpower. If I couldn't guarantee myself a supply of milk and cream – The thought sent me to bed, doubled up.

Well, that wasn't only cowardly, it was un-Christian. And besides, it got in the way of doing anything.

It took plenty of effort and plenty of prayer, but I got my stomach quieted down – and not for just that day, either. The thing was, I had to live *calmly*. I had to rely on God in an ultimate way, not for little things like enough milk or a miracle to save the crops. I had to believe that everything I did, as long as I did my best, was *for* the best.

Livestock, after all, were a luxury. It was August, which meant we still had time, but not time for experiments and failures. We burned off the blighted and bug-eaten fields, plowed up some pastures, and planted what would do us more good: carrots, turnips, beets. Our oats were doing well, comparatively – compared to our wheat, for example – but it was too late to plant more oats this year. We slaughtered stock as fast as we could use the meat or put it up. We salted and pickled as much as we could spare the salt for, canned as much as we had cans to hold, dried as much as we had room to spread in the sun, and smoked the rest. Plenty of people protested killing the stock and plowing up the grass, and the Farm Advisor protested that smoking didn't actually preserve meat; but we didn't have time to let everybody follow their own whims. Later we would plant winter wheat and keep our fingers crossed. We'd have enough grain and hay to winter what few livestock we were keeping.

Evergreen . . . After all, it didn't have to mean anything. Roley had picked up what sounded like American voices before, that had obviously been working for Arslan. Not a doubt in the world, whether I liked it or not, that Arslan's Americans were in Russia just as much as Arslan's Russians were in America. And it would be a miracle if some of those Americans didn't make remarks like 'Sorry about that, Arslan' now and then. Whatever were 'both sunk,' they might have been anti-Arslan as well as pro. 'Sorry

99

about that' – there might have been an order to capture instead of destroy.

Yes, we would last the winter, and every spring was a new start. Kraft County wasn't crowded – the population had been declining for years – and by the grace of God, or maybe the exercise of common sense, people just weren't having babies these days. There were the troops, of course; but, if anything, they were an economic asset now. On the average, they not only took care of themselves, but produced a little surplus that found its way by various means into the hands of Kraft County citizens.

Even if we couldn't do much farming, we could live. A few chickens for eggs, a few cattle for milk, a few hogs to keep up the breed; fish and game would be our staple meat sources. Every field abandoned meant that much more game-cover. And the game, like the bugs, thrived. The soldiers were permitted only very limited hunting privileges, but that didn't apply to us.

'Franklin, how the hell are you going to shoot anything without guns?'

'Who said shoot?' We weren't even allowed to have bows and arrows, but we did have traps and nets. It was a new style of hunting for us, but we learned it. The Indians had done all right in this territory, and maybe there was even more game now than there had been back then, when it was all deep woods. We held drives for the small game, rotating them around the district and learning as we worked. With good dogs, it wasn't hard to walk quail and rabbits and even doves into a fine-mesh seine. Getting it closed on them was a little harder. We used the seines for what they were made for, too, and got all the fish we could use, not to mention cleaning out a lot of mud turtles while we were at it. We hunted coons and possums with the dogs, trapped muskrats, snared rabbits – snared deer, too, when we'd learned the trick. We had long enough to learn it.

9

It must have been very near the fourth anniversary of Arslan's departure when a boy I didn't know came galloping into town with the news that a mechanized force was coming east on 460. His horse was still blowing when we heard their motors – a chilling sound these days, now that Nizam only used his vehicles for emergencies.

Starting home from the square, I saw a procession of jeeps and one truck draw up in front of my house. By the time I got there, the street and yard were swarming. Soldiers were prodding their way through the garden as if it were a minefield. The Russians were cheering from the school windows and popping out of the doors. My front door stood open, and a flock of women were trotting in and out helter-skelter, some of them carrying bundles and all of them chattering. One in a scarlet headscarf and a swinging blue skirt was directing operations, running from jeep to jeep, then halfway up the walk, then back to the street. Only one stood by silently, with a child in her arms. Arslan was leaning against the side of the truck, smoking.

I stopped beside him, and we eyed each other. He looked thriving. He might have put on a little flesh; otherwise he was the identical brash welterweight who had stridden out of my kitchen four years ago.

'Good morning, sir.'

'How's Plan One going, General?'

He grinned. 'Very well.'

'Then things could be worse.'

Luella stepped out on the porch. 'Franklin, come here!' She sounded excited and glad.

'But first, sir,' Arslan put in smoothly, 'you will meet my son.'

He dropped his cigarette and beckoned the quiet woman. I took a quick look at her face (she was on the far edge of middle age, and homely – definitely not the mother of Arslan's son), and he took the baby from her.

The nape of my neck prickled. There he stood beside me – Arslan Khan, and Genghiz's pyramid of skulls was no more than a steppingstone to him – there he stood, smiling, with a baby in his arms. 'This is Sanjar,' he said.

I focused on the child. 'Sander?'

'San-*jar*!' He rolled the name joyously, all but singing it.

Arslan's son. He was either small for his age or advanced for it. From a distance I had taken him for no more than a babe in arms, but he had the bright boy-face of a three-year-old. Now he put his hand commandingly on Arslan's mouth and said something that sounded very clear, though it certainly wasn't English. Arslan chuckled, shaking his head away from the little brown fingers. He might have been any proud young soldier-father.

Then Hunt Morgan walked out onto the porch beside Luella. He'd been gone four years at the fastest-changing time of a boy's life, but I knew him at once. I hurried up the walk to shake his hand, and Arslan followed.

He was taller than Arslan; almost as tall as I. He had grown a soft little fringe of beard, as dark as his hair, and with his big dark eyes and soft mouth he looked like a Persian prince out of the Arabian Nights.

'Hello, Mr Bond.' His handshake was solid. He wore Turkistani fatigues, with a sheath knife at his belt.

'Franklin,' I corrected.

Arslan set down the child, who promptly trotted over to the porch rail and started trying to climb it. With a clatter of heels, the red-scarfed woman flashed up the steps, swooped him up in her arms, and whirled on Arslan. I stood back comfortably against the house wall and watched. Arslan as a family man was a spectacle I'd never thought to see.

Whatever you could say for her temper, there was nothing wrong with her looks. Halfway through her tirade, she jerked off the red scarf, underlining her argument with a long loop of auburn hair. Her crackling eyes were blue, though her skin was the color of buckwheat honey. Arslan stood rocking on his feet, laughing at her. The child struggled down from her arms and went back to his rail-climbing unnoticed. With a final burst, the woman spun away and stalked into the house. Arslan lit a fresh cigarette and turned to Hunt and me. He was obviously charmed with the whole affair.

'I am taking the same room for myself, sir,' he announced. 'And the same room for Hunt. Sanjar and Rusudan will use the southwest room.'

'Nice of you to leave me my bedroom.'

I didn't realize at the moment how nice it was. The southwest room wasn't big to start with, and Arslan's orders crowded into it not only the mother and child, but four of the attendant women. The others – there were three or four more of them – disappeared in the course of the afternoon, touching off a general flutter of protest from the rest and a storm from Rusudan (if she had any more name or title than that, I never heard it). This time Arslan was roused to shout back at her, and she retreated up the stairs, spitting defiance with every step. *Rusudan* – her harsh name matched the metallic timbre of her voice and her harridan temper, but her features were clear and sweet. Arslan stood with hands on hips and grinned after her.

Not one of the women seemed to speak anything that could pass as English, though Rusudan made one or two stabs at it. Luella had her hands full, getting them settled in. I walked out of the confusion early, and into what would be Hunt's room again.

Hunt stood in the middle of the floor, gazing mildly around. 'Welcome home,' I said.

He gave me a sharp look – not sure if that was meant kindly. 'How have things been?'

'Not too good, Hunt, but we're surviving. Your folks are well.'

His mouth quirked with humor. 'Which of us invites the other to sit down?'

'It's your room.'

'It's your house. Let's sit down, shall we?'

We did, he on the bed and I on the one chair. 'Well, there's a lot to fill in,' I said. 'Where have you been, and what's happened?'

He spread his hand, palm down, a foreign kind of gesture. 'Bukhara.' That seemed to be the end of the sentence. He hunched forward confidentially, but he was looking at his hands, not at me. 'I tried to kill him once.' He shot me a glance, smiled faintly, and lowered his eyes again. 'Like old times, isn't it? Except that this time I can say I really tried to do it.' Now he drew the knife from his sheath and laid it across his knees, stroking his fingertips along the steel. It was a very practical-looking blade. 'Not with this one,' he said. 'This one was his own; he gave it to me, afterwards.'

No doubt there was a very interesting story there, as well as a very romantic one, but I didn't want to hear it – not right now. Hunt wasn't talking to me, he was playing a role, and, from the sound of it, one he'd acted out in his head till he knew it by heart. 'What did you see of Turkistan?' I asked him.

He raised his eyes to me. 'The Black Sands are gray. The Red Sands are pink.' He made the motion of a smile.

'Were you disappointed?'

He shrugged, eyes drifting downward again. 'It's a question of viewpoint. You can walk up and down hill all day and think you've gotten somewhere; but if you fly over the same area at ten thousand feet, you see that it's really only—'

'No, I don't!' He looked up, startled. 'If it *is* a question of viewpoint,' I said, 'then you can forget about that "really." I don't think much of the objectivity of anybody who spends his life on the ground, and then the first time he goes up in a plane he hollers, "Oh, that's what the world *really* looks like!" If he'd spent his life in the plane, then the first time he got down on the ground he'd say, "Oh, *this* is how the world *really* is!" That's all hogwash. Reality is whatever you've got to deal with.'

His eyes lightened a moment. Then he closed his hand on the knife hilt and stood up abruptly, sheathing the knife with a practiced motion. 'I ought to warn you. In case you're involved in any plots against Arslan, or happen to get involved, or happen to hear of any, don't tell me. Don't even give me a hint. I'm afraid there's nothing I wouldn't do to protect him.'

'If that were true, Hunt, you wouldn't have warned me.' We smiled at each other cordially, without contact.

'Ah,' he said. 'Do robots have souls? That's the question, isn't it?'

'You're not a robot,' I told him. 'Don't flatter yourself with that idea. You're a human being endowed with free will, and you can't get rid of it.'

'Ah.' He was – what? – eighteen now. '*The mind is its own place, and in itself can make a Heaven of Hell, a Hell of Heaven.*'

'That's not what I mean,' I said. 'I'm talking about responsibility. You're still responsible for your actions. And your decisions.'

He tilted his head in polite incredulity. It was one of Arslan's mannerisms. 'Aren't free will and responsibility distinct?'

'Not to me.'

He shrugged. 'I don't act. I don't decide.'

'You can't help it,' I said. 'You're doing both of them all the time. How do you know? You may have changed the course of history right here and now by warning me not to trust you with any plots. There are things you can't control, sure, outside of you and inside of you; but you decide what to do about those things, and you act on that decision – whether you know it or not.' He was listening closely. Hunt had always been a courteous boy. 'And not many people are decisive and active enough to try sticking a knife into Arslan.'

He couldn't hold back a pleased little private smile at that. 'Think about it, Hunt. And remember I'm always on your side. *Your* side, not Arslan's.' I patted his shoulder once, and I left him.

I wanted information, not bungled assassination attempts. I wanted to know what Arslan had been doing to the world for four years, and what brought him back here now. And what, if anything, *Evergreen* had been.

He had been back three weeks, spending most of his time with Nizam, when the changes started. One morning there was an unobtrusive placard on the notice boards. *Announcement*, it said modestly. *The curfew is abolished, effective immediately. By order of General Arslan.*

There wasn't any rush to take advantage of that order. For one thing, nobody wanted to be the first to test its validity. For another, people were used to the curfew; they stayed in after dark as much from habit now as from necessity. But gradually they began to try it – neighbors visiting in their yards a little later and a little later, people daring to go for the doctor when they got sick, and (because, after all, we were getting squared away for winter, and could make good use of the extra time) farmers and hunters working after dark.

By that time the billet rule was well on the way out. It was never officially suspended, but every week a few more of the billeted soldiers were withdrawn. They went first to the camp. After a few weeks, a company of them marched north out of the district, and later another detachment, a little larger if anything, went south. There was no doubt but that the whole atmosphere of the district was relaxing. Compared to Nizam, Arslan was making himself look pretty good.

At first I hoped we might eat a little better that winter; but Arslan's troops brought no supplies with them. They did bring something that promised to be more useful in the long run – seed corn that Arslan claimed was resistant to the blight. He kept his fleet of trucks and jeeps and armored cars serviced and ready to go, but he didn't use them much. The whole district was geared to horses now. The remaining Turkistanis constituted a cavalry troop, and there was another all-Russian one. Horse-breeding and horse-trading had become important parts of the economy again, and there was constant friction between troops and civilians over horses. The floodlights on the schoolground had been dark for four years, like all the other electric lights outside of Nizam's headquarters. Now Arslan formalized the situation by taking out the floodlights, and installed a windmill to supplement Nizam's oil-burning generators. On the other hand, he imported generous supplies of liquor, coffee, and tobacco for his own use, in fact for the whole household. I didn't mind having the coffee.

Arslan had set up shop in my office at school again, and he worked like any young-middle-aged executive bucking for a heart attack. His home life, to call it that, was something I couldn't fathom. Rusudan's appearance was generally the signal for a fight, which ended inevitably with slamming doors, but I would hear them laughing together in Arslan's room, boisterous and innocent.

He wasn't anything you could call a husband, but he was a real father. He took the child with him almost everywhere, and showed him almost everything. Nobody else was allowed to cross Sanjar in either the smallest or the most vital things; as a matter of fact, we were all under orders to obey (that was the word, *obey*) the child in everything. Naturally I paid no attention to that. Here was a bright, healthy, normal three-year-old boy, and of course he had no more idea of what was good for him than a hound pup. Luella was willing enough to spoil him, because she was starved for children, but she was always grabbing him away from the stove or out of her china cabinet or off the porch railing where he loved to climb; and every time Arslan caught her at it or heard about it, she was in trouble. I had to tell her finally, 'Just look the other way when he gets into something.' Nobody had laid a finger on Luella so far, and I intended to keep it that way.

'I can't look the other way,' she said. 'I don't care *whose* child he is. He's always trying to take the stove lids off.'

'He's got a father and a mother and a cavalry regiment to take care of him. If he wants to crawl in the oven, just hold the door open for him.'

Taking care wasn't exactly it. Rusudan would play with him and fight with him by the hour, acting like a six-year-old herself, but if he needed to be fed or washed or bandaged, she called her women – or Luella. Hunt Morgan led him around by the hand (or rather he led Hunt), took him fishing when summer came, and corrected his budding English. The troops doted on him, and spoiled him every way they could think of.

It was different with Arslan. Sanjar might be climbing all over his father on the couch, getting his muddy little boots into the charts on the coffee table. 'Sit still,' Arslan would say quietly, and the boy would slip to the floor without a murmur and sit there looking up with solemn eyes. And when, being a boy, he forgot again and started climbing onto the table, one sharp word from Arslan would set him back with a very chastened look on his face. He always spoke English to the boy now – at least, whenever I was within earshot – and Sanjar was developing a remarkable vocabulary. Most of it came from listening to Hunt read. Because, after all this time, Hunt was still reading to Arslan. I thought I understood that now. It was Arslan's own continuing education, the liberal arts that the *parvenu* dictator's son had never dreamed of; and now it was to be Sanjar's, too.

It was Arslan, appropriately, who taught him about guns. He showed him why he shouldn't pull a trigger by the simple, messy method of shooting a tame rabbit at close range with his pistol. After that Sanjar treated firearms pretty respectfully.

Still, by and large, Arslan with Sanjar was Arslan at his best. He fairly glowed with pride in all the child's little accomplishments. It was really pretty to see how carefully he pointed things out to the boy. 'Do you see it, Sanjar? Do you hear, Sanjar?' Dozens of times a day he would break off whatever he was doing to show Sanjar something. 'Can you tell what color that bird is, Sanjar? Then go that way – you see? You need the light a little behind you . . . Do you see how the mare turns her ears, Sanjar? She is wondering if we will be her friends . . . Look, Sanjar; these are two different maps of the same place. Do you see, here is an island, and here is the same island on the other.' And the boy knew that nothing pleased his father more than for *him* to notice something and point it out. 'Look, Arslan! Look, Arslan! You see the squirrel?' And Arslan would gravely follow the little waving finger and refuse to see the squirrel till it had been pointed out with bullseye accuracy.

Nobody ever disciplined Sanjar, but he had his hard lessons, and his punishments. The rabbit was only one of them. Arslan's rule against gainsaying the boy meant that he had more than his share of accidents. In fact, it was a wonder he survived the year he lived in my house without serious injury. That spring and summer, especially, it was a quiet day indeed that passed without Sanjar's shrieks of pain or fear, as he learned the hard way that mother sows will bite, that bulls will charge, that flatirons are hot and heavy, and a hundred other uncomfortable facts of life. None of these things disturbed Arslan; his only concern seemed to be that the boy should learn not to cry. 'You sound like a woman,' he would say scornfully. 'You sound like a baby.'

'It hurts me! It hurts me!'

And Arslan, hard-faced, hard-eyed, would shake his head.

'Sanjar, listen; remember. If you are strong enough, and smart enough, and brave enough, nothing will hurt you. Nothing.'

It was this kind of thing that made Luella the most indignant. 'He's ruining that child,' she said to me. 'He's trying to make him into a soldier before he's had time to be a baby.'

And she needed a baby to love. She should have been a grandmother by now.

You couldn't see much of Sanjar – I couldn't, anyway – without feeling a sort of fascination. I'd always hated to see a child completely alone in a world of adults. From what Hunt told me, Sanjar had never had a companion, or a rival, his own age. Naturally all good Kraftsville parents were careful to keep their children away from him. And it didn't seem to occur to Arslan or Rusudan that their child might enjoy (still less need) the company of any little plebeians. But Sanjar would stop whatever he was doing to stare at every bunch of kids who happened along – stare awestruck and intent, his black eyes as full of concentration as his father's and a lot more human.

Aside from acting as Sanjar's tutor and escort, Hunt apparently had nothing to do. He drifted from my house to Nizam's headquarters to school and back again. Information flowed through him like a wide-mesh seine.

'You can't tell me he hasn't run into a lot of active resistance movements, Hunt.' I knew for a fact he'd run into some. Roley Munsey's receiver had picked them up and listened to them die. It was why I knew I'd been right never to let Roley transmit anything.

Hunt's reaction to that kind of statement was likely to be literal: he wouldn't tell me. But a little later on, he would give his own kind of answer. 'It's essentially a judo technique – use your opponent's force and weight against himself. He's a very eclectic wrestler. Have you ever seen him wrestle?'

'No.'

'No, of course.' He mused on his secrets. 'He likes to use his own strength, too. That's like a religion with him. It would be terribly interesting to see Arslan disabled.'

'Terribly.'

'But brute force is only the *ideal*. In practice, he follows the principles of judo. It's not always easy, but it's very economical. He invites the resistance to organize, you see, so he can crush it conveniently. He doesn't object to resistance – only to organization.'

'What do you mean, "invites"?'

'Teases. Baits. It's a kind of sport – resistance-baiting.'

I nodded. 'So that's what he's been doing for four years – that and founding a dynasty.' Thank God, we had had the luck and the discipline to resist *Evergreen*. Still, it didn't necessarily follow that the KCR was undetected. And Hunt wasn't in a position to be trusted very far.

'It's not a dynasty. A dynasty is an organization.'

'I never noticed him objecting to his own organization.'

'His organization is designed to be temporary. He's going to phase it out as fast as possible.'

'I'll believe that when I see it. And I'll still call it a dynasty, Hunt. He's not above setting up a monument to himself.'

'Why should he?' Hunt's eyes went hot. 'Do you think he *wants* to be remembered by posterity? Do you think he'd go down in history as Arslan the Good? Arslan the Well-Beloved? He'd be Red Arslan – Bloody Arslan – Arslan the Terrible.'

'Isn't that the way he likes it?' From the sound of it, Hunt had savored that list of titles before.

He shrugged, mild again. 'Perhaps the question's a little academic.'

What the troop movements added up to was that about half the Russians and a smaller proportion of Turkistanis had been replaced by the new troops Arslan had brought in, which left us, numerically speaking, about where we were before. But in fact, things were a lot different.

It was probably a toss-up which of us was gladder to see Arslan – Nizam or me. I sympathized with Nizam, in a way; my hands had been as tied as his. The only thing that made District 3281 the possible site of an uprising was Arslan's presence in it. If we'd ever tried to fight Nizam, it wouldn't have made one bit of difference whether we failed or succeeded; the whole district could have been crushed from outside, like a flea between Arslan's fingernails. Now we had the heart and brain of the whole juggernaut within our grasp, and we'd had four years to develop our organization.

The problem the KCR had to face now – or I had to face for the KCR – was simple enough, but the answer still wasn't. As long as Plan One was in operation, we couldn't afford to make any mistakes. I knew enough now to be sure Nizam wasn't the only commander who would take it personally if anything happened to Arslan. And the new Turkistani battalion had the unmistakable look of an elite unit – hard and polished and too damned proud of themselves. There was no way the KCR could move, even now, without unleashing more hell than I wanted to be responsible for – no way but one. The only defense Arslan had been able to come up with against the threat of kidnapping was to tell me he wouldn't let me do it. That had been valid enough in the front seat of a Land Rover, with one gun between us, but it didn't apply any longer. Only we had to be very careful.

There was no lack of information and misinformation in the air, and Hunt wasn't the only source of it. Things had solidified under Nizam – petrified into a humdrum daily desperation. Now we were free enough to breathe and think. Things seemed fluid again, and stale old bits of information from the Russian camp suddenly began to branch and bloom.

'Of course he got the Russian government first, Hunt. But what the devil could he threaten them with – or bribe them with, either?'

There was a faint, abstracted frown he used for hypothetical problems. 'If the lever is long enough, it doesn't take much force to move the world.'

'It's got to have been some kind of a trick. They must have thought they were using *him*. But from there on, it's all downhill work. Somebody just picked up the hot-line phone and told Washington they could either fight a nuclear war or turn over the armed forces to Arslan. And all I can say is, everything we ever heard about Washington must have been true, the way they caved in. I suppose it doesn't matter much now whether they were traitors or just chicken. After that, he just started shifting troops around.'

Hunt nodded absently. 'That's approximately right.'

'What do you mean?'

'At least, that's approximately what he told me.'

It was no use getting mad at Hunt. 'Told you how long ago?' I asked him as mildly as I could.

He considered. 'About six years.'

'In other words, right after he got here.' And the whole town – the whole world – dying to know, buzzing with bewilderment and pain, while Hunt Morgan sat mum with his nice-little-boy face of ravished innocence. For six years. 'All right, how did he get the Russians to cooperate?'

'Magic?' he suggested. He met my eyes for a second, and hunched forwards in a movement of contrition. 'He didn't really tell me much,' he said seriously. 'I'm sorry. Would it have helped?'

'I suppose not. Forget it, Hunt.' His shadowy smile flickered, and it annoyed me. He was so damned determined to be an exile, cultivating every little irony like an orchid.

But it was in midsummer that the real revelation came, and everything crystallized into a new solidity. Luella tapped on the bedroom door and peeped in. 'It's Dr Allard,' she said. 'He wants to talk to you.' Her manner added, *privately.*

Jack Allard was already making his ponderous way upstairs, like a tired bear. Luella ushered him in and left us alone. 'What can I do for you, Doctor?' I motioned him to the armchair and turned my desk chair to face him.

He settled himself thoroughly down into the cushions. He didn't look cheerful. 'Torey McArthur and two of his kids are sick.'

'What about it?'

'Well, it looks to me like typhus. Not that we have typhus in Kraft County, but these new troops could have brought it in.' There had been troop movements – little, piddling ones, like fine-tuning adjustments – in and out of the district for the past two months.

'Didn't the McArthurs get their shots?'

'Oh, they got them, all right. Typhus – that's the one thing

Nizam's boys were the keenest about. They let me do the flu and the cholera, but they insisted on giving the typhus inoculations themselves. You know they've been through this district door to door.'

I nodded. 'So what are you saying, Doctor?'

He took out his pipe and looked at it. 'Well, nothing gives one hundred percent immunity. I'm not saying anything.'

'If the vaccine doesn't work, how do we keep it from spreading? Quarantine?'

'Quarantine, sanitation. It's louse-borne, you know. Shouldn't be much of a problem if I can have the authority to stop people from living like pigs.'

'You just take all the measures you need to, Jack, and if anybody objects, send them to me.' I looked at him. 'All right, what else is on your mind?'

'I tried to get some more vaccine or some serum from Nizam's boys, so I could at least revaccinate the rest of the family. Nothing doing. They not only claim they don't have any – they obviously don't give a damn that there's typhus in the district. Which strikes me as odd from the same bunch who were so steamed up a couple of years ago about everybody getting protected against typhus – especially women and children.'

'Jack,' I said, 'tell me one thing. How long since there's been a baby born in the county?'

'That's the right question. It's very close to a year. The last was Pearl Miller's baby girl.' He leaned forward, playing with his pipe. 'Oh, I could tell you some interesting things.'

'Such as that the birth rate started dropping fast about nine months after Arslan first got here?'

'Well, not quite that soon. But you remember how Nizam inoculated about half the population right away and then ran out of vaccine? And didn't get enough to finish the job till last year? Well, I've been going over my records since this McArthur thing turned up, and I can show you that every maternity case I've had in the last three years has been a woman who missed the first round of inoculations.'

I was pacing the floor by this time. *Relax, relax,* my little automatic warning system was telling me stupidly. 'Jack, is that possible? Is there a shot to induce sterility?'

'Well, I'm not the world's leading authority on the subject.' He tried to light his pipe, and failed. 'The Pill's a very temporary thing, of course. There's quite a spectrum of drugs that'll prevent conception in various ways, but the effect is ephemeral, or the dosage required is massive, or the side effects are pretty bad. But a lot of people have been working on it. Somebody was bound to come up with something like that sooner or later. And it looks like it was sooner.'

He sat silent, looking down at his hands and his cold pipe, while I paced down the room, and back, and down and back again. I stopped. 'Anything else, Jack?'

He glanced up and shook his head.

'Okay. Thanks. Be sure you keep me up to date.'

I found Arslan alone in one of Nizam's side offices, drinking coffee and dictating into a machine like any normal businessman. Lieutenant Z had brought me to the door with some trepidation, but I was admitted promptly, and Arslan greeted me with his blandest silence.

'General, are you aware that there's typhus in the district?'

He looked interested. 'Who?'

'Torey McArthur's family. They're poor and they're dirty, but they've had your typhus shots. The whole district's had your typhus shots, General; and now we've got typhus. What we don't have are any babies.' His smooth face didn't change. He only looked at me and waited. 'Is this Plan Two, General?' He began to smile, just a little. 'Was there ever a Plan One?'

He stood up, putting out his cigarette in his cup. 'Plan One was obsolete before it could be applied,' he said easily. The smile broadened all at once. 'Your country, sir, has been one of the easiest to deal with.'

Relax, relax. But I had held the gun on him, and thrown it away for the children's sake. And now the only children would be Arslan's. 'What is it?' I asked him. 'How did you get hold of it?' *How far has it gone?* was what I wanted to know.

'It is a virus.'

'Virus? You mean it's contagious?'

114

'Minimally, if at all. You will understand, sir, that there has been little time for research. But no cases of natural transmission have been observed. It was developed in a Chinese government laboratory.'

'Chinese?'

He nodded. 'Yes, it is true that the Chinese were very loud in praise of fertility. They developed the virus as a weapon, and I have used it as a weapon. The report of the virus came to me in Kraftsville, sir, in the first month of my stay here.'

So the night he had crossed his dirty boots on my bed, the night he had expounded Plan One with such blazing eyes and vibrant conviction, it was already a discarded shell. 'What makes a country easy to deal with, General?'

'Organization and centralization. The more centralized, the simpler to capture. The more organized, the easier to control.'

'So a lot of other places are giving you more trouble.'

He shrugged. He crossed his arms and leaned comfortably against the wall. 'There are problems of logistics and security. Colonel Nizam has been invaluable to me.' He smiled. 'District 3281 is totally sterile, sir. There is no harm in your knowing, now.' He tilted his head with that juvenile cockiness. 'North America is totally sterile.'

'Including your family?' I asked viciously.

The look that came into his face was the look of a snake drawing back upon its coils. 'I have a son, sir,' he said. 'I do not plan to have more; but I reserve the power of choice to myself.'

'And what about your son? How much power of choice are you reserving for him?'

The black eyes stared expressionlessly. 'None.' He straightened up and fished a cigarette out of his pocket. 'No, sir, I have not sterilized my son. If I fail, he will have his choice. But if I succeed, there will be no woman able to bear his children.' He lit his cigarette, and repeated, as if it was a mild joke, 'His children.'

'I imagine one of your logistical problems is just producing enough of your – your – What do you call it?'

'Vaccine,' Arslan said savoringly.

A warm wave of relief went over me. I knew, as surely as if I'd seen the documents in Arslan's own handwriting, that it wasn't only his son he hadn't sterilized. *One entire sex*, he had said that night in my bedroom. Vaccine, yes; he was trying to vaccinate the human female against pregnancy. 'How do you know it's permanent?' I asked him.

'What is knowing, sir? I have never seen an absolute proof of anything, but I have seen conclusive evidences. I conclude that my vaccine is permanent in effect. You, of course, are at liberty to hope otherwise.' And he grinned at me confidentially.

'It's none of your *Evergreens* and Resistances that'll solve the problem,' Jack Allard said to me, later. 'It's medical research, if it's anything.'

'You think so?'

'I'm convinced of it. After all, it's a medical problem. And you know as well as I do that there are physiologists and geneticists and virologists and biochemists and plain old general practitioners all over the civilized world working on a hundred different approaches to it right now. Somebody's bound to find an answer – most likely, several answers.'

'You know the trouble with that, though, don't you, Doctor?'

'Oh, sure. Insufficient time and inadequate communications. Oh, sure.' He sucked his pipe. 'But somebody will find it somewhere, and apply it somewhere, and that's all it takes. The human race has had setbacks before – take the Black Death, there's an example for you. The human race is going to outlive Arslan by at least a few centuries, don't worry. He may even have done us good in the long run.'

Well, that was the faith Jack Allard solved his part of the problem with – and it was about as unrealistic as any I'd ever heard. Conditions all over what had been the civilized world didn't figure to be exactly ideal for scientific research. And if one of those suppositious somebodies did find one of those hypothetical answers, how in God's name could it be put into practice? Logistics was on Arslan's side now. He was over the hump.

Now that I knew about his virus, it was a lot easier to make sense out of his maps and messages. What he had in mind, and in progress, was pacification with a vengeance. He certainly hadn't divided the whole globe into county-sized districts to start with.

Instead, he had sealed off key areas, divided them, and sterilized them. After that, it was a matter of annexing new districts, so that his sterile areas spread like patches of leprosy. The chilling thing was that he had *started* with America, Russia, and Western Europe.

But he was forging a chain that had to reach around the world, and every new link increased the chances of its breaking. How many of his officers would really push Plan Two to the end? How many of his men would go along with it at all if they realized what they were doing? If they could be offered an alternative at the right time, everything might change in a hurry. That was why he feared organization. It would be no civilian resistance that would ever break him; it would have to be an organized movement that could detach whole units of his patchwork horde. No, what we needed now wasn't faith, but works. And that was my business.

10

In spite of everything, Hunt was my best source of information, or anyway my most valuable one – and Arslan himself was a pretty close second. It was worthwhile talking to the Russians, too, and up to a point they were very informative. And not even all of Nizam's talents had kept a few facts from seeping across the border.

Arslan had told a piece of the truth when he called himself the leash that held back his wolves. Only what most of them were probably raring to do was hurry back where they came from. Of course there would be officers with private ambitions, ready to carve out their own little principalities or just to fill their own pockets. That was one danger – bad enough, but not too serious in the long run. The other was the officers who would stay loyal to Arslan. But Arslan's conquest itself was living proof that most armed forces would obey whoever spoke through the chain of command. And, this time, that would be us.

In fact, what we were preparing wasn't exactly a revolt; it was a coup d'état. One thing about Arslan – one thing that would work for us, finally – was that he was a very personal commander. That meant the ones who were loyal would be under our control by the simple law of blackmail, once we had Arslan, and the ones who were merely obedient would go on obeying. Furthermore, we would have the communications to bypass any uncooperative links in the chain.

It meant incidentally that he couldn't keep his hands off the adjacent districts. He was forever dashing across the border in one direction or another to handle some new problem. That was fine with me. It didn't make my work any easier – Nizam was less of a problem when Arslan was in town – but it was a weakness in a man who was trying to run the world, and any weakness in Arslan was something to hang onto.

He had been gone since early morning, presumably into the next district west, the day Rusudan disappeared. About five o'clock that afternoon, she had started out for a stroll with two of her women. It was just turning dusk when they got back. She had sent the women upstairs, walked through the kitchen, picked up an apple, and stepped out the back door, and that was the last anybody had seen of her.

When Arslan came in about an hour later, looking very pleased with himself and yelling for Rusudan, we were just realizing she was gone. The women were in a flutter. Arslan's face hardened; it was against his orders for Rusudan to go anywhere alone. But she had lived in Kraftsville almost a year now, and that particular order had been disobeyed a hundred times. He didn't say much to the two women who had been with her, but whatever he said was effective; their faces were sick with dread as they scampered out the back door and went separate ways into the dark.

After them went the soldiers – half a dozen who had come back with him, and three of his own bodyguard. Hoofs pounded and tires squealed. Arslan himself was across the street to school and back again four times in ten minutes. Obviously he was losing no time in mounting a full-scale search.

'What do you think?' Luella asked me quietly.

'I think you'd better go upstairs.' I wanted her out of Arslan's way. He had driven Hunt upstairs already with one savage gesture. Only little Sanjar stood by gravely, gazing up from the level of his father's knee.

'They'll be wanting their supper,' Luella said.

'Well, let them call for it.'

She put her hand on my arm. 'All right, but you come up with me.'

It must have been about nine o'clock when I heard the front door open after a period of quiet, and came downstairs to see a Turkistani sergeant frozen in a salute that Arslan did not return. The man's face was blank and hard as a glazed brick. Arslan stood in front of the couch, his shoulders a little hunched and his eyes dogged. There was dead silence in the room.

'What is it?' I asked the sergeant. Most of them knew a little English by now.

He dropped his salute, and spoke a few stiff words to Arslan. Arslan gestured silently towards the door, and was through it himself before any of his bodyguard had time to open it for him.

They brought her in within the hour. Sanjar had run downstairs in his pajamas when he heard the jeep, with the women fluttering after him. Arslan in the doorway shouted; one of them scooped up the boy, and they rushed back up the stairs.

His arms were full of her. She looked grotesquely big; she should have been doll-size, she seemed so broken. Clothes and hair, tangled and soiled, stuck out every which way; here a limp arm, there a dangling foot. He laid her on the couch and straightened her.

She was mired with her own blood. Whatever she had been beaten with had smashed full across her bright, queenly face. She was unquestionably dead.

'Vodka,' Arslan said flatly. He backed away from the couch and sank into the armchair. He was staring steadily at Rusudan. The bodyguard flashed into clockwork action. One produced a bottle, another a glass. Arslan took the drink in his left hand and looked at it; and slowly, deliberately, he clenched his hand upon it, till the glass broke with a snap and he crunched the pieces in his tightening fist. Blood spurted, squirting between his fingers. He opened his hand slowly, shedding glass fragments and liquor and blood, and still looking blankly at it.

Two of the guards had sprung forwards, one of them jerking out a handkerchief and the other one grabbing Arslan's forearm, but he shook them off with a wordless grunt, and they backed away. His right hand fastened and tightened on his left wrist, the nails and joints of the fingers standing out pale, and he bowed intently over his locked hands. His blood dribbled slower and slower.

There was a flurry of action at the door. The jeep charged away. Arslan raised his head at last, and his face was absent as a death mask. Now he began to talk, asking questions, giving orders, but his voice was soft and distant, and the eyes in that blank face stayed fixed on Rusudan.

In a few minutes, Dr Allard was escorted in by the jeep driver. He looked perfunctorily at Rusudan, nodded to me, and turned to Arslan. One of the hovering bodyguard pointed unnecessarily to the wounded hand.

'Now, why do a stupid thing like that?'

I stood up quickly; I thought the doctor had really put his foot in it this time. But Arslan only looked at him, a bleak, defensive look I'd never seen. The doctor spread out Arslan's hand on the arm of the chair, getting blood on Luella's doily. 'Sure, broken glass is all right; but it can't compare with tire chains, can it?' He pulled up a chair, settled himself domestically, and went to work. 'Stings, doesn't it?' He was pouring something into the cuts. 'Here, I'll give you a good dose. Now see if you can hold that still while I sew you up.'

The bodyguard crowded close, suspicious and helpless. In a little while the doctor stood up and waved his hand casually towards Rusudan. 'You want me to do an examination on her?'

'No.' Strength and timbre had come back into his voice.

'Okay,' the doctor agreed with a shrug. 'Let me know if you change your mind.'

He sprang up, bumping the doctor backwards. His eyes blazed and his face was flushing. 'Get out! Out!'

Jack Allard wasn't the man to be hurried by a tornado. He closed his bag calmly, nodded to me again, and moseyed out. Arslan had stood silent and vibrating. Now he spun on me. He took a handful of my shirt front, and I was on my feet instantly. I didn't know I could move that fast, but I wasn't going to be jerked up.

His voice was low and staccato. 'Tell me anything that you know about this, tell me anything that can help me. Do not quibble about words now. You understand. Tell me.'

'Nothing,' I said. 'I know nothing about it, thank God, and I don't want to know anything.'

He let go of me slowly. 'If you learn anything, at any time, by any means, you will tell me at once.' Something blazed suddenly in his face. 'If you betray me, sir, you will beg me to let you die,' he cried, and whirled away from me. A moment later he was snapping out orders. One of the soldiers waved me brusquely towards the stairs. The last I saw of Arslan, he was sinking back into the armchair, and he was still talking.

No, I didn't want to know anything about it. That night I lay awake, trying not to think. I couldn't afford it. And lying there with open eyes in the dark, I felt an ugly joy in my soul. If only it had been done outside of Kraft County!

I took a deep breath and willed that joy away. I was ready to stake my life that it hadn't been done by anybody in the KCR. Nobody in my organization would make such an all-out mistake. Not now, above all, when we were so near to starting the upheaval that was to put the world back on its track. Revenge was sweet, sure; there'd be plenty of people who felt the same vicious little joy I did when they got the news, plenty of nice ladies who'd nod their heads and say, 'It served her right.' But Kraftsville had taken on an expert. *If you betray me* . . . It was the first personal threat he'd ever given me, and unfortunately I had no doubt he could make it good.

All through that night they were coming and going. There were hoofbeats – usually one or two horses, sometimes more. A jeep drove up, later another; after a while they left. Rusudan's women had been brought down early, and Hunt shortly after. I had fallen into a sickly doze when I heard a cry from below, and then a whole chorus of shrieks and moaning wails. Luella sat up and clutched at me. 'What is it?'

'Put the pillow over your head.' And pretty soon she did. There was something funny about those shrieks; they didn't have exactly the wholehearted spontaneousness of cries of pain. After a while, they stopped as suddenly as if they'd been cut off by a switch.

I had slept and waked again to hear the first roosters crowing, when Arslan's quick step drummed up the stairs. He paused at our door and said something (the sentry must have been posted there while I was asleep) and went on to his own room. From then on, there was an irregular stream of footsteps up and down. I went to sleep again to that ragged beat.

Luella woke me with breakfast on a tray. 'This is just to get you started,' she said. 'There's plenty more downstairs. I would have let you sleep, but I thought you'd better have something in your stomach.' She was right; I could feel the warning sensations already. 'You'll have to go down for your coffee. I knew if I brought it up you'd drink it the first thing.'

It was already nine o'clock. Arslan was still in his room, where he'd had breakfast. Hunt was locked in. Luella had tried to take him some breakfast, too, but the soldiers wouldn't let her get near the door. She thought Arslan had forgotten about him. The women had fared better. A couple of them had been allowed to bring Sanjar down to eat, and Luella said they'd gone back with enough food for a week. Arslan had come out just long enough to claim Sanjar. The boy had been in his father's room nearly two hours now.

The sentry let me pass with hardly a look. Downstairs the house was deserted. Rusudan was gone. There was a clean afghan on the couch.

My coffee tasted very good, rich and warm and heartening. There was no use fretting over the hours I'd wasted. The thing now was to get out and try to find out. I'd enjoyed the comfort of ignorance as long as I wanted to.

I had more to tell the KCR that morning than they had to tell me. But there were a few items of information. She had been found in the edge of the woods on the old Karcher place, not far from the road. That whole area had been sealed off, and Nizam's men had been in and out all night. Dr Allard's off-the-cuff diagnosis wasn't the only evidence that she'd been beaten with tire chains; a set of them had disappeared yesterday from the camp. Just about anybody could have picked them up. The Russians tended to get sloppy whenever they were allowed to, and the chains had just been piled in a heap of gear outside their fence.

The Turkistanis had been very busy. They were going over the district with a fine-tooth comb, questioning everybody. Whether they'd found the tire chains, or anything else, nobody knew. Nobody was allowed to budge out of his home without special permission – apparently I'd been granted the special permission. Nevertheless, news was getting around. The KCR was functioning, like the lungs of a sleeping man.

The Russians were confined to camp. Maybe they were getting the same comprehensive once-over as the civilians, or maybe

Arslan just wanted them out of the way. If a Russian soldier had done it (and nobody would have had a better chance), we would have to write him off; the Russians were, for the moment, totally out of our hands, and at best they were too numerous and too anonymous. We had to work on the assumption that this murder was a native product.

One thing you could just about bet on: when there was anything really nasty going on, Ollie Schuster was going to be involved in it.

Kraftsville had always had pretty nearly its share of shiftless no-accounts. Ollie had been no good even when he was young, and age had made him meaner without making him any smarter or more industrious. A lot of people, including me, thought he had been mixed up in what we still referred to as Kraftsville's crime wave, a few years before Arslan appeared, when quite a series of local businesses had been hit by vandalism and even arson. He had certainly been arrested, at one time or another, for everything from drunkenness to indecent exposure. He lived now with his widowed niece in one of the shacky little houses on the north edge of town, not far from Torey McArthur, not far from Leland Kitchener.

I visited Jack Allard, and he made a house call to the McArthurs – as a doctor he was able to get the necessary permission – and somehow word seeped across the back yards from there. By midafternoon Susie Mitchell's house had burned to the ground, and Susie, with a wet rag on her forehead, was resting on her neighbor Leland Kitchener's couch, while her Uncle Ollie sat in the kitchen with Leland. It was a pretty drastic method of winning half an hour's direct conversation, but we were pressed for time.

That was Tuesday. After the fire, we sat tight. But Arslan's machine rolled on, through that day, through that night. 'I don't think he's eaten anything since breakfast yesterday,' Luella said to me Wednesday morning. 'And he surely hasn't slept at all.'

'Don't tell me you're worrying about Arslan,' I said.

'Well, I suppose he's human.'

He hadn't left the house. He hadn't spoken to me or to Luella since Monday night. We had never been questioned, and nobody had offered to restrict my movements in any way. In all likelihood, Arslan was eager to have me play detective; I might serve as a telltale to lead them to the quarry, or as a sponge to soak up information and then be squeezed.

But that morning the sentry at the front door sent me back to my room. And when all the breakfasts were over with, Luella was sent up to join me. She came and stood beside me at the window, and together we watched.

The town was filling up, the way it used to do on Saturdays when I was young, when all the farmers would come in for the week's trading and gossip. But today people weren't coming by choice. They were being herded. There was a cordon of soldiers around the schoolground, standing along the far sides of all four streets with their guns at the ready. They made a very deadly-looking cage. And from all four directions people were pouring into that cage.

'We can go out any time now,' Luella said after a little while. 'We're supposed to go over there.'

'Where's Hunt?'

'In his room, I suppose. I don't know, Franklin.'

She sounded very subdued. I asked her if she'd heard anything new downstairs, and she shook her head.

'I just feel like it's the end. What's he going to do now?'

'Let's find out.'

Everybody I talked to had the same story. Arslan's men had routed them out of their houses and fields and ordered them to go to the school. They were coming in waves – the folks from Baptist Creek, the folks from Reeves Mill, the whole town of Carey in a solid line of wagons. It looked like a clean sweep. Even the bed-ridden had been loaded into the wagons, and now they had to be unloaded and carried onto the schoolground. All the horses and wagons had to be hitched along the side streets. It was going to be another hot day; the whole neighborhood was already starting to smell like a barnyard. I wondered if it was physically possible to get the entire population of the district into the two square blocks of the schoolground and the adjacent streets.

The sun was high. The early-comers were getting restless – thirsty and sweaty and wanting to go to the toilet. There was still no word of what was going to happen, except for the rumors that churned the crowd. Maybe Arslan was going to produce the murderers. Maybe we were just going to be exhorted, or more likely threatened. Or maybe he was preparing to do a really thorough job of local extermination.

Lieutenant Z appeared at my shoulder, gently urging Luella and me along onto the east walk. Rusudan's women stood in a dejected knot, with a little space left clear around them, and then a circle of curious and hostile faces. Hunt stood at the edge of the space, not quite a part of the crowd. He looked pale and haggard, but cheerful enough. We nodded to each other.

Then a little procession came down my front walk and speared its way into the crowd. First two soldiers with dogs on leash, then Arslan with Sanjar in his arms, then Nizam, then Arslan's bodyguard. The crowd split frantically, almost silently, to let them through. They reached the east steps, and the men with the dogs cleared them of people in a matter of seconds. Arslan mounted the steps without pausing and turned to face us. A stillness rolled out over the crowd, and we stood waiting. Now the guards were spreading out, pushing people back, clearing an open space in front of the steps. I put an arm around Luella and held my ground in the jostling, so that when the movement stopped we were near the front rank of people. Nizam mounted the steps to stand a little behind his master, and, as he passed, Arslan put Sanjar into his arms.

He looked at us a few moments longer. He lifted his arms a little way and flexed them in a curious gesture and let them fall. His face, from where I stood, looked like a mask of sorrow, drawn and bleak. Then he lifted his head a little, and his voice rang out: 'Ollie Schuster!'

The crowd quivered, as a flash of horrible relief ran through it: *Thank God it's just Ollie.*

'Bill T. Carmichael!' Uncertain eddies of sound and movement were beginning here and there. 'Fred Gonderling!' Beside me Luella gasped. 'Morris Schott!'

That was all. He stood easy and quiet, his arms barely swaying at his sides, and minute by minute his face cleared, as the crowd milled and twisted and muttered, and here and there his men worked their way through it, and at last, across from where Luella and I stood, Ollie Schuster was disgorged into the open space.

Fred Gonderling came forth under his own power and stepped out on the walk, being careful to keep his distance from Ollie. But it took about ten minutes more, and a lot of poking through the crowd with bayonets, before Morris Schott and finally Bill Carmichael were brought out. Fred had tried to say something two or three times, but a gun in front of his face had stopped him.

Now the crowd was quiet again, quieter than ever. People were straining themselves into a desperate silence. In the depth of it, Arslan looked down on the four men and spoke.

'Ollie Schuster and Bill T. Carmichael' – their names sounded quaint and exotic in his foreign mouth – 'you have committed murder.' There were bayonets at their throats before they could begin their protests. 'Fred Gonderling, you have helped these two. Morris Schott, you have known this and tried to hide it.' He looked up, and out over the crowd, and his chest swelled like a singer's, and he cried in a voice that rang with exultation, 'Now I will kill you!' and only then did his eyes come back to the four men.

The guards fell away to the edge of the open space and took their places in what was now a double circle like concentric gears, the outer ring of rifles facing the crowd, the inner the four scared men. Arslan came down the steps with a movement that made my neck prickle and my arm tighten on Luella's shoulders – the hard, flowing motion of a dancer, muscle without bone. The holster on his hip was empty; the sheath knife was gone from his belt.

They backed and bunched before him, and Fred Gonderling was making one more try at formal protest. But before their indecisive movements had brought them into any defensive position, Arslan was already on them. With the unhesitating assurance of a trained herd dog cutting out a sheep, he pulled Ollie Schuster away from the others, a long one-handed yank on Ollie's right arm. The first cry went up from the little arena, a hopeless yelp of pain, or fear, or both; and before it died, Arslan's other hand rose and fell, and again, in two streaking hammer blows to the back of Ollie's head as the first pull jerked him past. He crumpled, half on his slack knees, half dangling by the arm in the iron grip. *He's dead*, I thought. But instantly Arslan ran his free hand into Ollie's left armpit, lifting him bodily, and smashed him sidelong down onto the walk. The noise of it was a solid crunch, mechanical and lifeless as breaking machinery or the chunk of a butcher's cleaver. Luella turned against me.

Arslan spun back to the others, his face drawn taut with a passionate smile. Morris Schott, unexpectedly resolute, dived forward; Arslan met his tackle with a stooping embrace. They skidded and rocked in the dust. Carmichael started forward, hesitated. It was already too late to help Morris. Arslan had flung him loose and was systematically demolishing his head with kicks and stamps. *A very eclectic wrestler*, I remembered Hunt saying.

Strange noises came from the crowd – cries of protest and exhortation and horror and rage that united and emerged as an inarticulate muttering groan. Carmichael and Gonderling had fled to opposite segments of the circle, as if neither one of them had any hope beyond seeing the other killed first. Gonderling was almost directly in front of us. I leaned forward and bellowed at him, 'Stay together, you damned fools! Fight him!'

Fred looked at me with startled eyes. He jerked a glance at Arslan, still occupied with Morris, and took off at a scared run around the circumference of the circle. Pausing in his work, Arslan stood still and watched him. Morris lay twitching; his wrecked head in a puddle of blood. Gonderling and Carmichael braced themselves, shoulder to shoulder. Arslan set one foot deliberately on what had been Morris's face, and swung across him with a vaulting stride.

He walked into them as if he expected no resistance at all. But Carmichael almost managed to sidestep his belly-punch; it took him grazingly under the ribs, and even at that, it staggered him away from Fred. Now they were separated again, but by the same token Arslan had to turn his back on Fred to follow up Carmichael. From our position, I couldn't make out the action exactly. I only saw that Arslan waded into Carmichael with fists and knees, and that Fred Gonderling threw himself wildly onto Arslan's back, flinging his arms around his neck to jerk his head backwards. Arslan hunched under the onslaught, turning spasmodically back towards us. His left hand was knotted under Fred's gripping arms – saving him, maybe, from strangulation or a broken neck, but otherwise useless for the moment. With his other hand he was reaching behind him to get at Fred. Bill Carmichael righted himself and plunged at Arslan's unguarded front. A howl went up from the nearer ranks of the crowd as Carmichael's knee found Arslan's groin. Bull-like, Arslan swung right and left, right and left again, moving forward staggeringly with every swing. Fred – I thought it was Fred – screamed suddenly, and at the same moment Arslan fell forward bulkily, bearing Carmichael down beneath him. For a few seconds the battle heaved on the ground, three men deep; then Arslan was up and out of it, stepping lightly backwards. He stooped and grabbed Fred's ankles, just as Fred was rolling onto his side and pushing himself up. One jerk put him flat on his face again. Arslan backed, dragging him partway across the sidewalk; then, with a lifting twist, he half turned him over, dropped his ankles, and leaped forward onto him. He banged Fred's head on the edge of the walk, and then his hands were on Fred's throat.

The crowd was screaming. It was as if all the feelings of all these past years had found voice at last. But the only words I could make out in the uproar were the ones in my own throat: 'Get up! Get up!' And they were aimed not at Fred Gonderling – no use to yell at him – but at Bill T. Carmichael. He had dragged himself up to hands and knees, or nearly so. Blood dripped from somewhere on his face, but he looked fairly intact. Suddenly the yelling seemed to reach him. He got his feet under him with surprising speed and lunged at Arslan.

Arslan knelt like an incubus on Gonderling's chest, one knee and foot on the ground for stability. Carmichael hit him like a tidal wave hitting Gibraltar. Arslan's head was bowed, his lips drawn back in an animal grin. His hands were rooted in Gonderling's neck. He crouched there immovable, while Carmichael clubbed and tore at his unshielded head with fists, knees, fingers. The crowd throbbed with hope, and in the froth of sound I heard myself howling, 'His eyes! Get his eyes!' The faces of the double ring of soldiers were set grimly; every rifle seemed trained on some appropriate target, one of which was my chest. Nizam on the steps with Sanjar in his arms stood like a statue of poised vengeance. The child stared, motionless. I caught another glimpse of Arslan's face through the welter of blows, and I could have sworn he was laughing.

Then in an instant the battle was reversed once more. Carmichael was down again. It took me a moment to realize Arslan's hands had come up like lightning and yanked him down by an arm and knee. Now he had his own knee in Carmichael's back, one arm binding his arms and chest, the other wrapping his head and dragging it back in a series of brutal jerks. The noise of the crowd swelled painfully, off-key, and died. Arslan clambered upright, shedding Carmichael's body across Gonderling's.

Luella stirred in my arms, and I realized I was gripping her painfully tight. I relaxed my hold. The crowd was still.

Arslan stood breathing in hard gasps, mouth open, arms hanging slack. He said something hoarsely, pointing at the ground. Then he turned toward the steps, and Nizam came quickly down them and put Sanjar into his arms. The boy's little arms went around his neck and held fast. Without another look at the bodies at his feet, he started back the way he had come. This time he went first, and only the men with the dogs followed. The crowd split away from his path as if some electric field had hurled them back. As he walked he swayed, and once I saw him stumble.

Even before he was through the crowd, some of the soldiers had brought out shovels from the school and started to dig. And long after Arslan and his child and his dogs had disappeared into my house, we stood like a herd of cattle in the sun and watched them dig the four neat graves and tumble in the bodies with their feet, and fill the graves again and tramp and stamp them down.

11

He must have slept the rest of the day and through the night. The house was very still, with a closed feeling. All the bedroom doors stayed shut. Next morning I was up early, before Luella. I was just starting downstairs when he came out of his room. 'Good morning, sir,' he said – his commonplace greeting – and went on towards the bathroom. He was still wearing the dirty fatigues in which he'd killed the four men yesterday, very rumpled now. His hair was awry, his face was bruised and his right eye swollen, and the ragged scratches where Bill T.'s fingernails had dug his face were blood-caked and inflamed. But he looked rested.

We were eating breakfast an hour later when he came in, clean, shaved, with Hunt at his heels. Luella jumped up to pour coffee and slice ham and fry eggs, and while Arslan plunged wordlessly into his meal, Hunt opened a book and began to read: 'In regard to tunicated bulbs, those consisting of broadened and fleshy leaf-like coats, as in the onion, no one not absolutely certain of his diagnosis should ever attempt to eat any which lack the familiar odor of onions . . .'

So it was business as usual – but business with a difference. There was a kind of fury in Arslan's actions, in his voice, his laugh, his stride. Every movement he made looked like a blow held back. He'd never wasted time before, but he'd never seemed pressed for it, either; he'd had the leisure to enjoy everything. Now, suddenly, he was in a hurry. Business as usual – but he plunged into that business with a very unusual fervor, burrowing his way into mountains of work that seemed to disintegrate under his attack and leave him unsatisfied, unprotected again. And after dark, pleasure as before; even beginning that first night, with

Rusudan hardly cold in her grave under his window, he dove into the black sea of his old pastimes. He had his two bottles of vodka every night, and every night now he had to have a new girl. He wasn't interested in the esthetic niceties of rape any longer; he took whatever the daily dragnet brought him. One of his lieutenants was in charge of picking up a new girl every day and getting rid of the used one. So day by day I saw a procession of the pretty kids who had been in second and third grades the last year of school, delivered and discarded like daily newspapers. A girl would be picked up sometime during the day, whenever the roving lieutenant spotted a likely prospect, and held at Nizam's till evening. Then the lieutenant would escort her over to Arslan's room, as forcibly as necessary. In the morning he was on duty from five o'clock, ready to whisk her away as soon as Arslan emerged and deposit her where he had found her.

But there were also nights when Arslan turned away from his door and crossed the hall with two quick steps. In the morning, the girl would be turned loose as if she had served her purpose – and, judging from what I heard in town, as often as not she was a little disappointed. Those mornings, Hunt would be a-quiver with the same fury, as if Arslan's pain was contagious. His voice, as he read about Hittite cuneiform or coefficients of expansion, was throbbing and throaty with bitterness. It was the voice I heard one night, through my closed door and his, cry wildly, '—*never* will!' I wondered who it was that never would. *I never will. You never will.* There were other possibilities, but they seemed less likely.

The nights with Hunt came more often, and so did the mixed nights, when Arslan went into his own room after supper and came out of Hunt's room for breakfast. There were days when the circles under Hunt's eyes looked like bruises, and more than once there were real bruises showing on his arms and neck. He had started drinking during the day.

Two days after the killings on the schoolground, Rusudan's women were gone. They loaded their multicolored booty mournfully into a truck and were driven off eastward. The crowded room where they had hovered around little Sanjar was now Sanjar's room exclusively.

He spent a lot of time there, just sitting, tracing rust lines on the windowscreen with his fingers. The bottom had been broken out of the world for him. His mother was underground in the front yard. His nurses were gone. The men he had watched his father slaughter were buried across the street. That father had turned away from him. He was alone, and the world was shifting and violent.

Luella gave him all the time she could, and all the loving he would take. But he never went to her now; she had to go to him. Only when he woke out of his nightmares he called for her, and that was every night for weeks.

He still went to Arslan, but he went cautiously, expecting the worst, and Arslan's reactions were brusque and harsh. They seemed to make their only contacts physically now. Sanjar would worm his way inch by inch into some firm position where he could press against his father, and stay there, silent and watchful, till Arslan's business dislodged him. Arslan hardly seemed to notice him, but again and again his hand would brush swiftly over the boy's hair or close hard for an instant on his shoulder. And maybe a minute later he would stand up, talking to one of his men, shaking off his son like a clod of dirt.

He had tortured nobody, unless it was Rusudan's women – and they hadn't looked any the worse for wear, physically. He had done it by simple, thorough detective work. In about thirty-six hours he and his men had questioned something like three thousand people, and (at least as important and a lot harder) found and compared the relevant answers. The questions had been very standardized and very few: *Where were you between five-thirty and eight? What were you wearing? Whom did you see? What were they wearing?* Meanwhile they had confiscated the shoes and clothes allegedly worn by every able-bodied man in the district that night. It was a massive job, but very effective if you had the manpower to do it fast and thoroughly. One of its virtues was that it touched everybody. It didn't much matter whether Arslan's conclusions were accurate or not, either. Kraft County had been impressed.

It was plausible enough. Everybody knew that Rusudan had talked to Fred Gonderling pretty often, in spite of the fact they didn't speak the same language. And in a way it was easy to imagine what Arslan's mistress could see in Fred Gonderling. He might have seemed, in comparison, downright courtly. Some people thought Fred had masterminded the whole thing. He would have thought he was smart enough to get away clean. Others figured it was Ollie Schuster's idea. Some said it must have happened on the spur of the moment – that Fred didn't have the meanness or the guts to plan such a thing, and Ollie didn't have the brains. Nobody imagined that Carmichael had been more than a willing henchman, and nearly everybody felt that Morris Schott – a respectable man who had never made any kind of trouble in his life – had gotten a very raw deal.

Of course there was plenty of outrage over the killings, but nothing that Arslan couldn't have turned to his own advantage. It had needed something exactly like this, I couldn't help thinking, to make him the veritable king of Kraft County. But he had thrown that possibility away by his behavior since then. He wasn't just asking for trouble; he was building it with his own hands.

But Rusudan's murder had stopped our timetable cold. For the first time in as long as I could remember, I honestly couldn't make up my mind. Maybe this was the perfect time to strike, while Arslan had other things on his mind and the flood-tide of feeling was running against him. But maybe it was the worst possible time, with Nizam's crew wound up to the highest pitch of alertness and suspicion, and all the troops ready for blood – ready, too, I noticed, to stand by and let Arslan risk his own neck against four men.

The whole district was like one raw wound. Not all the shootings of the past six years had had the effect of that one morning's work on the schoolground; and now every family with a teenage girl had a very personal stake in getting rid of Arslan. But by the same token, people had never been so demoralized, so distrustful of each other and so in awe of Arslan. I felt it myself, and cursed myself for it; normally I wouldn't be hesitating like this. What we needed – what we all needed – was something to pull us together. Something simple and immediate, a rallying point, a straight road, a slogan.

Day and night, for the first two weeks, two of Arslan's own bodyguards stood watch at Rusudan's grave, incidentally commanding a good view of the schoolground. Then one day they were gone. The next morning there were flowers on Fred Gonderling and Morris Schott's graves.

Quite a few people found reasons to pass by the school that morning. None of the soldiers paid any attention. It was Arslan himself, on his way across the graves to the school, who nudged the two Mason jars over with his toe, shattered them with his heel, and carefully ground flowers and glass into the bare, packed earth under his boots. I watched from the living-room window, and I felt a beat of hope. We had our slogan!

12

Decorating the graves . . . It was ticklish. The graves were in full view of my house and yard. I let the word get around that the KCR would take care of the decoration, if interested parties would supply the bouquets. That way we could keep it a popular movement without jeopardizing too many people too much. I put Leland Kitchener in charge of collecting the flowers. After a little experimenting, we settled on the three Munsey boys to do the decorating. From the corner of their yard they could see my bedroom window, which made it easy to let them know the best time to move. I would stand at that window for hours sometimes, watching the shrubbery and the shadows and the open places in the moonlight, the wind stirring the close-packed branches of a juniper beside the school steps. It always made me think of muscles moving under an animal's skin.

Every morning the flowers were there. Not in jars any more – there weren't that many jars to spare – but just laid in bunches, big or small, neat or sloppy, beautiful or scraggly. Usually every grave was decorated, and always at least one.

It was a little war that went on in silence. Every morning Arslan walked across the schoolyard, and every morning he paused at the graves and methodically trampled the flowers. He was careful to crush every blossom. After a few weeks the graves were covered with a mulch of broken, withered flowers. I never saw or heard of his exchanging a word with anybody about the decoration – or, for that matter, about anything connected with Rusudan. Sometimes I saw a couple of soldiers nudge each other and nod towards the latest decorations, but that was all. It could be they were under orders to pay no attention to the flowers, or to the thin parade of Kraft County people who passed along the streets by the school every morning. It could be they were under orders not to bother Leland in his rounds or the Munsey brothers on their nightly strolls. Arslan was capable of that.

Day by day the mulch deepened. Marigolds and zinnias gave way to chrysanthemums. The last roses bled under Arslan's heels. Night after night I listened for the shot that would mean the end of the Munseys. Morning after morning the graves were decorated. And every morning Kraftsville was a little stronger.

The first light frost came the first week in October. Then we had a warm spell – Luella always said we had our nicest weather in October – and then it began to get steadily more chilly. We had our hands full, citizens and troops alike, getting in crops and laying in meat for the winter. Along towards the last of the month, we had frost four nights running, hard enough to finish off the tomatoes and all the tender flowers. Sprays of bittersweet started to turn up in the bouquets. A lot of the ladies had been drying cornflowers and everlastings and pampas grass and all the other things Kraftsville ladies did dry. If Arslan was counting on the weather to win his battle for him, he was going to be disappointed.

Sanjar had started to venture out a little more. The horsemen were giving him riding lessons – something Arslan had insisted on doing himself, in the old days. Hunt had taken to horseback, too. On the bad mornings he would wash down his breakfast with a swig of vodka, saddle up the chestnut colt that Arslan had reserved for him, and flash down the road at a frantic gallop. Arslan himself rode everywhere now – rode, to give him his due, as well as he'd ever driven. Once I saw him, cantering past the school, suddenly dig his heels into the horse's sides and circle the long block at full gallop, dragging the horse's head sharp around the corners, and then canter quietly on down Market Street, straight-shouldered and blank-faced.

The flowers were getting to him. For once – maybe – he had started a fight he couldn't win.

He chose the fight. He could have stopped the decorations any time by guarding the graves, if not by more dramatic means. Instead, he chose this long, quiet struggle. He had taken me down the Morrisville road once to show me he could do things for himself. The evidence of something he had done for himself lay under the trampled flowers. Apparently he meant to win this fight the same way, by raw force of his own will and muscle. He was telling us he could trample all the flowers Kraftsville could grow. I thought not.

'You going trick-or-treat, Franklin?' It seemed like nobody's idea; it seemed like everybody's. By the middle of October, enough people had said it to me, with the right kind of grin, to make me decide this was it. Instead of a midsummer D-Day, we were going to have a bang-up Hallowe'en.

Only the older kids remembered going trick-or-treat, but they were all enthusiastic when the KCR spread the word it would be safe to go out again this year. I wanted Arslan and Nizam to be expecting a little innocent activity. Hallowe'en fell on a Sunday, and quite a dispute developed over whether it was right to allow trick-or-treating on the Sabbath. It was the nicest little smoke-screen we could have asked for.

We had set the Saturday night for the Trick; but for insurance we would be ready to go the night before. There would be a few kids out on Friday night – closely followed by nervous parents – and a few more little ones on Saturday afternoon. At sundown the KCR would pass the word at top speed, and an immediate curfew would go into effect. At seven o'clock most of the troops would be eating supper; those on duty would be expecting to see people on the streets; Nizam would be in his lair; Arslan, if he followed his recent pattern, would already be in his room with a girl. At seven o'clock we would hit.

All our hope was to strike fast enough to secure the two necessary prizes: Nizam's headquarters, and Arslan. With Arslan and Nizam neutralized (dead, or preferably alive under lock and key) there would be nobody competent to command the whole body of troops. More important, we would have control of communications in the district, and contact with Arslan's headquarters all over the world. And we would have a little language problem.

We had – maybe – our traitor, if that was the right word, among the Russian officers, ready to declare himself commander of the troops and broadcast our message. But all our contacts had been very circumspect, and I wasn't counting on him too much.

We would tell him what was going on when it was under way. I counted more on Hunt Morgan. Hunt could make himself understood by the Turkistanis, and one way or another – either to save the world or to save Arslan's life – I was sure he would act as interpreter for us.

If we got that far, we were just coming to the hard part. What we were betting was that nobody, not even the Turkistanis, really gave a damn about Arslan's Plans. Either they were serving Arslan personally, or they were serving under duress. In the first case, they'd be our men as long as we held Arslan hostage (and if he had to be killed, they wouldn't have to know it); in the second, we could tell them about Plan Two and offer them the freedom to go home. But we had to face the possibility of hostile units. That meant raising the local population against them, or turning other units against them, or both. Whether Kraftsville turned out to be the Concord of the new American Revolution or just the first skirmish of Armageddon would depend very much on what kind of contact we made with Arslan's armies and with the American people during the first few days.

And if we failed at any point, I would have let loose the hell on earth that I had sold my soul to prevent, seven years ago on the Morrisville road. But it was Arslan who had broken the contract.

Friday night, as it happened, we all ate together. Arslan swung into the house early, shouting for Hunt and his supper. Hunt was in the living room, pouring himself a drink. Luella was just sitting down with me to eat before the rush. She had been deep in making applesauce and apple butter all day. The stove was covered with steaming pots, and the whole house was full of the rich, spicy smell. 'I'm using up the last of the cinnamon,' she said. 'It loses its flavor, anyway; you can't keep it forever.' Supper was about as simple as it could be – baked ham, baked beans, and fresh hot applesauce. 'That's one nice thing about a wood stove,' Luella said; 'if you're cooking anything on top, you might as well put something in the oven, too.' She smiled at me tiredly.

'It's delicious.' I smiled back at her. This was probably the last supper I'd be eating with her here for a while. It might very well be the last of all. And the smell of the apple butter was very good.

But Arslan and Hunt came in, Hunt carrying glass and bottle.

'Coffee,' Arslan ordered. He was on the make tonight; the fury was avid, and everything in sight was fair game. He took Hunt's bottle and poured vodka into his coffee till it brimmed the cup; his teeth showed as he lifted it and drank. 'You are very trusting, sir,' he said to me. His eyes flashed. He dug into the beans with a vengeance.

'That depends on who you ask me to trust.'

'I ask you to trust no one, least of all my soldiers. But you have approved that your people's children should go out alone in the night. Would it not have been wiser to consult with me before you approved this?'

'We'll be watching them.'

He smiled cruelly. 'As you watched, the day I came to Kraftsville?'

I shoved back my plate. 'If anything happens to any of those kids, General, you've got a revolution on your hands.' It was the literal truth. My pistol shot – or any other – would be the signal to start things rolling.

Light leaped in his eyes. He turned his square hands above his plate, half-smiling. 'No, sir,' he said softly. 'But perhaps a revolt. There will be more important revolts.'

I got up. 'You'd better see that they're left alone. Be careful if you don't want to lose me, General.'

He gazed up at me, balancing, daring. 'Do you imagine that this is important to me?'

'If it isn't, you've gone to a lot of trouble for nothing.'

He smiled slowly. 'Ah,' he whispered, and went back to his beans.

Luella bent her head over her plate, but not before I saw her drawn mouth and look of misery. I hadn't eaten very much. I was sorry. Hunt sat stiffly upright, eyes down, swirling the liquor in his glass. Arslan smiled around the table; he was pleased with his work.

It couldn't have been more than twenty minutes before Arslan was at my bedroom door, bottle in hand. He stood eyeing me a moment before he came all the way in, kicking the door shut behind him, and stretched himself on my bed, propped on his left elbow. 'Have you considered the significance of flowers, sir?' he asked softly.

'I've never given it much thought.' Thirty-six hours from now, one of us would be a corpse or a captive. It was easy enough to picture Arslan bound hand and foot, blood and sweat on his face (there'd be no other way), with his black hair lank on his forehead and his black eyes watchful and undefeated; but I couldn't picture him dead, any more than I could myself.

He was a young man – a very young man to have destroyed so much. But his skin was weathered, and his eyes haggard. 'What is a flower in itself, sir? It is an organ of reproduction, and like other organs of reproduction, it gives pleasure. No doubt the pleasure of the bee is greater than the pleasure of the gardener. Pleasure, sir' – his face grew fierce, intent and serious – 'pleasure is the supreme immediate end; but in the economy of the world it is only instrumental. The flower of the pea is as exquisite as the flower of the rose. The scent of the lilac is a tool with which the lilac constructs its seeds.' He looked down into his bottle with an expression of intense wonderment, and slowly, feelingly, drank.

'And yet there are sterile flowers, sir. The flower of the potato, the Japanese cherry blossom; to what end do they bloom? This is the monstrosity that man has bred: the sterile flower. And yet there were already sterile flowers when man ran on his knuckles with the apes. Who bred the wild yam? Who bred the saxifrage?' He glared at me as if he could compel an answer. Then he drank again, and his face smoothed. 'Is this not beautiful, sir?' he asked purringly. 'The flower that gives pleasure fruitlessly? Is it not beautiful that nature is so – unnatural?' He showed his teeth in a slow grimace. 'Why do your people put flowers upon graves, sir? What is the meaning of this custom?'

'I suppose, like most customs, it means about whatever people put into it.'

He hunched his shoulders forward a little, searching my face. 'I tell you a curious thing, sir,' he said confidentially. 'I am in pain. You understand that I am accustomed to facts; facts do not trouble me. But there is a pain that does not cease.' He grinned savagely. 'Ah, this gives you satisfaction, sir. Good. Good.' A hot look glowed in his taut face. He lifted three cigarettes from the pack in his shirt pocket and plugged the mouth of the bottle with them, and in one powerful, deliberate movement he swung his legs down and his arm in a sideward arc. The bottle smashed against the opposite wall, spewing liquor, and he was sitting upright on the edge of the bed. 'Hunt!' he roared.

Vodka dripped down the wall. A piece of flying glass had landed on my knee. I flipped it off with my finger, and it hit his leg and dropped onto his shoe. He picked it up and looked at it searchingly.

Hunt opened the door. 'Bring me another bottle,' Arslan said suavely. Hunt nodded, taking it all in with a little scornful smile, and lifted his hand into sight. It held an unopened bottle of vodka. Arslan's laugh exploded. He dropped the glass fragment onto the bed beside him and accepted the new bottle. 'Shut the door.' He opened the bottle swiftly, took a long swig, and nestled it between his knees. 'Therefore, or in part therefore, I am going.'

Hunt took a step forward from the door. 'Where?'

'To Russia. Probably then to India.'

I didn't care where. 'When?' I asked harshly.

He gave me a smile of luminous sweetness. 'Tonight,' he said. He lifted the bottle by the neck and swung it gently back and forth. 'The main transmitter and receiver have been dismantled. The rest of the communications equipment' – he glanced at his watch – 'has just left headquarters. Sanjar,' he added smoothly, 'is already out of the district.' He set the bottle on the floor and leaned forward confidingly. 'You see, sir, that I wish to save Kraftsville.'

He had spread his hand a little too soon. But I had to be on my feet and out of reach, and I'd better be between Hunt and the door, and my first shot should be by the window, to put the KCR into action.

Hunt brushed past me and confronted Arslan. 'This time are you *asking* me?' he cried huskily.

Arslan's face went cold. 'No. You stay, Hunt.'

Hunt swayed on his feet. 'I'm going with you.' His voice was hard and shrill with desperation. Three strides got me to the window; as I turned I had the gun in my hand.

That instant the world stopped turning for me. The whole room seemed illuminated with a terrific clarity. I felt every muscle in my body. I was contented. There would be no more lying now.

Hunt had turned his desolate face towards me. On the far edge of the bed, Arslan had to look almost over his shoulder. He made no move, but his face was afire with excitement. 'Ah, there it is,' he said quietly.

I turned the gun a little away from them, to fire the signal shot. But as I turned it, the long moment ended, exploded in a splintering burst, and flying specks of my blood and bone sprinkled my face. Flickeringly I saw Arslan fling himself across the bed, rolling over and up onto his feet in front of me, and stoop and rise and dance back. He stood before me with a pistol in each hand.

I knew two things in the smeared dimness that throbbed through the room: *he* had fired the signal shot; and with all the guns on his side, I had nothing more to lose. I plunged towards the door. Keep him cut off from his men till the KCR got here – that was the last-ditch idea that moved my legs.

Hunt met me in a rush, and we grappled together. I heard myself remarking, up in some attic of my brain, *He's stronger than I thought*. Now the shock of the bullet was wearing off, and one wave after another of hot pain washed up my right arm. I threw Hunt down and slammed against the dresser, driving it in front of the door. Through the drumming in my head I heard feet on the stairs. I gave the dresser a last thrust and caught Hunt as he came up again.

He hadn't tried to use his knife – the famous knife that had been Arslan's own. My vision cleared as if a curtain had risen. I hugged him to me with my left arm, catching his right hand between our chests. Arslan's men were at the door.

Hunt had stopped struggling. He stood trying to control his breath. Arslan was standing a little back from the window. He holstered one of the pistols casually and called out something; the sounds at the door stopped.

'You can let me go now,' Hunt said composedly. 'Consider me *hors de combat.*'

I wasn't about to let him go. Other things being equal, Arslan would maybe rather not kill me, but he would almost certainly go at least a little out of his way to keep from killing Hunt. And the only thing Hunt had showed me so far was that neither of us could afford to trust him.

Then the first shots sounded from the schoolground. Arslan

143

smiled at me expectantly. A machinegun answered under the window.

'Sir,' he said, 'I am leaving Kraftsville to you.' He lifted the lamp from the table. The machinegun spoke again. I heard running footsteps outside; the Land Rover started up; something else – one of the trucks – was coming down the street. My whole right arm to the shoulder felt swollen and half-solid, like a balloon full of blood. I was getting dizzy. He shouted one more order, and then he hurled the lamp in a looping overhead pitch that lifted the shadows and shook them over us. He swept the curtain aside, and struck the screen a sidearm blow. Fire swarmed up the cotton spread, from the shattered lamp at the bed's foot. The screen clattered on the porch roof. I let go of Hunt and lunged forward, carrying him along with my rush till he pulled away from me. Arslan was already out of the window.

The fire was to keep us busy, maybe, but neither of us was having any. Hunt dived through the window. How I got through I didn't know.

Arslan was running lightly along the edge of the porch roof, fuzzy in the darkness. At the corner he half turned to us, and his hand came up in a quick gesture of salute or warning. The light of the flames from the bedroom glinted on his face. Hunt had almost reached him when he dropped over the edge. Instantly, it seemed to me, the truck motor roared. There was one more burst of machinegun fire, somebody yelled something, and beyond the roof's edge I saw the truck and the Land Rover scream into Pearl Street, their lights coming on like explosions.

We teetered on the gentle slope of the shingles. I waved my good arm. 'Joel!' I bellowed. 'Pete Larner! All of you get up here! We've got to put out a fire!'

Hunt came back to me with a step, facing me close. He shook with racking laughter. 'That's right, Mr Bond,' he said. 'Your house is burning. You'd better take care of your Goddamn house.'

'A few weeks, a few eons – in other words, presumptively never. *That's* when Arslan will come back.'

That was what Hunt said. He had made his movement of self-preservation very promptly. He had attached himself to me the instant Arslan deserted him, but he had also asserted his independence, or at least his aloofness, by doing it with a very scornful air.

And for half an hour on the porch roof, it was Hunt who had taken care of me. He had caught me when I swayed and eased me down away from the roof's edge. He had held me back when I half sat up and raved at the KCR men to leave me alone and get to work on the fire. He had put the tourniquet on my arm, and he had jumped off the roof and gone for Dr Allard.

Later I found myself lying on a strange bed in a strange room. But it was Arslan's bed, Arslan's room. 'Is it out?' I demanded.

'Yes, yes, it's out,' Luella answered.

'Where's Joel Munsey?'

'He's dead,' Hunt said from somewhere in the shadows.

'He's the only one,' Luella added quickly.

'Then get me Leland Kitchener – or anybody that knows what's going on.'

Hunt put himself forward. 'Okay, I can tell you. The town's all yours. The troops are apparently all in camp – those that are still here. Nobody's fighting anybody. The school is cleaned out. Nizam got his unit out with practically no action. Joel Munsey's dead, Leland Kitchener has a few bullets in him, and you're the rest of the casualty list.' His voice was brassy. 'You had a nice little revolution going, Mr Bond, but it never had a chance to get off the ground. Oh, yes, and your bed's ruined – that's all. But you have a couple of extra rooms now, anyway.'

I looked at my arm lying beside me and was a little surprised to see fingers at the end of the bandages. Luella was holding my left hand. 'I'm sorry I couldn't let you know beforehand,' I told her.

'Thank goodness you didn't.'

'Where's Leland?'

'Downstairs. The doctor's down there with him.'

I took a good breath and started to get up. There were a lot of things to find out.

We couldn't tell how many Russians were still in the camp. The only men we saw were manning the machineguns along the fence. We had no way of attacking that kind of fortress, and I had no intention of trying it. There was no sign of our friendly officer. Either Nizam had got him, or he'd chickened out, or he'd been Arslan's man all along.

Except for the impacted Russians, the district was empty of troops; but, as the KCR soon found out, the border was as solidly guarded as ever, only now it was guarded from the other side. We had gained nothing but the half-mile-wide border strip. It wasn't that our coup had failed; it had just ceased to be applicable.

The bemusing thing was that Arslan had *escaped* from Kraftsville. He had known the plot, or at least known of it. He could hardly have doubted he could smash it. Instead, he had secretly packed up his valuables and fled. He had come into Kraftsville like a young lion, rampant and triumphant, but in the end he had climbed out a window and run down a roof, and his getaway car had been waiting.

There was a weird feeling everywhere, like the shock when an unpleasant noise you've gotten used to suddenly stops. No more soldiers! The Russians stayed inside their fence. On Tuesday Kraftsville boiled over. Boys romped through the school and Nizam's headquarters, breaking windows and tumbling desks down the stairs. By midafternoon an orgy of visiting was in progress. The wagons were coming to town again. Impromptu picnics and covered-dish suppers were being put together. Reunions were being planned. The churches were announcing prayer services. Quite a few people were looking for Arslan's liquor supply, and several of them came to me about it. As far as I was concerned, he'd either used it up or taken it with him – and in case anybody looked through my furnace-room window, I sent Hunt down to cover the cases with some boxes of Luella's fruit jars.

He had left the district to me and the KCR. But it was still a sealed box, with an explosive charge in the middle of it. We might have twenty-four hours of respite or forever; there was no way to know except by living it.

As it turned out, we had five years.

PART 2
HUNT MORGAN

13

I had dreamed, asleep and awake, so many variations of his return. I had even considered the possibility of not recognizing him. And when he came at last, the only shock I felt, standing unnoticed in the twilit doorway, was at seeing a stranger in our living room. Then the question arose in my mind, as it were abstractly, *Is this Arslan? Yes*, I answered, and felt nothing. I saw that he was not a large man – something I had known before, but not realized. His face was plain – a face without attraction or notable characteristic, a face with nothing special in it. Then he turned his head a little, and I thought definitely, *No. Not Arslan.* Not only his anonymous countenance but his whole build seemed different. The Arslan who inhabited my nightmares was a more massive person. Then he spoke to Franklin, and his voice was strange to me, and then, in the same moment, all familiar, and I knew him. And still I felt nothing. Or, rather, I felt an empty excitement, an emotion without content; aroused, but to nothing; awaiting the contact that should fill me with fear or with desire.

He was ugly. He had gotten a little stringy beard like Genghiz Khan, and his right hand and arm were horribly mutilated, transformed into a scar-striped claw.

And then he looked at me.

Ah, that was what I had forgotten – had thought I remembered, remembering only words; when Arslan looked at you, he looked at you altogether, and anyone else's most penetrating stare was a casual glance in comparison. I felt his look go through me like an X-ray (that burned, pierced and burned, sweet as *Liebestod*); and knowing everything he wanted, he smiled at me, his inescapable smile, all joyfulness. 'Hunt,' he said. And he said, 'Sanjar is with the horses. Help him bring in the saddlebags.'

If I could have refused him, he would not have commanded me. I went out in the blue dusk to the shed and found Sanjar watering a gorgeous pair. In the twilight their coats were slatey-black; bays, perhaps. He must be nine now. I would never have recognized him. 'I saw you go by a minute ago,' he said. 'We got some things for you in the bags.' He looked very tired, but he grinned merrily at me. He was a beautiful boy; and, seeing that, I saw how like Arslan he was; and Arslan was beautiful to me again. 'Don't you have any horses?' he asked.

'Not this year.'

He frowned with quick concern and gestured around the shed. 'Did they die?' I noticed that he had served the horses from our chickens' supply of oats. Not, however, prodigally.

'Don't worry,' I said. 'Nothing contagious.' And he smiled again, a very winning, open smile. He stood hardly higher than my waist. 'How was he wounded?' I asked. Soon I must say *Arslan* aloud again; but not yet.

'Phosphorus,' he answered cheerily. 'North of Athens. That was the only real fighting we got, that and in Canada. We got these' – he patted a sleek flank – 'from Nizam in Ontario. Your corn looks good. When are you going to harvest?'

'About two weeks.' I wondered if he talked so easily to every-one, or if he thought of me as an old friend.

'They're tired,' he said fondly. He was so tired himself that when he picked up a pair of saddlebags his arms trembled. 'We rode from Marshalltown since daylight. We left the regiment at Colton.' I picked up the other pair of saddlebags. 'Look.' He steadied his against the doorframe and flipped one open. 'We're going to learn Spanish.' He pulled out two small books and handed them over to me. They were beautiful – leather-bound, printed in Madrid; one volume of Lope de Vega, and one of Garcia Lorca. I had to smile. Yes, he was real; he was altogether Arslan, unqualified and undeniable.

A little girl lay curled asleep in the corner of the couch. Arslan opened the saddlebags beside her, displaying his largesse trium-phantly. 'Salt; the baggage train will bring more. Seeds: tea, barley, opium poppy, rice. Vodka: two liters only. Needles. Cloves. Whetstones. Penicillin. And this for you, Hunt.' It was a packet of notebook paper. 'Novocaine. Solder.' The salt aside, they were all luxuries, the most useful and satisfying luxuries, the very things whose lack we had cursed a thousand times.

He laid his left hand on Sanjar's shoulder. 'Now sleep,' he said.

Sanjar stood up, with that clear smile, and all the rest of him hazy with weariness. 'Upstairs?' The true crown prince.

Arslan nodded. 'The old place. Do you remember?'

'I remember.' They grinned together, a contact very beautiful.

Franklin rose, grim and displeased, to lead the way upstairs. It was an act of – what? compassion? conspicuous gallantry? – that he did not detail me for the job of chambermaid. And I was alone with Arslan and the sleeping girl.

'Come here,' he said, and I came. I was afraid that he would touch me first with his ruined right hand; and, seeing my dread, that was what he did. But after all, it was a hand that could be lived with. The last two fingers were gone, and the next stiffly hooked, but it was still Arslan's hand. He curled it around my bare forearm, and looked at me. When I began to tremble, he smiled and let me go.

I went back to my chair. He flipped one of the little books at me, and I caught it, and he was pleased. Yes, oh yes, now I remembered; it was exactly for this that I had loved and hated Arslan, those eons ago – that everything pleased him, like a child, or like a child intensified and exaggerated. 'Read to me,' he said.

'I can't read Spanish.' The first words I had spoken to him in five years.

This time he laughed aloud in his pleasure. 'Hunt,' he said. And he rocked forward a little, laughing at me. 'Read,' he said.

It was the Lorca. There was a little introduction, and I began with that. Of course I knew no more about Spanish than how to say *mañana*. But to be made ludicrous by Arslan was an old, accustomed thing; and, after all, I had undertaken to teach myself Latin once, and Turkmen, without total failure. So I read, as intelligently as I could, and he listened, serious and intent as ever he had listened to Mommsen, or Milton, or Samuel Eliot Morrison. Franklin was back before I had finished. He stood almost between us, looking first at me, then at Arslan, with impersonal, expressionless interest – the principal's look, only a trifle pallid now in the comparative presence of Arslan. And having weighed and measured me to the pound and foot, Arslan to the milligram and millimeter, he nodded with judicious frown and asked brusquely, 'Will you have a glass of beer?' And Arslan – soberly, soberly – with glowing eyes and lifted brows, replied, 'This will please me very much, sir.' A decision of state.

Did Arslan ever offer toasts? None that my broken memory showed, yet now he lifted his mug smilingly toward Franklin. 'To you, sir.' A singular *you*.

'We have our little brewery in the basement,' Franklin said explanatorily.

'Is this a change of principles, sir, or only of practice?'

'Only of practice. We've always said a little moderate drinking was all right in Biblical times, because of the different conditions. I figure conditions have changed back again.'

Arslan chuckled. 'Thus you permit yourself to drink – good. But to drink with me?'

'I'm not going to fight you, General, unless I have to.'

'Ah. And you command here?'

'I'm Mayor of Kraftsville and Supervisor of Kraft County.'

'And no doubt relatively better armed than when we parted. Why not arrest me now, sir?'

'It's a possibility.'

'Then I must discourage you. Earlier, my death would have had significant consequences for the world. This is no longer true.'

'Why not?'

'Because I have succeeded.'

Now break, break, break, on thy cold grey stones, O sea. Franklin sat still, large, and ominous. Arslan had spoken. *I have succeeded.* The universe adjusted itself.

'I didn't know we were talking about your death,' Franklin said. The granite cliff hadn't flinched.

'You don't kill prisoners yet?' He smiled the old sweet smile. 'If you try to manipulate my troops by using me as a hostage, you may have some temporary success. But of course I have left orders to cover this possibility. Does the prospect satisfy you, sir? Have you anything to gain now that is worth the risk of – of what, I do not tell you?' He studied Franklin eagerly, humor bubbling in his look. 'But you will do as you wish, sir. Now it is immaterial what you do, or I, or any man.'

'Not to me. Not to Kraftsville.'

He shrugged and drank. 'No. Doubtless no. But it is immaterial to the world. You can play out your games as you like, now. The course of the world is fixed. You have no power to destroy it.'

Franklin considered him drily. 'It's not immaterial to you either, General. You told me once that at the end you had to fight. I imagine that still goes.'

Arslan smiled appreciation. 'Abstractly it is immaterial to me. Practically, no.' He looked whimsically into his drink. I knew the look; the pleasure that stirred him now was almost too much to contain. 'I, too, play my games. And at the end, yes, I fight. Therefore consider carefully, sir. As for Sanjar' – his look tilted ceilingward; he shone with pride – 'Sanjar is my aide-de-camp and my bodyguard. Do not expect to manipulate me through Sanjar.' He drank deep. 'I've had beer much worse than this, sir.'

'Hunt's the brewmaster.'

I braced myself for Arslan's look. But his eyes only flicked me weightlessly. 'So you still have a food surplus.'

'We don't *still* have one, we have one again. This has been the first good crop year since you left.'

'An omen?' He drained his mug, and I rose to pour him more before he could demand it.

'How long are you here for?' The principal's voice, definitely a tone sterner than the supervisor's.

'Don't worry, sir. I am not taking Kraftsville from you. I am on my way to South America.'

'What are you up to there?'

'It is a tour of inspection.' He looked up into my face as I filled his mug. I kept my eyes fixed on the gushing beer. It was warm beer from the kitchen. There was a keg cooling in the wellhouse, but that was outside the sound of his voice. 'Nizam has given me a very favorable report of you, sir.'

'Nizam? Don't tell me he's been skulking around in the bushes somewhere!'

'Rest assured that he has kept several eyes on you. Now, sir; what is the condition of the camp?'

'Annihilated,' Franklin intoned with relish. 'After the Russians pulled out, people had a field day out there. Everything's been burned or smashed or hauled off. Didn't Nizam tell you that?'

Arslan only grinned. I put down the pitcher carefully and looked at him with fresh consideration. That he had appeared thus, unheralded and frivolously unprotected (*And, save his good broadsword, he weapons had none. He rode all unarmed and he rode all alone*) did not in itself surprise me; he had his games to play. But why should he ask about the camp unless he intended a second occupation? And something in me surrendered, resolved into peaceful tears that did not rise or fall, and I abandoned myself hopelessly to hope.

The child stirred, kittenlike, on the couch beside him, and in a fond, absent gesture he ran his maimed right hand along her leg. Till now I had not thought of her, except to note her presence. But I found, with distant amusement, that I had assumed what now his casually obscene caress confirmed. I observed her: my rival, my replacement. Her features were hidden in the snuggling crook of a thin arm and a tumble of hair; but that hair was alienly black as Arslan's own, and her skin a color not made by sun. Where had he found her? India, perhaps, or North Africa.

'Unnecessary, sir.' (I had not heard, with any part of my brain that counted, what they had just been saying. Adult talk. For the past five years I had functioned as a real person in a real world; it had only required Arslan's entrance to reduce me again to the irrelevance, to the freedom, of a spectator, of a child.) 'Leila sleeps with me.'

'Not tonight,' Franklin stated definitively. 'When you've got an army to back you up you can turn my house into a pigsty. We've seen that. But not tonight.'

Arslan ran his good hand under the sleeping child's back and scooped her upright. She swayed like a heavy vine, her head tilting and swinging, flutters of darkness showing where her eyes fought to cope with the light. He looked, incredulous but tolerant, from her to Franklin. 'As you like, sir. But you should consider two points. One, I desire only sleep tonight. Two, Leila is a professional, indeed an expert.'

'And three,' Franklin said equably, 'tomorrow you'll have your army to back you up again. But tonight she sleeps on the couch.'

14

The third night, in the early quiet after the lights were out, while the nervous house settled its boards uneasily, Leila came to my bed. She turned back the quilt and began to slide in beside me. 'No,' I said positively. In the dimness her smoky small face showed the pale light of a smile. 'Arslan,' she explained.

I turned my face away into the pillow, disabled with regret, finding it pitiful that he had sent this child to me. In his mind, would an obligation be discharged – or at least deferred? Did he recognize obligation? He was Arslan. He might have chosen to punish me for my presumption, to punish me with the smallness of her cool narrow arms; I should not have dreamed of obligation. 'Arslan?' I said, talking into the pillow.

She came sometimes early in the night, sometimes when I slept, sometimes in the dawn. She came always silent as a dream, appropriately fairylike in her smallness, miraculous in her power. The laying on of hands. And I understood, and I was reconciled, and the bitter buds of pity and regret opened peonylike into gratitude and joy. It was a gift – a gift that Arslan had put into her hands to give to me. It was exquisite, it was glad; and I wept, and I laughed, and her delicious small body and her lithe wise fingers lit multicolored joys through all my nerves. And 'Arslan,' I sang silently into her hair, 'Arslan, Arslan,' against her smooth brown body. This came, too, this unexpected universe, under the heading of the small word *sex*. This was pleasure, a thing I had never known, a thing pole-distant from the black urgencies that Arslan knew how to rouse, the blinding explosions that resolved them in wreck.

He had no business of state in Kraftsville now. He had come to give me this, and to tell Franklin a lie. *I have succeeded.* But when the dust-colored regiment had settled in the ruined camp, and the bodyguard of hawk-eyed Turkmens hovered devoutly in the house, he announced, 'The last pockets of fertility are in South America.'

'In other words, you lied to me.'

'A simple deterrent, sir. I was relatively unarmed, and I wished to avoid unprofitable complications.' Franklin, too, no doubt, wished to avoid complications. Arslan had eaten reclined on the couch – his old place, his old style – served by his bodyguard, attended by Leila, while blithe Sanjar dined with us in the kitchen, bubbling questions and information. Now Sanjar had taken Leila to show her the camp, and I had brought in the cold keg. I looked into my mug and considered beer. I was very grateful for beer. How much ease there was in it, and after all, how much strength. There were still pockets of fertility. Arslan was a pocket of fertility.

'Is South America giving you trouble, General?'

'Yes, sir. It is the jungles – the *extent* of the jungles. The more accessible areas present no worse problems than other continents.' He dipped more beer from the open keg. He was affable, conversational, informative. 'I have dealt with jungles elsewhere, of course. But the methods that worked in Burma and the Congo are not working well in Brazil. And not to work well is not to work at all. Ah, you look hopeful, sir. But it is very probable that I shall succeed. The areas are large, but they are isolated. It may be necessary to use more severe methods.' He broke off, looking at Franklin's face, and in a swelling rush of exuberance he flung out his arms, half rising, and burst into a chortle of merriment. 'Do you remember, sir, the night I left Kraftsville?'

I laughed. He flashed his look of all-knowing glee upon me, a moment's mutual touch that left me motionless. Franklin leaned back in his chair, his face dark. And Arslan cried (turning upon himself that eager vivisectionist interest which was like mockery), 'I have lost my pain.' He subsided smiling into the cushions. 'Somewhere between Athens and Stalingrad.'

'That'll be fine news for Morris Schott's widow.'

Arslan watched from the bastion of his amusement. 'You no longer put flowers on the graves.'

'Only on Decoration Day.' Franklin stretched his legs pontifically in front of him. 'That's our custom, General. We decorate all the graves then.'

'And Rusudan's?' Arslan asked softly. 'And your wife's?'

Franklin's voice, when he answered, was heavy. 'My wife's, yes. Rusudan hasn't had any mourners around here lately.'

The eyes hooded, but the telltale dimples of the invisible smile remained. It was touching – or horrible, or ridiculous – that Arslan should have dimples. They were unobtrusive, they were faint, they were perhaps deniable; but I saw them. 'How did your wife die?'

'Are you asking for information, or just for entertainment?'

'For information, sir.'

'All right, then, General, I'll tell you. She died for lack of some of those drugs you once assured me would be manufactured locally. She died of pneumonia. A simple dose of penicillin would have saved her.' (Although he had talked bitterly enough of ready-made excuses for doctors' mistakes.) And he added, a gratuitous bonus of non-entertaining information, 'It'll be two years this November.'

Arslan lifted his drink with a motion like a shrug. 'But you have managed well.'

'That's right,' Franklin said savagely. 'Considering the circumstances. Now *I'd* like some information. What was your idea leaving the Russians here as long as you did and then pulling them out the way you did?'

'The way I did? Why do you ask this, sir?'

'I mean secretly. I think I can understand why *you* sneaked out with your headquarters, and I think I can appreciate it. But why bother to leave the Russians here all winter, with nothing to do but watch the border and fraternize with us natives? And then why go to all the trouble of sneaking them out by night?'

Arslan gave him a meditative half-smile. Just beneath my diaphragm I felt the interesting beginnings of fear. Nizam's reports had not satisfied him; I was doomed to describe to him personally those months of fruitless intrigue. 'They were needed elsewhere. They had fraternized too much. Also, sir, it is my habit to move without advance notice. Every habit involves a weakness; what is predictable is exposed to attack. But by its nature, a habit of unpredictability is less dangerous than most.'

'And then it turns out not to make two cents' worth of difference whether the border's sealed or not. We get goods and we get news from pretty far up the Mississippi and the Ohio, too, General, but I don't see where we're any better off than before the Russians left.' Or, in short, Plan One was a posthumous success. He leaned back in his chair and fixed Arslan with a monitory stare. 'We could live with the Russians. They earned their keep.'

It had always been entertaining to observe their conversations: Franklin truculent and unbending, unabashedly asking his impertinent questions; Arslan with his accidental air of courtesy and his deliberate candor, forever expatiating his profoundest secrets as if there were nothing outrageous in the counseling of conqueror with conquered. It was like old times – the bitter truce, the threadbare couch, the presence (quiet, full of signification and portent) of the soldiers. Like old times, except that we all drank together, though independently; except that I was almost a quarter-century old; except that there were thread-like lines of gray in Arslan's coarse hair, and webs of lines about his eyes, and the straggle of beard, and the white freckles on his right cheek where phosphorus had splattered; except that Franklin Bond was Mayor of Kraftsville and Supervisor of Kraft County.

15

Now what had been our real life was suspended. Arslan was here; we existed in relation to Arslan. Franklin and I passed in our orbits, speaking like hostelers, all discussions adjourned, all quarrels in abeyance. Kraftsville receded, a cycloramic setting for Arslan's movements. The little war that had so occupied me for seven seasons lost all personal interest. Kraftsville would kill no more of my horses; I rode Arslan's horses again.

Yet, expectably, chance set me alone with Franklin after a late supper, Sanjar and Leila abed, Arslan and his bodyguard on some midnight errand, and nothing petty to talk about. 'He's changed,' Franklin said.

Not even to my physical sight, since that first night of his return. Arslan's mouth and Arslan's eyes were unscarred and unaged. But there was a difference around him. 'He's over the hump,' I said.

'That may be partly it.' He snorted thoughtfully. 'It's all over but the dirty work.' Franklin L. Bond, ever fair. But his convictions were otherwise. 'And of course,' he added, 'he was very young then.'

Very young? I closed my eyes against it. Very young, when he crushed me beneath him on the green couch in the school gymnasium, and I heard him laugh in my ear, and smelled the ugly smell of him, and blazed and all but burst and splintered with hate? No, Arslan had never been very young. But I, I had been very young.

I was so young, indeed, that a little after, when I began to pull together my lacerated soul, I thought, *So that's how it's done*; and only later I learned, with surprise, that that was not necessarily how it was done at all among genteel modern homosexuals. But Arslan was not a genteel modern homosexual. He was outlandish, archaic, indifferently male.

That was the easy time. I lived quietly in hell, and things were done to me. But already within a few weeks something was required – my single, ludicrous, several-times-daily act: to catch the book that sprang from the flashing bow of his arm. Reading was not an action. It was rest, it was restoration – sore labor's bath, balm of hurt minds, the compensation that was granted for my laborious sleep. Night after night I climbed the same desperate mountains, thorny crags that crumbled and stabbed, staggering, crawling, naked and hideously torn. I woke disordered, with jerking nerves and quivering heart, to traverse the equally unsure footing of reality. I was learning his looks, his movements, as a downed flyer on a raft might urgently learn the looks and movements of the cryptic sea. There were the keen smiles, joyous when I had shown pain against my fruitlessly stoic will, eager when he was about to inflict it. (Later he was to tell Franklin Bond very soberly that he had never been cruel, that the pain he gave was incidental, a waste product of the process that gave him his victory or his pleasure. But if he abstained from the crasser crudities of sadism, it was because I suffered enough in the course of simple violent perversion. A by-product, perhaps, but never waste.) There was the concentrated look with which he turned to a map or a soldier or a thought, releasing me for some moments or hours; the swinging, dancing stride that meant he would tease me a little before he laid me; the deliberate, gentle motion with which he reached for my shoulder when his desire was serious. Among them all, the one that lightened my heart like a fair breeze, a shower of pure rain – the whiplash flick of his forearm that sent a book spinning toward my hands.

I considered, with serious and equal care, the cultural requirements of tomatoes, the stagnation of seventeenth-century Russia, the artillery of hell. My soul was restored. I mounted up with wings as of, say, a pigeon. But soon, risking glances from under the flimsy protection of my eyelids, I learned that there was something I could do. I had the power to produce, by my own action, an actual result in Arslan; the reading pleased him. And, by a retroactive causality, reading became act.

So it was with a kind of triumph that I would see his taut face lighten, his deep eyes grow live with intent concern. I, I had done this. It was insignificant that his concern was for the battle of Poitiers or of Jericho, the poisonous principles of the Umbelliferae, black little Pip a-bob in the white-toothed sea; it was my act, my voice, my reading that had roused the concern. I could do something. I could do something to Arslan.

In early summer he began to take me hunting. The first time, it was to the abandoned woods just east of town. The old Karcher place. The name of it came to me as a recollection of another era. Childhood revisited. We walked into the woods – Arslan and I, and his bodyguard fanning out behind us. Arslan himself put the rifle into my uncomprehending hands, that almost let it fall before they grasped it. 'Do not shoot me, Hunt.' It was not a joke, but a command. Lightning-struck, I took it. Such an invitation smashed down walls on every side. Wild light and stormy winds poured upon me. We went into the woods.

It came to me slowly, as I stalked beside him, that I would not be permitted to shoot him. There would be half a dozen bullets in me before I could pull the trigger. Arslan watched me with interest. He was considering the way I held the gun and my face, gauging how much I wanted to kill him, calculating the probability of my trying to do it. The soldiers were to keep me harmless while he made his observations.

And presently he was so well satisfied that he sent them away.

I did not shoot that day – not at Arslan, not at the game we started. There were no closed seasons for him, no licenses or limits. His smooth face shining with a happy lust, he took squirrels, rabbits, doves, a bemused daylight possum, two brown thrashers, a curving mink – filling his bag and loading me with the excess, cursing sweetly in Turkmen when he missed a shot. But he missed few. (Once, later, Mr Bond asked him why he never used a shotgun, even for birds, and he laughed: 'Sir, if I could, I would carry the bullet in my hand.') He was a good marksman – of course, of course; but through that summer and fall I watched his marksmanship improve.

Sometimes he brought one or two of the hunting dogs, but evidently more for their education than for his pleasure, and I understood that he preferred not to share his attention between the dogs and me.

It was not the first day, it was a near one, when the first question was thrust to me, and necessarily I had no answer. We were alone in Karcher's woods (after the first hunt we were always alone, though two of his bodyguard waited, bored and smoking, in the jeep), and we were looking for deer. We made no kill that day; but in the dew and innocence of sunrise, on the heartbreaking plush of moss below the oaks and in the shelving shales and sandstones of the creekbanks, we tracked the spoor of a harem of whitetails. And while the dew exhaled and the gold sun undid the pink and grayness, and the mosquitoes gave way to gnats, and the birds bustled from matins into business, we tracked them slowly yet.

Arslan a little ahead and left of me went with grave eager eyes and ready gun. Suddenly he paused and touched my arm, a touch to stop and still me. I turned to him; and he gave me a gentle, smiling look, a look of such intimacy that my heart and my whole being turned and stirred, and I understood at last and saw as beautiful that verse in the Song of Solomon whose meaning had been cramped into the vulgar dialect of my childhood. It was a look of shared secrets, a look that drew me toward him more powerfully than ever his savage embrace had repulsed. I felt that he was offering me something dear to him – he who gave nothing, to whom nothing was dear. Then he turned his eyes, showing me which way to look, the motionless gesture of a soldier, of a hunter. And I looked, motionless too, looked into the dense, always quivering congeries of leaves, heard the sizzling hum and rustle of young summer, saw the oak branch that swept downward on our left, the tangled arches of bayberries, the scraggy cedar seedlings like discarded Christmas trees, the limp, blistered, delicately apple-colored leaflets of poison ivy. His fingers still lay upon my sleeve, without warmth, almost without pressure. I looked at him again, and now he was waiting for my response, for the look that would tell him I had understood, had received and accepted his treasure. And I was molten with longing to accept; but I had not received.

I was thirteen. All else ignored – as you might ignore the earth beneath your feet – he stood beside me a man, a grown man and a soldier, offering me with that smiling look a comradeship to dazzle any boy.

And seeing that I had not seen, he smiled a new smile, kindly withdrawing the offer; kindly, but so certainly that I caught my breath and leaned, stumbling at the verge of speech. But I had nothing to say to him.

That was one day. And that night he had a girl – I forget which girl. But there were other days. And I began to learn that the eddying stream of time brings round and round again not the same opportunity, but, over and over, opportunities for the same answer – like a thousand billion waves, each new, each different, each formed by its own causes, and yet all recognizably one.

There was always death, sometimes sickening, sometimes so neat and sweet that he gathered the body in his hands like a sleeping pet, running his fingers caressingly through the fur of coon or cottontail, squirrel or possum. I had hunted before, though never much – with my grandfather, with my country cousins. I had shot rabbits myself, and doves, and missed squirrels. I had fished every summer since I could remember, and gigged frogs since I was old enough to stay up after dark. And I had been soft-hearted and a little squeamish by the savage standards of boyhood – but not really squeamish, not really soft-hearted. Now everything was different. Now every pain I witnessed, I felt; and with every dying I cringed nearer to my death. As the hook went through the minnow's back, I felt the rending stab in my own. Before the threshing of the wordless deer, my own limbs ached with thwarted jerks, and the red heat of the bullet lay burning within my chest. It was a curious malady, which I tried to conceal; and though he knew that these things bothered me, I thought – it pleased me to think – that he never knew exactly how.

There was death in his hands, the gentle hands with which he hurt me, and death in the still eyes that watched the deer. But there was another death that filled the summer air, that made each breath an exercise in tension. At first I wondered what he found in the hunting that made it worth the risk, or if (he was a man, a soldier, a general, he knew so much more than I) there was really no risk worth considering. Then I saw the electric pleasure that kindled in him with his first shot, saw how he stalked more cautiously after each kill than before it, and I understood that the joy of the hunt was precisely in the risk. These woods, which had been tame as gardens to me all my life, were suddenly perilous as jungles. He was alone, except for me; armed, yes, but un-protected, vulnerable in the green mazes of the unconquerable woods; and with every shot advertising himself to all the vengeful-ness of the countryside.

So he moved, tense with his mortal pleasure, hunting, hunted, between two levels of death; William Rufus in the Saxon forest. And after the shot that brought our first deer staggering down upon its neck, he reached across the gun and laid his stilling fingers again on my arm. And I, hunched with the crushing pain in my neck and shoulders, turned to look at him, and found again the offer in his eyes. 'Look,' he whispered.

What was it I was to see? Was there some animal crouched among the leaves? Some spoor I should have noticed? I shook my head at last – explicit answer to the explicitness of his word. So, at least, the time might come when we could talk.

There were other days. There were other moments. But it was not in the woods, it was in my bed, alone, in the room that had been Mr Bond's son's, holding in my hands the soft pelt of a rabbit, that I understood.

When I was a child, we had had a sort of formal garden behind the house, and I had always rather liked it – liked it, in fact, a great deal more than I had ever admitted. It was exactly the formality of it that I liked; and the flaw, the secret reason for the real contempt for which I feigned other reasons, was that it failed in its formality – it was incomplete, inconsistent, too small or too open. But in midsummer and in fall, coming into it from the south side, I had momentarily loved it. It was calm. Calm. Beautiful in its calmness. The healing, smooth, content, contained, closed endlessness of the circle. And with the downy softness of the fur against my face, I knew, and quivered with hopeless regret for my dullness, that it was this he had offered me – the very calm of the circle.

Too late. Too late. The waves had ceased to flow. I sat up in the empty bed, clenched all over like a fist. *Our strange and self abuse is the initiate fear that wants hard use. We are yet but young in deed.* And I, indeed young, abused, initiate, got up and pounded on my door, pounded and did not answer the sentry's objection, pounded until my fists felt numbed and pulpy and Arslan's own hands turned the key in the lock and pushed me back. Afterwards we would talk.

16

It wasn't to understand Turkistani that I began to study it, but to understand Arslan. In time I would grow fond of that hot, smooth tongue, and proficient enough to silence his gossiping officers with my presence. But their cabals bored me. It was more interesting, and more significant, that what was officially called Turkistani was in fact Uzbek; that Arslan spoke by preference the Turkmen of his hand-picked bodyguard, and spoke it like a common soldier; that it was Colonel Nizam who spoke the elegant Uzbek of the schools.

I had learned by that time, too, the tactics he used to make his command of English seem greater than it was. No, not his command – for he commanded it truly and superbly – but the range and accuracy of his understanding. I had been reading to him for weeks when he first began to ask me the meanings of words – sometimes words he himself had used earlier. He never, as far as I could tell, admitted ignorance of an English word to anyone else. Confronted unignorably with a phrase he was unsure of, he would turn it back, with a straight face, in question, threat, or provocation, to elicit more data. I thought, too, that one reason for his inscrutable looks, his reluctance to show surprise or annoyance or enthusiasm, was a simple fear of betraying misunderstanding by an inappropriate reaction. In his own tongue he behaved as in his own bedroom – responsive as quicksilver, eager, impatient, and irritable, throwing off little explosions of scorn and admiration.

In that crowded, bustling house I lived alone and silent. The raucous poultry of the yard, the thick-tongued soldiery, alike confident of their validity, filled day and night with urgent communication. Betty – Miss Hanson to me before my promotion to auxiliary adulthood – emitted signals of agony and ecstasy from Arslan's room. Mr and Mrs Bond communed conjugally, upon a band narrow but apparently clear. Cats wove their intricate society through the useful obstacles of humankind and its hounds. The monkey, *sui generis*, scratched his piglike skin and pattered forth rattling streams of helpless exhortation. Individuals addressed communications to me: Darya sang, in a language whose very sounds I never grasped; Mrs Bond presented to me kindnesses, fruit pies, clean linen; Arslan's soldiers delivered retailed orders and original mockery; Mr Bond kindly preached; Arslan laid upon me his light hands, his heavy body, his intolerable informations. I did not respond. Only in certain roseate darknesses – the laughably, pitiably frail virginness of dawn, the dying violent power of sunset, the glory that attended midnight in Arslan's sweated bed – did I speak, give answers, question, and then to Arslan alone. A certain mechanical heaviness invested otherwise my speech centers.

'Light, Hunt,' he said. I lit the lamp: the match blared its small headstrong explosion; the patient wick took the fire quietly and lifted a tall pale flame, ravelling into a tangle of dark smoke. I set the chimney, fixed in its perfect curve, over the equally perfect and ever altering curves of combustion. The flame settled; the smoke vanished; the room was lit. 'Is not light beautiful?' Arslan said.

I considered. All the all-but-infinite hues of the spectrum were beautiful; and every intensity, from the coalmine dark to the retina-searing brilliance of a star unmasked, had its peculiar beauty. He took my wrist as I returned, and I sat beside his neatly sprawled body on the bed, and nodded. How, then, could any visible thing be unbeautiful?

'Yes, beautiful,' he said – the voice that swam in dark sweetness, that purred, that without music sang. 'And strong, Hunt; light is strong. Do you know the laser?'

Personally, no. I nodded anonymously.

'A beam of light of such—' his hand groped air until he found the perfect word '—*integrity* that it pierces steel.' He loosed my wrist and turned to me on his elbow, his face eager and exhorting, Arslan's native posture. 'As a weapon it is only a weapon – you

168

understand? It has its own limits – of range, of speed, of accuracy, of maneuverability. Another weapon, Hunt, nothing more. But every new weapon has its hour, the period when its power is multiplied by its newness. Therefore to use a weapon most efficiently, it is necessary to strike during its hour.'

And if there was nothing at which to strike? But Arslan could create his own victims. Now he tamped his pillow into a solid backrest. His shoulders curved against it as he lit a cigarette (swiftly, impatient of his self-interruption). 'Consider, Hunt. If the United States had struck, intelligently and with decision, at the hour when she alone possessed nuclear weapons and her delivery capability exceeded the defensive power of every other nation, she could have conquered the world.'

I looked at him, interested at last in the content of what he was saying. He touched me, and thus unspellbound I asked, 'Did you do it with lasers?'

He let his head fall backward, draped from the rolled pillow, not in indolence but in enjoyment. He talked around his cigarette; gentle rivulets of white smoke accompanied his words. 'The laser had been developed as a defensive weapon. Unfortunately its offensive potentialities will never be realized. But consider, Hunt! When two men face each other with drawn knives, who will live longer? He who wears armor. The shield was as decisive an invention as the sword. And what is the shield against the sword of full-scale nuclear attack? Either a counterstrike force too massive and dispersed to be neutralized, or a defensive network that is virtually one hundred percent effective. Nothing less is adequate. The advantage of the laser, the beauty of the laser, Hunt, is its speed. The antimissile missile has one chance to destroy its target: the laser has four, five, six! No, nothing is perfect – but we can approach perfection as a limit. Given a complete defensive network of lasers, the damage that can be inflicted by a nuclear strike approaches zero. Most certainly, for a large country, it falls within the limits of acceptable damage. Therefore—' he half straightened, jabbing his cigarette toward me – 'your country and the Soviet Union competed for years to perfect an antimissile laser – competed quietly.' He smiled at me, the playful smile. 'Conveniently for me, the Soviets succeeded first. Do you understand now?'

He touched me nowhere; but my whole right side was warmed because of him, the principal heat exchange occurring in the region of my right hip. He reached past me to tamp out his cigarette; returning, his arm brushed across me, his hand caught gently below my armpit. 'A little,' I said.

He chuckled lowly. 'A little,' he mocked. 'A little, little. Hunt,' he said, urgently if cavalierly. His fingers sank into me (five bruises tomorrow) and I said, mightily aloud, 'I want to understand.'

He paused, his fingers still tight in my side, eyeing me with humorous surprise. 'You want,' he said interestedly. 'Good. I shall tell you.' His gripping hand eased slowly. 'I knew – and your government knew, Hunt, in much more detail than I could know – that the Russians had perfected an anti-missile laser. It followed that they were installing a laser defense network as rapidly as possible. Do you understand, Hunt? It is very simple. The shield – the first shield – is a weapon of offense.' I understood. It was very simple. 'I went to Moscow to talk to the Chinese, yes, as the papers said, but much more as an escort to Nizam.' His eyes, unmoving, withdrew from me a moment. It was dull and cold to realize that he thought more of Nizam than of me. Recollection united them, occupation welded them. They were made one by years (five? ten? fifteen?) of shared effort, intense not with love but with life and death. Conspiracy and combat – two fields as far beyond me (considered as a point infinitesimally distant from the neutral center) as, say, experimental biochemistry and steamfitting – were the elements of their weathered intimacy. 'Nizam was a student of the Soviets,' he said reminiscently. 'Therefore he was able to apply appropriate modifications of their own methods to themselves. We were half certain before we set out for Moscow, almost certain before we reached Moscow, entirely certain before we finished a week in Moscow, that the Russian laser defense network was complete. No, Hunt, you could not have known. Certain parts of your government knew that the Russians had perfected the laser, and were installing it, but how far the installation had proceeded they did not know.' He sank his head back into the pillow. His face rounded and sweetened; his smile played like summer upon earth. 'There were two men,' he said.

There had been two men. I remembered them very well from eighth-grade Current History. Their names were Glukhovsky and Kerbabayev, and it was hard to keep in mind which was the technical head of state and which the leader of the Party. I remembered the stout businessman face of one, soulless and broad, and that the other was a little man. But as Arslan spoke, low and luxuriatingly, the blurred pictures sharpened and came alive to me. Two men. And I shuddered, stroked with the razor-edge of actuality. It was more strange and thrilling that the man beside me had seen, conversed with, dealt with those miraculous beings – men and yet powers – who had swayed nations, destroyed lives, inspired headlines, than that he, Arslan, was himself such a being raised to a higher power. For I touched him, I knew the taste of his breath and its sound in sleep, his flesh had wounded mine, I saw him yawn, scratch, spit, his stomach rumbled, he repeated himself and mispronounced words; he was Arslan to me, absolute Arslan, but he was familiar to me as the potent air.

It was Glukhovsky, the man with the business face, who had been Chairman of the Supreme Soviet and thus effectively Tsar of all the Russias. 'Ah, he was good, Hunt. Good!' *Good*: praise from the cockleshelled lancer for the featureless wall-face of the turning whale, backed with kilotons of oiled muscle and buoyed with the endless ocean. 'It was the hour of the laser, and of Russia. The world was hers to take, if she had the courage. It could be a long hour for her, perhaps. But for me, Hunt, the hour was very short. It was necessary to do two things. First, to encourage the Russians to take this world that they had earned. Second, to persuade them to give it to me. Not so difficult, Hunt – not so very difficult. There was a disagreement within the Russian government.'

And in blazoned clarity I saw the scene: the two Russians with distrustful eyes, the smooth wood of the table, the smooth faces of the Chinese, the red telephone ominous and ludicrous, and Arslan, Arslan in his hour. I saw the tiger glint of his prowling eyes, the crouched short-muscled power within (born for the stalk and spring, not the long lope of pursuit), the glow of joy that made his squat solidity beautiful as Praxiteles' gods. 'Nizam,' he said, 'had made these things possible.' Nizam making the ways straight. I looked for Nizam in that picture, and distinguished a shadow on the outskirts. 'He had – isolated – insulated – the room. Thus I could make my proposal without interruption. And could enforce an answer.'

He spoke Russian, presumably well. 'Enforce an answer how?' I asked him. Gem-eyed Arslan, two thousand miles behind enemy lines, armed with a silent whip named Nizam, enjoying himself. Arslan at climax, all but imperceptibly quivering, alight, afire, ablaze. Shabby princeling of a beggar state, stretching his hand to manipulate the crowned chessmen of world politics. 'With a gun,' he said.

I would have laughed, if laughter had been among my current capabilities. At least I registered the words as amusing. *I could enforce an answer. Enforce an answer how? With a gun.* Premier Arslan Khan of Turkistan in the capital of the world's vastest nation – and, for the hour that might have been long, the world's most powerful. 'Naturally our belongings had been searched; but I had carried it always on my person.' Arslan's bedmate, Arslan's bath-mate. 'Naturally we had been examined electromagnetically; but there are convenient devices, which were known to Nizam, that defeat such examination. Thus I had the gun with me in the conference room. It was necessary only to point it.'

But already the scene was fading. It had been merely a projection of colored light, not one of the etchings of the mind. The red telephone would not have been in that room, probably not the Chinese. I frowned, trying to follow the legend he unrolled for my education, trying to regain the interest I had felt or claimed to feel. He had pointed the gun. He had made his proposal: that the Chairman of the Supreme Soviet deliver to the President of the United States an immediate ultimatum demanding immediate response – capitulation (though not in that unacceptable term) or nuclear war. 'And in either event, Hunt, I asked for myself only the command of the armed forces. More than that I could not hope to be given.' That was all he asked. Later he would not need to ask.

'It was not unreasonable, Hunt.' No; insane but not

unreasonable. Silent-eyed Glukhovsky had heard all the reasons long before he faced Arslan's pistol. And brisk little Kerbabayev, who watched them both with equal attention, burned with belief in those reasons. There had been a disagreement within the government. *Irony*: somehow the word had always brought me the picture of some unidentifiable curio, carved in ivory. It was a beautiful irony that Kerbabayev should hear urged upon Glukhovsky at pistol point, by the premier of Turkistan, the very act that he had been urging for weeks past. It was reasonable, reasonable. It was the terminus of all the logic of defense and counterdefense, of strike and counterstrike. For what else (except-ing only the great ends of Communist teleology) had they worked, contrived, expended, sacrificed, risked? How could they lack the final courage now to take the final risk, a risk so much less than many they had triumphantly run? Thus he had surely argued. And now they would take that risk perforce. Arslan was the gadfly to drive them into the promised land, and then be brushed away.

Or, alternatively, to be crushed at once, before the heavy thews began to move. And Arslan's audacity, if it failed of success, would have ended the arguments forever. He, Kerbabayev, would be silenced with the same blow that destroyed Arslan.

And the man who faced the pistol – had he been charmed, somewhere within, by this swift brash grace and youthfulness, the outrageous speed and ease with which this trivial opportunist had pierced the guarded heart of their strength? Or had he only raged, Philistine confronting the minuscule host of inspiration, at all the petty, irrevocable stupidities, of his underlings, predecessors, col-leagues, that had left him suddenly at catastrophe's brink? Or, executive to the last, had he been weighing truths and con-sequences all this while, premeditating the muscular actions that should inflect his face, produce words from his breath, explode or petrify the world?

'He did not accept.' So there had been a man, a member of my very species, who had refused Arslan – a character as unreal, in that aspect, as Arslan's mythical parents, as the teachers in whose classrooms he had presumably sat, as the woman for whose love he had considered committing follies. Why had he not accepted, that man? I did not well understand, then or later, his teleology;

perhaps to him it implied the necessity of the current phase of international relations. Or, ideology aside, did the status quo appear, in the curled computer of his brain, more advantageous than the newborn risks and harvests of a new world conquered? Or, simply and humanly, was he unwilling to exchange the ritual of his daily problems for the cataclysm of a revealed truth?

'Therefore I shot him.' And, patient and cold (it was the previous sentence that had chilled me), I looked at him. It was the first time such words had been addressed to me, and to my ignorance they sounded abnormal. But the logic was real. Arslan had enforced his answer.

It was, of course, desperate. He had begun the plunge, the crimson sky-dive of Macbeth. If Kerbabayev, too, 'did not accept,' where could he turn to find his next sacrifice? Isolated in that still room as in the hurricane's eye, he had no weapon but murder, no exit but triumph. A second Glukhovsky would have defeated him. But if there had been two Glukhovskys, he would not have attacked.

And Kerbabayev, of course, had accepted. Doubtless it had seemed to him a dazzling gambit. The goaded muscles would move, more suddenly than decision alone could make them, and the whole momentous bulk of his nation be set upon the path of righteousness. As for Arslan, without question he could be eliminated or neutralized; or (questioned) at worst he, Kerbabayev, would be able to keep a hand on the reins; and if all somehow failed, if the path were missed, or led awry, then Arslan should be sponge enough to sop up all the guilt.

He had made the call. He had delivered the ultimatum. The mountain had been climbed because it was there. No doubt the world's end would have been different if there had been no red telephone – or, say, no Arslan, or no human race. The evolution, at least, would have been longer.

But these things came to me later, far later. Beside Arslan, in the lamplight, nothing stirred in me – nothing until the sullen slow warmth of an unexpected resentment (disappointment? shame? – some degradation product of a residual patriotism I had thought I never had) roused at his casual disposal of my country's honor. 'The United States, of course, capitulated.' Why *of course*? Why was all the uncertainty, all the risk, in Moscow? I looked down at my hands in my lap, and Arslan, hunching toward me, laughed. A momentary pulse of desire to argue rose in my throat, beat once, and died. Later, in the still hours before sleep, I was to cherish that little urgency as one more hopeful twitch of my paralyzed soul. *Confusion of the deathbed over . . .* There was still a future tense.

17

Measuredly, by a gentle gradation of brutal degrees, I was being weaned away from slavery. He took me hunting, and I breathed. He struck me, and I spoke. He left my door unlocked, and I was afraid. It was not night I feared (*Come, seeling night*), but the great ghost-filled day. Daylight and Kraftsville swelled and swirled around the house, infiltrated the staircase, eddied outside my door. Tendrils snaked and vined through cracks and keyholes, every exit and entry let in a puff, and I sat bleak as Arctic stone in the knowledge that I would have to go out into it, out into all of it.

At first I went only with him, at special order. 'Come, Hunt.' It would be no farther than the yard. The horses were ghosts to me. I looked through them, or looked away. I had learned to ride, seriously, two summers before. He caressed their solidity with a touch luxurious and sure, feeling for faults. From the outside Mr Bond's house looked alien or unreal. Warm breezes rustled the dusty flowers. Yellow sunlight poured in heavy swathes from the exhaustible sun. It was simply hot.

'Come, Hunt.' It was not an invitation; he merely commanded my attendance. *Thousands at his bidding speed, And post o'er land and ocean without rest.* I also served, apparently; though for what, in the sunlight, was obscure.

'Come, Hunt.' In the newly finished stable, in the good smells of horses and raw lumber, he talked his plausible Russian, criticized equerriel architecture by eye and hand, and turned on me with a sudden order to mount. The horse stood just-saddled; the Russian groom was laughing. I muffed it, naturally. But once in the saddle, hot with shame and dread, looking down at Arslan (a fantastic viewpoint), I felt my body take over. I remembered how it was to ride. He looked at me – looked up – and laughed. And looking down I smiled my first smile.

And still later, Mr Bond's gentlemanly and unpronounceable lieutenant was deputized to chaperone me. I liked his worried expressions and his diluted devotion to Arslan. He regarded me with the eyes of a conscientious nursemaid who didn't much like children. He was a mild challenge, a natural object for harassment; but I wasn't up to it. I was debilitated, the good invalid child glad of its leading-strings.

He led me, on Arslan's precise instructions, farther and farther into the ghost-filled day. Two blocks south (the stables, to fetch the horse of Arslan's whimsical choice); four blocks east (Nizam's headquarters, to deliver some trivial, perhaps nonexistent, message; to look, or not to look, one block onward to my father's house); three blocks north (shorter but farther, a different neighborhood, to Gullick's the harness-maker, for a rather interesting modification of a halter). And outside Gullick's house he courteously instructed me to wait a few minutes for him, and turned the nearest corner.

It was the first time I had been alone in the open, and I was at a loss. I dangled Arslan's halter and admired the air. Did a colt feel the same dull resentment at being trained? Or, for that matter, the same dull satisfaction? I would perform my lessons, accept the bit, follow the reins. The line of least resistance, spidery clue through the funhouse labyrinth of actuality.

And alone in the open air, perceiving the world leafy and flowery, full of space in which the displaced personality could spread arms and turn about, sun-shone, solitary, I felt myself grow cheerful. Future tense aside, there was most definitely a present – a present in which it was possible to move, smile, respire, ride horses, understand harness, study Latin.

The tranquil street was unpeopled but alive. Hadn't there always been people on the streets, before Arslan? No, I remembered now, and the scene around me sharpened into a keener focus, unmodifiable, indescribable in its realness and rightness; lovely and real. It had been exactly like this before Arslan, on such a sidestreet, on such a summer day – the life and quiet bustle all in the houses and the trees, only an occasional flitter-between or resident-on-threshold (passer-by, porch-chatter, rug-shaker, harness-customer, tomato-picker), nobody in very much of a hurry. Nothing had changed. And I felt for the first time a wholehearted homesickness for my own people (cracked, contused, lacerated, but whole) and in it, temporary but stabbing, an instant ache for fellowship, for the kids of Eighth Grade, Room One.

And on cue, real and right, with the coincidental inevitability of fate-in-the-dice, two figures emerged from the green shadows of the next cross-street north, coming my way on the other side of the street. They were Gene Michaels (not, indeed, of Room One, but he had played first trumpet beside me) and Simon Teffertiller, universally known as Bud, kind-eyed and potato-faced. They were in eager conversation. I stood and waited until they were nearly opposite me. Then, 'Hi,' I said, and lifted my hand.

They were very, very busy with their conversation. Not until they were definitely past did a half-glance come my way, and Bud exclaimed, in a voice that filled the attentive universe, 'Hey, Gene, do you believe in fairies?'

I waited, hot but frozen, very busy in my turn with the harness, until they turned the corner, and then while I counted ten, twenty, forty-seven; and considering this a sufficiently angular and realistic number to justify me before any lingering atoms not yet convulsed in snickers, I turned and walked slowly – to very hell with instructions – back the long three blocks to Mr Bond's house. Some part of my brain (was it the cerebellum?) had cravenly deserted under fire, leaving the management of all my muscles to my unpracticed consciousness, so that I traveled in jerks and wavers where all should have been smooth but firm, and stubbed my toes.

It wasn't the impersonal fact – I had anticipated, imagined, and armed myself against such taunts, indeed much worse, even to violence – but the source of it, which so unstrung me. Gene and Bud were not among the jackals from whom I had expected such, nor quite among the friends whom I was prepared (having lately learned the ruthlessness of self-defense) to forgive it. They represented the rational and indifferently sympathetic Better Class my bitterest apprehensions had assumed; and that they had turned upon me demonstrated, with mathematical finality, that all the world at large was hostile.

It was one of the turning points. Not my turn, since I had not altered in self or in direction, but the world's turn. I was only the pivot pin upon which the visible universe wheeled. And feeling cramped and restless for a pin, I resorted to merely physical motion. That was the first time I walked boldly, so to speak, into Arslan's stable and saddled and harnessed one of Arslan's horses, and mounted and rode off, wordless before the mock salutes of my watchers. Not one moved to stop or question me. And on the road I leaned the horse slowly into a flying, floating gallop that eased my chest. I quartered the town, tattooing down Bud's street and down Gene's, making long corner loops along the country roads. Then I rode back, the horse and I heaving together, to gather the fruit of my first disobedience.

Yet I was so obtuse, the universe so little visible to me, that eight weeks later I walked like a lamb to my father's house. And lamblike I was bewildered and surprised when the club fell. 'You are a Goddamned hypocrite,' I said – the valor of the lamb – and walking back through the forbidden dark, I heard the rifle crack and felt an outrageous thrust drive through my thigh.

I had been taught that there were good people and bad people. The good subscribed to certain theoretical tenets and abstained from certain actions. The bad faulted in one way or both. There were also rumors of peculiarly loathsome creatures, the worst of the bad, who pretended to subscribe to the required tenets, the better to perform the forbidden actions with impunity. Scorn and righteous indignation were fired at these absent monsters from the batteries of pulpit and school-book fiction, but none were ever pointed out to me in the flesh. For Kraftsville's ancestral piety had not been shaken by the seisms remaking the face of America. The Sunday School literature spoke fashionably of society's sins, and the Social Studies books confessed that westward expansion had been a little hard on the Indians; but what citizen of Kraftsville could have questioned that Kraftsville citizens were nice people, and that nice people were good?

So it took a convulsive effort to realize that it was exactly the good people, it was especially the better people, who were the loathsome hypocrites. My father and my mother, and all the other reasonably intelligent, reasonably nice, reasonably successful people I had ever known – *they* were the ones who spoke out so dogmatically for truth, beauty, and goodness, while with every action of their lives they cast votes for falsity, ugliness, and corruption. And Mr Bond, of course – Mr Bond was a particularly prime specimen, because he made his living teaching hypocrisy to children.

It was Arslan who showed me the possibility of living honestly. Even his deceits were straightforward – tools as simple in purpose and exquisite in design as the guns he equally loved. He lied; but he did not pretend.

'You give me much pleasure, Hunt.' Yes – except that I gave nothing; he took, took with both hands. The stuttering metaphors of my mind were silent before the concentrated consciousness he brought to bear upon his pleasure-taking. It was this – not his deeds, but the passionate and concerned intelligence that powered them – which struck me dumb and helpless, naked before his ruthless interest. Brutal but un-animal, wholly aware, wholly deliberate, he probed again and again for one more pocket of resistance, one more unwillingness from whose bursting another spurt of pleasure would flow. That was what I saw of him. It did not occur to me that he had other concerns as well.

It was against my will – it was against my very flesh – that I read *Tamburlaine* to him. I did not know the story. I had never heard of Timur the Lame, I did not dream that Arslan had paced the polished floor of Timur's own tomb with pudgy legs, his hand in his father's. But before I had read far, the words thickened in my mouth, and I saw Arslan doubled, before me on the couch, before me on the page. Surely to read this to him was to pour oil upon the fire that was devouring me. *Over my zenith hang a blazing star That may endure till heaven be dissolv'd, Fed with the fresh supply of earthly dregs* . . . Yet he listened with an earnestness that might have been anxiety if it had not been calm. Later, out of silence, he would speak the word that had touched him. 'Triumph. Triumph is public, is it not?' I nodded doubtfully. 'Yes. And it is temporary, Hunt.' His eyes were very quiet, very open. 'I do not deceive myself. I have finished my triumph.' It was spring, his lush first Kraftsville spring. I was very young, I did not guess that he was more and less than Tamburlaine (the conquering shepherd, invincible by sheer intent, noble by sheer brutality, marching forever forward to new wars). 'Now there is only work.'

Those were words I forgot, for months, for years, while I remembered all the standard, stirring taglines of Marlowe's limpid bombast. *Come, let us war against the powers of heaven And set black streamers in the firmament* . . . No, Arslan would need no second triumph. His triumph was with him forever.

No doubt it was grievous to be unable to respond, practically, to inquiry or assertion, friendly or hostile. Yet, on the whole, response seemed to me frivolous. There was nothing to say; or the things sayable there was no point in saying. 'Arslan says you're free to go,' Mr Bond informed me. That was communication, and valuable, or at least effective. But *Go where?* would have been the only feasible response, and it could have evoked no effective answer. Therefore I gazed, and was silent.

And in the dusty music room – though I felt such a sweet stab into my vitals that everything inside me was, in a moment, dissolved and flowing – I only listened. The room was so small. Exactly here (or there, or there; my memory ran liquid and swirling as the eddies of spring creeks) the instrumental scores had been kept, here the vocal, in those two cabinets the school's instruments (the dingy, dented brass, the dilapidated woodwinds, the new drums we had been so proud of); there, in that corner, I had kissed Patty Cummings after the year's first basketball game, because I liked the wild grace of her and because she teased me – my first kiss, my only kiss, except the hundred that Darya had demonstrated to me, except the condimental tendernesses with which Arslan spiced his assaults.

I had been a good trumpeter, by Kraftsville standards. And it was that thought, ramifying, that brought tears to my eyes while I listened to my mother. My mother, Hunt Morgan's mother, Mrs Morgan, Mrs Arnold Morgan, Jean Morgan – in any aspect, not a woman to sentimentalize. She was all business; but the sentiment was notably present – very neatly boxed, very properly veiled, very ostentatiously unmentioned – a thing set as on a table between us.

She looked so thin and so old – not truly old, of course, but I had never before recognized the marks of time upon her, or imagined she could be subject to them. It surprised me (I was still that young) that she had actually and physically suffered. Parents were immutable.

'What became of my trumpet?' I asked her.

She radiated stifled pleasure. 'It's in your room. As far as I know, it's as good as it ever was.'

And it had been a good trumpet. 'What ever happened to Patty Cummings?'

Now she was surprised – staggered, in fact. Was it good or bad for me to ask about Patty Cummings? Good, for me to express interest in anything; good, for me to be interested in a girl as opposed to Arslan; good, for me to speak at all. But bad, for me to be more interested in a girl than in my long-awaited home-coming; bad, for me to have any interest that implied sex, however innocuously; bad, for me to be interested specifically in Patty Cummings, an empty-headed innocent without family prestige or intellectual pretension.

'Patty *Cummings*? Nothing, that I know of. All the Cummings girls are still living at home.'

Living at home. What a world of homeliness that phrase implied, a world enormous, solid, and sweet, in which 'home' had a meaning beyond 'the place where I live.' I had forgotten. I gazed at her, staringly, touched and awed, and the word *Mother* came to me, and I thought that I understood it. And I wished, knowing it an adolescent wish, that she would ask me some important question to which I could answer, 'Yes. I am coming.'

But she talked of mealtimes and underwear, of my father's health and my old dog's death, presented me with a pseudo-leather toilet bag and advised me how to pack it, tucked her handkerchief into her well-kept purse and adjourned the meeting. She was a grown-up.

And Arslan, also, was a grown-up. Grown-ups might give, at unpredictable intervals, anything else; but not drama, not dignity, and not freedom. He did not come to see me go. With neither congratulation nor recrimination, with nothing but a pseudo-leather toilet bag, I stepped into the cool sweet air of the first breeze of evening. Yet, in the end, all the drama and all the dignity were on Arslan's side; and there was no question of freedom. Hot and sour I walked back through the bitter night, ballasted with incredulity and contempt (which would be worse, that they had forgotten the curfew or that they had remembered?), waiting for the bullet. And when it came I staggered, less with physical shock than with the strong wash of relief, of satisfaction, of preconceived anger now justified and released – and, later, with the dragging undertow (annoyingly real) of fear.

And Arslan was there to see me come back, there to heal me with his hands. It had been a false departure, a real return. When the time came for true departures, he would be there.

He threw himself stomach-down on the bed where I lay, and my own stomach contracted in the accustomed cold cramp. Propped on his forearms, a very boyish posture, he dragged a fingertip across my chest. 'You understand, Hunt, that I make a whirlpool around myself. There is no one who can come to me' – he considered for a word – 'naturally. I must always deal with people who are in a condition of strain with regard to me.'

I felt a small smile detachedly form itself on my face. He looked at me with confident expectation. 'A condition of strain.' My voice sounded to me husky and childish.

'Greater or lesser,' he said, grinning, and laid his palm on my diaphragm by way of demonstration.

'Rusudan,' I said, and the blackness her name roused in me was, in comparison, soothing.

His other hand flicked; the knuckles caught me under the chin, snapped my mouth shut very effectively. Not, with regard to Arslan, what you could call a blow. Just a mild warning, a touch of the lion's paw. Just a gesture to inform me that I must not contradict his dogma with the fact of Rusudan. She was not a part of the world which I was permitted to consider.

'Therefore I discount the strain,' he said, 'in one who would be a friend without it. Do you understand?'

I investigated with my tongue for blood before I spoke. I had a notion that the sight of blood excited him. 'I don't know.'

'You say to me, "I hate you." But without the strain you would have said something different. I consider that you have said the something different. Hunt, I tell you this tonight for a reason.'

I closed my eyes. I didn't want to hear his reason. But I was too vulnerable in that blindness; I had to look at him again.

'I return to Bukhara,' he said. 'Tomorrow.'

Instantly the world flashed and rang, as if I had been colorblind, tone deaf, for a season, and those few words had cured me. My heart sprang; my lungs drew one delicious breath of pure freedom, like pure oxygen, before everything shifted, like one of those optical illusions in which high is suddenly low and low high, and I felt myself abandoned in a world to which I had been made a traitor. Christ had volunteered; but the scapegoat was a conscript.

'I want you with me,' he said.

So it was back into the frying pan, and nothing had been given me but the prospect of old tortures with new instruments. And falling back into the crumpled husk of myself, I felt tears under my eyelids. I closed them. 'And if I say no, I suppose you'll consider that I said yes?'

He was silent, until I had to open my eyes and look at him. At once he smiled and spoke. 'I am not asking you to choose, Hunt. You come with me. When I ask, I do not dictate the answer.'

'Okay,' I said. 'Okay. Okay.' I closed my eyes again, going down for the third time. And this time (elementary tactics, invite a relaxation of vigilance and then strike) his hands shut like steel on my upper arms and I felt his breath on my ear as he said softly, 'Remember.'

18

And I remembered. Through the four terrific years, the fast years, the years of my true initiation (for what happened in Kraftsville had been only the test, the preliminary ordeal, which I had passed, because I had survived), I remembered that he did not accept my hate; he returned it to me, so to speak, unopened. I remembered that he chose not to endow me with free will. I remembered, seeing her for the first time the day he brought her to the palace, that my mouth was incompetent to speak her name. Seeing him look at her, I remembered the taste of his tongue. Seeing him rock with laughter, hearing her passionate shouts of anger and of joy, I felt again the little tap that had clapped my jaws together; and I thought – small, sour, spiteful, old-man's thought – *Well, I was right.* Rusudan did not exist in a condition of strain.

She was not beautiful, no. She was garish, she was cheap, she was third-rate Technicolor – not even *nouveau riche*, as Arslan so patently was, but overpriced toy of *nouveau riche*. Yet she was whole; she was integral. And I, a disarticulate collection of fragments, awash in the bile of envy, watched. She was the only person with whom I had ever seen him quarrel. With the rest of the world his arguments were rational, his angers dictatorial. But with her he struggled and raged. With her he was unjust, brutal, indignant.

I thought I understood. She was, in some way, his unique equal – the one living being with whom it was unnecessary for him to condescend, to explain or domineer. Not even Nizam the Ineluctable Shadow merited abuse or importunity – how much less I. I watched at first with bewilderment and shame, but later with admiration. No, it would not occur to him to muffle his noisy struggles; there was no danger of rousing revolt or contempt, for it was inconceivable that any other could dare stand against the flashing force of his confidence. All the openness of his furies, his frustrations, his delights, said to the world, *My weakness is stronger than your strength.*

Bukhara was a trap. In those bleak halls, under that blank sky, Arslan's retinue drew into itself, re-formed, transmogrified, and spread netlike around him, a full-fledged court. In the exercise yard he wrestled with soldiers from the garrison, challenging one after another, embracing every man who gave him a fall. Cigarettes drooping, eyes askance, the jealous majors stirred and shifted. They were aligned in only two things, distrust of Rusudan and devotion to Arslan. The world was divided and distributed every day in the casino, while Arslan, sweating and tousled, dictated endless orders in the radio room, scribbled his maps with ever-spreading lines like crackling glaze, shoved away his lukewarm coffee and called violently for hot.

He was happy. This was his home. He had his woman, the chosen vessel. *Never yet have I found the woman by whom I should like to have children, unless it be this woman whom I love: for I love thee, O Eternity!* She was eternal, at least, in her pestiferousness. She mocked, interrupted, scolded, demanded. It was unnecessary to understand the language of her complaints. So-and-so had insulted her. She wanted new clothes, more jewels. The cook must be replaced. Arslan shouldn't drink so much.

He drank more. He began with coffee and raki at lunch. The steel schedule of Kraftsville – a long day's driving work, an evening's intense debauch, a short night's childlike sleep – crumbled and vapored away. More coffee, to be gulped or forgotten. More raki, until light-foot Arslan slipped and scrambled on the treacherous marble floors.

It was the traitor's hour. In this palace, the bloody powers of Bukhara – emirs and viziers, and all the Turkish generals who had anticipated Arslan by half a millennium – had succeeded each other upon waves of treason. Generations of his forefathers' betters had caroused here to their own undoing. But there were no traitors among Arslan's men. The schemers were faithful.

They came and went, dispatched to this sector or that, still plotting. The cook stayed. Rusudan was arrogantly pregnant. Arslan knocked a lieutenant down the stairs for bringing him the wrong report. But after the three-day carouse that left him immobilized for the fourth day and night, while the palace buzzed with varying tones of dismay and frenzy, he reformed by the unexpected expedient of cutting himself to three cups of coffee per day.

In the winter of Bukhara, the great wind flowed like a tide across the plain. Wild flights of snow boomed like storm birds around the minarets; sprays of coarse, dry flakes spewed through unsuspected crevices and scattered down the barren halls. (There were no comforts among the marble luxuries of Bukhara; small wonder that Arslan had settled so complacently into the meager ease of Kraftsville.) In the streets, the shivering dogs chewed the snow hopefully. Symbolic more than real, it stated winter and disappeared. But the wind rolled on, the cold sank ponderously through the blankets, the dull pink bricks of Bukhara were hazed with an arid and delicate frost.

At his orders, I gave English lessons to his officers. I, whose classification in life, for as long as I could remember, had been 'pupil,' found myself elevated to full professor, an authority and source of knowledge looked up to and earnestly consulted by the commanders of regiments. All my ineptitude and confusion to the contrary, it was very steadying. Rusudan came a few times, curious and impatient – jealous, perhaps, of the alien language into which he withdrew from her – eager, most of all, to show herself off to me. Rusudan, at least, did not reject my hate.

Grotesque among the pilasters, in rooms designed for cushions and hangings but bare now as new-built prisons, stood the last emir's gestures toward technological civilization (or was it Arslan's father who had installed them, or even Arslan himself?): a nonfunctioning air-conditioner, a stereo console with ready-made collection of unplayed records. For the first time there came home to me, exiled in Bukhara, the banal horror of Arslan's great work. One could not honestly grieve for the loss of future Mozarts – there would have been no more Mozarts in any case; but Arslan had destroyed forever what I, backwatered in

Kraftsville, had never known: the whole ebullient and evanescent world of performance. There would be no more concerts.

In Kraftsville, Mr Bond had left beside my bed his little record player and a stack of records in shabby jackets. Now and again, Arslan had pulled a random disc from the pile and thrust it at me – background music for the sports of the evening. Otherwise they had sat unconsidered, silent, accumulating the dust of that uncleaned room. *Rigoletto, Don Giovanni, Fidelio.* In Kraftsville I had not noticed. But in Bukhara I remembered and was moved. 'Do you think the electricity will ever come on again, Hunt?' Mrs Bond had inquired anxiously, at a slightly later epoch. 'I know he misses those records. It's the closest thing he's ever had to a hobby.' Mr Bond, the self-contained, self-satisfied, the Gibraltar on whose stolid crags my new-born soul had steadied its bruised first footsteps – had he offered me, like Arslan in the woods, drink from the very springs of his own strength? Had he once bowed, as I did now, intently over the music, searching out the rich phrase that should nourish him through another day? And pell-mell, simultaneous perhaps, regret and resentment welled up, and I burned against him, remembering with momentary hatred his lofty shoulders and rock-rough face, remembering Kraftsville with hatred, because he had not been my father.

In Bukhara, the music seemed miraculous to me, the machine no less so. Nightlong I would sit hunched beside it, touching my budding beard with small proxy caresses, while the floating tone-arm softly bobbed and gradually pivoted, spinning great ripples of sound from a flat black circle. The tremendous swag and sway of Verdi, the joyous patternings of Mozart, gave back to my memory now the odor of Arslan's lust, now the concerned and disapproving eyes of Franklin L. Bond. In the morning there would be coffee, raucously strong; and at midday I would lie flat, spread-eagled on a blank bed, my teeth locked tight and fragments of arias furiously rotating through my brain.

I was lonely. In Kraftsville three people had been kind to me: Mr Bond with his mute gifts and unseasonable advice, Mrs Bond with her promiscuous motherliness, Darya with her harmless corruptions. In Kraftsville I had had Arslan, inexorable and close, a surrounding presence in which I struggled warmly. But it was in Bukhara the pale city that I felt the first doomed stirring of desire.

He had not touched me in Bukhara. And at first, thankful, I had shied away from every chance of touch. But I looked now with an abstract cupidity upon those blunt, soiled hands, seeing in them my only hope of human attachment.

As in Kraftsville, so in Bukhara, he purveyed me a girl. I didn't want her. I was incapable of the simple prophylactic contact with which Arslan's bachelor officers solaced themselves; and affection for one of Arslan's poppets was futile, futile. Where now was Darya?

But she was billeted in my room ('Hunt, I have given you a girl'); she was serious, gentle, and persistent. Her name was Chalyu. Dutifully I studied, not the art, but the mechanics, of lovemaking. Two drinks, taken in a period of forty to forty-five minutes, and with her help I could manage it, like a diligent paraplegic lover. It had been better with Darya. I tried to teach her English, which she tried to learn. We talked in a halting pidgin Turki. She was sixteen. She didn't know where America was. She admired Arslan.

One night she was gone. I sat on the bed and practiced rolling cigarettes while I waited. I had finished seven when he came. He walked straight to the bed, his hands coming out to take my shoulders. 'Now, Hunt,' he said.

Rusudan was five months pregnant. It would have been consistent, I thought, for Arslan to retire her from his bed, to put her in storage until the heir was safely born. Instead, he had retired Chalyu from mine. I never saw her again, and I asked no questions. I was busy. For what opened around me now was a new world: Arslan's Bukhara, the inner sanctum of a universe, the pale city I had seen hitherto through the veils of solitude.

We talked. In the exercise yard, now, he called me, too, to wrestle with him. To me they were desperate battles, fought in fury and shame under the hooting laughter of his troops. He expounded maps to me. He appointed one of his best pilots to teach me to fly. For hours in the dense-aired night he interrogated me on the intrigues of his court. I had become his spy. Under the caravan stars he schooled me in his language, rich and simple as a poem. And when, dizzy and defeated, accepting that I myself must be the traitor, I plunged the knife with all my force, and fell back stricken as Arslan's veritable blood welled upon his naked side, it was in his own language that he cried furiously, 'You dirty little fool, you don't know how!' Indeed I had done very badly. I had had to get up to get the knife, and by the time I struck he was awake, twisting out of the way. There was plenty of blood to set the palace buzzing again in the morning, but the wound was, as he said, 'very inadequate.' I learned that night that I had never before been thoroughly afraid. In the end, when he kicked the broken knife away, he came back to English, leaning over me in one last blaze where I cowered like a quivering hound, jerking his own knife from the tumbled clothes beside the bed. 'Next time' (lilting the words) 'use a better one.' And I took it from his bleeding hands.

There were gifts. There were recompenses. I had not expected (I had not considered it) that piloting a light plane would be the opening of a new world. *A New World*. And I understood at last (the realization flashing in and out of existence at first, then steadying, focusing, becoming examinable) something of what that phrase must have meant to Europeans of 1500, to Columbus himself. *A New World*. As one might say, *a new universe*. No. *A new continuum*. No. There was no word, since the beginning of the era (just ended) of multiplication and renewal, so final and whole as *world* had been.

To fly: the consummation of the most exquisite longings, the reality of the most delicious dreams. The whole globe of the world showed itself to me two-dimensional but enveloped in the perfect third. I bent myself to learn, to be quickly rid of my instructor. To fly – it was by definition to be alone.

It was flying in the dazzling void of the desert air that I came to terms with death. All the mortal hardware that surrounded Arslan had given me a brief mechanical thrill, like that of a carnival ride; the bullet wound in my thigh had been interesting but trivial, disappointing as much as pride-engendering; the bodies in the dump had seemed fraudulent. For the rest, I had poeticized suicidally, misusing Keats to ease my own midnights, and pondering the merits of knife and noose. It was suicide, not murder, I had meant when I dreamed in Kraftsville of shooting Arslan (the most certain suttee), though I had earned my new knife another way. But under all the romantic frenzy my unperturbed and patient self had known that I had other engagements. And the silent slogan with which I greeted the days and the nights – *I wish I were dead, I wish I were dead* – was as hollow, and as comfortable, as the *Now I lay me* of my childhood.

> Yet always when I look death in the face,
> When I clamber to the heights of sleep,
> Or when I grow excited with wine . . .

I had smiled at what seemed to me Yeats' boastful simplicity, the casual implication of daily encounters with extinction. But now, above the Black Sands, in the enormity of the humming air, I had my daily encounters. For the first time I teetered on the knife edge, not merely of possibility, but of temptation. Nothing held me up. Nothing above, nothing below. Sometimes a miniature cloud crawled forlornly along the outskirts of the tremendous sky. Otherwise I was alone. It was only a straining, groaning, quivering, squealing effort, a frantic laborious whirling, that kept me precariously aloft from moment to moment. It was easy, it was inevitable, for me to lift the plane's nose into the unbounded blue, until she stumbled and hung, a momentary floating star, and the uselessly flailing propeller growled a new tune, and suddenly hollowed I was falling, backward into the nothing below.

It was enough. 'Nobody dies of a stall,' my instructor had taught me; 'only of fear.' I tilted the plane's nose downward . . . downward . . . still downward . . . Whimpers rose in my throat, and my neck and arms prickled helplessly. Against the stiff resistance of my wrists I pushed the plane's nose still farther in the direction of death. Still downward . . . And now she caught the air, and I was flying again.

My hands on the wheel trembled. I was running sweat, and in the cold blue sky I was chilly within a moment. I turned the plane and climbed slowly, in wide circles, wheeling my way, with an eye on the fuel gauge, gradually back to Bukhara.

It was to become an exercise. I learned half a dozen ways to stall and recover. I learned to dive toward the scorching sands and pull out when it was almost too late. It was very calming. I looked with new eyes upon death, knowing now what Arslan's very existence should have taught me; shrugging off, unregarded, the destruction of multitudes, myself among them. Myself among them. There was no more to learn. The door of my death stood ajar, and a touch would open it. Beyond, Arslan's hands and soldiers' laughter did not enter.

On foot, once past the towers and foliage of Bukhara, the cloudless sky of Turkistan oppressed me. I would stare at the un-qualified blank (the inside of the small end sliced from the cosmic eggshell), trying to remember that what I saw was itself a cloud – not clear space, but a tangle of bewildered light, the blue rays lost and hurtling among thickets of jiggling dust. But it was useless – the polished shell remained; and I was hungry for the buttermilk skies of Kraft County, dawns as rosy-fingered as any Homer could have dreamed, sharp-edged and layered sunset clouds like the stone-made sediments of past ages.

Bukhara was a fever. In the dense shade of the trees, the oven air baked, the furnace breeze seared. It was surreal to pluck a peach from the tortuous branches and bite into that exquisite juiciness, while my eyes ached with drought. Arslan's deep laugh burst like fireworks bombs. The reports flowed in, the maps were netted with ever finer meshes, Rusudan was approaching her time. He was parched and hard, with gleaming eyes. He would never leave. Here was his home, the root of his nourishment, the hard nest of all his loves.

Who had noticed or cared, in eighth-grade Current History or the labyrinths of the CIA, that the Republic of Turkistan was developing one of the world's most efficient armies? 'It is a question of men, not of money; of morale, not of equipment. This is not wishful thinking, Hunt; I have proved it. Also,' he added pensively, 'we were not badly equipped.' It was the Russians who had re-equipped them – not badly, but not well – as their British arms fell obsolete. It was Arslan who had ordained that men outweighed equipment. 'It is not important – not for long – that a man should be trained to use this tool or that one. It is important that he should know that he can learn quickly to use any tool.' Supple and proud, they were a far cry from the tindery battalions of most of the third world. And to their suppleness and their pride he had added the crucial third ingredient. 'A soldier is alone, Hunt, more alone than other men. Do you understand? Because he lives with death.' The trite phrase was new in his mouth, making him smile with pleasure and knowledge. Yes, as I died with life. 'But also, if he is truly a soldier, he is never alone. His army is always with him.' Even unto the end of the world. It was unjust that Arslan's eyes, brilliant and treacherous, over-shadowed his mouth. It was a mouth worth watching, supple and proud. 'They are good, Hunt. Good,' he said, and his lips curled fondly about the word, telling me that they were his children, his brothers, his lovers, his creatures. The cadres of the army he had inherited as dictator's son had been unremarkable – half trained, half experienced, half rebellious, and thoroughly venal. It was not the least of his feats that he had, in that subterranean era before the revolt that made him Premier of Turkistan, infected every one of them (every one, at least, who had survived) with what in the interests of accuracy, might have been called love. I tried to imagine a world in which Arslan's ruthless enthusiasm was con-tained in so small a scope: to train – to create, rather, an army that would make him unqualified master of a certain arid acreage in Central Asia. 'I had seen the Russians and the Chinese, Hunt. I knew what I must measure myself against.' He was talking about armed forces, and he was serious. First, it had been necessary to neutralize his father's air force; but his immediate next move had been to take firm possession of his country's ill-defined borders. He had fought a little, unnoticed war with Afghanistan – a war that could have tempted him into conquest, but had not. Through the vacancy of the Black Sands, where the Soviet Union had been content to leave an uncertainty for future exploitation, he had drawn his emphatic line of fortifications and patrols – and Moscow, startled but sanguine, had given him vodka and con-firmed the line by treaty. On the east, he had sat down with relish to some four years of skirmish and argument. That – the Chinese border – had been his recreation. Within the boundaries, bidding East against West for oil rigs and teachers and irrigation projects, stockpiling his silky cotton while the mills went up, he had not neglected his first loves; the army was never idle. Like emirs and sultans before him, he had pacified the tribal Turkmens with bribes. ('My father's people, Hunt. A difficult people.' Arrogant, irascible, joyous, and cruel, a people dear to his heart.) All other tribes had been pacified Roman fashion. *Ubi solitudinem faciunt, pacem appellent.* The Kurds and Kalmucks, still following their ancient feuds and herds, contemptuous of boundaries, had been corralled, decimated, partitioned, and resettled with staggering speed and thoroughness. The nomads of old Turkistan became part of the growing proletariat of Bukhara and Merv and Khiva, and Arslan's troops added rural and urban riot control to their list of practiced skills.

So that when his great hour came, unexpected but destined, he was prepared. It was not in vain that he had sworn the oath of blood-brotherhood with Nizam – Argus-eyed Nizam, whose foresight provided the corps of interpreters through whom Arslan's officers were to command the world's troops. And the army had shared. The songs that rose from the Kraftsville grade-school gym had been true paeans.

It had been his feast of Persepolis, the single hour of triumph. And if, more moderate for once than Alexander, he had ignited no city (his conflagrations were later, measured and purposeful), he had had no less his accidental sacrifice; it was I who had been consumed in the peripheral blaze of his glory.

And only now I began to understand what lightning stroke had changed Kraftsville from a crossroads bivouac to the capital of the world (for Bukhara could never be more than the capital of Turkistan). He had driven west – the instinct of Timur, the inverse of Alexander – into the physical vastness of his untried conquest, leading his personal army into the heart of mid-America as he had drawn his personal gun in the Moscow conference room. It was not yet a matter of baiting the incipient resistance – there could be no resistance until the conquest was real. It was a challenge, a risk, an exploration; he did not yet know what he had done, nor what he would find. The world (there, *there* was the rub, the nub – I beat my palm against my brow and cursed like Hamlet over Hecuba) the world had still been free to choose its answer to him.

But driving west on Illinois 460, he had received the answer. Nizam had caught up with him, bringing the confirmation that he could accept from no one else: Moscow was docile, Washington was well in hand; those generals who had shown themselves uncooperative had been rendered harmless. For the first time (perhaps the last), Muzaffer Arslan Khan knew himself the master of the world. The place where he found himself became the universe's center.

So that the Arslan I first saw – swaggering down the aisle of Mrs Runciman's eighth-grade class, face aglow and body afire and the hand that touched my shoulder vibrating steel – was not, as I had assumed, the normal Arslan of his everyday past or his everyday future; just as the Kraftsville he saw that day, and all that it contained, were illuminated by an incandescence not their own.

Again, again, again; my muscles would bunch, my blood leap, and for the instant it would seem determined that I was about to plunge, simply and physically, for whatever freedom my legs could find. Assaults of escapism, they took me more often and more keenly in Bukhara than they had in Kraftsville. They were pangs of returning life, not spasms of dying (so, at least, I concluded); perceptions of reality, not rejections of it. Between convulsions, I was growing unsteadily more aware that flight was not so much impossible as pointless. *Hell hath no limits, nor is circumscribed In one self place; for where we are is Hell; And where Hell is, there must we ever be.* Milton's Satan was a general; Marlowe's Mephistophilis knew what it was to march in the ranks.

He moved always with the urgent skill of a professional. His plans were as secret as the wrestler's in the ring; the movement announced the decision to move. The child was to be born. Rusudan's plans were elaborate. Yet, 'Hunt,' he said, 'you will come with me.' I thought it would be to India, where the great camps were – the labor camps where, contrary to all his announced doctrine, the surplus rice crops were grown, the medical supplies mass-produced. There were always problems with those camps, and with the sterilization program that accompanied them – this the overt, even publicized sterilization program, using only surgical methods, that busied his henchmen for a time in India as in China. And indeed we were to visit some of those camps before our journeying was done. But first, out of a pink dawn, our jet tilted downward to the convoluted islands that had been Japan.

I saw now, as we sank roaring through the air, one of the beautiful horrors of which he had told me – an invested city. Through the outskirts of Tokyo ran an irregular band of devastation, a knotted black sash binding the city against the sea. In places it merged into broader spots of wasteland – the love knots of Arslan's ribbon. Well-set fires and well-planted bombs had drawn that siege line. Tokyo, caught in a tightening belt of flame, and inspired by memories of old conflagrations, had saved herself (other cities had been less skillful or other-starred), to strangle more slowly in the cordon of blackness. Here, it had been Chinese troops who patrolled the perimeter, shooting down fugitives from the city. At certain checkpoints, a citizen could buy his way out with any deadly weapon. (In Tokyo, guns were scarce, but swords were equally acceptable.) Such people were packed off to the farm districts being laid out in Mongolia and Siberia. There were escapes, of course. There were sorties, organized and otherwise. In the depths of the city, there were riots, new fires, cannibalism. When the Chinese marched in at last, there was very little resistance.

It was from such cities, docile with agony, that Arslan had drained off all the surviving males. All evidently pregnant women and mothers with male infants were ghettoed in convenient prisons and hospitals. Their men and boys were marched or shipped away, to farm the unappealingly virgin lands of northern Asia or Australia, or sometimes – if they passed the scrutiny of Nizam's agents – to serve Arslan more directly, as drivers, mechanics, technicians, clerks, interpreters, administrators, seamen, soldiers. In such a city, only the inmates of the inevitable brothels required sterilization. It was, on the whole, an efficient way to dispose of several million people.

There in Japan, to my relief, I fell ill. I was to learn on that zigzag journey that the health of mankind had already deteriorated. A surprising variety of plagues afflicted the concentrations of population, plagues that Arslan accepted gladly and manipulated with growing skill. Under the circumstances, diagnosis and prognosis of my ailment were alike uncertain, and not worth bothering with. I was content with the indefinite consolation of a schooldays phrase, 'just a bug that's going around.' The practical result was that I was spared setting foot on the barren ground of Tokyo. But after a few days of helpless peace I was well again.

And by that time he had finished his dispositions in Japan ('It is very simple here, Hunt. But there are problems elsewhere'), and we were ready to put still more distance between our backs and Bukhara. *But ere the circle homeward hies, Far, far must it remove.* The route was circuitous, not circular, and in the end we were to come back to Bukhara from east, not west. But I took care not to anticipate any return.

I was seeing the world. What surprised me was that it was indeed a world – globular, and covered all over with seas and continents. The sun went around and around it (Copernicus was irrelevant), and a mouse or a human being might go around and around it, too – by rocket, by plane, by ship and train, by swimming and walking if he chose. Maps could be drawn of it. Beams of electromagnetic energy could be bumped along its surface. It was real; it was finite.

Finite, and not only divisible but already divided. Water was Arslan's ally: the great rejecting oceans; rivers that cut nation from nation; the final ice of the mountains and the poles, blank, white, and perfect. And I was pleased. What Arslan was doing was fitting. I began to see the tangled web of twisting, heaping life in which this globular world was awkwardly netted. And I saw how Arslan with his square-nailed fingers worked at it, stretching and cutting and piecing and smoothing, so that someday, the scraps discarded, the web should fit neatly over every painted continent.

Lying in alien beds, awaiting the dull tides of shallow sleep that would flow and ebb across the mudflats of my mind, I was oppressed by the futility of all my hours. Remembrance, anticipation, experience, all were shadows in the night. Nothing was real to me but weight, the resistance of the dark medium in which I moved. And in Delhi, Marseilles, Kinshasa, it appeared to me still in images of Kraftsville summer: days filled with linty wisps shed from the cottonwoods, like the lung-muffling waste from some industrial process, nights with the horrid blunderings of gross beetles, junebugs monstrous in pathetic stupidity. And a passing jet, mysterious and purposeful in the night, that in other times would have relieved awhile the pressure on my heart, now only grindingly moved and mumbled, crossing the sky with a long tearing sound, and left for a little a rasped furrow upon the flesh of mind.

Worm-belly skin of the creeping oceans beneath us, clouds repurified of life beyond our wingtips. 'You will see, Hunt. All wounds heal. The world will heal very quickly.'

'All?'

'Death heals the last.'

King's fool or kempery-man, I served in other functions. Aimless, jerked idly along his hectic track, I carried his books and listened. Dimly I glimpsed, perhaps, what it would be to call Arslan my friend.

He took care, after all, to be on hand for the birth of the child he had never so much as mentioned, except in his battles with Rusudan. Sanjar; the name came from out of the air, or from some secret sanctum, immediately and unmodifiably. There was never any talk of 'the baby.' Once, before we left Bukhara, Rusudan had followed him into my room to scream at him, and he had turned to her a face coarsened with rage, while I stood widening myself in futile imitation of an angry cat. It was a violation that roused in me resentments and disgusts I thought I had lost – and in fact they melted in the warm pleasure of their recognition. It was good to feel outraged; but since it was pointless to object to the outrage, I relaxed and observed it. The woman's face streamed and dribbled (when Rusudan wept, she wept wholeheartedly), her wild hair, beautiful sometimes in its munificence, was fuzzed and snarled now; and yet her body, like Arslan's, and for all the topological distortions of cramming one human being inside another, moved and held and moved with the authority of beauty. What she alternately begged and demanded was that she be allowed to name the child. He did not argue; he called her whore, bastard, beggar, sow, and a good deal else that got past me. And all the while, untainted by their strained ugly faces and guttersnipe voices and stupid peasant spite, their bodies played out a ballet of majesty and grace. It was one of the times when I thought I understood.

Arslan's son. Rusudan's baby. I made an effort, once the birth was accomplished, to consider the child as a human being. Surely the offspring of these parents must be torn apart, wrenched by two such forces. And yet, apparently, he was not torn. Arslan accepted, as he accepted the hyperbolic weather of Bukhara, all the pampering jujuism with which Rusudan's over-heated court of handmaidens featherbedded their infant master. He insisted only on his right to claim Sanjar at any time of day or night and to handle him without interference. I found to my fleeting horror that it was I, not Arslan, who felt and showed the traditional discomposure of the male confronting the infant. It was so small, so frangible, and so irreparable. It seemed made of rice paper and jelly, a miniscule misrepresentation of human-ity, at once exquisite and obscene. But, 'Come, Sanjar,' said Arslan, and tucked the silken monsterlet into his bent arm with all the quick casual care he extended to his guns and his animals. Rusudan shrilled at him from her bed (deprived, for the time, of her body, she was all ugly now), and her women fluttered quietly like a border of voiceless birds. They were aban-doned disconsolate.

Day by day, month by month, in the crook of his father's arm, perched on his father's shoulders, dragging with pudgy-footed stumbles from his father's hand, Sanjar was introduced to his profession. He was accustomed, in order, to every branch of Arslan's transport system, from the ponderous cargo jets to the stony-footed mules of the mountaineers. Weaponry and com-munications were the meadow of his infant play. I always, and I only, spoke English to him – Arslan's educational scheme, designed to promote native and uncontaminated bilingualism. 'Paperwork,' Sanjar explained to me solemnly, burying his slight arms in the day's unclassified residue from Arslan's wastebasket – a phrase I did not remember having given him, and which he might well have constructed for himself. He was quick-witted, sometimes thoughtful, delighted to please – traits that boded well, to my ignorance of little children, for his future development. I was not very patient, but I was not spiteful with him. He was so very small.

19

Odi et amo. Quare id faciam, fortasse requiris.
Nescio; sed fieri sentio, et excrucior.

I claimed the right to be young; to be moved by Catullus. I was trying to translate that poem – my first exercise in authentic Latin. The story of my life in two lines. 'I hate and I love.' Those words were the data, incapable of alteration. Odious, amorous; yet the verbs of English had their taproots in deeper soil. 'Why I do that, perhaps you ask. I don't know; but I feel it to be done.' *Et excrucior.* another datum. If I could translate that, the rest of the poem would be merely bricklaying. But if there was any direct English equivalent, I had so far failed to find it.

'I hate and I love. Why, you may ask. I don't know; but I feel it being done.' The passive infinitive (the inactive indefinite; or, say, the suffering unlimited). *Fieri sentio*: 'to-be-being-done I feel.' I sense the happening. *Et excrucior.* 'And I am crucified.'

But that was wrong, both in its literal inaccuracy and in its lack of a certain refinement. Or was it falsely that 'excruciate' tinted *excrucior* for me? Was it indeed a fact (one of those observable concepts of which the world and science were constructed) that the greatest pains were the fruit not of bludgeons but of needles – not the crushed bone, but the delicately raveling nerve – so that, in the tortuous course of two or three millennia, what had meant simply the extremity of pain had come thereby to connote exquisiteness? What had Catullus felt? That (I had read) was the true translator's question. Well, the cross was an instrument combining the principles of bludgeon and needle.

The *ex* troubled me. My knowledge and my books were

inadequate to explain it. *Excrucior.* 'I am taken down from the cross'? Or had *ex*, like *per* (thoroughly, thoroughly), its aspect of completeness? Outerly, utterly; 'I am crucified out-and-out'?

But it was futile. (Another Latin word; *futilis, futile*, it would be. But what exactly did it signify? What was futility after all – one of the basic states of human existence, undefinable except by pointing, part of the impenetrable bedrock of etymology?) For crucifixion, since the Crucifixion, was irreversibly changed, dyed with the purple of sacrifice and glory. What Catullus had felt, rereading his stylused words, I could not feel. The shadows of his world were different, the punctuation different, and crucifixion as commonplace and as repugnant as hanging. And to translate from his mind, rather than his words, would be to write a new poem, or the poem anew – impossible, unless I were Catullus.

Futile, all futile, when in truth I could barely scratch out the literal meaning. Futile to be concerned with shades of skin color before I knew the structure of the skeleton. Grammar (knobby, articulated, concealing in stone-walled cells the leaveny life within), grammar refuted my pink and slovenly mis-shapes.

'I hate and love.' I had never seen him comfort or soothe or tend a woman – not even Rusudan; least of all Rusudan. That sort of tenderness he reserved for his soldiers, for men wounded in body and spirit. I had had a few flashes of it, in Kraftsville and in Bukhara; but then I was certainly his man, and certainly I was wounded.

And in time of crisis, what woman would cling to Arslan for comfort or protection? No; if they turned to him, it was as a tracking antenna to the missile that will smash it. And a wave of regret and pity went through me, to think that of all the women who had felt the pressure of that hard chest against their breasts, not one had clung there for security; and I was sorry for Arslan, my poor and terrible Arslan.

> 'I hate, I love. You may ask why I do it.
> I don't know; but I feel it done, and it tortures me.'

He had spoken so often and so matter-of-factly of our returning to Kraftsville that I had long since ceased to believe him. 'When we go back . . .' he would say, as if Kraftsville were his point of origin as much as mine. 'When we go back, we will show Sanjar the cave in the hill.' My mind set sullenly. That had been my cave, one of my secret places, only big enough for one boy. 'When we go back, Hunt, you will be useful to Nizam.' Not, *You can help Nizam*; willy-nilly, active or passive, I would be useful. Used. In the beginning, my heart had twisted at each of his magical *go back*'s; but it no longer occurred to me to consider them as real possibilities. Thus, though no doubt my potential usefulness had increased (I had lost scruples, gained cunning, advanced linguistically and diplomatically), I did not bother to imagine how I might be used. The only point worth examination was Arslan's motive in rasping the skin of my soul with this particular tool on this particular day.

So that when Rusudan's bustle of packing began, I speculated with the ludicrous sobriety of a three-in-the-morning drunk. He was preparing to send her somewhere out of the way (and certainly at the last minute he would keep Sanjar with him); or we were all embarking on a royal progress of his dominions; or he was preparing to lead an actual campaign or defend against a threatened coup, and Rusudan and the child were to be sent elsewhere for safekeeping or, contrarily, as bait; or no one was in fact going anywhere, and all the preparations were one of Arslan's smokescreens for some gigantic or minute maneuver. I failed to consider that the announced schedule might be simply true. And even when we reached Kraftsville, realization had not overtaken skepticism, so that I labored with feelings of belatedness and surprise, and perceived what I looked at only after a moment's delay.

Everything was altered. I had left as a victim, contemptible but pitiable. I returned as a henchman. To fulfill the role Kraftsville had assigned me, I should have died, or escaped, or found refuge in suicide, murder, or madness. It was ungrateful of me to have reappeared, intact and even cheerful, at Arslan's side.

Everything was altered, from my viewpoint as from Kraftsville's. There was the trite and tediously inevitable change of perspective known, no doubt, to every returned native; but I myself had changed, so that the difference lay not only in point of view but in organs of perception. I too had thought myself a victim and seen myself fail in that role. But my conclusions were not Kraftsville's.

Mr Bond, the image of a wise disappointed father, was glad to see me and offered no recriminations. It was he who introduced me to the practical realities of Kraftsville life. 'We've had a lot of trouble with the deer.'

I could resolve the sounds into words, but not into meaning. I smiled inquiringly.

'Of course, we don't have anything to shoot them with. We've turned into pretty good Indians – but you know something, Hunt? I don't believe the Indians ever kept the deer down very well, either.'

It was true, if ludicrous: a good deal of Kraft County effort was devoted to the serious business of 'keeping the deer down.' Or, considered more constructively, of keeping the district in good meat. Kraft County had moved a long way toward a hunting economy, though it still had far to go. Venison had practically replaced beef; and yet deer were, in popular opinion, vermin. 'The deer seem to have adapted better than *Homo sapiens*,' I said. Although *better* was a matter of definition.

'They're thriving, that's the truth.' But 'thriving' was not necessarily the same as adaptation; and in fact, hadn't the deer been always better adapted, even in *Homo sapiens'* heyday? They had done more than survive; they had kept the balance. It would have been valuable, once, to know their secret.

Already on the first day, Mr Bond began the offer of his pastime intrigues. He was to play Good Angel to my Faustus; but it was, of course, too late to burn my books. I had made that attempt, in Kraftsville and in Bukhara, without celestial prompting; and the first time he had dissuaded me (there were politics in heaven), and the second – when I needed whatever I could get, dissuasion or assistance – he had not been there to save me from proving myself incompetent. So that now I could be titillated, but not seduced. (Raped virgins, in St Augustine's opinion, were as pure as any.) Still, his tone opened old and new possibilities.

My usefulness to Nizam was wholly passive. When I was full, he squeezed me, and the pores of my mind, dutiful not to the greater glory of his Turkistan but to the principles of elasticity, gave up their drops of stored observation. But to serve Franklin L. Bond would have required activity. I had no doubt that he led the most powerful, at least, of whatever submerged forces moved beneath the dull ripples of Kraftsville's mud-dark surface. It was tempting to think of offering my services – tempting but impossible. No man could serve two masters. That was not a moral prohibition, but a statement of fact. I could not choose to betray Arslan.

No, nor conceive betrayal, however I struggled toward it. Meshed in his heavy nets, all maneuverings were futile. For all roads led to death, all species evolved toward extinction.

Bukhara the Pure, Bukhara the Mine of Wisdom. *So is every wise man a Bukharan.* I had not realized, in the deep fever of Bukhara, what it was that he displayed to me so proudly, with such love. His city, yes. It was in Bukhara that I heard him called Al Hadj and learned that he had made the Great Pilgrimage with his mother when he was very small. But it was complacently, almost with pride, that he assured me he knew no Arabic. Bukhara the Dome of Islam, the Crown of the True Faith, the City of Many Mosques. His city, his country. 'For four years I worked hard . . .' He had left the mosques still standing, as the churches of Holy Russia had still stood in the Soviet Union. But the light had gone out of the dome. And in Kraftsville I recognized at last that the Bukhara through which he had led me, his left hand locked on my wrist and his eyes luminous with joy, was already a ruin. He had cut, methodically, remorselessly, his own roots. And the nourishment he planned for his heir was drawn from other soil.

It was part of his scheme of education that Sanjar should learn, willy-nilly, all the prowess of Huckleberry Finn. For that, too, I was useful. Arslan did not hunt this year, nor the next. (Had it been only a summer's sport, a bachelor's game?) It fell to me, Chiron to his infant Achilles, to initiate Sanjar into the art of killing. We were not very successful at hunting together – he was impatient and noisy, too small to help, too young to care – but I supposed he had fun in the woods. 'I seen a bluebird, Hunt! I seen roses!' He mimicked my turns of phrase and Arslan's (diversely stilted), but his grammar was pure Kraft County.

Fishing was better. 'Later he may hate me,' Arslan had said to me. 'There will be hard times for him.' But Sanjar would croon his little wordless songs and jiggle contentedly the line I had set for him, or sink absorbed into some private game at the water's edge, while I gazed bemused on the running ripples, a little eased to think that the brown cowponds of Kraft County were moved with the urges of the Pacific. The wavelets of these flowing breezes, baffled on every side, were the very image of those immeasurable surges swept by the Trades around the endless curve of ocean. And I would gaze until, broken from my roots, I felt myself, and the bank I sat on, running like a ship athwart the motionless ripples.

But if motion was relative, could it be real? And anchored by doubt, my bank would brake abruptly, and the ripples run again. Drop fused with drop, the inseparable crumbs of water swung in their trivial orbits, here as in the open sea, a fall for every rise, a retreat for every advance, no particle escaping its tiny province; so that what flung itself at last, heaping and rending, against the helpless shore, was not a thing so much as a force. It was like the headlong incessant lunge of mankind, transmitted by the feeble and frustrated circlings of an infinity of atoms, unendurable in its strength.

That was what made Arslan unique, human but not merely human. How could he be a bobbing droplet in the waves, he who was himself the waves embodied? He would sweep on, carrying all before him, pounding the wreckage of his enemies against the stubborn cliffs of earth until they crumbled at last and the restless waves swept past. He and his own.

Queen of the universe; mistress of its sole master, mother of its sole heir. Tenderness aside, Rusudan stood now, in Kraftsville as never in Bukhara, within the full circle of Arslan's embrace. They were comrades, bound by a kinship deeper than love, bonded by Kraft County's alien fields. And I, disconnected and withering on my home soil, felt here as never there the stifled anguish of the concubine. Laden with Arslan's disregard, goaded by Rusudan's contempt, I plodded my treadmill way, deeper into desperation. Dutifully I uttered my drops of useless treason (what could I tell Nizam that Arslan did not already know?) and dutifully begrudged them. For the sponge remains wet, the last drops are always unexpressed.

It was possible to look into the chill air for a long time without realizing that rain was falling. Only the whitish blurring of a thin mist intervened, like a dingy windowpane, between eye and landscape. Then, refocused, the ever-falling drops showed faint and cold, like delicate beaded chains sliding and slanting across the blue.

Again, it was spring. Weary and irreversible, again the world heaved round. Autumns were falsely sad, patting the fat tears of success. But spring rose always again like a beaten fighter stumbling from his corner for still another round. There was nothing to say to the universe; it *was*; one could only turn away.

But could not. I breathed, and the air was spring. In Karcher's woods, the trees stood definite and angled as black crystals; yet a scattered few were hazed with mists of color that showed, through the white rain, uncertain as illusions – faint green, fainter pink, like the pastels of an impressionist. I stood under the stable eaves, leaning and waiting. Arslan might come with Sanjar, to ride in the young rain. Or might not. And my mouth made the small, standard smile of acknowledgment, for I felt the weed of hope rising again, for one more spring.

20

Rusudan lay dead on Franklin Bond's couch. Awkward with fear, an apprehensive covey of women jostled behind Arslan. He had sent the guards beyond the doors. He bent deliberatively over Rusudan and began to strip her of her clothes.

First one, then two, then all, the women shrilled. They wavered; the boldest stepped forward to offer help. Arslan turned on her with a voiceless animal sound, lips shrunk back from his teeth, and she dissolved into wailing cries. He bent again to his work. The women swayed and shrieked, willows with tambourines and sirens. What did it express, this racket of anguish? Perhaps nothing more or less profound than their ache to perform the last offices of their mistress. Perhaps grief, certainly shock. I was shocked myself.

He examined her very thoroughly, and he took care not to obstruct our view of her. Or was 'it' the proper term for one so emphatically dead? No; Rusudan was unalterably female. For the first and last time I saw her naked, and the sight stirred something within me, though not (as I had mildly dreaded) necrophilia. I was surprised by the broad aureoles of her nipples; I was impressed by the solid curves of her breasts; and I was strangely touched by the dark turf of hair, scanter than I had expected, at the vulnerable meeting point of thighs and belly – the tender crotch where Arslan's hands had lain, into whose recesses he had rubbed himself with the authority of love. Now he soberly examined the dead flesh for bruises. It was with a kind of medical-student coarseness that he flopped her broken limbs. And with each manipulation of the silent corpse the women screamed, as though Rusudan's nerves functioned now in them.

When he had finished, he went to one of the women – the nearest, and also the oldest, who keened a desperate and ritualistic cry – and struck her. She tumbled backwards, all dignity abased. He said to me, moving his mouth laboriously, like one to whom speech returns as a lesson forgotten, 'Bring in two men.' I stepped onto the porch. 'The general wants two men,' I told the Turkmens in English. It would have been presumptuous now to present myself as anything more than conquered alien. They were accustomed to me as Arslan's messenger, but they gave me this time the hard looks that uniforms were invented to authorize, the looks that warned, *Everything you have ever said is already held against you.*

Arslan had covered what he could of Rusudan with the filthy dress he had peeled from her. 'For Colonel Nizam,' he said, consigning the women with a gesture. One guard escorted them. Arslan turned to me. 'Tell me everything. Everything. Everything.'

Far less prepared for this inevitable moment than for that of death, I felt my eyes go wide, my tongue stiff. All my innocence and ignorance, so valid a minute before, crumbled and evaporated, and I was cowering again in Bukhara, incompetent even in guilt. Stumblingly I told him everything I could remember or imagine that might serve, not to solve his mystery or assuage his pain (helpless with fear, I had instantly forgotten that such purposes might exist), but to protect me from his violence. His eyes blazed out of some distant enmity. He listened, he questioned, and at the end, 'Upstairs,' he said to the remaining guard, nudging his head at me. It was the command I had known a hundred times before I understood it literally and grammatically. I was surprised that my heart did not grow cold at the sound of it. But I was chill enough already.

So again I sat the long hours on the bed's edge, listening, drifting. But I was older now, and knew how to hope for a better thing – that when reality came through the door again, it would be with what I had earned, the possibility of contact, of mutuality. So that when in fact it came, nights later, after Arslan's hands and heels had wrought the execution that was, for a time, to lose him Kraftsville, there was another hope to be crushed down.

He came to me, those nights, with the unplanned, unplanning, conscious intensity of an elemental. I remembered that démodé phrase, 'crime of passion,' and understood it in a new light, glaring and garish. For they were crimes that he wrought upon me in the narrow room that had been Mr Bond's son's, crimes in intent and therefore in effect. It was not sadism, in the pure sense, that struck me from my waiting sleep and wrenched my joints into a new and still a new distortion; it was revenge, that Satanistic atonement. He pressed from me not only the immemorial noises of the wounded, but speech, but argument. For I was wounded by his cruelty, but I was outraged by his unreasonableness. It was not appropriate to Arslan to snarl accusations, to sneer insults. Threats were something else again; but it was wrong for him to whisper them. 'Your mother, too – she is one of them. I will deal with her personally – personally. Do you wish me to tell you how?' I lay quietly outside my listening body and waited for him to finish, to sleep, to go away, to kill me. 'Do you think that you are one of them, Hunt? Wait, wait until they have drained you dry. I protect you now, while you plot with them, while you crawl on your belly to do their errands, and pour for them your little drops of information. But wait, wait until I throw you to them, these jackals. When they have finished with you, *then* I will destroy them. And perhaps I will take what is left of you again. Perhaps.'

Those nights, he broke upon me like a tempest, waves of lust and fury that overran each other and died not in satisfaction but in collapse. I was roused and tumbled, buffeted with the excitement of the gale that is past pain and near to glee. And in the spent surf of such a dying storm he turned on me a look of so much gentleness that I sank, desolate, forlorn past hope at last. He cared for me; somehow, in some sense, I was of importance to him, a subject for tenderness, a source of joy. Therefore I was lost.

21

Somebody's child came idling down Pearl Street, in grave pursuit of this season's resident tomcat; an older child than Sanjar, without Sanjar's aggressive grace. He looked apprehensively at the raw palings of the new fence – fences were not common in Kraftsville – drubbed his fingers experimentally along them for a moment, and stooped for a throwing stone. The cat sprang without visible effort, like a sailplane rising on a sudden thermal, posed a brief second on the gatepost, and descended, ponderous and lithe, upon Franklin's front walk. The boy flung his stone side-armed toward the other side of the street and trotted past. The cat paced halfway down the walk, turned, seated himself, and began to wash. He was impressive in rear view – thick-necked and chunky-shouldered, like Arslan.

'What do you call that one?' Franklin's memory for the names of cats was short.

'Bruce,' I said huskily. 'Robert the Bruce.'

'I'm glad we put the fence in.' He ran his hand approvingly along the porch rail and turned back toward the front door. 'You call me when you get that paint mixed, and I'll help you paint it.'

What was it Hesse had said in *Der Steppenwolf*? Something in scorn, or perhaps in envy, of the Faust who complained merely because he had two souls struggling within his breast. (Every book I read had seemed to me momentarily the fated answer to my question, before I learned that literature was an insignificant sham, shallow to its very depths – that there was no vicarious experience, none; that I knew nothing I had not felt in my own flesh.) One of the sparse benefits of having an indefinite number of souls was that one or more of them could find some glint of silver in almost any catastrophic cloud. So that there was a small pleasure in being abandoned by Arslan, an enemy alien in my home town. It was challenging. It had its aspects of unaccustomed freedom, somewhat like being parachuted alone into a jungle. I did not realize at once that he had exactly fulfilled his threat; he had thrown me to the jackals.

One thing I had already learned: it was useless to ask for help unless you didn't really need it. There were no free gifts possible in a functioning universe. Those who gave, took payment; and as the truly helpless had nothing to tender but their helplessness, they could pay only with their suffering, or (if they had the luck to petition a lover of responsibility) their dependentness. Long ago I had asked for help, in every way possible to me, from Mr Bond – this at a time when I was in physical pain and spiritual anguish and simple desperate daily fear of death, while he, my host and my principal (ex officio protector and automatic father image), was the only man in Kraftsville with will and power to stand against Arslan. I had begged for mercy (surprising how readily one was reduced to begging for mercy, that contemptible self-confession of schoolbook dastards) from Arslan himself. And I had received, in response or in inattention, kindly exhortations to have courage (I would have been glad to have it) and sweetly mocking laughter. (But Mrs Bond, from whom I had asked nothing, had given me egg-nogs and offered me hot compresses; and though I had gagged on the first and declined the second, I appreciated their practicality. It was, however, vain.) I had asked for bread from my father, and he had given me a stone. Only much later, when my soul had healed and grown strong, like the terrible cripples of folklore, did I receive what I no longer required.

Therefore now I pressed my tenders with the firmness of desperation. I must run with the jackals or be torn. Arslan had taken all and given all; but Franklin Bond did not batten upon suffering. To him and his KCR I offered myself as a non-aligned Mephistopheles, one of hell's rejects, a useful servant at a minimum wage. To my parents I presented myself politely as the independent son, in business for himself but well disposed toward his origins.

I saw them, now, merely as two more citizens of Kraftsville.

They had made their own adjustments. My father was a pillar of the respectable branch of the non-KCR anti-Arslanists (so far had sectarianism advanced). As such he had weathered the variable gales of the past years, unscathed, secure in his harmless intransigence. He was Kraftsville's independent lawyer. Arthur Kitchener (tenuously, if at all, related to the equally notable Leland) was the KCR lawyer, and Greeley Simms had once been Nizam's entry, until the KCR had quietly bankrupted him.

In turn ravished, perverted, abandoned, and brutalized, the school stood dirty and forlorn. Undismayed, my mother went on teaching. She had gathered two classes of vocal students, separated by age, and gave private lessons in piano and a few other instruments. Things wore out, things atrophied; and yet so much of Kraftsville remained, essentially intact.

'Come see my primary chorus, Hunt. You know, the little ones really have better voices than the older kids; it's always that way. Your dad will be home for lunch, and then you can stay and listen till you get bored.' And so I lunched with them, and stayed and listened. The children arrived promptly, in clusters, obviously experienced pupils – feral out of doors, noisy but tractable as soon as they crossed the threshold. It was true that their voices had not yet lost the sweet clarity that their souls, being human, had never had; and she had schooled them into a lusty approximation of accuracy and order. They sang 'John Peel' and 'Auld Lang Syne' and 'I've Been Workin' on the Railroad.' They sang, pristinely as an inspiration:

> Oats, pease, beans, and barley grow,
> Oats, pease, beans, and barley grow.
> Do you, or I, or anyone know
> How oats, pease, beans, and barley grow?

I stayed longer than I had expected. They sang 'America the Beautiful.'

How long since I had heard that song, or any such song? At least ten years, it must have been. I tried to recall some real or plausible last occasion from my disintegrated memories of the

Time Before, and could not. And since that lost last time, my ears had been filled with the sad, wild anthems of the sterile plateaus.

> Oh, beautiful for heroes proved
> In liberating strife,
> Who more than self their country loved,
> And mercy more than life.

And suddenly a real beauty trembled vainly up from the foolish words, and I was homesick, soulsick, for those alabaster cities that had never been and would never be. There people lived whose right name was *patriots*, and fed upon the golden wine of pride, the snowy bread of love. But there had never been a past from which that future might have come.

Had there been? I had been a child, too young to do anything real, too young really to understand; and when I began to understand, and to be old enough, it was too late for doing. That was easy to say. *They* should have done it: the grown-ups, the genuine citizens, the ones with the newspapers from which to understand and the votes and money with which to act. But that was too easy. Every citizen had had his own helplessness. Where had the power been? Could there be responsibility without power? Free will without free action? The responsibility and the power were easy to locate now; Arslan had taken them upon himself. (Unto himself? What was the word? *The king, the king's to blame.*) But taken them from where – from whom? Children and ignorant, we had been responsible then, I as much as any. We should have understood. We should have found a way to act. If we had not, that was our fault, not Arslan's – our fault not collectively, but individually. I was to blame for Arslan.

We have turned every one to his own way. And the Lord hath laid on him the iniquity of us all. We were free now; the drunken freedom of the slave, of the cog, of the world rolling in its orbit. Our sins were as white as wool. But I shook with belated anger at myself, at all other lethargic cowards and all zealous imbeciles. *Mock mockers after that, Who would not lift a hand maybe . . .* Was one responsible for the past? Could there be any responsibility for what did not exist? I had been responsible *then*, when no one had called me to answer. Now I was ready to present my true account (One talent: Lodged with me useless); and the books were already closed.

Oh, beautiful. This woman who had been my mother, honorable and brisk, freckled but tidy – was it still beautiful for her? Possibly so. Mrs Jean Morgan, last surviving singer of 'America the Beautiful.' I looked at her, with her mouth vigorously open, and I was touched. She was a kind and honest lady. The cruelties and falsehoods she had inflicted on me were no more than the duties of motherhood. *I did love you once.* Kind lady, she would do better to forget that beauty. These were the last children, loud and docile, with their uncertain throats and visionary eyes, that she would have to teach; and already these were not Americans. Where but in bitterness could she lodge all that good will and courage, when the children were gone and the beautiful stillborn nation was forgotten? *Why wouldst thou be a breeder of sinners?*

It was with the Bonds that I lived on familial terms, in various senses. I was not yet the household menial – that was to come later – but I was Franklin's instrument in his gestures of worried kindness toward his wife. 'Hunt, would you carry out that laundry for Mrs Bond?' On the other hand, she fulfilled for me (as, I increasingly thought I saw, for Franklin) the role of devoted and honored servant, privileged to criticize, to manage, and to share, but neither to initiate nor to command. It was the sort of personal relationship that one might have with a beloved animal, and in that way, I concluded, very like most maternal relationships.

Between her husband and me, the intimacy was of a different order. (It did not occur to me to be surprised that it had not, apparently, occurred to Kraftsville to impute any variety of improper relationship to us. Such unsuspicion was a tribute, from Kraftsville and from me, to the force of Franklin Bond's character, or at least reputation.) For a long time now, I had argued with him from the privileged position of the favored graduate student. But our daily contacts were on a rawer and more urgent level. Who was to water the horses? How were the corn borers to be stopped? Why was the septic tank in danger of overflowing – and what, and by whom, was to be done about it? And after Mrs Bond had failed us for the first time, by inconsiderately allowing herself to die, all our dealings were aggravated and exasperated. The last courtesies crumpled from our theoretical discussions as the last distances were squeezed out, and though 'I never argue about religion' was one of his mottoes, we were more and more embroiled in savagely impatient disputes on immortality, the nature of dogma, the roles of reason and revelation. I could recall only darkly a time when I had believed in some divinity; and yet I found myself beginning so many heated sentences with 'Granted the existence of God . . . ,' shifting my ground again and again and yet fighting for every inch of that batable and marshy terrain. In mundane matters, he was as shrewd an organizer as Arslan (if a more open and unsubtle one) and scarcely less hard a master. Irregularity offended him, neither abstractly nor practically, but in his personal feelings. An esthetic reaction, perhaps. Or a memorial of affection. Mrs Bond had been regular. I was not. 'I thought we'd agreed that if we're going to keep this house together, we've *both* got to do our jobs!' I bowed before his dams as before Arslan's floods.

Yet sometimes, unexpectedly, Franklin touched me with a perceptive kindness. 'Where have you been, Hunt?'

My clothes were saturated with dust, my eye swollen all but shut, my shirt torn and a little messed with blood. 'Walking,' I said, 'in the corn.'

I liked to walk in the corn. From August on, when the great stalks stood higher than my head, the corn fields were a world apart, a world aloof and alien as pale Bukhara. I walked in the corn alone, or sometimes with a dog as a convenient switch by which to connect myself now and then with reality. After a late-summer rain, the field steamed. I walked in a dense green heat, my feet in the mud, my body and soul washed with sweat. Midges and mosquitoes twinkled. My ears hummed. And all around me the enormous grass-leaves hung and crowded, rubbing their moist rough blades against my clothes, shouldering and slapping as I pushed through the rows, spilling their drops upon my hair.

But it was in waiting autumn that I liked best to walk in the corn. It was dry then, colored like the yellow dust, a gold without luster. The blades still curved and drooped in the easy postures of life; but with every stir of air they clashed faintly, a sound of thin brass. Their edges cut, cruel grating cuts like those of stiff paper. I paced slowly through the dusty stillness, surrounded, surrounded – ahead, behind, to left, to right, above – by the great tawny leaves, alone in the harsh ripe corn.

I was teaching myself to see and hear in the dim world of the corn, as Arslan had taught me in the woods, and in the dazzling nights and colorless days of Bukhara. In the lion-colored noonday dusk of the corn, the eye lost itself. The brazen rustling had the very quality of silence. It was easy to drift in a hot, buzzing dream, down aisles cross-laced with ragged swords. But I was learning. So I heard, in the unresonant clangors that ran like muffled alarms through the corn with the changing breeze, a more purposeful rustle. I stood at gaze. Ahead, behind, the tall files closed in. The blades clashed. The bronze shadows crossed and waved. I walked on, stirring the blades carefully out of my way.

Again. But this time it was the wind. Again. A mist of gnats hung quivering in the heat. Dogs ranged sometimes in the corn. I waited.

He was two rows away from me, a dark shape without outline. I wiped my hand carefully and drew Arslan's knife. One row. It was the dark Russian uniform. I stood with the knife held behind me. He stepped into my aisle, four yards away, perhaps. I had seen him before, I thought – a middle-aged lieutenant, big-eared and stupid-faced. I discarded my experimentally friendly greeting. All doubts were removed by the light in his pale eyes, the clubbed pistol in his red hand.

The corn slashed at me as I ran – head down, to save my eyes from the blades and my feet from the roots. I heard, over the pounding of my steps, the slower pounding of his. It seemed not unnatural to be hunted in the corn, and it seemed to follow (seemed, with the distorted clarity of heat waves) that if I could escape from the corn, the hunt would be over.

A stunning shock thudded my back, between my right shoulder and the base of my neck, a blow outrageously hard and heavy. I was scrabbling angrily in the hot-smelling dust. He must have thrown the gun at me; ergo, the gun was somewhere near. But my right arm refused to act, my neck and shoulders were heavy as stone. I heaved myself over, seeing the prop roots of the near

217

stalks standing out like flying buttresses. The Russian plunged upon me like a falling cloud, and I realized that I had lost the knife.

I was initiated long since in the actuality of physical contact; it was old familiar business, serious, deliberate, and there could be nothing more real. He had the advantages of weight and position. But I had been thrown by Arslan. I knew all the art of the underdog.

He had my left wrist. Before he could gain the right, I got a grip on his left thumb, and bent, and as his right hand twisted and crushed, we strove in mutual torture. With furious joy I felt my wrist spring free. I writhed, gouged, suffered his clubbing fist. I was tipped – folded, rather – upon my side, my still-free hand (the immediate jewel of my soul) crushed under our double weight. He pulled busily at my clothes. My left eye was in the dust; my right contemplated a blond cornstalk. A terrific decision enacted itself: *no!* And I exploded in the self-forgetful fury that had burst me in the beginning so long ago. And though it had failed me then (even in total war somebody loses), now the Russian hunched backward off me, grunting. I spraggled up to knees and elbows. Arslan's miraculous knife winked in the dust. My hand sprang to meet it, and I crouched and panted.

He backed away, shaking his head, grinning, stumbled on his gun (to each his own), paternally dusted and holstered it, and disappeared gradually through the successive curtains of the corn, still backing, still grinning, still shaking his head.

I tidied myself triumphantly. My nose was bleeding. (*Had he his hurts before? Ay, on the front.*) I sat among the shattered stalks and nursed it patiently, while the long shafts of sunlight broke among the corn.

Franklin looked at me with care. He didn't ask, 'What happened?' He didn't ask, 'Who was it?' He didn't ask even, 'Are you all right?' He set his chin and turned away into the kitchen, his back broad to my gratitude. 'Why don't you wash up,' he said, 'while I fix the fire?'

Winter came, passed, with the beautiful ashes of wood fires under the grate, to be carried out and shed like hushed snow-flakes or blessings on the frigid earth; with dried corn, hard and dimpled, the seeds that could not sow themselves (corn, that hapless species, reproducing only by the service of man). The deer pushed thicker into the easy browsing of the fields and fencerows, and were shot with our clumsy arrows. And the Russians departed, sudden and noisy as a migration of purple martins, with great pretense of secrecy. Spring came, speciously wholesome, feeding eyes and tongues while winter-lean bellies grew leaner still. Merely, winter rains changed to spring rains. Yet it was true that the skewed earth thrust us ever deeper, for a time, into the sunshine; and it was presumable that these green shoots would bear again the golden fruits of their fathers.

After the long, vague days of mist, I loved the sleek sky; loved especially the clear and brilliant clouds, truest white on their heights and ridges, shadowing their own slopes with the blue of ashes. They stood pure and definite like piled snow, unneatly firm as some engraving by William Blake. What had Blake said about line? Outline is reality. He had said it Blakishly, of course. Standing in far air, the real clouds shone and shadowed. But at close range they would be edgeless, lineless – a vague mist, obscure and obscuring. Yet that very obscurity was the sum of myriad surfaces, the entangled glitter of a billion crystal spheres, each comprised in a bounding line of mathematical trueness and demonstrable reality; so that (unless, as was probable, my grasp of Newtonian physics was infirm) the slovenly gray of Kraftsville's mists and heaven's exploded clouds was only, in generalized form, the radiant precision of the misty rainbow.

I watched the nobility of the ranked clouds, passing, with that stateliest motion perceivable by human eyes, across the high hemisphere of Heaven. *Oh, lift me as a wave, a leaf, a cloud.* Well, it was not the thorns of life that had drawn my blood, and I was, to all perception, tame, slow, and humble; but certainly I could feel my leaves falling. (Oops, there goes another – hectic red, that one.) *Drive my dead thoughts over the universe Like withered leaves to quicken a new birth.* Alas, poor Shelley. It took more than withered leaves. And no doubt Pluto, as much as Earth, had its forever-sequent spring.

Patterns of leaves upon the wind, billowing flights that went nowhere, sails of green lace that moved nothing, moved me. Through March and April I drifted, my horse unguided, along fencerows and woods' margins. *As burnist silver the leaf onglidez That thick con trill on everich bough.* The little leaves, furred with their delicate birthcoats, colors of silver, colors of wine, and the heart-touching innocence of young green, misted the great elastic branches that surged and sprang in ponderous sweeps above my head. Every species had its shape – the lifting fountains of the dying elms, the broad layered pyramids of oaks, the rustic bouquets of the little blossoming redbuds. Already the eager maples spread broad leaves, like flocks of green stars, upon the wind.

They were not my friends, the trees. My friend was the chestnut horse that moved under me, warm in the sterile air. But I admired the trees, those static galleons, rooted like me in the graves of their ancestors. They drank the traveling air, the dead radiance of a star. They shadowed their shapes upon the passing wind and light. Every leaf held its place, a stitch of the tapestry, disordered by every breeze, primly returning with every calm. And when at last it fell, its one flight, spinning and beautiful, bore it to the grave of its birth. Year by year the epicycles wheeled. The trees remained. They bent; they broke at last; but they did not budge.

Under the trees, my chestnut's hooves among the thick gold stars of dandelions, I took relief in the slow, traveling spiral of the world, the great pacific resultant of how many billion impassioned problems, the moving equilibrium of all forces. Humanity was a plague. Locustlike, we ripped holes in the world's fabric. The locusts met their controlling limits – birds and starvation, fungi and disease – and the fabric healed itself; and mankind had met Arslan. But as the plague was more ravaging, so the control was more drastic.

Passive and exquisite as the fretwork of Taj Mahal, the viruses laid their irrefutable pattern upon the world. Whatever we saw was through that screen. Yet by what perversion of language was *passive* the opposite of *active*? The viruses did not suffer, did not allow, were not done to. It was they that, without action, performed: performed their existence and their replication upon the struggling active world. Passive, impassive, unpassional, they cancelled the activity of passion. And passionate men who suffered and inflicted would, marked with that multiplying pattern, vanish in incorrigible uniqueness.

Royal in nothing else, I forgot nothing, I learned nothing. All my meditations moved around him, returning to their premises unimproved. Other things faded, leaves in seasonal decline; the trunk remained, imperceptibly enlarged, armored in fissuring scabs.

'I have made you ashamed,' he had said. *Shame* was a trivial word for it. He had looted me of boyhood, manhood, freedom. The key to my door was in his pocket. 'But someday, Hunt, you will be able to say, "Arslan is my friend." And you will be proud.'

He would be drunk when he said these things to me – the real drunkenness that closed down upon him after the second bottle was opened, when for a moment anger flickered in his eyes and he weighed once more the hazards of uncontrol in the scales of his enormous *Realpolitik*, and relaxed with a small but total shrug. Or it would be passion, the real desire that was to his everyday lust as moon to morning star. 'There is a woman that I have loved.' His look was luminous, his hands as steady as a singing string. 'Do you understand?' No, I did not understand. 'That was a year ago – eight thousand miles away. But I shall see her again. And if I love her again, that will be good. That will be good, Hunt.' I did not understand, I could not conceive, what such a verb as *love* might mean to Arslan. Had he held her, that fabulous woman, against his square, blunt body, and said into her ear the actual words, 'I love you'? No; it would have been another language, eight thousand miles away. What language – and what intonation? Had he looked into her eyes? But he would not have spoken. Lying with his bare feet cocked on the bedpost, his drink neatly clasped on his belt buckle, 'I have been afraid to father a child,' he said. His seed was sown like the cottonwoods'; battalions of his children must have sprung already from the raped planet. 'Because I loved her.' *Father*, then, was a word he understood better than I. But *afraid?* 'Rusudan,' he said. 'Her name is Rusudan.'

Love. The word became transparent to me, and I saw it empty

of all signification. A sound so used and misused should have had a multitude of meanings – contradictory, by nature, imprecise, but real. Yet it stood in my mind as uncontaining as a nonsense syllable, and I puzzled seriously and honestly at it. Verb transitive: *I love* – but what, or whom? No feeling I could find or imagine in myself seemed to couple me as subject appropriately with any object.

Rusudan. They were syllables in a void, and yet the name was dark with meaning and power. He would not have spoken to Rusudan of friendship. Did I want ever to say, 'Arslan is my friend'? No; I wanted him in some relationship utter and forthright – lover or master or enemy – nothing so complex and temperate as a friend.

Yet it was Arslan and Rusudan who put content into that dry vessel for me at last; so that, returned from Bukhara, I could tell Franklin Bond, 'I love him.' They were complete, those two, each alone; but when they touched, they struck fire. That was what I saw; and what my greedy heart asserted (I can *so* ride no hands, and my bike is just as fast as yours) was, *I can feel that, too.*

My place in the pattern of things was, apparently, to serve beside the throne, one of the perquisites of royalty in Kraft County. Franklin had inherited, by force of some cosmic law of survivorship, the position for which he had been born, meshing the rusty gears of civilian government to the subterranean motor of his KCR. But his ambition was closed in its own nutshell. His kingdom was an enclave in the unbounded universe of Arslan's curved world.

It was after Mrs Bond's death that my floating position in Kraftsville solidified (obscure insect in posture of flight, suspended for inspection in clear plastic). It was more than a year later, after the troops' withdrawal, that the last veils fell away from it. I was (since the Russians, faithful in their fashion, had taken the brothel with them) the only visible vestige of Arslan's regime. I had notably failed to repudiate him and all his works. I had declined the helping hand of Kraftsville custom. I was queer. Neither my parents' virtue nor my patron's power could shield me from the fallout of outraged propriety. There was a certain civility in my reception by the adult population, ranging coldly from the Cut Courteous through the Snub Outright. My horses were less fortunate.

The first was shot from ambush, and I assumed that the arrow was meant for me. Indeed, perhaps it was – the local standard of accuracy was not high – and the campaign may thus have launched itself accidentally. The second was lamed by a simple pit-trap. Then I understood, and became cautious. It was months before the third was killed, and that by a somewhat desperate night attack whose perpetrator I almost caught. (But the mare was crying, her belly slashed, and in Arslan's absence I had forgotten the trick of turning from one pain to inflict another.) Winter favored me; but with the spring my last mare and her foal were hamstrung, and a little later the four-year-old chestnut I had bought from the Munseys was poisoned. I was resigned. I would keep no horses that year. Next year I would be ready; I studied my defenses and began, very slowly, to prepare my counter-offensive. But with rich September came Arslan, and touched me with his marred right hand.

He stayed for four weeks and three days, an exact month of the calendar. And closely and distantly, in and out of focus, I considered him. Sometimes he presented himself to me as a mathematical diagram, the Platonic idea of Arslan, sometimes as a reality of close and radiant flesh. He was, take him for all in all, a man – *menschlich-allzumenschlich* – and I was also, oddly enough, a man.

When he went, there was no talk of my going with him. What was perhaps the first genuine and independent action of my life was wholly negative, passive, and imperceptible – all the more genuine for that. Out of turmoil and dread, joy of Leila, jealousy of Sanjar, I collected a quietness, I enacted a decision: I did not choose to go with him.

Sanjar and Leila were all his household now. I had canceled Rusudan, as she me, and that in itself was a victory more honorable than triumph. For the first time I began to see the past as past, the future as possible. The probability that he wanted me with him approached the infinitesimal, but that was irrelevant. I did not choose to go; *therefore* he would not ask, still less command me. Hourly, momently, my world refocused, my eyes blinked off dry tears and fading illusions. I acknowledged truth after truth – the shabby usefulness of his depleted regiment (pockets of fertility, unarmored and feebly arrowed, lurked in the dilapidating jungles of a broken world), the convenience of Kraftsville (a road, a memory; rest and recreation, the playing out of games), the aptness of his shrunken meiny and shriveled hand (the perfect end of Arslan's success must be inglorious).

It was a wholesome feeling. I had made the elementary discovery that marked, perhaps, the beginning of maturity as of childhood: *This is myself. I am separate.*

Through that month, knowing that he would go but not knowing how soon, I schooled myself for his departure. It was educational. I understood now how deeply I had counted on his return, and what little grounds I had had to expect it. Like a jilted lady of romance, I had staked my life on the farthest of outside chances, resigned myself with enthusiasm to a oneway journey into the ultimate pale realms of fantasy. He had come and halted me. He had put a body of solid flesh into my bed – and if it was not his body, it was all the more certainly real. He had come, and refocused the world for me, and he would go again. So far was certain. But not even the most heterodox predicted a third corning.

PART 3
FRANKLIN L. BOND

22

I came downstairs one morning before sunrise and heard movements in the kitchen. The dog had barked earlier, but not as though something was wrong. Still, it wasn't often Hunt was up before me, and these days anything was possible, so I came along as quietly as I could and just looked around the corner of the door.

'Good morning, sir.'

It was Sanjar. He stood beside the window, looking very straight and small. It was too dark to see his face, and he had grown, but I knew him by his voice and the way he held himself. 'Where's Arslan?'

'Not very far from here. He wants to know if you can hide us for about two weeks.'

I came in and reached for the candle we kept on the table. The cracks of the stove showed red; Sanjar must have built up the fire.

'No light yet,' he said, and as neat as you please he whisked the candle up before my fingers touched it, and stepped back out of reach behind the table. 'Nobody must know except you and Hunt.' He hesitated. 'Arslan wants me to tell you he's *asking* you. He wants me to tell you he says, "Please." ' He held the candle clasped against his chest.

'What's the trouble?'

'It's not trouble. We're on our way north, Arslan and me. We just need a place to rest awhile.' He set the candle down again, but he didn't let go of it.

'Who's he hiding from?'

Again he hesitated a little, before he said coldly, in his sweet, boy voice, 'That's the message. I've got to give him your answer.'

'Sanjar,' I said, 'take it easy. You know I can't give you an answer that means anything till you tell me a whole lot more. Now sit down and let me get you a drink of milk.'

'No, thanks.' But I heard him swallow.

'Well, sit down, anyway. Don't worry, I'm not asking you to give away any secrets. But I've got to know what happens if I say yes, and what happens if I say no.' He sat down. 'Now I'm going to slice us some bread.' In the darkness I didn't want to make any sudden moves he might interpret as hostile. He was only a child; but he was Arslan's child, and he was keyed up.

'If you say no,' he said softly, 'we'll go someplace else, that's all. If you say yes, I'll go get Arslan and we'll stay upstairs – or anywhere you want to put us. We can keep quiet. It'd be probably ten days.' He paused. 'We think nobody knows where we are.'

It was two years since they'd been in Kraftsville – seven, if you didn't count the month-long stopover on their way to South America, or wherever they really went. I wondered who the somebody was that had reduced Arslan to a fugitive in that time.

'And what if somebody finds out?'

He took a piece of bread from my hand. 'Then you might get hurt. But it's not likely.' He munched hungrily, but even so he was quiet about it.

'I'll tell you, Sanjar. If anybody came looking for you, this is about the first place they'd look. That's one thing. Another thing is, this is Hunt's home, too, and I can't speak for him. But the main thing is, I'm not even going to consider it unless I know what's going on – why he wants to come here and what he's planning to do. And maybe you can't tell me that.'

He put the bread down on the table and stood up. 'No, sir,' he said, but he didn't move to leave.

I stood up, too, and came around the table to him in three steps. 'Who's after him, Sanjar? Where are his troops?' I took him by the left arm. 'What's going to happen in ten days?'

He was Arslan's child, all right. Absolutely before I knew he was moving, I felt a hair-light touch on my wrist, and looking down in the dimness I saw the dull gleam of the knife in his right hand. 'Nobody's after him,' he said steadily. 'His troops are north of here. In ten days he'll be rested enough to go on.'

228

I didn't let go of my hold. 'What's happened? Why all the sneaking and hiding and begging favors? That's not like Arslan.'

I felt the knife-edge quiver against my wrist, but his voice was still steady. 'He's disbanded the armies.'

'What armies?'

'All of his armies. All of them.'

'You just said his troops are north of here.'

'Those are irregulars.'

I shook his arm just a little. 'What's happening up north of here, Sanjar?'

'There's a battle to be fought,' he said evenly. 'Maybe more than one. Now, that's all I'm going to tell you. If you don't let go of my arm in thirty seconds, I'll cut you.'

'Will you listen to me a minute if I let go?'

'Yes.'

I dropped my hand. 'You can tell Arslan this: I'm willing to hide *you*, Sanjar, for this ten days or so, but before I decide to hide *him*, I'd have to talk to him face to face.'

'I'll tell him.' He started melting away towards the window, but halfway there he stopped, silently poised. I listened, and heard Hunt's footsteps on the stairs.

It only took a few words; Hunt was always quick to understand a situation when he wanted to. 'Where is he?' His voice was rough with eagerness.

'Not far from here,' Sanjar said quickly.

'Is he wounded?'

'No.'

'Are you on foot?'

'No. Got a horse down the road.'

'Wait a minute while I saddle up.'

'No, Hunt.' The difference in their ages didn't matter, no more than it would have between brothers. They talked straight at each other, on the same level. 'He told me to come back alone.'

Hunt hesitated. 'You'll bring him here, then.'

'I'll tell him what both of you say.'

Hunt whipped around to me, looking for someplace to take out his frustration. 'He's *disbanded* the armies! I assume you know what that means. Can't you perform one generous act in your life?'

'Sure I know. He said himself there'd be revolts.'

Sanjar stepped between us, lifting his face towards mine. 'Listen, Mr Bond, I'll tell you something.' He spoke fast and low, every word stinging clear. 'He disbanded the armies because he was through with them. He's done exactly everything he planned to, one hundred percent. There's some trouble, yes. I can't tell you what, I'm under orders; but he's going to stop it. We got word some of his old troops are gathering, up north of here. He wants to get there before it comes to a battle. Sir, he *needs* rest. Sir' – he seemed to grow an inch or two with sheer intensity – 'do you think Arslan would be asking you just for – for *fun*?'

'I wouldn't expect it, but I can imagine it. What I can't understand is Arslan rushing north to stop a battle.'

'Stop it?' he cried, surprised. 'No, sir – win it!'

I had to laugh. 'All right, and after he wins his battle, Sanjar – then what?'

He didn't answer. Maybe he was considering what to say, or more likely it hadn't really occurred to him, up to now, that time would go on beyond the next battle. I put my hands on his shoulders and felt the skin-and-bones of him through his shirt. 'Is it Nizam?' He didn't say anything, but his shoulders stiffened. So Nizam was making his bid to take over – Nizam with his wolf's face, Nizam who had carried Sanjar in his arms and sworn to avenge Arslan's death by annihilating Kraft County. Another proverb turned out to be right – thieves' honor. I let go of the boy and stepped back. 'All right. Tell Arslan to come. I'll hide him.'

He swayed toward me a little – from gratitude, maybe, or else faintness – and then he sprang to the open window and poured over the sill like a shadow. We both looked cautiously after him. I saw him once, already near the shed, before he disappeared. 'That's quite a boy,' I said.

'Which room are you putting them in?' Hunt asked briskly.

We talked about that, and decided inevitably on Arslan's old room. The window was a reasonably good escape hatch, and they could hear something of what went on in the living room and keep an eye on the street and the Morrisville road. I went upstairs to get things ready, and Hunt went out to the well-house to fetch milk and butter and eggs and a bucket of fresh water.

I got back to the kitchen just in time to see them come through the window – a beautiful performance. Hunt stood by the cabinet, with his hands full of dishes. Arslan came straight on into the middle of the room and stood there like the king of the mountain. 'Good morning, General,' I said.

'Good morning, sir.' He turned to Hunt. 'Bring me food upstairs. Sanjar will help you.' This was his greeting after two full years of absence. I was a little sorry I hadn't decided to keep him in the shed. He passed me, heading straight for the stairs, with Sanjar hurrying in front. I followed, and Hunt trailed mutely after.

Pale daylight poured down the stairwell, and for the first time I got a good look at him. In the dark he was definitely Arslan, but I didn't know whether I'd have recognized him in the light, except by the crippled hand. He was sunburned nearly black, and he wasn't just thin, he was shrunken, like a fugitive from a prison camp. 'You've been sick.'

He laughed huskily. 'I *am* sick. This is why I have begged your bed, sir. You need not worry. It is not contagious, and I will not die on your hands. Not this time, at least. I want two things only, rest and nourishment.' He grabbed the bannister with his crippled hand, swinging from it like a boy swinging around a lightpole. Sanjar was halfway up the stairs, leaning anxiously on that same bannister. Arslan grinned at me like a death's head, swung himself back to the stairs, and mounted them slowly, with steady steps. Sanjar waited, all but quivering, till he reached him, and hovered at his elbow the rest of the way up. Hunt slipped past me and followed. They didn't need me. I went back to the kitchen to wait for breakfast.

Sanjar was right; it was ten days, almost to the hour. They had come through the kitchen window in the dawn of a Monday morning; and a week and a half later, a little before the dawn of the Thursday, they went quietly through the back door. Arslan brushed against me in the darkness, and I felt the heat of his lean body, still fired from the fourth bout of fever since he came. It had been a nervous ten days, but quiet. There were no alarms. He slept; slept night and day, apparently. Sanjar stood guard over him like a tame tiger. He ate. Maybe ten times a day and three or four in the night, Sanjar would materialize in the kitchen to carry away a bowl or plate full of the nourishing messes that Hunt continually stirred up. And in those ten days I never once saw Arslan. It was like having a ghost for a tenant. All the news of his progress came through Hunt from Sanjar. Hunt had washed and ironed Arslan's clothes, such as they were – the threadbare blouse and pantaloons of a peon. Sanjar had washed his own, in stages, borrowing a pair of Hunt's pants while his dried in the basement, belting them in to fit and rolling up the legs so that he looked like a boy playing pirate.

And now Arslan, hot with his fading fever but steady on his legs, brushed past me in the dark, and Sanjar slid through the door like a breath of night wind. Hunt stood shoulder to shoulder with me, occupying the space Arslan had vanished through. 'I'm going,' he said conversationally. 'Maybe I'll be back. Thanks.'

I stopped him with an arm across the door. 'What are you talking about?'

'I'm going with Arslan.' He paused. 'I didn't ask him. I'm not asking you. I own the horse.' Then, Huntlike, 'You can make a note of anything I owe you. If I live long enough, I'll be back to work it off.'

'You don't owe me anything, Hunt.' I dropped my arm. 'Good luck. Come back.'

'Thanks.' He passed me into the night. I watched till the three horses moved out of the shed, shadows in darkness, and then I closed the door and turned back into the lightless house.

The truth was that I missed Hunt. For one thing, I cared about him. And for another, he had been *there*, a human presence in the house. Now, for literally the first time in my life, I was living alone.

When Luella died, it was a terrific blow to me. And yet there was something in my feeling that surprised me. It was a while before I could even admit to myself what it was, and it was this, that I felt only a very little personal grief. As far as Luella herself was concerned, my overriding feeling was thankfulness that she had gotten out of it as easily as anybody could in these times. In the past years I'd watched her getting tireder and tireder, more and more discouraged and resigned, and I had grieved for that. Now the grief was relieved.

No, the real blow was entirely practical and selfish. Luella had kept everything running smoothly. No wonder she'd been tired. She had cooked and canned, washed and ironed, sewed and mended, swept and dusted and scrubbed, built fires and carried water; and hardest of all, she had coordinated all of those things, so that we never lacked for anything it was in her power to provide. And on top of everything else, she had helped with the garden and the chickens and the cow. She was even more a part of my life than I'd ever known.

The day after we buried her in the old Cedar Hill cemetery, I walked into the kitchen for the first time since she'd died. It was a real shock. The sink was piled full of dirty dishes. There were dirty pans on the stove and dirty napkins wadded up on the table. The whole place smelled of garbage and burned grease. 'Hunt!' I yelled. He came in hastily from the dining room. 'Look at this filthy mess! How did it happen?'

He shrugged. 'There's been nobody to clean up,' he said mildly.

I stared at him. 'But good Lord,' I said at last. 'It's only been four days. Three days.'

He shrugged again. 'This is what happens in three days.'

I couldn't stand to look at it. I went back to the living room, and Hunt followed slowly, closing the door behind us. I sat down and scrubbed my hands over my face. 'What about the women?' It seemed to me they'd been all over the place. When anybody died, now more than ever, the women friends and relatives would come over to do the cooking and cleaning and all of that.

He didn't answer at first, and when I looked at him he had an odd expression on his face, partly sly, partly defiant. 'Didn't they bring food?' I asked him.

He nodded. 'That's what you've been eating.'

'Didn't they offer to help out?'

'They offered.' He smiled a little puckered smile. 'I accepted some of the food, because I couldn't ask you to eat my cooking. But I didn't accept anything else.'

'Why not?'

'Because I've known for ten years where I stand with Kraftsville, but this is the first chance I've had to show Kraftsville where it stands with me.' He came a little farther into the room to face me better. 'I hate to bother you with this when you're in the midst of your own trouble. But since it's come up I'll just say that I'm ready to leave whenever you give the word.' He waited a moment and went on. 'But the only dealings I'm going to have with Kraftsville people from now on is to tell them to go to hell.'

'I'm Kraftsville people, too, Hunt.'

'Except you, of course. You've been very good to me.' But he said it oddly.

He had stayed, of course. He had turned out eventually to be a pretty good cook, and we had shared out the other household jobs between us. There was a certain toughness in Hunt, and along with his intelligence and his enormous coolness it made him a good manager, and sometimes a good worker. Nothing was too trivial, or too dirty, or too complicated for him to undertake. He didn't have to ask questions, and he had the initiative to start things on his own. The trouble was, he couldn't be relied on. He would drop a project in the middle, not from boredom exactly (it was never the really dull and monotonous jobs he gave up on), but because for some reason he suddenly lost the interest necessary for him to carry anything through. If he cared about a thing, he could be determined to the point of stubbornness.

There was no shortage of work to do. I'd kept my house and grounds up, and I meant to go on doing it. 'Your place looks like old times, Mr Bond,' Leland had said to me once. 'Got yourself a real old-time well-house now.' What Leland actually understood better than most people, though he might not have known how to put it, was that the way my place looked was modern now. Where too many people were letting things wear out and run down and just sit there, I got rid of the obsolete items and installed whatever would be useful from here on out. After the water system broke down, I had dug a good well and a complete septic tank system. A lot of people told me that if I wanted that kind of facilities I should have bought a country house that already had them; but I was damned if I was going to move out of my own house for no better reason than that. We had plenty of room, with the Carpenter lot. I'd had the KCR's help, of course, but Hunt had done all the calculations and his share of the manual labor – more than his share, because he worked faster than most. Hunt was no weakling. He might be slender-built, but there was nothing flimsy about him, and I noticed he took care to keep himself in shape.

He'd said he wasn't going to deal with Kraftsville people, but that turned out to be the exact opposite of the truth. In the last two years, starting from scratch and with all the odds apparently against him, he had built himself a very successful little business in horse-trading – a very exclusive business, too, because he dealt only in select breeding stock. It suited his restless temperament and his aloofness. He would ride far out of county to scout good prospects, and arrange deals sight unseen, acting as a go-between for men who'd never heard of each other. Then he'd ride off again with a string of his client's horses and come back leading a string of new ones. Everybody was amazed that Hunt had turned out to be such a good judge of horseflesh and such a shrewd and honest trader (he got very few real complaints, at least in Kraftsville), but the only thing about his success that surprised me was that he'd gotten so many people to trust him. I figured we could both be proud of that.

The horse-trading was all on his own, but I'd already done what I could to give him a livable position in Kraftsville. I didn't try to coddle him – that would have been no kindness – but I made it public knowledge that he was part of my family and a confidant in most of my business. After I was elected to my second term as County Supervisor and concurrently my first as Mayor, he served me as an unpaid private secretary, and I had let it be known before the election that he would do just that. Some people didn't like it.

'I stood by Hunt when his own father turned him out, Leland. He's not going to let me down.'

Leland tilted his head ruefully – a sort of sidling negative.

'Maybe not *you* he won't. But he don't seem to think he owes the rest of the county nothing.'

'He's working for me, not the rest of the county. And just what harm do you think he could do, anyway?'

'It ain't me,' Leland protested. 'It's just what I hear around town.'

'Well, what the hell do you hear? I know it's not you, Leland.'

'Well, you know there's still Russian troops up north, and God knows where all. It's not like the war was really over.'

I'd quit arguing about that word years ago. *War* was what people chose to call the state of abnormality Arslan had created. It was a shorthand way of saying that standard regulations didn't apply. 'All right, get it out, Leland.'

'Well, Arslan's someplace, and Nizam's someplace. Some people just figure Hunt's in a pretty good spot to spy on things.'

'On me, you mean – if he was going to spy on anybody. And I know damned well he's not going to spy on me. You just tell them to figure again, Leland.'

He pushed his scrap of a hat farther back on his shabby head. 'Yeah, I can tell them you vouch for him.' He grinned. 'And I don't reckon the Turks is much interested in Kraft County no more, anyway.'

'And another thing, Leland, you make it clear to everybody I'm not using any public funds to pay Hunt. That's a saving they'll see reflected in the next budget.'

But I paid him something, all right: I broke his mother's heart for him. He didn't quite have what it took to do the job single-handed. His father had been in poor health for some time, and Jean had taken to dropping in on the excuse of telling Hunt how Arnold was. Hunt was civil enough, but never much more. And after the elections, when, to give him his due, he had his hands pretty full of work, he began to be a little less.

'Could we just clarify something, Franklin?'

'We could try, at least.'

He was turning back from the door where he had just shown Jean out. His face was a little flushed and his lips a little tight – Hunt's irritated look. 'I'm curious to know just what are the visitation rights in this house.'

'I suppose any decent person is welcome here, if that's what you mean.'

'I see,' he said pettishly. 'In that case, where would you like me to do this work for you?'

Jean's visit had interrupted something, but it wasn't all that important. 'Now what do you want, Hunt?'

'It's what I don't want.' He went back to his chair, demure and gloomy.

'I could put it to your mother that you're very busy now, if that's what you really want.'

His head snapped up like a twanged spring. His voice quivered. 'I *want*. . . I *want* you to tell me you'll keep her out of here! Isn't the line drawable anywhere? Do I have to retreat to my bedroom for refuge? And how long before she'd be in there, too?' He grimaced in self-derision and beat the flat of his hand lightly on the chair arm. 'Yeah, yeah, yeah, I know, I know, you don't have to say any of it to me. Just let me submit that I've taken a lot of various things in my time, okay? And there are a few things that rightly or wrongly I can't take.' He bit his lips, and sat there still and collected, but trembling quietly all over.

I sucked in my breath impatiently. 'Exactly what do you have in mind, Hunt?' It was too bad it was his mother he just happened to be unable to bear, and I was well aware that he *let* himself tremble visibly, to demonstrate his earnestness. But that didn't make his trembling or his need any less real.

'It's your house.' Stubborn and meek.

'Hunt,' I said finally (I never knew how it was, but he could outwait me every time), 'I give you my word she won't enter this house while you're living here – unless you ask her to.'

Naturally, I didn't intend to put it to Jean in quite those terms, but she got it out of me anyway. She took it calmly, as Jean Morgan was bound to, but her face went deathly pale. 'All right, Franklin.' Her voice cracked a little. 'Don't tell me why. Let's just leave it at that.'

The house felt very empty, though Hunt had been a quiet person to live with. I fed his pets without enthusiasm. For a while – for years, in fact – I'd insisted on having no animals in the house, but when some people's hostility against Hunt had broken out in the form of attacks on his horses, I'd told him to bring his pets inside if he wanted to. (Not that every animal on the place wasn't a sort of pet to Hunt. He called the cow Lucinda. The old rooster was Saladin. Even the hens had names.) People who were capable of hamstringing a horse out of malice would do worse things to cats and dogs. That danger seemed to be past, now that Hunt was a practicing businessman; but I'd gotten used to the creatures – after all, it wasn't the pampered menagerie of Arslan's regime – and they had stayed. Now it was suddenly up to me to take care of them, and for Hunt's sake I did it.

I figured that 'north of here,' under the circumstances, was three or four days' ride from Kraftsville. If it were any closer, Arslan couldn't have resisted some kind of direct communication with his irregulars – always supposing they really existed. He would lose the third day in his next attack of chills and fever, unless he was fool enough to exhaust himself by riding with it. And, being Arslan, he'd make the most efficient use of his time; it was safe to assume he would give himself the maximum amount of rest, and arrive just in time to fight his battle before the next chill took hold. Of course, it might be farther north than that – another chill farther, or two or three; but Sanjar had given such an impression of immediacy, I was convinced otherwise. So I could begin the infuriating business of expecting them in a week and a half.

23

It was Sanjar again who came as scout in the darkness. This time he woke me. 'Sir! Wake up! Sir! A message from Arslan!' His light, sharp voice, hissing with urgency, entered my dream in the form of a knife thrust, and I woke up with the conviction I had been stabbed. He started back from the bed as I jerked upright. 'Sanjar, sir! A message from Arslan!'

The mists cleared away. 'What is it, Sanjar?'

'Arslan's sick, Hunt's wounded. Is it safe to bring them in?'

'Of course it is. How bad wounded?' I was out of bed and feeling for my clothes.

'Not so bad – a smashed leg. Horse fell on him.'

'Where are they?'

'In the shed.'

'Sounds like you pretty well brought them in already.'

But he was gone. I pulled on my pants, dug my feet into my moccasins, stuck a candle into my pocket, and felt my way downstairs. It was the dead of night. The back door stood open. I crossed the yard to the shed.

It was full of the smell of horses and the sound of their breathing. 'Hunt?' I said softly. His little dog was snuffling and fretting around our feet.

'Here,' Sanjar answered. He caught my hand and guided it to something solid.

'Hunt?'

'Hello, Franklin.' His voice was firm and sardonic. I ran my left arm under his right and got a good grip.

'Which is your bad leg?'

'The right. Otherwise known as the wrong. Let's go.'

I took most of his weight, and we staggered across the yard. I didn't let him pause till we had struggled through the open door and he could lean against the washstand. He was breathing in ragged gasps of pain and effort, and I could feel him sweating. 'Damn it, where's Sanjar?'

'Let's go,' Hunt repeated tightly.

Even with Sanjar's help it would have been hopeless to try to get him up the stairs. I crutched him into the living room and over to the couch and let him painfully down on it. In the darkness I didn't want to fool with his injured leg; I hurried back to get a light from the cookstove embers and planted my candle on the coffee table. One little flame wouldn't show through the heavy curtains. Together we got the leg lifted and straightened on the couch. It had been crudely splinted and bandaged, but I could feel the bones grating as we moved it. He lay back panting.

'Okay for a minute, Hunt?'

'Very fine.'

I headed back through the kitchen again, ready to chew out Sanjar and maybe Arslan, too. A minute later I was helping them. It was too much to ask an eleven-year-old boy to carry a grown man, however emaciated. Sanjar had gotten him – part dragging, part supporting – almost as far as the door, and they were both exhausted. Arslan was just conscious enough to try to keep his legs under him. He was shivering in short spasms; you could almost hear his bones rattle.

Between us we manhandled him into the dark house and upstairs to his old bed. He was so light it gave me a peculiar chill feeling in the pit of my stomach. 'He's all yours,' I told Sanjar, and went back down to Hunt. 'Well, did you win it?'

'We won it.' He was looking studiously at the ceiling.

I went on through into the kitchen and brought him back a drink of water. He poured it down eagerly and gave me a shy sort of smile in the candlelight.

'I'm going for Dr Allard.'

'No.' He tried to raise himself.

'Relax, Hunt. You can trust Jack Allard as well as you can me.' I patted him back down on the couch and went out again by the back door. I hadn't gotten very far before Sanjar caught up with me. He ran like a hunting cat – low, and all but silent. I turned to meet him. 'What's the matter?'

He caught hold of my elbow. 'Don't get the doctor. I can take care of Arslan.'

'You can take care of him all you want to. I'm getting the doctor for Hunt.'

He hung on, and I half dragged him along. 'You mustn't let him know Arslan's here.'

'Don't worry, Sanjar. You can trust Doc Allard not to tell tales.'

'No!' he squeaked, his urgency too much for his young voice. He jerked at my arm, and I stopped again and faced him. The moon was down, but I could see that his face was twisted with earnestness. 'I can't even trust *you*!' he burst out. 'You see? You're going to tell the doctor!'

Under the circumstances I couldn't laugh at him. 'All right, Sanjar. My story is that Hunt came in with a broken leg and I went for help without waiting to find out how it happened. You hurry back to Hunt now and figure out a nice plausible lie. Don't forget he's got to explain how he got here alone on horseback.'

'Thanks! Thank you!' He melted back into the darkness.

The story Hunt told was sketchy, but not unbelievable. He had been thrown and dragged in the neighborhood of Reedsboro, where there was no doctor, and the Reedsboro people had given him the doubtful favor of an amateur bonesetting job and tied him to his horse. People would do things like that these days. It was a funny thing that Arslan's plan of independent communities really had taken effect in some ways. There were business trips like Hunt's, there was trade, and news filtered around fast enough; but by and large, people stayed in their own districts, and they didn't take in strangers.

When the doctor was gone, I made sure Hunt was as comfortable as he could well be and went upstairs. There was no answer to my knock. I opened the door and stepped into the dawn-lit room. A curious noise was going on, a continuous soft rustle punctuated with irregular rasping sounds.

'Sanjar?' I couldn't locate him for a few moments. Then I

looked at Arslan in the bed and found Sanjar, too. He had fairly plastered himself onto his father, his arms locked around Arslan's chest, his face profiled against Arslan's throat. He was looking sidelong up at me with a look I knew all too well, the look I had seen in the eyes of dozens of wastrel's sons as they faced their inevitable paddlings – the hopeless, utter defiance of the outlaw's child. The noise was coming from Arslan. He was shaking, shaking helplessly in the grip of his cold disease, and he was not conscious now. His breath came in noisy heaves. Sanjar had put everything available on him – sheet and spread, the blankets he must have found in the old dresser, his own hot body.

I looked at them for a minute. 'You're pretty proud of your father, aren't you?' He gazed at me with his steady desperation, the look that accepted hell. 'Let me know if you need anything,' I said.

Those were a peculiar three days. It was hard to get used to the idea that Arslan might very well die in my house. I had to plan burial arrangements without mentioning the possibility to anybody. As for his northward expedition, I'd heard nothing but Hunt's 'We won it.' The physical results didn't look very triumphal. Arslan himself had changed from a South American peasant's rags to an equally ragged uniform – anonymous khaki, totally without insignia. Maybe that was a step up.

Kraftsville was willing enough to do business with Hunt, but he wasn't what you could call socially popular. The silver lining of that was that we were spared the normal flood of neighborly visits and inquiries. Jean Morgan came, of course. 'He's doing very well,' I told her. 'He's comfortable.'

'May I come in?' We were standing in the open front door. Hunt was just out of sight at the far end of the living room.

'Jean,' I said, 'you know I can't go back on my word.'

She set her jaw and looked at me hard. 'I'd laugh, if I felt cheerful enough. Just tell me, Franklin, did you ever hear of a more ridiculous situation? My son is in there with a broken leg, and I'm here on the doorstep begging admittance.'

But begging was something Jean Morgan couldn't have done.

When she saw I meant what I said, she went away without more ado.

I stretched my charity to the point of offering Arslan, through Sanjar, a pair of my pajamas. They were politely declined. As before I saw nothing of Arslan, but this time I saw more of Sanjar. With Hunt immobilized, he undertook to do all the cooking, after he'd asked my permission very prettily. As a cook he was a little less than inspired, but about as competent as you could want for an eleven-year-old. He took whatever I brought into the kitchen, and inevitably he boiled it. We lived on nondescript gruels and unclassified stews. And while his pots simmered, Sanjar squatted or sat cross-legged beside Hunt's couch, deep in cheery discussion. I left them alone; it was pretty obvious they preferred to speak Turkistani when I was within earshot. I hadn't seen Hunt so animated in years. And since Arslan had come through his chill, Sanjar was all smiles. He hadn't really learned yet that his father was mortal.

But except with Sanjar, Hunt had lapsed back into the inarticulateness of his first days with Arslan. I tried exactly once to ask him what had happened. He fixed me with that remote look of a visitor from another world, as if we faced each other through barriers not simply of language but of perception. 'It was a battle,' he said. 'We won it.'

'What happened to Nizam?'

He shrugged, and after a while he said in an answering tone, 'What happens to Nizams?'

'I expect they succeed or they die trying.'

He nodded slowly. 'Nizam's dead.'

'What was he trying for?'

'Exactly,' he said.

24

The third day, Sanjar was as restless as a young cat wanting out. Arslan's next chill was due tomorrow, and the prospect seemed to infect the boy with jumpiness. For the first time since he was a tot, I saw him get really mad, flaring up at Hunt in the course of their chats, swearing – multilingually – like a trooper over his cooking. But it was with an air almost of contrition that he came to me just after lunch.

'Mr Bond, I want to catch us some fish for supper. Arslan's asleep. He won't need anything for a few hours, and I'll be back by then.'

'In broad daylight, Sanjar?'

He gave me the humbly calculating look of a wise child facing the barrier of adult prejudice – considering how to convince me he knew his business without displaying a confidence that would look like overconfidence. 'I can keep out of sight,' he began cautiously, and I clapped him on the shoulder and told him to go ahead.

He flushed with relief and pleasure. All the same, he managed to delay for half an hour, fussing up and down stairs, he was so anxious to leave Arslan well provided for. When he finally went, he went through the kitchen window, surging out the way he always did, with the unreal grace of a shadow or a dancer. There was a certain crazy beauty about Sanjar. He preferred windows to doors – and he was entitled to windows.

It must have been about two in the afternoon when a wagon pulled up in front of the house. I was working in the side garden – somebody had to do Hunt's chores – and I straightened up to watch.

Three men were getting out. One of them I recognized immediately – Harry Flaxman, a trapper from over by Blue Creek. The other two I placed as belonging to the middle-aged generation of town loafers, but couldn't call their names to mind. Flaxman was hitching the horses to the gatepost. I headed up front in a hurry. This was a visit I didn't like the looks of. Flaxman was a loner, a childless widower who was said to have worked his wife to death. After Arslan's coming he had let his little farm grow up in brush and taken to trapping for a living. He was a drinker, a poacher, and a chiseler, efficient and mean.

By the time I got to the front walk I had placed the other two: J. G. Sims, a shiftless drunken no-account, like a milder Ollie Schuster; and Cully Johnson, a lanky, gentle-mannered loafer who lived on the charity of his relatives and whose only serious vice, as far as I knew, was absolute laziness. Hunt's dog was yapping and snarling around them, but that little dog wasn't worth two cents, and they could tell it at a glance. I stepped up on the porch, to get solidly between them and the door. There was a gun upstairs in my bedroom, but it might as well have been on the moon. Flaxman was leading the way up my front walk, and he swung a rifle loosely in his hand.

'Good afternoon,' I said. 'What can I do for you?'

'Well, now, Mr Bond,' Flaxman began. He was grinning widely at me. He mounted the porch steps and stood facing me, while the other two formed up behind him. 'Mind if we come in and talk about it?'

'I'll have to ask you to put the gun down,' I said. 'It's a little rule I have – no firearms in the house or on the porch.'

He nodded a little exaggeratedly and rested the rifle butt on the top step. 'We really come to see Hunt Morgan.'

I looked quickly at J. G.'s face, and Cully's. If it was only Flaxman's viciousness that inspired them, we had a better chance. But all three pairs of eyes were lit with the same vindictive fire. There had never been a lynching in Kraftsville, to my knowledge, but the conclusion was obvious: they had come to lynch Hunt.

'Hunt's resting, and he's not in shape to talk to anybody. I'm sorry I can't ask you in.'

'Well, Mr Bond, you just don't have to ask us.'

So there was no use being polite. 'Sorry,' I said, in a different tone. 'I'm busy. If you have anything to say to me, you can say it tomorrow in my office. If you have anything to say to Hunt, I'll take the message.'

'Seems like it's hard to find you in your office,' Flaxman said. He was still grinning. The dog had given up and sat down, still growling uneasily. 'Least that's what I hear. I don't have much occasion to come looking for you, myself.'

'Somebody says to me,' J. G. chimed in conversationally, ' "If there's ever another war in Kraft County, they'll never make the Supervisor surrender." I says, "Why not?" And he says, "They can't never find him." '

They all thought that was pretty funny. 'I'd advise all three of you to tend to your own business and let me tend to mine. You'll find out I'm in my office, all right.'

'Right now our business is Hunt Morgan,' Flaxman said.

'No.' I saw Flaxman's muscles shift as he tilted just a shade forward, ready to take the offensive, but Cully and J. G. were already losing their nerve. 'We've got laws in this town, mister, and you ought to know by now that I enforce them. You can't go around disturbing people in their homes.'

'We ain't going to disturb you one bit, Mr Bond. We ain't even got to come in if you bring him out.'

'Get back,' I said. Flaxman's face twisted as he tried to stare me down, and I felt a swell of comfortable warmth. They weren't so tough. 'Mister, you've still got time to leave quietly and there won't be any charges. But don't you forget, the KCR has an interest in preserving law and order, too.'

Now they were all three whipped. Flaxman half turned away, riding his hand loosely up and down the gun barrel, figuring out his parting sneer. The gun might not be loaded; on the other hand, if anybody still had cartridges, it would be people like Flaxman, too selfish to turn them in and too smart to waste them. 'We'll get him, Mr Bond,' he said with a travesty of pleasantness. 'Don't you worry, we'll get him. There's other ways.' He took the first slow step down.

'We got the proof, Mr Bond,' Cully blurted. 'That's the God's truth.'

A brown flush surged over Flaxman's neck, and he spat on the steps to clarify his stand on Cully's insubordination. 'Get off my property,' I said. Flaxman turned his vicious face, surprised. 'I mean you. Take that gun and get out, and don't come back here or I'll have you jailed.'

Flaxman teetered murderously, not sure whether to show his teeth before he slunk off, but J. G. and Cully, looking chastened, were already started toward the gate. 'You come back here, Cully,' I said. 'I want to talk to you.' He turned back hastily. Flaxman shrugged, and dawdled down the steps, passing him. 'What proof have you got of what?'

He came up close to me and said, in a husky, confidential voice, like somebody discussing a dirty disease, 'We just happened to find out, Mr Bond. All three of us, we seen him with our own eyes.' He nodded. 'Hunt Morgan's a spy for Arslan.'

Flaxman had stopped halfway down the walk, looking back. 'Out!' I called to him, and motioned with the back of my hand towards the gate, and he shrugged again and went on out to the wagon where J. G. was already waiting.

'What did you see, Cully?'

He shuffled a little, or managed to look like it without actually moving his feet. 'We was out on a fishing trip. First time in a long time, I mean a real trip like that. You know how it is, nobody goes out of county no more. Don't know why – do you?'

'How far did you go?' You had to be patient with Cully. Flaxman and J. G. were leaning against the side of the wagon, watching.

'Clear up to the Wabash. Nearly far as Clairmont, I reckon. Spent most a month, if you can believe it, Mr Bond. I mean if you count coming and going.' If he had had a hat, he would have taken it off now and turned it round and round in his hands. 'And it was up there we seen Hunt Morgan. Riding that there red horse of his. I'd of knowed him and the horse both, five miles off. Seen him ride up to a little old house there was, one of them little summer houses some people used to build up there, and he waited there most near half a day till somebody come and met him. And you know who it was, Mr Bond? A soldier. Yes, sir. One of Arslan's soldiers, I'll swear. He had the uniform and all. And they was talking there all evening from noon till clear up dark. We was watching the whole thing from the river bank, all day long, first to last. Then we seen them ride off again back the way they come, Hunt south and the soldier north. He wasn't just no private, neither; he was some kind of an officer.'

'When was this, Cully?'

'Near two months ago.' He screwed up his eyes and rocked on his feet. 'It was six weeks, Mr Bond. When we got home, we heard as Hunt was out of town again, so we figured we'd get him when he come back. Then when he come back hurt, it seemed like a God's judgment. We don't none of us figure you had a thing to do with it, Mr Bond. I know I don't.'

I stepped back across the porch to the front door and opened it, and held it open while I motioned to Flaxman and J. G. They straightened themselves and came up the walk grim as death, not a hint of a grin between them. 'I'll take the gun,' I said to Flaxman.

'No, sir,' he said, snapping his mouth shut. That meant, most likely, that it *was* loaded. Guns were a lot easier to come by than ammunition.

'Then you wait out here.' He nodded curtly. 'You two come in. You can say what you think about Hunt to his face. If it's more than hot air, the whole business belongs in court.' There were no treason laws in Kraft County – we hadn't been able to agree on how to word them – but the KCR had its own rules. It was one thing when Hunt was a virtual prisoner, with Arslan's hand on his throat; it was another to ride a hundred miles out of county to tell his little tales behind my back.

Hunt on the couch looked at us with eyes no more wary than usual. He didn't speak. He couldn't help knowing that something was up, but he was prepared to be polite if the situation allowed. J. G., not sure what had been told, wasn't about to say anything, either. As for me, I didn't feel much like doing favors for any of them. 'Tell Hunt what you just told me,' I said to Cully.

'Well, like I was telling you, Mr Bond—'

'Tell it to Hunt.'

He mustered some of the patriotic indignation, or whatever it was, that had slipped away from him. 'Hunt, we seen you up on the Wabash.'

He raised his eyebrows very coolly, but I'd lived with Hunt long enough to recognize the quick shrinking look in his eyes – hurrying to acknowledge defeat before the fighting started.

Cully was back on the track now; his voice shrilled and trembled. 'You been spying for Arslan all along, ain't you? There ain't nothing never went on in this town but what you told him, ain't that right? Living right here in this here house and everything. There's a lot of folks always said so, and now we know it. We got the proof!'

But it wasn't for Arslan, it was for Nizam. Hunt shrugged. He had been looking steadily at me, and I at him. 'Am I being charged with something?'

'I'll have to check out the legal aspects,' I said. 'One way or another, we'll see that justice is done.'

Fear and humor washed like rotating colored lights across Hunt's face and left him looking tired and injured. He nodded vaguely. Six weeks ago. He had believed then – at least he could have believed – that Nizam was still Arslan's selfless right arm. And four weeks later, he had ridden north again to battle against Nizam.

'I don't hear him deny it,' J. G. observed contemptuously.

'He can deny it all he wants to,' Cully shrilled. 'But we seen it with our own eyes!'

The door scraped open. Flaxman was well into the room before I took my eyes off of Hunt. 'Cully,' I said, 'you know Ward Munsey's house. You go tell him or his brother we've got a charge of collaboration to investigate. If you can't find them home, get me Leland Kitchener or—'

'You just stay put, Cully,' Flaxman said. Five minutes earlier he wouldn't have dared cross the porch with that gun. Five minutes earlier I wouldn't have let him. There was a kind of justice that replaced legality sometimes – the kind of justice that dragged a careless hand into the gears of a machine.

'Hey!'

I didn't understand for a moment what had happened. Flaxman, with his startled shout, had dodged back, jerking up his gun.

Cully wavered, then leaned his long reach forward and scooped up something from the floor. It was Arslan's knife.

He was leaning on the bannister. His face shone with sweat. His mouth was drawn into a grimace or a grin. J. G. was swearing softly.

'By God, it's *him*. Is it him?' Cully said, in a voice of awe, looking from the knife to Arslan and back. Flaxman leveled the rifle.

'Wait,' I said, and 'Wait,' said Arslan at the same instant. His hoarse voice rasped. As he spoke, he forced himself upright from the bannister, his arms trembling with the strain. 'I make you an offer,' he said steadily. 'You see that I am weak – even too weak to throw a knife properly. You see that I am alone. You want Hunt. Will you trade him for me?' His voice was gathering strength and color. 'I will surrender myself to you, in return for a promise.' I wouldn't have surrendered a tenpenny nail to those three for all the promises they could make. 'You will promise – you will swear – before Mr Bond and before your God, that you will never come to this house again, that you will never attack this house or anyone in it. Do you understand?' It was ridiculous, of course, but inside I was cursing whatever had made me keep the whereabouts of my gun strictly to myself. If I'd told Hunt about it, Arslan would have known by now.

They looked uneasily at each other, with dawning greed. Flaxman had lowered the rifle. J. G.'s mouth twisted. 'Looks to me like we got you both,' he said fiercely. 'We don't need to make no promises. What's to stop us just walking up there and getting you?'

'This.' Now the grimace was unmistakably a grin. He raised the second knife – Hunt's knife, it must be – turning it in front of his chest to make it glint.

Cully cleared his throat. 'Well, hell.' He sounded embarrassed. 'We can just shoot you, and take Hunt anyways.'

'I am dying,' Arslan reproved gently. 'Which do you want more: Hunt Morgan, or Arslan – alive, in your hands?'

They looked sidelong at each other, and suddenly they all three moved, drawing together and mumbling agreement. 'Okay, drop the knife,' J. G. ordered.

'When you have sworn. You first.'

'Wait a minute,' I said. 'Who says you can take anybody out of my house?'

'Mr Bond,' Flaxman said patiently, 'if you don't shut up, I'm going to shoot you dead. I ain't promised nothing yet.'

'Then wait just a minute. I'm going to get a Bible for you to swear on.' I started for the stairs.

'If that ain't a Bible on that there table' – the gun muzzle dipped towards the coffee table for half a second – 'my mama sure didn't teach me right.'

'You first,' Arslan repeated. I held the Bible, and J. G. laid his hand on it unwillingly, looking past me to Arslan.

'Repeat what I say. "I swear upon this Bible that I will never set foot in this house—" '

'I swear on this Bible I'll never' – he faltered over the words – 'set foot in this house.'

' "Or on its grounds—" '

'Or on its grounds.'

' "And I swear I will never try to hurt anyone—" '

'I swear I'll never try to hurt anyone.'

' "While they are in this house or on its grounds—" '

'While they're in this house or its grounds.'

' "And I swear I will never damage this house—" '

'And I swear I will never damage this house.'

' "And if I ever break any part of this oath—" '

'If I ever break any part of this oath.'

' "I pray that God will strike me—" '

'I pray that God will strike me.'

' "And all my family—" '

'And all my family.' J. G. had no family worth mentioning, but by this time he was speaking in deadly earnest.

' "Dead in agony." '

'Dead' – he balked a little, and finished in a strangled voice – 'in agony.'

I pulled the Bible away. 'Do you understand what you have sworn?' Arslan insisted.

'Yeah – to leave this place alone, and anybody that's in it – as long as they're in it.'

'Or on the grounds.'

'Yeah, or on the grounds. But that's only if you drop the knife and come with us.'

'Right,' Arslan approved, like a teacher who's finally dragged the right answer out of a dull class. 'Now you.'

And Cully, with his embarrassed air, mumbled through the same oath, impatiently coached by J. G. when he stumbled. 'I ain't putting my hand on no Bible,' Flaxman protested. But he did, while J. G. held the rifle for him.

'Now,' Cully said with relief. 'Drop that knife and get down here.'

'Back up,' Arslan commanded quietly. 'Open the door, and wait there.'

Shufflingly they did as they were told. I saw Hunt brace himself, bunching the muscles of his good leg, and knew he meant to plunge at Flaxman. But Flaxman knew it, too, and gave him a wide berth.

Slowly Arslan made his way down the stairs, stood swaying a moment, and crossed the room more briskly. He was barefoot. He smelled of sickness and sweat. The threadbare khaki clung to him in wet stripes. He didn't look at Hunt. Beside me he stopped and opened his hand, and the knife clattered dully on the floor. At the same time he steadied himself against me with his two-fingered right hand. I felt the hooked fingers tap my wrist, with something between them; I closed my hand over them quickly and they pulled away, leaving the folded paper in my palm.

He stepped forward. I squeezed my hand against the pit of my stomach, where waves of pain ballooned outwards in pulse after pulse. The three faces at the door beamed with triumph, with the lust of cruelty. And who could blame them? Who could blame them?

Flaxman kept the rifle leveled, not at Arslan, but at me. Cully reached for the crippled arm, but J. G. struck out with one foot in a sudden sideways kick, and Arslan sprawled, half through the open door onto the porch. Hunt made a sound, a piteous small moan of protest. J. G. reached down; cloth ripped as he pulled Arslan upright. Cully seized his arm, twisting it up behind his back, and they crowded through the door. Flaxman waited till they got to the wagon. Then he gave a cheerful wave of the gun, slammed the door, and hurried after them.

A thick ink line crossed the paper. Above it was written in Arslan's open hand, 'Wait With Hunt,' and below, 'Sanjar – Follow – If I am dead, try Spassky *at once*' and the last two words were underlined, the ink petering out into a pen scratch.

I brought down the pistol from my bedroom, and I got myself a drink of pure cream and sat hunched by the window. Hunt's voice was frantic and coarse. 'What are you waiting for? You own this town. Why the hell don't you stop them?'

'That's government. This is a private matter.' For all I could do, I kept wondering how Jesus had looked when He fell with the cross. *If I am dead* . . . 'Who's Spassky?'

'Spahsky,' he said, correcting my pronunciation, 'is the ranking Russian officer on this continent – or was when there were ranks. He's the one who raised the irregulars against Nizam and got word to Arslan.' His slim hands were folding, unfolding, smoothing, refolding the paper. 'One of the few loyal people left. He sent four separate crews south, far enough so that Nizam's receivers wouldn't pick them up, to broadcast calls to Arslan. And he was sharp enough to see what was happening and do that in time.' He folded, folded again, opened, read, refolded. 'So Kraftsville's going to burn after all.'

'Oh, God,' I said wearily. 'What's the use?'

He laughed harshly. 'What's the difference? Aren't we all dead?' He clenched his trembling fist on the folded paper and burst out, 'Nothing about Arslan is private!'

I looked at him. 'Try to get things straight in that brain for once, Hunt. Neither the KCR nor the government could possibly lift a finger for Arslan.'

'Well, Sanjar, at least. If your dainty stomach allows, why don't you get the hell out of here and look for Sanjar?'

'I don't put much faith in their Bible oaths, and I judge Arslan didn't either.'

'For Christ's sake! For Christ's sake!' he cried furiously. Tears were spilling into his soft beard.

I did go out to the shed and saddle Sanjar's horse. Arslan was still Arslan; he would take a lot of killing, and they would be in no hurry about it. Still, he had looked very frail. He had said, with all his pedagogic assurance, 'I am dying.' And the ugly thought never left my mind that if he died too soon to suit them, they would be back in a hurry for Hunt.

I was in the living room, looking at the old clock for probably the hundredth time, when the kitchen window rattled. I strode in to meet Sanjar as he pulled a heavy string of fish over the sill after him. His grin faded as he turned; I put the crumpled note into his hand. 'J. G. Sims, Cully Johnson, and Harry Flaxman. They came for Hunt, and Arslan persuaded them to take him instead. They went in Flaxman's wagon; looked like they headed for his place – that's just north of Blue Creek on the Morrisville road. An hour ago. Flaxman's got a rifle.' The paper fluttered downwards. 'I saddled your horse.' I held out the pistol.

He took it in both hands. For a moment more he held still, barely crouched, his eyes flitting wildly. Then he spun back to the window and was up and out. I watched him sprint to the shed; a few seconds later he was on horseback, tearing across the back garden and disappearing into the trees. When he showed again in the glimpse of road beyond the burned stable, he was going at a smooth gallop.

I gave Hunt the knife Arslan had dropped, locked the doors, and went the quietest way round to Jack Allard's. 'Well, who's getting murdered now?' he greeted me.

'I'm not sure, but you'd better bring everything you've got.'

By the time we got back to the house, Sanjar had been gone half an hour. That was plenty of time for him to get to Flaxman's. I told the doctor to make himself at home, and started after him.

I heard something coming over the hill and pulled my horse off of the road into the high brush. It was Flaxman's wagon, but Sanjar was driving. I hailed him. He pulled up and sat wordless while I tied my horse to the tailgate beside his and climbed in. 'You drive,' he said shortly, dropping the reins in my lap. He swung over the back of the seat, knelt beside a heap of sacking on the wagon bed, and pulled back the top sack. Arslan's face was unrecognizable. 'Go easy,' Sanjar ordered huskily.

Four times during that slow ride home, Arslan moaned – a thin, inarticulate sound, horrible because it was so helplessly unconscious. I drove into the back yard and stopped as close as I could get to the back door. The doctor came out, and we rigged up a litter from hoe handles and sacks and carried him in. Hunt was sleeping heavily. 'I gave him a little something to knock him out,' Jack explained. 'I don't know what you might be bringing home.'

What we had brought home had been pretty well worked over with the classic tire chains, though fists alone must have caved in the face. They had burned his naked feet, but apparently they hadn't had the time, or the imagination, to get into anything more refined.

'I'd say he'll live – if he weren't already about two-thirds dead of malaria. Mind you, you don't exactly die of malaria, any more than you die of flu; but when it's knocked out all your resistance, it can get into your liver or your brain, or it can just weaken you to the point where any little infection will finish you off.' He gestured with his pipe towards the ceiling. 'That's why we're not through up there yet. We're going to keep scrubbing him till he wishes he was back at Flaxman's. Every little laceration he's picked up probably in the last three weeks is infected already, and of course now there isn't a patch of undamaged skin on him any bigger than the palm of your hand. The burns aren't much to speak of. The main thing is, I can't tell yet just what's ruptured inside.' He puffed thoughtfully. 'And then of course he hasn't lost a hell of a lot of blood, but he probably couldn't afford to lose any.'

'How about transfusions?'

'Thought you'd say that, but I wasn't going to suggest it if you didn't. It's just a little bit riskier than it used to be since we've gone primitive. You know your blood group? That's all right, I'll just run a little direct agglutination test.' He got up. 'Sanjar gets first chance, but we may need all we can get.' In the kitchen doorway he paused. 'And when he comes to himself – if he ever does – I wish you'd point out to him that it's absolutely his own fault if he dies. Absolutely.'

The first transfusion was Sanjar's blood. The second was mine. There was no change that I could see in the swollen, multicolored face, but the whistling breath slowed and steadied, and the doctor grunted with satisfaction.

Hunt woke near midnight. As soon as the fuzziness of the drug wore off enough for him to understand what had happened, he lashed out at us desperately. He was furious at the doctor for having put him to sleep, at me for having let Arslan be taken, at Sanjar for no logical reason. What really hurt him was that he couldn't see Arslan and couldn't help him. Their blood was incompatible.

25

Now I found myself living in something like a state of siege. One morning I received a formal delegation of aldermen on the porch (they wouldn't come inside); they informed me that the board considered I had forfeited my position as Mayor as long as I sheltered Arslan. 'Suppose I got rid of Arslan. Would you consider me reinstated?'

They thought so, but the board would have to approve when the time came.

I told them they could go home and forget it. They had no such power, and like it or not, I was Mayor until elections next January. There wasn't even any provision for impeachment in the city charter. I was pretty mad. Then they wanted to have Sanjar tried for murder. They were on better legal ground there, and I told them that just as soon as they recognized my authority as Mayor, I'd let them charge him and I'd go bail for him. There wasn't much risk in that. I could delay the trial till the county cooled off enough to be reasonable. Cully's relatives were the only people who might really care about what Sanjar had done at Flaxman's place. The rest of the heat against Sanjar was just an overflow of the feeling against Arslan, and against me for shielding Arslan. It was leftover feeling. It might have applied well enough when Arslan was a foreign invader, but that didn't mean it suited the present circumstances.

I kept the boy strictly in the house and yard, and I stayed home, too. Sanjar complained that the horses needed a run every day, but I convinced him it was too dangerous. If he went out, he might not come back alive, and Arslan needed him. If I went out, there might be a raid on the house.

Dr Allard came every day. He'd had some unpleasantness on Arslan's account too, of course, but he didn't have to worry about any serious retaliation. A good doctor – any doctor – was too valuable.

I went in every day to have a look at Arslan, and it never failed to give me a peculiar feeling. So much of his aura of power had been physical. The thing that lay in the bed, dribbling from swollen lips, restlessly fingering the covers with shrunken hands – could this be any part of Arslan? The eyes in that discolored face, when they did open, were dull and drifting. The only sign of strength left was the violence of the shivering that racked him every third day. The whole bed rattled and inched along the floor. The blankets that Sanjar piled on him quivered like an earth-quake. Downstairs, Hunt would lie staring at the ceiling while that racket went on above him. But during the second of those chills the sunken eyes opened clear and burning and fixed on me. And slowly, improbably, the smashed mouth shaped into a smile – a smile with split lips and chattering broken teeth. Arslan still lived in that wrecked flesh.

For how long was something else again.

Sanjar was a good little nurse. He hung on everything the doctor said. He handled all the dirty sickroom business – feeding, bathing, bedpans, bandages. Under the circumstances I couldn't expect him to nurse Hunt, too. But Hunt didn't require much nursing.

He lay quiet and calm on the couch, as he had lain since his first resentful outburst. He was polite and cheerful, but he didn't want to talk much. He, the perpetual reader, hardly touched a book. He was content to rest, propped up with pillow, stroking a drowsy cat, gazing peacefully towards the windows or at the ceiling. Hunt had beheld his miracle. Now nothing, not Arslan's death nor Arslan's life, could destroy it.

One day he was still dying; the next, he was going to live. Like a savage – which was appropriate enough – Arslan seemed to consider death a matter of choice, or at worst an avoidable accident. His mind had turned some corner in the night, and there only remained the detail of dragging his body after it.

He went at it with patience and determination. I had to change my mind again, seeing how the authority of the man shone through the debris of his body. I had the feeling he would have discarded it as readily as any other corpse, if there had been anyplace else for him to go.

Now when I came to his room it was a visit, not an observation. We talked. At first it was only a few minutes at a time, he tired so fast – and he was so careful not to push himself any harder than was profitable. But for those minutes he was so much his old self I literally forgot his appearance, forgot even the rasping weakness of his voice. It was like familiar music on a bad recording.

I learned his version of what had happened 'north of here.' It had been really northeast, where the Wabash curves away through a rich plain, eastward from Clairmont into Indiana. Arslan's six hundred irregulars – the remnants of a decayed Russian regiment – passably well-mounted and well-armed, had surprised Nizam in the process of building what was to be his capital. I shook my head. It wasn't easy to imagine Nizam being surprised, still less Nizam or anybody else building a capital at this point of time. Arslan smiled – a painful act for his face, from the looks of it. 'It is not unreasonable, sir. Nizam might very well expect to live twenty, thirty years more. Why should he not choose to live in the enjoyment of comfort and power? Does life require an heir?'

Hunt told me later, citing it as an example of what he called Arslan's delicacy, that he, Arslan, had personally killed Nizam in the battle. But Arslan only remarked that Nizam's body had been found among the dead. 'I was able to identify him,' he said thoughtfully. That was the kind of remark Hunt would enjoy brooding over. It didn't contain much, but a lot of tall structures could be built around it.

Later it was Kraftsville we talked about. If any of the information Hunt had been feeding to Nizam for the last two years had ever gotten through to Arslan, he didn't want to admit it. The political situation interested him mightily – not to mention the personal situation of every prominent family in town, and some of the obscure ones.

He hadn't known – or pretended he hadn't – that Arnold

Morgan was dead. Even granting he hadn't watched us, and even knowing Hunt, that surprised me a little. But no doubt they'd had more urgent things to talk about than a father's death. 'I wasn't there,' I said dryly. 'I suppose he died as well as he lived.'

The last time I saw Arnold Morgan alive had been typical, in a way. I had stopped by the house out of duty, to see Jean, as I did sometimes. It helped give her the feeling Hunt took an interest in her. She wasn't home, and in common decency I sat down to talk to Arnold. We were all right till Hunt's name was mentioned.

'He seems to be happy there,' Arnold said, in the kind of tone in which people used to say So-and-so's boy was really much better off in military school. *There*, presumably, was my house.

I didn't ask him how he knew whether Hunt was happy or not. I said he was getting along well enough. Maybe it sounded a little cold.

'As well as he can, probably,' Arnold said stiffly. 'I *will* say this,' he added, warming up. 'I've never heard a breath of scandal concerning you and Hunt – and I think I would have heard. I hear all the rest of it about him. People are sweet enough to do that for me.'

I'd let him get that far because it had taken me that long to realize what he was talking about. I stood up and looked at him, and he shut his mouth. 'What the hell are you trying to say?'

'Say? Nothing. I'm saying that nobody says anything. Or thinks anything, as far as I can tell.'

'You mean *you* could imagine a thing like that? What's wrong with you, Arnold?'

'What's wrong with *me*? What kind of a question is that?'

'Forget it. It's stupid for us to be yelling at each other.'

'I didn't know there was more than one of us . . .' He let it die out, and we managed to part politely enough. Arnold did look very poorly, and I didn't doubt he suffered over Hunt. But in my opinion, Jean was better off when he died. As for Hunt, it was harder to say.

Arslan nodded slowly. His face was tight with thoughtful interest – so far as you could interpret its expressions. 'You are no longer the resistance,' he said abruptly. 'You are the rulers now.'

'Governors, maybe, General. Kraft County's not a kingdom.'

'Administrators.'

'Yes, I'll buy that.' We looked at each other. 'You're feeling better today.'

'Better, yes. And when I am well enough to want a woman?' He was grinning now, friendly and mocking as he'd ever been.

'Not in my house. You're not a prisoner here, you're a guest, and you'll behave yourself as a decent guest for as long as you sleep under my roof. When you leave here, you're on your own.' Even here and now, sick and broken and besieged, beaten within an inch of his life, and flat on his back in a hostile town, he had to show his goat legs. It was monotonous.

But he said no more about women. He still knew how to concentrate on the job in hand, and the job in hand was recuperation.

Maybe I'd built him up to legendary proportions myself, as I'd scolded so many other people for doing. Anyhow it seemed unlike him – unworthy of him – to take so long to get well and have such a hard time of it. Maybe, after all, nature hadn't given him quite the body to match his will. Because he was trying, trying hard, and it must have been quite a blow to him to find out he couldn't manipulate or coerce his abused flesh back to health.

There were the setbacks, the dreary plateaus after spurts of improvement, the bruises that wouldn't heal, the wounds that insisted on festering. The chills lost their regularity but not their strength. Blood appeared in his stool; boils developed on his back. Sanjar was exhausted and frantic with impatience. But Hunt's leg was knitting nicely. Jack Allard brought him a pair of crutches and told him to get up. He practiced for nearly half an hour downstairs before he undertook the climb to Arslan's room. It would have been hard to say whether Arslan's recovery went any faster after that, but at least Sanjar felt better. Now there was somebody else on duty who had the proper regard for his father.

I left them to their own devices. I had other things to tend to. There was quite a little backlog of city and county business building up, aside from the matter of Sanjar. As soon as Hunt was really on his feet, and Arslan was making his first dizzy attempts to stand, I called a meeting of the county board. Just as a precaution, somebody would be keeping an eye on my house.

That was a private arrangement. If the KCR involved itself officially at all, it would have to be on the other side. But purely as a friendly gesture to me, a few old members were willing to stand watch over Arslan and his young henchmen.

Effectively, now, there were two governments in Kraft County, and I was at the head of both of them. The KCR functioned first as the county's real police force (Kraftsville had one policeman on the payroll, who supervised what traffic we had and mediated disputes about barking dogs), secondly as a clearinghouse of information and a postal service. The elected government had gotten into the habit of not recognizing the KCR's existence, which saved a lot of inconvenience for everybody. It worked out, without much special effort, that very few people were directly involved in both. In Arslan's day, of course, there hadn't been any elected government, and we had developed our own personnel and our own methods. With the end of Nizam's repression, a lot more people were suddenly interested in joining the KCR, and over the years we had enlisted a few recruits; but generally we didn't welcome those who had found reasons not to join as long as death by torture was one of the occupational hazards. And by and large, with a few exceptions, people who enjoyed politicking and drew votes were a different breed from KCR people. So the organizations had stayed separate, and the KCR had stayed quiet, though it wasn't secret any more. But now there was a very nice harmony. The initiative usually came from the elected government. Questions would be raised before the board, and if it looked like a KCR matter, somebody would say, 'I think this kind of thing would be better handled in the private sector,' and the question would be dismissed.

I personally took care of the KCR budget. Even when we had been fighting for our freedom, our country, and our self-respect, there had been expenses, and now that the thrills and the virtue were mostly gone, people wanted wages. It hadn't seemed right, or smart, either, to make the KCR over into a paid Mafia. Instead, we had made it over into a mutual-assistance cooperative. Members were paid on the basis of their services and their needs – paid, in kind or in labor, by other members. Our income was in contributions levied on people we figured we had helped.

The budget was a piece of work I would have been glad to get rid of. It was complicated and laborious, and I could have used the time for the duties I'd been elected to. Hunt would have done a good job of it – better than anybody else in the county – and I had been tempted more than once to trust him with it. But I'd made up my mind long since that nobody but myself would ever see that budget. Now I thanked God for that.

The board met on a muggy July afternoon. I left Arslan and Hunt deep in private discussion upstairs, while Sanjar stirred up their dinner, as carefree as a meadowlark. When I got back, the three of them were over in the schoolyard. Arslan, with his head thrown back and his good arm clamped on Sanjar's young shoulders, was limping laboriously around the ruined west wing.

'Surveying?'

Hunt, a few feet behind the others, smiled humorlessly at me. 'When I leave your house, sir,' Arslan said, 'I propose to come here.'

'It's city property.'

'Yes. Who will stop me?'

'Probably a lynch mob.'

He laughed happily. 'Haven't I *been* lynched?'

'Well, not entirely.' I was looking at Sanjar's grave little face.

'Let them try. It will be good. But I am more interested in what *you* will do, sir.'

'I'll do exactly nothing, unless you give me a specific reason to. I told you you're not a prisoner. But as long as you stay in Kraft County, you're subject to Kraft County laws. And outside of my house and yard I can't offer you any personal protection. I suggest you stay put till you're ready to leave.'

The black eyebrows, broken now with scars, went up. 'To leave?'

'You aren't staying in Kraftsville indefinitely, are you?'

'Sir,' he said, 'I have come *back* to Kraftsville.' Maybe it was really that straightforward to him, or maybe he was explaining it in simple terms for simple minds.

'You're crazy. Don't forget that a crippled general without an army is just a man with a limp.'

He gave me a luminous smile, turning a little to share it with

Hunt. 'I am not a general, sir. There are no longer generals. Do you understand?'

'I understand that. I don't think *you* do.'

'Ah,' he said, and he turned back to the school. 'It is still the most defensible site in Kraftsville, and it is unused.' He gave me a sidelong look of amusement. 'I am aware that Arslan would not survive long in Kraftsville without – fortification. I propose to fortify your school and to live there. That is all.'

'And what do you propose to live *on*?'

He shrugged. 'We will hunt.'

'Well, you know where I stand. What you do from here on is your business – as long as it isn't public business.'

'And if I appropriate city property?'

'A lot of other people have been doing it. I won't interfere on that ground alone. But I'll use it if I want to interfere for other reasons.'

He nodded soberly. He took a breath and squeezed Sanjar's shoulder, and they moved on. Hunt gave me a studying look as he trailed past. 'I brought the ham in,' he said.

That night Arslan shivered again in his bed. But the next morning he was out behind the house, watching sharply while Sanjar saddled Hunt's colt. Hunt eyed me – ready to say, if I looked like objecting, 'It's my horse.'

'Where to?' I asked.

Sanjar shot a look at his father before he answered, 'It's for Arslan.'

'Going somewhere, General?' He didn't look in any shape to ride, but I'd learned not to make bets on what Arslan couldn't do.

'I need exercise,' he said cheerfully. 'Also I wish to see the district.'

'The district's going to see you, too.'

'It is good for the district to see me.'

'Well, it's your neck, and Hunt's horse. But I'm going to wish you luck.'

He laughed. 'Why?'

'Oh, I don't know. I'd like to see you back in good health before they kill you.'

264

'Good,' he said warmly, but he was talking to Sanjar, who had just finished his job. Arslan took the bridle and began to walk the horse away from the house. It was the first time I'd seen him take more than two steps without help. He went slowly, talking to the horse, his face lined with concentration. Presently they stopped, and Arslan bunched the reins in his hand, and, after several false starts, got his foot into the stirrup. Even from where we stood by the shed, I could see how he gathered himself for a major effort. He swung himself up, but didn't quite make it into the saddle: hung awkwardly for a moment, half lying on the horse's neck, and then slipped back down.

The horse stepped nervously. He quieted it, hopping a little and twisting his foot on the grass for better purchase. For a moment horse and man stood waiting. Then in one sweeping chain of motion he swung himself astride, the horse moved, they were turning towards us, and Arslan swayed and toppled and caught himself on the startled horse's neck, straightened and dug in his heels, rounded us in a tight circle, and drew up, laughing in harsh gasps.

Hunt seized the bridle. They gazed at each other, immobile. Then Arslan struck with his open left hand and shouted. The horse leaped away. Hunt staggered against me and recovered. He was cursing quietly, nursing his right wrist. Arslan was headed down the Morrisville road at a ragged trot, getting the horse and himself under control by fits and starts.

Hunt was looking at Sanjar so intently that I looked, too. The boy's face was stricken. 'Why don't you saddle up and go with him?' I said.

'I'm under orders!' he flashed at me.

Arslan was already out of sight. Sanjar scuffed the dirt and shuffled sullenly into the shed. The horse would be his consolation. Hunt turned towards me – past me – a face so blank and tired that I was shaken. Arslan's family.

It didn't matter much now what Hunt had done. Nizam was dead, and Arslan was back under my roof, and nothing any of us could do would make the past any better. Forgiving people their trespasses wasn't just Christian charity, it was common sense. There might be imitation Nizams still to come, and double-dealing was part of Hunt Morgan's nature, or at least of his education; but I couldn't see him as a threat to Kraftsville. Hunt had found his orbit again, his old orbit around Arslan. It was from Arslan the next move was bound to come.

He was back within an hour, and he was exhausted. Hunt caught him as he slipped clumsily down from the saddle – the closest thing to an embrace I'd ever seen between them. Arslan's drawn face was radiant. Sanjar capered beside him, aglow too and all little boy again. Arslan caught my look and advanced between them towards the back door, the horse neglected for once. 'So, sir; today it was only a small part of the district. Tomorrow, perhaps, more.'

As a matter of fact, it was two days before he went out again. Arslan, in his own way, was a cautious man. It had always struck me that most people's approach to a risk was to open their eyes to the eighty percent chance, or whatever it happened to be, of safety, and close their eyes to the other twenty percent. But Arslan never staked anything he wasn't fully prepared to lose. And if he pushed himself, it was never quite to the limit – except maybe that day when his knife had clattered on my floor.

He did ride out again, and come back again, and twice more after that, before he settled down to the business he'd laid out for himself. By that time it was well enough publicized.

26

From the first day of their remodeling operations they attracted observers. All of the immediate neighbors who were home had a good look from their windows or gardens, and the Munseys stood out in the street for a better view. The next day, and every day from then on, a few people drifted over from other parts of town. They would stand in idle groups of two or three or four, smoking, passing a few words, mostly just watching. After half an hour or so, a man would knock out his pipe, hitch up his pants, and move on about his business; but in a little while somebody else was likely to come along, so that while the groups shrank and grew, broke and re-formed, there was seldom a time when Arslan was without his spectators.

He gave them a pretty good show. What with his scars and scrawniness and lameness, and the too-loose hang of the ragged uniform, he made a nicely heroic laborer himself; and Sanjar as the picture of innocent devotion and Hunt as the fallen aristocrat didn't hurt any, either.

At first, people stayed in the street or the neighboring yards. But after a few days, some of them started drifting up the east slope or into the parking lot for a closer look. They didn't speak to the workers, and vice versa. Not for a while.

He ignored them just the right amount. Whenever he turned, whenever he spoke, he was ready to include them; you could almost see the blanks he left for their responses. Every time he hammered a nail or lifted a plank or laid a brick, every time he sang out an order or paused for a drink of water, he played it for all it was worth, reaching hard for his audience. And getting them.

First their interest, then their admiration for a job well done under difficulties, then – with some of them – a little more than that.

Pretty soon people started making comments on the work, near enough and loud enough for Arslan to hear. He made no pretense of not hearing. If a remark pleased him, he smiled; if it didn't, he made a little comic grimace that did a lot more for him than the smile could. Still there was a gap, a little something lacking to make the connection complete. He looked at them, they looked at him – but never quite at the same moment. They spoke, he spoke – but never directly to each other.

It wasn't what you could call a relaxed situation, but in a way it was peaceful. As long as that connection remained uncompleted, nothing was going to happen, and that meant nobody had to make any inconvenient decisions. Kraftsville was uncommitted. Arslan and his ménage and his project had been granted, by popular will or by default, a kind of diplomatic immunity.

It was Ward Munsey who finally completed the connection. He had left the group of four that had settled that particular morning on the ruins of one of the parking-lot dividers and strolled up close to the workers, getting himself between Hunt on the one hand and Arslan and Sanjar on the other. He watched a little while longer, with his fingers flat in his hip pockets and his elbows stuck out behind. Then he asked conversationally, 'You trying to make a fort out of it?'

Arslan turned to him with a sociable smile, as if it was an everyday exchange between old friends, up-ended the board he was carrying, and wiped his face with the back of his wrist. 'Just a place to live.' He leaned on his board and gazed at the school, giving his handiwork a fond appraisal.

Ward gestured. 'How come all the fortifications?'

Arslan shot him a confidential grin. 'To prevent insomnia.'

It took Ward a minute to get that, but when he did, he answered it by spitting appreciatively into the grass and turning away with a one-sided smile. Nobody was about to forget that Arslan's bullets had cut down Ward's brother, or that Ward had risked his neck every night for weeks to give Arslan another little floral stab in the only place where it hurt. Whatever relationship was going to emerge now, it had to be built on that.

It was a new variation on Arslan's old theme: first the rape, then the seduction. He was wooing Kraftsville now. The difference was that this time the strength was on the side of the victim.

But for good or ill the connection had been made, and Kraftsville was committed to the extent of accepting Arslan into fairly polite conversation. After that, people talked to him. It wasn't that they were friendly; they were curious. And Arslan was always happy to explain his project.

'Yes, permanently. Later we can demolish what is left of the west wing. For the present, it is enough to seal the fire door.'

'You figure you got to seal it like *that*?'

'I would prefer a solid wall; I settle for a door that no one can open.'

In fact, the great fire door was probably the solidest part of the west wall. With the state of its tracks and bearings, welded with rust, there wasn't much likelihood of anybody being able to open it, but Arslan wasn't satisfied with that. What he was doing was literally bolting it in place. For lumber and hardware they were pillaging the railroad line. Hunt and Sanjar used the horses to drag the soundest rails and ties, travois-fashion, across town and into the school parking lot. They did it piecemeal, fetching another section whenever Arslan was ready for it. 'We have no time to guard a supply depot,' he told me. 'Sleep is more important.'

When they got through with that door, it would have taken a platoon of men with blowtorches to get it open. By that time, people were getting right up close, talking to all three of them, offering advice and argument – everything short of actually lending a hand.

'Come in and take a look.' Arslan's English, like his manners, was mellowing. That invitation was made more and more often, and usually it was to the youngsters – the teenage boys who were taking more and more to hanging around the school-ground. Those kids were growing up pretty wild, in some ways. All that saved Kraftsville from a mass outbreak of juvenile delinquency was the amount of necessary work there was for everybody to do and the shortage of opportunities for getting into real mischief. We didn't have to worry about drugs and peace politics any more, but the young people didn't have much to hold them down or give them direction – except the ones who had joined the Last Days movement.

What had happened in religion was funny. The regular churches had just faded away without much fuss during Arslan's first occupation – oh, some of them had shown signs of life longer than others – as if the ban on meetings had been the excuse they were waiting for. Most people had either lost their religion or preferred to exercise it privately. Even when meetings were possible again, the churches hadn't come back to life, in spite of all the attempted revivals. But the Last Days was different. It started out as just another revival, but people were swept up by it. It had one main doctrine: that Jesus Christ would come to judge the quick and the dead pretty darn soon, while there were still some quick left. Which made as much sense, when you came to think about it, as a lot of other doctrines I'd heard in my life.

'What's he telling those boys?' I asked Hunt, and he answered dryly, 'Whatever they want to hear.' Hunt didn't like the way the boys had started to flock to Arslan like flies to honey. For a little while Arslan had been all his – profoundly and poignantly his. 'Isn't it obvious?' he added. 'He's collecting a gang.'

No, after all, maybe the strength was on Arslan's side again. At least he had certain advantages. He offered those restless kids a freedom that amounted to riot and the discipline of the wolf pack. I couldn't match that.

Sanjar was finding Arslan's new role a little hard to take, too. He was doggedly adoring – whenever he had a chance to be – but the betrayed look in his eyes told it better. Arslan's new playmates were a far cry from the troopers who had made Sanjar their mascot. These boys were boys; that was the long and the short of it. They didn't have enough years on Sanjar (and, God knows, not enough security) to see him as anything but a competitor. The fact that he could do practically anything as well as any of them – anything that didn't demand weight or sexual development – just made it worse. And Arslan was no help. I'd used to think, when Sanjar was a three-year-old with a talent for finding trouble, that Arslan was trying to toughen him up. Now I was beginning to wonder if he just didn't give a damn.

By the end of September they were moving in. Arslan had

finished his fortifications and fixed up enough of the interior to make a little livable spot. It was like moving into a half-built house, but he knew what he was doing. The boys he was wooing had to have work to do – otherwise the whole setup would have fallen apart in a hurry – and this was the only work he had to offer them. So far, at least.

I wasn't surprised when Hunt silently packed up his belongings and plodded across the street. I wouldn't have been surprised if he'd stayed put, either; but since he'd made up his mind to go, it behooved him to go early and get himself established on Arslan's right hand.

Once Arslan, Hunt, and Sanjar were well bedded down in what had been the A-V room on the second floor, the boys started moving in, two or three at a time. A few of the parents came to me, either threatening or appealing, to try to get their sons home again, but Arslan was ready for that, too. If the boys were eighteen, they had a legal right to live anyplace they chose; and if they were younger, he didn't let them actually move in unless they got their parents' consent in writing. He wasn't prepared to fight Kraftsville.

'People ask me why the dickens we didn't shoot him when we had the chance.' Leland Kitchener was too tactful to put his question more directly. 'Looks like we could have had a trial to make it legal.'

'We could have.'

'Had to hang him then, I guess,' Leland added thoughtfully. 'But I reckon he'd find his way home either way – sniff his way along by the smell of the brimstone.'

'Leland, when I accept a man into my house, he's entitled to all the protection I can give him.'

He rubbed his jawbone pensively. 'We might of had somebody waiting for him when he come out.'

'Well, the thing is this, Leland. Arslan hasn't committed any crimes as a private citizen, and we don't have the authority to try him for war crimes. And even if we did, what good would it do? From here on in, he *is* a private citizen, and nothing more than a private citizen. He's entitled to the same rights as anybody else.'

He thought that over and then grinned his sly, sweet grin. 'You

271

mean when he's got a army we *can't* get him, and when he don't, we ain't supposed to?'

'That's about the size of it.'

Of course Arslan would never be exactly a private citizen. But he'd come a long way down since the day he drove me out on the Morrisville road.

'At least you got Hunt Morgan to tell you what goes on in there.'

'I don't rely too much on what Hunt Morgan tells me, Leland. He's let me down a few times too many.' Which wasn't entirely accurate. Hunt was useful enough, but even without him, it would have been pretty clear where Arslan was heading.

He was a politician now. A real politician. It wasn't hard to make fun of everything the government did, and mockery was one of Arslan's specialties. People were ready for that – people were always ready for that kind of thing. He didn't make fun of the KCR, though; in fact, to the extent that he had any public position on the subject, you could say he supported the KCR.

He kept his boys well enough in line not to cut himself off from the rest of the population. (Plenty of hard drinking and hard riding, but no vandalism of private property. Plenty of flirting, and probably seductions, but no rapes.) The next step would be to start offering the same services as the KCR. Already people with a grudge or a gripe – and there were always those – were starting to think of Arslan as a man who might know how to run things better. 'Nizam was behind a lot of that business before.' I don't know how many times I heard it. 'Things are different now. Arslan knows he's got to behave himself. He's only alive by the good will of the county.' That was as much as they needed – just an excuse for not shooting him on sight. Arslan's position in Kraftsville was a little like Hunt's, now; people didn't have to accept him to do business with him.

'He's on city property, Mr Bond. Looks like we got a right to evict him.'

'Maybe we've got the right, Leland, but he's got the arsenal.' As soon as he'd collected enough reliable recruits to garrison his new quarters, he had dispatched Hunt and Sanjar with a couple of boys to some cache farther east, and they had come back loaded with automatic rifles and ammunition.

What Leland was really asking, and a lot of other people, too, was why I'd stood by and *let* Arslan set himself up as an independent power. Well, there was no way they could have understood the answer – or appreciated it if they had. Arslan wasn't going to take over the world a second time, and I was ready to swear he wasn't going to take over Kraftsville. If it ever came to fighting, I knew how to crack his famous fortifications (Hunt was useful, all right). And besides, there was a lot of solid power in that school, and I didn't want to see it wasted. Putting Arslan out of action for good would be too much like cutting off my right hand.

27

Leland Kitchener himself brought the alarm, and Leland never wasted much time on introductory remarks.

'There's a gang riding down this way from somewhere upstate. We're in trouble, Mr Bond. Only good thing, the General could be in trouble, too. Looks like his little plan went *pffft*.'

'Lets have it.'

'A girl up there got pregnant.'

My throat and chest tightened. My stomach felt frozen. 'How do you know? What happened?'

'Got the word from Colton. Don't know where they got it from – nor how much you can believe of it. Must not have been a very smart girl. She tried to get rid of it. Killed the baby, and herself, too. Or maybe that's what she had in mind. Anyway, the thing is, she wasn't what you'd call a decent girl. And they got a theory up there, somebody got a theory, it was by her having so many *different* gentlemen friends she got the baby.'

I turned my head in disgust and spat into the dead grass (something I wouldn't have done, anywhere, while Luella was alive). 'It won't hold much water, Leland.'

'No, I guess not. Not when you think about the girls in the houses. But I hear that's the theory.'

'What are they doing about it?'

'What they're doing about it is, they've organized themselves a kind of a army. A bunch of them are just riding around the country, taking a town at a time.'

'I don't get it.' But I did get it, by premonition.

'Seems like they take that theory as gospel. And they're spreading the gospel.'

'Where are they?'

'They'd have been here by now, only they veered off north of Colton. You know they got to stop and recuperate now and then.'

'All right, Leland, pass it on. Not everything you've told me – just a KCR alert. I'm going to see Arslan.'

It was apparently news to him, and interesting news, but it didn't seem to bother him. He said nothing – politely – but the corner of his mouth tucked in with amusement. The idea of a troop of dedicated rapists, riding out to save the world by force, had to appeal to him. Salvation through violation – it was a concept that suited Arslan, even when it meant salvation from him.

'So much for Plan Two,' I said as viciously as I knew how.

'Perhaps. At worst, it was worth a try.' And he gave me the old bland look of half-surpirse. It only needed the caption: *What fools these mortals be.*

I stood and leaned my palms on his desk, leaned far over to him. 'You stinking bastard,' I shouted into his face, 'I'm going to round up all the women and children in this county and I'm going to bring them here, and you're going to defend them or die trying, and if you don't I'm going to kill you – I don't know how, but I'll kill you by quarter-inches!'

And he laughed – a big, open, joyful laugh that tossed his head back and pointed his beard at me. 'Hurry,' he said. 'No men, no boys who can fight. We can't take more than a thousand. Sanjar will go to scout out these raiders of yours.'

It was the biggest single operation we'd had to handle in years, and we weren't really geared for that kind of an operation any more. I'd said 'all the women and children,' but in fact we only needed to bring in the women of child-bearing age – stretching it a little on both ends, of course. We released as much ammunition as we could afford to people with families to protect – those that wouldn't be likely to waste it – but we took nothing to the school. The rest of our little stock would be safe where it was, and Arslan could spare bullets better than we could.

Well before sundown we had the school crammed full. We had brought in practically all of the girls – the very youngest, after all, were already twelve – and women and girls were all over everywhere. Every room, every hall, every other step of every staircase. It would have been impossible to conduct a defense, or anything else, in such a mob. Arslan's answer was to set two of his boys to painting boundary lines. (They had turned up some usable paint in the course of their remodeling, and Hunt had done good work with it.) A bright stripe down every staircase reserved a broad passageway 'for authorized personnel,' as Arslan put it. Stripes on the floors packed the crowd into the rear of the classrooms and against the corridor walls; the window areas were off limits to them, along with generous aisles that would make it easy for the defenders to get around in a hurry.

One of the things Arslan's gang had done was take out most of the basement floor. The concrete slabs had been put together on the remaining part to form a rainwater cistern, fed from the gutters by a pipe that came in through a convenient chink. In the dank subsoil they had excavated a large-scale latrine. The school was ready for a siege.

If the raiders had guns or explosives, there might be one; otherwise, it looked like no contest. Arslan was as serious about the Battle of Kraftsville School as if the fate of the world depended on it. He hadn't hesitated to hand out automatic weapons to my men, with a little lecture on how to use them. The KCR was manning the first floor and the basement, with a few monitors scattered through the crowd of females to keep them in line. Arslan's boys were bubbling like a pot of soup, full of pepper and hotter than sin. This was what they'd been waiting for all their lives – all summer, anyway. Arslan himself looked a good ten years younger and ten pounds heavier.

'What happens if nothing happens?' I asked him. 'These kids can't keep the steam up very long. Ten to one there won't be any attack tonight, and tomorrow they'll be down.'

He fairly chortled. 'There will be an attack tonight. At least, it is very probable.' And it occurred to me that Sanjar had never returned from his scouting.

'When's Sanjar getting back?'

'When he is ready.'

So Sanjar was dropping some kind of bait to bring the raiders hot on his tracks. There was a lively blaze now in the big fireplace where the furnace used to be, and there must have been plenty of smoke coming out of the chimney. They wouldn't have any trouble finding us – and just in case they did, Arslan was already having the lamps lit on the top floor.

They came without much commotion, riding down Pearl Street at an easy pace. There must have been about a hundred. They pretty nearly filled the block, not solidly, but in ragged clumps. At the southwest corner of the schoolground they stopped and bunched up into a dense mass. 'Why not fire now?' I didn't see how we'd ever get a decent shot, otherwise, in the dusk.

Arslan shook his head. We were watching from a second-floor window. 'No. We shall get a better return for our bullets.' And he added, not as casually as he seemed to think, 'Sanjar may be with them.'

For all the orders of silence, the crowd inside kept up a steady buzz of noise. Everything considered, they were being pretty quiet, but you couldn't expect that many women to be soundless. The horsemen were talking, but there was no hope of hearing anything they said.

Now they started their move, still not in much of a hurry. Maybe twenty-five or thirty of them peeled off and came across the parking lot at what started as a walk and ended as a fast trot, bringing up at the south door in a flurry of shouts. 'Now!' Arslan bellowed. His boys were hanging half out of the second- and third-floor windows; the line of fire was practically straight down. Arslan himself was fairly mortised into the window frame, his hip on the sill, the light rifle making one stiff vertical rod with his left arm and shoulder. One momentary burst of fire was enough; then he was yelling, swearing at his boys furiously, and the shooting sputtered out. The poor fools outside hadn't exactly expected this kind of treatment, judging from the screams. A belated volley of missiles came from the main body in the road – rocks, or something just as futile. I felt like the US Cavalry in an old western.

Not many of the women were really squealing, but it was enough to make quite a racket. Arslan was at the stairwell, roaring them quiet, yelling at his boys to follow orders, then back to the window. The attackers were lugging their casualties back across the parking lot. The main body milled and shrank away from the school. A few loose horses ran or stood aimlessly. Right beside the door, a wounded horse – I hoped it was a horse – was making a terrible noise. Obviously, they were taking too long to begin their next move. Arslan's lips swelled with pleased contempt.

Somebody on the third floor started shooting into them, and Arslan went up the stairs three at a time, clubbing the rifle in his hands as he ran. The thudding of his blows came down through the woodwork. Maybe he was expressing fatherly concern; Sanjar might still be out there. By the time he came back down, they had rallied and started their move. They split into three parts, one group tearing north and east around the block to attack the north side of the school. There, they would have the disadvantage of the steep north bank, but maybe they didn't know that yet. The second group was supposed to hit the south side at the same time, presumably, but they got there first. They couldn't have hoped to do much more than smash in the doors and first-floor windows, and to do that they had to get right up to the walls again. This time they got it from all three floors, hard. They wouldn't have tried it if there'd been enough light to see how those doors and windows were barred. Their rocks and clubs were entirely wasted.

But the third group – the biggest one – were dropping off their horses and ducking into the ruins of the west wing. Arslan had said he was going to demolish that wing, but he hadn't been in much of a hurry to get around to it. There was no immediate danger there – they'd have to knock a hole in the brick wall, and that would take a little while – but they were protected from our fire. There was enough of the roof left to provide considerable cover, and the west wall of the main building was blind – not a window in it. (Arslan's answer to that problem had been to install a trapdoor in the roof, and I wondered if there was anybody up there now. But the top floor was in his jurisdiction.)

Arslan had hot-footed it across to a north window to be in on the juiciest slaughter, so he missed the steady stream of automatic rifle fire that cut into the south-side raiders from across Pearl Street. They must have felt as if they were caught between the upper and the nether millstone, but it was only one gun, and I thought, *There's Sanjar*. It took me a little while to realize it was coming from my house. By that time, the horsemen had broken completely, at least on this side. They weren't even pretending to try to get their wounded out. I had already called off the KCR fire. But Arslan was out for something else. His boys kept pouring it on – not to finish off the wounded and the dehorsed, but to cut down as many as possible of the fleeing.

In the back of my head I heard Arslan yelling something with Hunt's name in it, heard feet racketing down the stairs. Once they were bolted, the doors were awkward to open, but a few of the basement window bars had been planned for quick exit. I saw the flying shadows in the schoolyard – Hunt running clean and long-legged in the lead, and half a dozen more trailing behind him. Somebody on the roof fired a burst into the waiting horses at the far end of the west wing; then Hunt and the first few others got there. I couldn't see what was happening any longer, but at any rate the men in the west wing had just lost their chance to get out. A light flared, too close to the west wall for me to make out what it was. It must have been a mistake; I could hear Arslan's curses over the hubbub. Then a solid lump of flame pitched through the darkness and bounced its way down through the broken west-wing roof. A minute later another followed; this one caught between a jutting beam and the solid part of the roof and hung there blazing. Rifles or no rifles, Hunt's detachment would have their hands full. Most men would sooner risk a bullet than burn.

The west wing had to go, that was inevitable; but I didn't intend to let my whole school burn for Arslan's Plan Two or any other reason that came to mind. If that fire got out of hand, we'd have had all our work for nothing. Luckily it was a still night. I got my men busy rounding up everything that could hold water and organized a bucket brigade from the basement cistern up to the second floor, in case we needed it. There was shooting in the west wing, and the middle part of it was well afire. What raiders were still alive and on horseback had scattered down the neighboring streets, and some of Arslan's boys were catching riderless horses and racing after them. Behind me, the school was in an uproar. The crowd of women had broken across their painted limits, shrieking to know what was going on. The riflemen were yelling in glee. Arslan reappeared beside me, thumping his fist against my shoulder. 'How do you feel, sir?' he shouted over the tumult.

'Great!' I yelled back at him, and straightened up from the window. 'All over on the north side?'

He answered me with a nod, already on his way out. It was no surprise that he wanted to finish off the wounded himself. My job was with the school, putting the fire out and getting that mob of females organized to go home again.

I ran into Arslan a while later on a stair landing. 'Finished?'

He turned his eyes towards me, but I could have sworn he didn't recognize me for a second. Sixteen years had begun to tell on him, after all. 'So it wasn't perfect,' I said. He kept on looking at me. 'Your virus.' He was so expressionless I wondered if he'd heard my words. The noise level was still pretty high. 'Some of those guys are going to get away. Quite a few years and a lot of people dead, General, to have it end up just a matter of chance.'

He took a breath like a man about to speak, and those black eyes came alive again, but he still didn't say anything. The women's chatter was seething all around us. Then Ward Munsey came hustling up the stairs, grasping Sanjar's arm. 'This here damn crazy kid!' He was almost yelling in his awe and delight. 'He come in through that spillway hole on the cistern, and nobody knowed he was coming! Hey, General, I thought you told me nobody couldn't get in there!' He paused to shake Sanjar's arm. 'Hey, boy, why don't you come in the door like anybody else? Don't you know the war's over?'

Sanjar grinned wanly, his eyes reaching for his father. He looked as if he were walking on tiptoe, every move he made tense and poised. He was keyed up to a new pitch altogether, and it was hard to tell whether, if you touched him, he would be tough as steel wire or brittle as thin glass. Arslan limped easily down to meet him, halfway up the flight, saying something in his own language, shifting the rifle to hug the boy's shoulders with his good hand and shepherd him up the stairs. Abruptly he turned to me. 'It is not chance.' His voice was hot. 'There is no chance. There is always risk, but there is never chance.' They started past me up the next flight and stopped again. This time Arslan had to turn his head over his shoulder to look at me. 'We accept the risk,' he exclaimed almost indignantly. 'We do not abandon ourselves to chance.'

Outside, some kind of order and progress was beginning to emerge. The fire was reduced to a few smoldering beams, checkered with bright gold embers. Bodies were dragged away from the doors; men were detailed to escort the women home by neighborhoods. The male civilian population – to call them that – were turning up in droves to claim their womenfolks or bring in a strayed raider, dead or alive, or just to exchange the news. Hunt came slowly from the direction of my house, a rifle sloped on his arm. He walked with deliberate grace, like a woman in a room full of strangers. Two or three people called to him, and he answered casually, tallying the dead raiders like a game bag. He sat down on the doorstep, barely out of the way of the open door, and looked up at me. 'We used your horses,' he said. 'I've taken care of them.'

'Thanks. They're all right?'

'Yes. And I apologize for taking them without your permission.'

'I imagine Sanjar did that.'

'Yes.'

Somebody had planted a torch a little way out in the parking lot to search the bodies by, and the night was so still the flame hardly flickered. I sat down beside him on the step. For all the noise and movement, all the people brushing past us, we were as alone there as we would have been in a desert. 'Franklin,' Hunt said. I waited. 'I know you don't appreciate people walking in and out of your house—'

'You don't have to apologize for Sanjar,' I said. He took it the wrong way; his mouth tightened. And suddenly I was sick of all the games he played. 'Does he know you killed his mother?'

His eyes widened, and winced almost shut again. After a few seconds he said patiently, 'I didn't kill his mother.'

'What I really can't figure out is whether Arslan knows it.'

'Why . . .' he hesitated, then went on decisively. 'If you thought I killed her, why did you turn the KCR loose on Ollie Schuster?'

'We needed a conviction. Like Arslan – except he wasn't satisfied with just one.' I looked at him. 'Tire chains,' I said. 'Good God, Hunt.'

He watched me evenly, but there was a tired horror in his eyes. 'Don't worry,' I told him. 'After tonight, we won't have any trouble working with Arslan. I'm not going to rock the boat.' We'd have trouble, all right – Arslan was born to create trouble – but nothing we couldn't live with. The KCR had found its groove.

Hunt took a little deeper breath. 'What I was leading up to,' he said firmly, 'was a proposal to move back into your house – if you think I'd be sufficiently useful to compensate for whatever needs compensation.' He paused again. 'Incidentally, I am not a murderer, but I don't intend to argue the question. And besides,' he added softly and quickly, 'it's true that I've killed people.'

'Always welcome, Hunt. I told you that a long time ago.'

'Yes,' he said. 'Among other things.'

PART 4
HUNT MORGAN

28

Sanjar and his red horses – the chestnut roan mare and the bright bay and the sorrels sired by Arslan's starfaced stallion – flashed down the hillside like a meteor shower. This was his sport – to drive the little herd alone, struggling to turn them at full gallop, by voice and whip and example; so that when he rode among his followers, it was the horses, almost more than the boys on their backs, who rallied to him and obeyed him.

He was fourteen, and he had his first girl, installed now in the school among Arslan's. He had picked her himself – Peggy Rose, perfect exemplum of her name – but Arslan, in his own harvesting, had left her to be picked.

Later he may hate me. Later, perhaps, he might. Now he rode his roan mare amid the herd, rode sometimes alone with me, hunted and raced and wrestled with his companions. They were the young ones, his own age or one year older or two, who chafed now at Arslan and his arrogant muscular gang. They would be forever the babies of their families; old men in the young wilderness, they would wither unmatured, spoiled brats to the end, the darling buds of May enduring fruitlessly into December. They were desperate and innocent as lemmings, happy as bees. They gathered to Sanjar as to their single hope.

The herd flared wide across the field, grudgingly turning to his shrill whoops. He rounded their outskirts, driving the little mare hard, bunching them gradually closer; pulled ahead of the herd and then slowed, calling to them by name as they overran him; and the rush dwindled and dried as they passed me along the fencerow, the riderless horses stepping knee-deep in broom sedge that matched their own colors. Sanjar raised his hand to me, the half salute that was his greeting, and I rode out from under the trees and walked my horse beside the blowing mare.

'Want to come north with me?' His eyes sparkled, but it was a half-hearted invitation. He was saying, *I'm going north. Come if you will, I don't want you.*

'No, thanks. Will he let you go?'

'I'm going!' But it was the joyful defiance of the beloved son. *I could be stopped, but not by him; he could stop anyone else, but not me.* They had quarreled for weeks now. He was too young, Arslan said – Sanjar who had been eleven when he killed three men single-handed, who had been nine when Arslan boasted, 'He is my aide-de-camp and my bodyguard.' It was a little late to shelter Sanjar. But Arslan's eyes would redden with anger as he shouted, 'Not this year!' It was already October; he would ride, if he went, into winter. Spassky had pitched his wigwam towns among the forested hills of the Great Lakes, where good hunting outweighed bad weather; and to visit Spassky and scout out the territory between was Sanjar's excuse for seeking his fortune. 'You'll go next summer.' Next summer would be more reasonable, yes; but it would be permitted and therefore unsatisfactory.

We rode slowly into town. The wind was in our faces, droning and singing in our ears. The sky was the original of blues, scraped and sanded clean by that scouring air. The dazzling maples shed their gold rags around us. A pieced landscape, crazily stitched with its rail fences, opened before us as we turned through the gate into the road: woods multicolored and splotched with bare darkness, the touching spring green of new wheat, fields molten with goldenrod and Spanish needle, fields rusty with the broom sedge that would stand all winter, embroidered with the tarnishing purple of ironweed and loosestrife; the pale even stubble of mown wheat, the harsh stripes of trampled cornfields, the dully shining thatch of haystacks; Kraftsville itself, beautiful from here, a speckled parkland of trees in whose colored shades occasional roofs glinted.

The low sun was deepening into red, and every perishing lawn was a green-rubbed gold. We pulled up beside Franklin's house. Sanjar's eyes danced. 'We're going tomorrow,' he cried suddenly. Blithe Sanjar, whose secrets were all innocent. He leaned over the mare's head, naming to me the boys who would go with him. 'Hunt, I'm telling *you* this.' He straightened. 'I'm telling Arslan tonight.'

'Take care, you hear?' We grinned at each other.

'You mean tonight, or tomorrow?' he said, and laughed. *Later he may hate me*. Not yet; no, not yet. He had planted wild roses on Rusudan's grave, blithe Sanjar, without a word to anyone. Dog roses, their arcing stems furred with spines. I looked at the flowerless tangle below what I had been accustomed to think of, so many years ago, as Arslan's window. Come May again, and rosy June, those ungraspable briars would flower with the simplest and loveliest of blooms, and wild bees sing around the pink and gold. 'See you, Hunt,' said Sanjar, and he clucked the mare into a sudden trot.

By morning the town glowed with expectation. It was Sanjar's followers, the chosen troop and the disgruntled rejectees, who had spread the news. The prospect of a showdown quarrel was as good as a holiday; at daybreak the loafers were gathering around the school. Franklin closed himself in his room with a stack of paperwork, while I loafed as eagerly as any, leaning with elbows on Arslan's windowsill. But the quarrel began late, and when it moved out onto the schoolground it was already past climax. Only then I came down the stairs, and out, through Franklin's porch, down the well-patched walk, across Pearl Street (unrutted still, for all the rains of spring, the summer wheels), unhurrying.

Sanjar swung into the saddle, his courtiers demurely following suit, and wheeled the little roan to face us all. In the gold of the high morning sun he seemed luminous himself. He thrust one hand into the mare's mane, a gesture unconscious and beautiful as the cataract of coarse red hairs that poured upon the arching neck. Arslan limped forward a wounded pace. Girl Peggy stood forlorn, rumpled by the wind.

'Any messages?' Sanjar sang out. Certainly with the muscles of his back he felt the watchful attention of his retinue; his legs were warmed as much by the attendant crowd as by the mare's round sides; even the hand in the red mane must be aware of Peggy. But the flushed young face was all concentrated on Arslan.

And Arslan, stern and grave, with basalt eyes, answered presently, 'Ask Spassky if he can send me a good pipe.'

'I will!' It was a cry of exultation. He lifted the reins, raising the red mane like spray, and spun toward the road, heeling his body around and bringing the mare to follow, as a young centaur might turn and bound away. With scrambling hooves the courtiers followed.

Arslan's hand had risen in the mild ghost of a salute. His lifted bronze face glowed with the grim furnace-light of pride. Now he would watch until the little troop was out of sight and hearing. But he did not. They had barely rounded the turn, a compact knot of motion, when he swung upon sobbing Peggy. 'Go kill the broilers and roasters! And start dressing them!'

Stupid and shaken, she stared. 'Now!' he barked, bell-mouthed Arslan, the voice that had wheeled the irregular cavalry at Clairmont like a flight of swifts. She turned mechanically under the force of it, and – in mid-step at last realizing what she was commanded to do – gasped tearfully, 'How many?'

'All of them!' He swept her away with a gesture that eddied the other girls with its backwash. 'Fay! Judy! Get on there and help her!' And, swinging back, 'Jerry! Buck! Take as many men as you need and butcher the slaughter hogs. Hunt! Go bring me a deer.'

Go bring me a deer. And without a break he completed his wheeling maneuver and moved schoolward, swinging left and right to fire orders, driving the watchers like schools of shiners in a creek. He had imposed on me not a set of instructions, but a responsibility. All right. I would bring him his deer.

In the room that was his bedroom, study, and arsenal (I could not even remember, now, what classroom it had been) I sought and found his hunting rifle and the treasured cartridges with which to load it. The everyday bow and quiver that stood beside my bed in Franklin's house were too prosaic now for this day's hunt. I put my own saddle on the big dun and led one of the quarter horses. The cool October sun was high. Every deer in the district would be bedded down for the long rest. I tied the horses under the first trees of Karcher's woods, beside a leaf-padded pool. For a little way the woods were open. Hickory, oak, ash, persimmon, sassafras, stood like good neighbors, a little withdrawn but with interlocking branches. It was the best of hiking weather, the worst for hunting. Dry leaves crackled at every step. Bare twigs curved in endless facsimiles of antlers. I went up the round swell of the hill that rose like a wooded cenotaph from the place where Arslan's true love had died, and paused below its crest to ready the gun and let the noise of my tramping soak away into the quiet and be forgotten.

Beyond, the woods thickened. The down-slope was cut into deep, irregular gullies – midget ravines that merged and inter-sected, their channels choked with many autumns' leaf falls. Buried at the slope's foot, a nameless creek felt its forgotten way. I crossed its dank-smelling sandstone below one of the windfall dams that broke it into pools, and moved by slow gradations up-stream along the wilder slope of the far side. Layered outcrops of stone and the miniature boulders cracked from them, and here and there a still-sound fallen log, gave me silent footing through the rustling welter of autumn. At each step I paused, scanning the barely altered scene until every element of it declared itself clearly, and choosing the next few feet of my route. It was a stooping, twisting way, picked to avoid the tangled brush and branches rather than to bend them aside; movement visible was even more hazardous than movement audible. An automatic pleasure, like that of the monotonous routines of sex, possessed me. *The sweet dark woods, the dear dim woods, the wonderful woods and glades.* But it was a labyrinth that led to death. A necessary end, I came (eluctable and rambling) toward some victim no less stoic and unforeseeing than Caesar.

In the light air, the faded leaves hung stiffly, gray-green and brown, palest beige and sallow. Here and there a single leaf spun and quivered, tinkling like a dry-mouthed bell. The creek below glinted at me occasionally through the brush, where meandering sunlight struck up from some clear minnow-pool; occasionally, even, a whisper of running water sounded. Between, stretches of sandstone and of silt (more exquisite than coral sand, scrolled with the tracks of the stream) had been swept clear of leaves by the wind. Where a bend had undercut a tree root, a late frog sang from his grotto. Elsewhere the creek lay silent and hidden, thatched with leaves.

Squirrels eyed me from the upper trunks. Persimmons, plum-sized, pumpkin-shaped and pumpkin-colored, hung like the lights of a garden party along the threadbare umbrella-ribs of their branches. I was beyond all sight and sound of humankind. The birds of the fencerows and open woodlots had given place to the shyer, drabber birds of the deep woods. Sweet-voiced, nameless to me, they flitted with little suspicious cries about the fringes of my vision – the only creatures in the woods whom my presence troubled. *They* would give warning (or so in my conceit I believed) if any warning was given. Only the mourning doves, imbecile and mild, ignored me.

I had neared the top of the creek's gentle gorge, the dangerous point where I must cross the ridge into the next tiny valley. Again I took my cautious step, and paused, and scanned. An old oak tree stood at the head of the gorge, and from my latest viewpoint I could see a single ascending column of dull crimson rosettes up the visible edge of the thick trunk – the palmate, five-fingered leaves of the Virginia creeper, neatly graduated from large to small. Beneath and behind the oak, the undergrowth was hung with the open clusters of a young grapevine. The small black grapes, most of them already a little shriveled, were like lackluster eyes among the leaves. I stared at them, and they, pregnant with mighty vines upon which no boys would ever swing, stared steadily back. Then without alteration of the scene another eye was staring. Larger and brighter, it poised motionless among the grapes. Slowly, as in those puzzle pictures in which the outlines of hidden beasts gradually reveal themselves to the concentrated sight, certain branches resolved into the beautiful forward curve of a raked antler.

From the height of the eye, he stood a good four feet. For minutes more, I could make out nothing of his actual fleshly presence – only the symbolic eye and antler, like the grin of the Cheshire cat. I counted four points; adding a conservative two for concealed branches, and doubling for the other antler, I could assume a twelve-point buck – old and wise and in all probability the master of a considerable harem. That antler raised a very practical question: Should I try for the glorious-headed stag, or for one of his more succulent dependents? *Bring me a deer*. It was a requisition for provisions (Hunt Morgan's commissariat, Buffalo Bill to Kraftsville, Illinois), but was it not also a test of my prowess?

Then the line of his back came into focus, and I stiffened with silent lust. In those still woods, he and I were the stillest things. The creek whispered; every leafed thing burred and rustled; the birds exclaimed in quiet voices; the indifferent insects sang and whirred. What wind there was (a stirring in the damp earth's cover, a life in the hanging leaves) favored me. It was possible, for all the directness in that dark gaze, that he did not see me. I began to raise the gun.

There was no change in the solitary eye or the stretched outlines. Creepingly from inch to inch, with pauses, I lifted the rifle, until my cheek nested peacefully against the stock. Now I could see, or imagine that I saw, the even tan of his pelt showing in background patches between the patterning leaves and twigs. I chose a spot that offered as clear a trajectory as any (Arslan had taught me how slight a thing could hopelessly deflect a bullet) to the broad target of his chest, and began that most delicate pleasure of the hunter – the gradual squeeze that is to trip the trigger exactly at one of those unprolongable instants when the swaying sights are mated perfectly upon the target.

But my stag, too, was cocked, and his triggering instant came an instant sooner. As the stock struck my cradling cheek and shoulder, and my ears rang with the shot, the buck was already in motion. He crashed across the slope into the next gorge.

I plunged wildly after, paused upon his track to look for blood, and followed far enough to be sure he was not wounded. There was no need to follow farther now. Later, much later, when the calm hours of afternoon had lulled him, when responsibility had netted him round and routine emergencies disarmed him, my chance would come again. There were other deer in the woods, but he was mine.

I circled back to the edge of the woods where I had entered. I checked the horses, drank, relieved myself, gathered a double handful of persimmons, and stretched out with them and a slab of my own bread to rest and wait. By now he would have fled far enough. He would gather his harem, while I lay munching tranquilly in the thick dry grass. Herder, warder, leader – lover last and first – he would return to his familiar bonds. He would not wander far; like me, he had his bounds. And bound – oh, *bound* . . . oh, bound. The swelled and shuddering word engorged my mind. The spring and fall of haunches in the leap, ridges and gullies of unleaving autumn, the maps of love, the ropes of life, trees rooted in the towing tides of air . . . oh bound, bound, the leap of the heart, the limit of the deer. Until, released at last, the word found words and drained itself in the relieving trivialness of poetry. *And, bound for the same bourn as I, On every road I wandered by, Trod beside me, close and dear, The beautiful and death-struck year.* 'Bound to stir up a fuss,' my grandfather had grumbled (or was it my great-uncle? Some old man, grumbling once, a time and scene forgotten), though I had been the quietest of children. My eyes were open, the same persimmon trees hung their fruits before me; I stretched myself in the dry grass of Karcher's woods and finished my bread.

In Karcher's woods, here at the foot of the first hill, I had found one spring a shin-high stalk spiraled with cloud-white flowers. I had gazed, disturbed because I could not put a name to my pleasure, a long time into the tiny depths of the twisted blossoms. They were minute, fly-sized – and yet, in intricacy and grandeur, monumental, like expert miniatures of the Great Buddha. Slowly and sweetly I recognized that they were orchids.

That spring and others, I had found, too, the standard school-book wildflowers – Dutchman's breeches, snowdrop, hepatica – academic beauties that were somehow touching, rooted in Kraft County dirt; touching but unreal. More to the point were the flocks of sturdy little upright violets that we called rooster-fights, purpling sunny hillcrests unregarded, mowed and trampled like the grass. And my orchids. Anomalous, unpredicted, and secret, they illuminated the woods.

I had wondered, sometimes, if Sanjar had known those orchids. Perhaps he had seen them and passed on, unrealizing, he to whose homeless eyes all flowers were exotic. Solomon's seal, cinquefoil, heal-all – he had delighted to name and touch the rugged blooms of Illinois. Smartweed, ironweed, butterflyweed – season after season, he named, he touched, but he did not pick. Yet I had seen him race and roll with a puppy's craziness in the red clover, and one day he had cut armloads of wild honeysuckle and ridden home triumphantly bedecked, in clouds of sweetness, with trailing stems twined in his vexed horse's mane. But honeysuckle or columbine, mullein or pigweed, they were no more native to him than the flamboyant flora of monsoon Asia, he who was born to the twisted scrub of Arslan's plains. To Sanjar, the unyellowing ivory of miraculous orchids in Karcher's woods must be no more, no less, significant than the casual dayflowers whose blue blossoms and supine stalks we trampled every summer long. No, the orchids were mine forever.

And Sanjar, Sanjar was gone – Sanjar whose shining eyes opened sometimes into a look of blindness. Confiding, quick Sanjar, afire with indignation as he struck with his riding whip, and struck again, and struck again ('You don't kick *any* of those dogs, you hear?') while the disgraced courtier whimpered and backed, head hunched behind his flapping arms. Singing Sanjar, Sanjar who had tumbled the books off the table, laughing – 'Oh, what's the use, Hunt?' (I thinking, but not saying, *Someday you may want to read.*) When Sanjar argued, he was candid, receptive, eager to learn; but his commands were arbitrary, his angers as flashing and frequent as summer lightning.

My fingers curled in the stiff curled grass, and my mind rode back to the blaze of Bukharan summer, where Arslan lay, drenched with his sweat and mine, one bright arm flung like a wave-cast across his face. It was not likely that I would see him so again. In Bukhara, everything had been intensified, concentrated by a process of dehydration. Essences of day and night, of summer and winter; spring itself, too faint and swift to grasp, wringing the heart with one outrageous spasm; these things had suited the passions that lived within them, the hoarse and howling rages that swept down the shining stairs, the abandon (loose and laughing as drunkenness, but unblurred) of joy. That – if, of course, I could only have known it – had been our honeymoon.

And he had been young then, very young. He had begun his work early, as a man should (as men were born to do before the artifices of civilization had prolonged childhood past puberty), and in his hour of triumph he had still been very young. He was not old now. He was total, arrived, all his powers at peak; and it was right that his work was finished. When Nizam lay dead in the grass at Clairmont, Arslan had looked at him, not long, but so intensely that I clenched my hand upon my belly as Franklin Bond was wont to do in his moments of horrible crisis. His worn face was without expression, as if all feeling and purpose had withdrawn from it, and only his eyes burned upon dead Nizam. Later he squatted beside me, steadying himself against the still-warm body of my horse, and touched my leg thoughtfully. 'Fuck Nizam,' I said – the pain was so inescapable. Arslan's face, cracked and sunken, warped like an old scrap of bad leather, softened once more into his dimpling smile. 'Nizam,' he said gently. 'Nizam was right.' Tears persisted in seeping out of my eyes. Yet six days later he was to barter his ravaged body for mine.

Yes, Nizam had been right. Arslan's ephemeral empire had passed, like a running prairie fire. Nizam's devotion, like Arslan's plans, had served its purpose and could be discarded. Work was over. It remained only to live.

And Nizam's style of living had crossed Arslan's; therefore he had died. But Franklin Bond had built himself a solid hold on undisputed ground. Nobody's servant, he had not run Nizam's danger (the shadow's death, the fatal disease of fidelity), and he had seen his own danger in good time and trimmed his ambitions to fit the space allotted. Like me – I thought – he had taken the step backward that enabled him to stand upright. There was a certain family relationship between our positions. It was therefore that I had chosen to live in his house; chosen in the teeth of those fierce abstractions – treason, murder – that were realities to him; chosen to live, or, if that were still denied me, to wait. And when I lay raging in the tranquil nights, it was for that, almost alone: that all obstacles had been passed, all walls broken, and yet he declined to recognize so simple a relationship.

I had been resigned long since to the look in Arslan's eyes, the look that lay far back like the silent shapes under deep water. A look of concern I could have forgiven, of anxiety, or of love; but it was more and worse than these, a look of vulnerability; I could not forgive him the fact that Sanjar could hurt him. Yet I had been resigned, for – surely as the inevitable, uncertain spring – Sanjar would go, Sanjar my almost friend, my something less than brother. Sanjar would go, and the alien burden of fatherhood would be lifted from Arslan, the far shapes die out from his eyes.

For Karcher's woods stood witness that his vulnerability could pass, that if his brain remembered, his heart could forget. Here, somewhere between the bramble-clogged roadside ditch and the scattered flat seeds of my persimmons, Rusudan had died among the leaves, opening the wound that would close at last, unnoticed, somewhere between Athens and Stalingrad. There were no memories of Rusudan in Arslan's eyes now; and it was Sanjar who had planted roses on her grave.

Idling on the road, leaning against the chain links of the Russians' fence, they had watched me pass. I did not even know their names (*Schuster* was one?), though I knew their eyes. I rode slowly, not to avoid them. And when one hailed me, 'Say, Hunt!' something made me draw rein – something not suicidal, but aggressive. Their question surprised me. So I was not, after all, their quarry. Yes; I knew (as what did I not know?) where Rusudan had gone to tease Fred Gonderling in the dusk. 'Well, Hunt, if you meet Mr Gonderling on the way, why don't you pass the time of day with him a few minutes? Just so he don't get there too soon, you know?' 'Wouldn't want him to have to wait out there in the woods by hisself,' said the other. Shadow men, they were not real. What was real was what turned inside me, pointing like a weathercock. 'Right by the road,' I said. 'Not really *in* the woods.' Later, beneath the lash of Arslan's tormented voice, it was Fred Gonderling's name I stammered out first, before my haphazard descriptions of the shadow men.

I did not know, until he turned away from the four corpses, that I would not be the fifth. Until that moment I had waited, with anxious anticipation and a hollow sickness in the gut, to learn whether I would fight him – and how, if I did not, he would destroy me. But as he turned, slack and satiated, sheer joy bubbled within me, and I trembled like a fountain. Rusudan was dead, and I would live. Nights afterward, when in my agony I dared to tongue Rususdan's name, he leaned the heel of his hand upon my mouth, saying for all time, 'That case is closed,' and I read in the jet transparence of his eyes that I was absolved of my own sin, called only to suffer for others.

'Dreams are funny,' Sanjar had said once, touching me with his humanness. (For all the billions of babies, the first cry, the first step, the first word. Yet why should it be touching that life was cyclic?) 'Sometimes I dream about' – he broke off, gently embarrassed – 'you know – kids. Children. I mean, I just see them; walking around and everything.'

'Playing,' I said. 'That's what children do.'

He nodded gravely, his eyes searching inward.

Like secret orchids, the children bloomed; native strangers, humble and precious. I too had dreamed of them, the children that would have been, the children that might be. Certainly it was in quest of children that Sanjar was leading his little troop northward. Surely in all the fertile sweep of the rich land, at least one child must lurk. And I felt the intangible pulse of the earth against me, the immortal dirt of Karcher's fecund woods, squirrel-eyed, bird-voiced, grass-pelted, cloven and rutted with the gushing generations of the deer.

I rolled over and sat up, remembering something Sanjar had said once, coming contritely back to me after some trivial quarrel. 'I wish you could have been with us all the time.' *All the time.* The memory struck like a revelation, so that I heard the tones of his voice, reviewed the expressions of his face, hands, shoulders, all his guileless muscles. I had taken it then as an offer of conciliation to a subordinate, no more. But it was more. *I wish.* Awkward with boyishness, unaccustomed to confession. *You could have been.* Helpless before the huge impossibilities of past and future. *With us.*

I checked my gun – Arslan's gun – and stood up.

I knew my road now, and followed faithfully along it; up the hill, down the slope, across the creek, and upstream beside it. Below the head of the gorge I stood awhile, staring at the grape-eyed vine under the oak. He had his paths as well as I, and this was our only proven crossroads. But I did not meet him there, nor, working my way downhill, in the next valley. The lower reaches of the third were broad and ruggedly flat, a section that had been cut over more than once when this land belonged to somebody. Clumps of crimson sumac and little cedars made a low forest among the stumps and tall saplings. I stood for a long time surveying the gaps among the foliage. I could not afford another mistake. Slow waves of certainty succeeded one another: he would be here; he would not; he would be. Without surprise I grew aware of a certain brownness among the browns and reds and muted greens. I eased my head sideward a little, and made out the sleeping deer, folded snugly as a cat. A deer, but not my buck. One of his harem, perhaps; and in that hope, and expert with desire, I trod Indian-soft among the leaves, too busy to be moved by the intimacy of the scene that revealed itself to me.

He lay among his loves, his splendorous head resting at ease along his foreleg. Moving with the faint pulses of the breeze that washed in slow ripples down the valley, I found my way to a vantage point against an ash tree and raised Arslan's gun. Heat throbbed in my face, nested my heart. He had been hunted before, this stag. But who, even in his incautious youth, had seen him thus helplessly abandoned to peace? I would have wagered my life, at that moment, that no one, since the Shawnee had tracked his ancestors through the virgin scrub of aboriginal forests, had witnessed this secret domesticity in the woods. His ancestors, not mine; immigrant in my very homeland, I could only imitate the ancient lords of the land. But the unbroken stream of his breed ran back, birth by birth, through wooded centuries before the first footfall of those first immigrants of whom the Shawnee had been the illegitimate heirs. I lowered the gun.

I could not take him so. In the end, I could not take him unawares. It was not, certainly, the classic perversion of sportsmen, obsolete from the moment of its conception, that morality demanded for the victim some chance of escape. No, my morality was older, more classic yet, the morality that distinguished between sacrifice and slaughter and had not yet dreamed of sport. In the end, it seemed to me, no death could be so cruelly unfair as the unfelt death in sleep. I leaned against the ash and waited. Time was my ally. Time: not the fourth dimension, but the first, the essential, without which the mere dimensions of space could not be born. Time: the matrix wherein we traced the shapes of beauty and of power. For it was shape that gave significance. Form was beauty – the classicists were right – and power was form. Starlight swept along the curved lanes of the closed universe; planets wheeled in the grooves that Newton had not seen. Swinging down the paths of time, my deer and I would meet – rightly, as our predecessors had met, here beneath other trees, round centuries ago.

And after all, I was not simply an imitator – or not, at least, an imitation. If I wore moccasins, they were of my own design and making; and though for years past I had delighted to play with bows (making of civilization's wreck an excuse to return to my childhood's toys), for this hunt I chose a graver weapon. It added both power and risk. Arslan's gun had not been fired for many months, though he cleaned and nursed it beyond all practical need; and the cartridges, however lovingly they had been guarded against assaults of weather, were older than Sanjar – twice, three times, perhaps, the age of the buck they were to kill. But in return for such precision and potency, it was only fair to accept the risk of a misfire.

Fair: a sweeter, truer word than *just*. All justice aside, was it not keenly unfair that I had scrambled for crumbs beneath his table with his other minions? – that the place I had earned by such fierce apprenticeship was reserved to that mindless salamandrine queen of fire and earth? What had she to offer him, beside the match of passion? Where could they meet, but in the furious and volcanic dark? What, in simple fact, could they talk about?

It was absurd, of course, to be still wrestling with the gorgeous shade of Rusudan – Rusudan whom Arslan had forgotten. But I wrestled now not for his affection (had that ever been the prize?) but for understanding. By what right had he suffered for Rusudan? It was I, not Rusudan, whom he had led through Karcher's woods, to whom he had whispered, 'Look.'

And now, leaning in the very heart of the still circle, looking with wordless patience upon the nested deer, I turned the curve of recollection for the thousandth time, and saw, for the first time, everything in its place. Yes. It was I whom he had led through Karcher's woods, to whom he had whispered, 'Look.'

I took a deep breath that swelled my chest like pride, and my eyes focused to a new intensity on the great stag. A thrill, slow but electric, passed through me. He was awake. I must have moved (perhaps I had breathed too vehemently), for he was aware of me. By infinite split seconds, time was draining past us.

Then he rose. One fused sequence of movements, heavy and lunging and yet effectively graceful, brought him to his feet and on his way. I had swung the gun up with all my speed, guessed an arm. It jerked against my hands; the cartridge had been good. He sprang.

Aborted and perfect, like the eternal gasp of violent art, his final spring hung before the leather-colored brushwood of his bed – hung, altered, and fell. I pushed forward, afire with the one hope that he would need no second shot, while my provident hands prepared the gun for it. The woods around me burst with exploding deer, the does scattering in panic out of the depths of sleep. He lay crashed upon the broken underbush. The dark vast eye loomed above his cheek. The sinewy prongs of his antlers (woodlike neither dead nor living) skewed his head into an awkwardness that seemed to guarantee the honesty of his prop-osition: *I am dead.* I squatted beside him and drew my knife, holding it ready to the warm, golden throat. Death, in theory so final and so certain, had mocked me before. His legs were stretched, a little more than half tense. I lifted one of the beautiful cloven forefeet and teased my knife into its depths, grazing the point against the black quick, but I did not plunge, not pry. I would not force him to betray his life, if he lived. Only, I gazed into the round brown eyes. There, if he lived, he would betray himself. There life would gleam, or flicker, or deeply glow, or fire up at me some uncontrollable bolt of intelligence or enmity. So I gazed into that dark globe, dived it, navigated it, sank and surfaced and swept along its curve. He was dead.

And I remembered only then to notice the wound. My bullet had pierced the skull at its vulnerable point and thrust into the secret soft core of his brain. My right hand had brushed, unknow-ing, the little unsealed opening in the warm pelt, and small dark clots of his blood clung to me. He had been dead already when he sank upon the leaves.

I rode into town against the light of the setting sun. Market Street was afire. A narrow blaze stretched down the long block of the schoolyard. From the slopes, with hilarious whoops, Arslan's boys were hurtling blunt missiles into the flames. Behind them, and on the other sides of the school, lesser demons tended lesser fires. On the walk near the eastern one, a thin swarm of old men hovered about the naked carcasses of three hogs, ritually waving their flywhisk hands.

I rode up the low east face of the yard, where Arslan waited, fists on hips. He laid his hand on the dun's nose and walked past me to the packhorse. Turning in the saddle, I watched him inspect the buck, saw his eyes seek and find and judge the wound. When he began to untie the ropes, I dismounted. Together we heaved the shining body up and off and let its sudden bulk pour between us to the ground.

'Good enough?'

He grinned at me in silence and turned away, calling for volunteers to butcher the deer. I headed for the school, to return his rifle to its place.

Inside and out, the feast was under way. The chickens were already cooked and the pork was roasting. My deer would be the final surfeiting course, toothsome and succulent. Kegs of beer stood open, for anyone with a cup or a cupped hand to help himself, and more were being hauled out. The town was gathering to the school, as it had gathered before.

Beside me on the east walk, Franklin swung his spread hand in a slow horizontal arc, taking in the fires, the feasters, and the rolling kegs. 'Do you know what this is, Hunt?'

A wake? A jubilee? 'The winter stores,' I said.

'Exactly. Our food and fuel supply for the winter, going up in one big blaze.'

'Plus the liquor supply. All the renewable resources.'

'I don't take it as a joke. We'll have a hard time renewing them by December.'

Hard times come again. But the fact was that they *were* renewable, as we were not, and my deer had planted his seed already in Karcher's woods. 'The sabbath was made for man,' I said.

The indigo twilight deepened, deeper already than the hearts of jewels. Arslan strode to the eastern fire, his last limp dipping into a swoop, and lifted a long brand. In stately loops, trailing a fiery friz, it traced his path to the steps. And standing where he had stood to pass sentence on Kraftsville's martyrs, he whirled the torch around his head once, twice, and pealed the undisobeyable order, 'Listen!' At that enormous shout, the trivial shouts below subsided in a rush. There was no sound louder than the crackling of the fires, until he cried his ringing cry, 'Is it good?'

There were no words distinguishable, or needed, in the cheer that answered him. It was good. He stretched his torch out over them, a fiery shepherd's blessing, and they hushed – docile, expectant, and eager. 'Enjoy it!' he sang at them. 'Enjoy it! This is for Sanjar!' It was a voice that called and celebrated, that might conjure Sanjar himself out of the twilight. 'Whatever you drink tonight, you drink to Sanjar. Whatever you eat tonight is the gift of Sanjar. All your games tonight are in honor of Sanjar. All your songs are in praise of Sanjar. Tonight you laugh for Sanjar. You make love for Sanjar. Remember! Remember! This is the Feast of Sanjar!' Again the firebrand circled, this time a wide slow curve, and flew meteorlike across the yard to plunge with a golden burst of sparks upon the street.

Reluctantly, in the new darkness, the sounds surged up again. A mutter of talk, peaked with soft yells; the songs beginning anew, a little self-conscious now and defiantly obscene; the light thuds of running feet; and – crown and seal of all, Sanjar's investiture, Arslan's mandate – the many-keyed concord of laughter.

I waited as he came down the east steps. He threw his arm around my shoulders and steered me toward the south side. He said nothing, only waved and grinned to the groups we threaded through. The grip of his good hand on my moving shoulder was comfortable, fond, the limping swing of his body beside me easy. I walked carefully, not to lose my balance upon the precious knife-edge of tranquillity. I saw that Franklin had started home and that we were unhastily following him. In the street he turned and waited.

Here the moonlight fell upon our faces, but we stood in a moat of darkness. The glow of the nearer fire cast moving hues of yellow-red over the bright black of Arslan's hair and the hard planes of Franklin's temples. 'Now what?' Franklin asked. Unexpectedly his voice was rough and bitter.

Now what? It was a question to be answered with panoramas,

not with sentences. 'I stay here,' Arslan said, as if his staying had been the point in question. He tightened his arm about my shoulders for a moment, and let me go, and took out his pipe, and began to fill it – gently, casually, fondly, gently.

'Why? To wait for Sanjar?'

'To wait for Sanjar.' He was tamping his tobacco with his thumb. 'Also, I am a citizen of Kraftsville.' He put the pipe in his mouth, took an experimental pull, and tamped again. 'Also, sir, I am your friend.'

'I wish I could be yours.' He said it very soberly. The authentic voice of Franklin L. Bond. I wish I could be your friend. I wish I could be your father. *But this inconstancy is such As you too must adore.*

'Will he come?' I asked.

Arslan shrugged. 'Will tomorrow come? Who knows?' He was still looking at Franklin.

One of the groups on the south bank began to sing again, meltingly out of the darkness. 'He's a good boy,' Franklin said abruptly, and he turned again toward the old house.

'Sir!' Arslan called softly. And Franklin turned once more, a little ponderous and square, making a full half-cycle where Arslan would have pivoted dancer-like far enough and no farther. Now Arslan swung forward a step, and I knew by the movement of his shoulders that he held out his left hand. 'On that?' *When I ask, I do not dictate the answer.*

'On that.' The clasp of their hands was in darkness. Then the granite head nodded, the portentous budge of the cliff. At three paces, in the trivial moonlight, his eyes were too shadowed. I would have given something – say a hand – to know if he was looking into my eyes or Arslan's. 'Good night.'

And Arslan, who had not watched his only son ride out of sight into the wilderness of earth, stood silently gazing while the Supervisor of Kraft County finished crossing the narrow street and mounted the broken walk and blackened into the darker darkness of his porch.

I hadn't moved. Arslan threw his right arm around me in passing – the clawed clasp, the soldier's caress – and released me, and moved on. Up out of the moon-defined moat, up the black bank, up into the harvest light of bonfires, where his citizens crunched their feast bones and licked their fingers, where his boys and girls sported in the moonlight and fornicated in the shadows in the purity of their young lust, he walked with his dancer's limp, red Arslan, Arslan; and quietly I followed him.

M. J. Engh was born in 1933. A science fiction author and independent Roman scholar, in 2009 she was named Author Emerita of the Science Fiction and Fantasy Writers of America. She lives in Washington, USA.

SF MASTERWORKS

* no longer available

* no longer available